Romancing Robin Hood is dedicated ~~to the~~ ~~academic~~ and administrative staff of the History and Archaeology Departments of Leicester University. Particular mention must go to Prof. Norman Housley, Dr Neil Christie, and Mrs Lynne Wakefield, and their colleagues, with whom I worked as both a student and a member of staff between 1990 and 1999.

I would also like to extend a special thank you to Anthony Horowitz, Richard Carpenter, and the entire cast of the 1980s television series *Robin of Sherwood*. Without your wonderful writing and performances, my Robin Hood obsession would never have started in the first place, and this novel would never have been written.

Jenny x

Author's Note

As a teenager I was as obsessed with Robin Hood.

I devoured any information I could find about the famous outlaw legend. Then, as an A Level student, I studied the reality behind the criminal organisations that plagued England's Midlands in the thirteenth and fourteenth centuries.

By the time I was in my early twenties my obsession was unstoppable – I wrote my PhD thesis about the subject, a factual work which consumed my life for five head-thumping, Latin-reading, happy, manically busy years. This study can now be found hiding under a layer of dust in a university library somewhere. *Romancing Robin Hood* has shamelessly borrowed from – and somewhat corrupted – my doctoral research.

Within this novel I play fast and loose with history. Although I don't stray unreasonably far from reality, this is a fictional story which shies away from too many historical terms and phrases. So whatever you do, don't go using the 'history' included in this novel to answer questions in the pub quiz!

To absolve my historian's conscience, which I have to confess has found 'messing' with history every bit as difficult as Dr Grace Harper does within the following pages, I have provided a set of references at the end of the book to set help the record straight!

Jenny x

Romancing Robin Hood

Jenny Kane

Map of Mathilda's Leicestershire

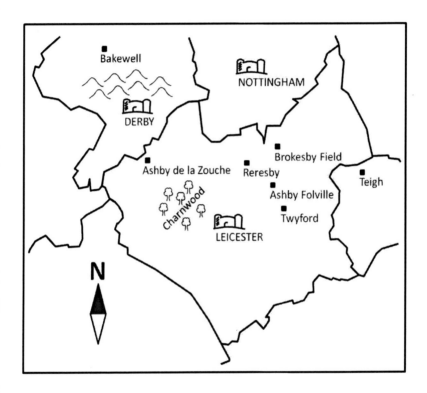

Chapter One

Raising a cup of tea to her lips, Grace Harper leaned back against her pine chair and blew carefully through the steam which rose from the liquid's surface before taking a sip. It was the first cup from the third pot of tea she'd ordered that afternoon. The scalding drink slid down her dry throat, a throat which her friends joked must be coated with asbestos, such was her ability to drink tea almost directly from the kettle.

Staring through the teashop window, Grace watched the shoppers stroll by in a never-ending stream of flip-flops, T-shirts, and a staggering variety of different lengths of shorts. It was as if everyone on England had decided to expose as much flesh as possible, and as wholeheartedly as possible, just in case the burst of late June heat was the only sun they saw all summer.

Grace drew her wandering attention back to the reason for her weekday escape from the office. With constant interruptions from research students and fellow academics alike, she had been finding it increasingly difficult to marshal her thoughts for the opening chapter of the book she was trying to write.

Two hours ago she'd gathered up the printed sheets of what made up her manuscript so far, and headed for the quiet of Mrs Beeton's tearooms. She'd read it twice already, and now sped through it again. A notebook lay next to her teacup, and Grace added an additional point to the rough list she'd made of things to check out and expand on, before sighing into her cup and turning back to watch the stream of pedestrians pass by the window.

Writing a book in the academic world was a bit like

running an incredibly slow race. With your legs glued together, and at least one arm tied behind your back. Everything took so long. The research, the checking, the double-checking, the making sure you were one step ahead of everything else already published on your subject, and then racing (tortoise-style), to get your book out there before a similar historian, in a similar office, in a similar university, produced their book on an identical subject in a similar fashion. Then, of course, there were the constant interruptions. Students and fellow lecturers *always* wanted something. Not to mention the secretaries, who were forever after some pointless piece of administrative documentation that the occupants of the ivory tower had decreed it necessary to add to the already overwhelming mountains of paperwork.

At least, Grace thought to herself as she picked her sketchy plan and first draft back up, fanning herself with them in an attempt to circulate some air in the stagnant café, *no one else studies what I study in quite the way I do.*

Admitting defeat, and stuffing her work back into her large canvas bag, which was more suited to the beach than landlocked Leicester, Grace pulled out the square envelope that had arrived in the post that morning, and pulled out the card within. It showed a guinea pig wearing a yellow hard hat and driving a bulldozer.

The card could only have come from Daisy. Grace read the brief message again. Daisy's familiar spidery scrawl, which would have been the envy of any doctor, slopped its way across the card, illustrating that it had been written in haste. Grace could picture Daisy clearly, a pen working over the card in one hand, a packet of pet food in the other, and probably her mobile phone tucked under her chin at the same time. Daisy could multi-task with all the prowess of a mother of three.

Daisy, however, wasn't a mother of any sort. She had long since vowed against having children, human children at least, and after her degree finals had swiftly cast aside all she had studied for in order to breed rabbits and guinea pigs, house stray animals, and basically become an unpaid vet. Daisy's home, a suitably ramshackle cottage near Hathersage in Derbyshire's Peak District, had become her animal rescue shelter, the base of an ever-changing and continually growing menagerie of creatures, which she always loved, and frequently couldn't bear to be parted from. Grace smiled as she imagined the chaos that was probably going on around Daisy's welly-clad feet at that very moment.

It had been the card's arrival in the post that morning that had made Grace think back to her youth; that strange non-teenage hood she'd had, and of how it had got her to where she was now. A medieval history lecturer at Leicester University.

Grace had met Daisy fifteen years ago, when they'd been students together at Exeter University, and they'd quickly become inseparable. Now, with their respective thirty-ninth birthdays only a few months ahead of them, Daisy, after a lifetime of happy singledom, was suddenly getting married.

She'd managed, by sheer fluke, to find a vet called Marcus as delightfully dotty as she was and, after only six months of romance, was about to tie the knot. The totally unorthodox (but totally Daisy!) invitation Grace now held announced that their nuptials were to be held in just under two months' time at the beautiful Hardwick Hall in Derbyshire. Daisy had then added a postscript saying that she would personally shoot Grace if she didn't turn up, with some mild torture of an especially medieval variety thrown in if she didn't agree to be her bridesmaid.

'A bridesmaid!' Grace grimaced as she mumbled into her cup, 'Bloody hell, it makes me sound like a child. If I was married or had a partner I'd be maid of honour, but no, I'm the bloody bridesmaid.'

Swilling down her remaining tea Grace got to her feet, and carried on muttering to the uncaring world in general, 'Robin Hood, you have a hell of a lot to answer for,' before she hooked her holdall onto her shoulder and began the pleasant walk from the city centre, down the picturesque Victorian New Walk, towards the University of Leicester, and an afternoon of marking dissertations.

It was all Jason Connery's fault, or maybe it was Michael Praed's? As she crashed onto her worn leather desk chair, Grace, after two decades of indecision, still couldn't decide which of the two actors she preferred in the title role of *Robin of Sherwood*.

That was how it had all started, 'The Robin Hood Thing' as Daisy referred to it, with an instant and unremitting love for a television show. Yet, for Grace, it hadn't been a crush in the usual way. She had only watched one episode of the hit eighties series and, with the haunting theme tune from Clannad echoing in her ears, had run upstairs to her piggy bank to see how much money she'd saved, and how much more cash she'd need, before she could spend all her pocket money on the complete video collection. After that, the young Grace had done every odd job her parents would pay her for so she could purchase a myriad of Connery and Praed posters with which to bedeck her room. But that was just the beginning. Within weeks Grace had become pathologically and forensically interested in anything and everything to do with the outlaw legend as a whole.

She'd watched all the Robin Hood films, vintage scenes of Douglas Fairbanks Jr and Errol Flynn, Richard Greene, Sean Connery, and Barrie Ingham. As time passed, she winced and cringed her way through Kevin Costner's comical but endearing attempt, and privately applauded Patrick Bergin's darker and infinitely more realistic approach to the tale. Daisy had quickly learnt to never ever mention Russell Crowe's adaption of the story – it was the

4

only time she'd ever heard Grace swear using words that could have been as labelled as Technicolor as the movie had been.

The teenage Grace had read every story, every ballad, and every academic book, paper, and report on the subject. She'd hoarded pictures, paintings, badges, and stickers, along with anything and everything else she could find connected with Robin Hood, his band of outlaws, his enemies, Nottingham, Sherwood, Barnsdale, Yorkshire – and so it went on and on. The collection, now over twenty years in the making, had reached ridiculous proportions and had long since overflowed from her small terraced home to her university office, where posters lined the walls, and books about the legend, both serious and comical, crammed the overstuffed shelves.

Her undergraduates who'd chosen to study medieval economy and crime as a history degree option, and her postgraduates whose interest in the intricate weavings of English medieval society was almost as insane as her own, often commented on how much they liked Dr Harper's office. Apparently it was akin to sitting in a mad museum of medievalism. Sometimes Grace was pleased with this reaction. Other times it filled her with depression, for that office, its contents, and the daily, non-stop flow of work was her life – her whole life – and sometimes she felt that it was sucking her dry. Leaving literally no time for anything else – nor any*one* else. Boyfriends had come and gone, but few had any hope of matching up to the figure she'd fallen in love with as a teenager. A man who is quite literally a legend is a hard act to follow.

A knock on her office door dragged Grace from her maudlin thoughts of permanent spinsterhood.

Professor Davis, the head of school, stooped to allow his tall slim frame through her door. Grace liked the professor, and was often thankful that she had such an easy-going boss, unlike many of her sister departments,

5

which seemed to be run along the lines of private dictatorships.

'Sorry to disturb you, Grace,' Davis smiled, flashing his dazzling white teeth at Grace as he gave her office his usual amused look of disbelief. 'I've had a call from Nottingham Uni, they need an external examiner for one of their PhD student's viva exams and I thought of you. It's a bit of an emergency, they've been let down by their previous examiner and the viva is soon-ish.'

Grace sighed inwardly; this was precisely what she didn't need. Her time to write was precious enough without the amount of work involved in supervising a viva eating into it. Assessing a research student and their work during the most important exam of their careers was not something Grace would contemplate taking lightly. It would take hours of careful preparation. Keeping her opinion to herself, her voice was light as she asked, 'What's the subject?'

The professor read from a sheet of paper he was carrying, 'It's entitled – wait for this! *The Sheriff of Nottingham; suppressed and oppressed over-worked civil servant, or out-and- out villain; the story of a fourteenth-century official.*'

'Good grief! Sounds like the work of a future tabloid journalist.'

Davis smiled again; his gleaming grin clashing with his dark skin. 'That's pretty much what I thought. He's supposed to be a good student, this Christopher Ledger. His supervisor is Dr Robert Franks.'

Grace frowned; she thought she knew all the medieval academics in the country, but his name was new to her, 'Who's he?'

'A new chap they've just got in. He's been spreading the knowledge in the USA. He did four years in Houston, and now he's taken on a post at Nottingham.'

It was ridiculous to feel worried, but Grace couldn't

keep the mildly anxious edge from her voice as she asked, 'What's his speciality, this Dr Franks?'

Davis pulled out a chair, understanding exactly why his colleague was enquiring, 'He's an expert on medieval landscapes and architecture, and the nobility that came with them.'

'Ah, hence the Sheriff of Nottingham-themed doctorate.' Grace was relieved that her academic territory hadn't been invaded so close to home. 'Is he good?'

'Very, apparently. He could help you with your own research, maybe. I believe Franks has access to the remaining land and forestry records of Nottinghamshire for the fourteenth century.'

Grace nodded, 'I admit some extra original evidence in that area would be useful.'

'How's your magnum opus coming on anyway?' Davis rose to his feet, 'Bit slowly right now I should think, after the admin avalanche that's fallen upon us from a great height over the last few weeks.'

Hiding her crossed fingers behind her back, Grace replied, hoping she wouldn't blush and give away her major exaggeration from the truth, which was that only a very sketchy draft of it existed so far, 'It's been tricky fitting it all in, but I'm at the second draft-checking stage. The skeleton is there, just needs the padding out to go now.'

'Excellent. I know there's no set deadline for it yet, Grace, but the sooner you finish your textbook, the sooner we can get it on the course reading list, and the better your career prospects; but I'm not telling you anything you don't know! Well then,' her boss heaved himself away from the filing cabinet against which he'd lent, 'I'll leave you to it. I'll tell the Nottingham lot you'll do it then, shall I?'

'Sure. Why not?'

'Thanks, Grace.'

Chapter Two

The sky was the sort of brilliant blue that primary school children happily daub in thick stripes across the top of any outside scene they happened to be painting. Free from a single cloud, it shimmered with a hazy heat from a piercing sun, whose rays were only diminished by the cover of a group of aged oak trees which huddled together at the end of Daisy's vast garden.

'I'll make a deal with you,' she said to the sky, 'you stay like this for my wedding, and I'll let you rain as much as you like for the rest of the summer. Deal?'

Laughing at herself, Daisy arranged a large wooden-framed run on one of the only patches of grass that her guinea pigs hadn't yet gnawed down to the roots. Despite the lawn's size, Daisy hadn't ever bothered to purchase a mower. With her ever-expanding livestock there was no need. Chatting to the animals as she placed hutches, pens, and runs in position, Daisy started the daily task of carrying the various furry creatures from their indoor to their outdoor accommodation. Glancing back up at the perfect sky, her mind returned to its preoccupation with her forthcoming nuptials. The fact it was happening at all was a miracle really.

Daisy hadn't grown up picturing herself floating down the aisle in an over-sequinned ivory frock, nor as a doting parent, looking after triplets and walking a black Labrador. So when, on an out-of-hours trip to the local vet's surgery she'd met Marcus and discovered that love at first sight wasn't a myth, it had knocked her for six.

She'd been on a late-night emergency dash to the surgery with an owl a neighbour had found injured in the road. Its wing had required a splint, and it was too big a job for only one pair of hands. Daisy had been more than a bit surprised when the locum vet had stirred some long-suppressed feeling of interest in her, and even more amazed when that feeling had been reciprocated.

It was all luck, sheer luck. Daisy had always believed that anyone meeting anybody was down to two people meeting at exactly the right place, at exactly the right time, while both feeling precisely the right amount of chemistry. The fact that any couples existed at all seemed to Daisy to be one of the greatest miracles of humanity.

She pictured Grace, tucked away in her mad little office only living in the twenty-first century on a part-time basis. Daisy had long since got used to the fact that her closest friend's mind was more often than not placed firmly in the 1300s. Daisy wished Grace would finish her book. It had become such a part of her. Such an exclusive aim that nothing else seemed to matter very much. Even the job she used to love seemed to be a burden to her now, and Daisy sensed that Grace was beginning to resent the hours it took her away from her life's work. Maybe if she could get her book over with – get it out of her system – then Grace would stop living in the wrong timeframe.

Daisy knew Grace appreciated that she never advised her to find a bloke, settle down, and live 'happily ever after,' and she was equally grateful Grace had never once suggested anything similar to her. Now she had Marcus, however, Daisy had begun to want the same contentment for her friend, and had to bite her tongue whenever they spoke on the phone; something that happened less and less these days.

Grace emails were getting shorter too. The long paragraphs detailing the woes of teaching students with an ever-decreasing intelligence had blunted down to, 'You ok? I'm good. Writing sparse. See you soon. Bye G x'

The book. That in itself was a problem. Grace's

publishers and colleagues, Daisy knew, were expecting an academic tome. A textbook for future medievalists to ponder over in the university libraries of the world. And, in time, that was exactly what they were going to get, but not yet, for Grace had confided to Daisy that this wasn't the only thing she was working on, and her textbook was coming a poor third place to work and the other book she couldn't seem to stop herself from writing.

'Why,' Grace had forcefully expounded on their last meeting, 'should I slog my guts out writing a book only a handful of bored students and obsessive freaks like myself will ever pick up, let alone read?'

As a result, Grace was writing a novel, 'A semi-factual novel,' she'd said, 'a story which will tell any student what they need to know about the Folville family and their criminal activities – which bear a tremendous resemblance to the stories of a certain famous literary outlaw! – and hopefully promote interest in the subject for those who aren't that into history without boring them to death.'

It sounded like a good idea to Daisy, but she also knew, as Grace did, that it was precisely the sort of book academics frowned upon, and she was worried about Grace's determination to finish it. Daisy thought it would be more sensible to concentrate on one manuscript at a time, and get the dry epic that everyone was expecting out of the way first. Perhaps it would have been completed by now if Grace could focus on one project at a time, rather than it currently being a year in the preparation without a final result in sight. Daisy suspected Grace's boss had no idea what she was really up to. After all, she was using the same lifetime of research for both manuscripts. She also had an underlying suspicion that subconsciously Grace didn't want to finish either the textbook or the novel; that her friend was afraid to finish them. After all, what would she fill her hours with once they were done?

Daisy's mobile began to play a tinny version of *Nellie*

the Elephant. She hastily plopped a small black guinea pig, which she'd temporarily called Charcoal, into a run with his numerous friends, and fished her phone from her dungarees pocket.

'Hi, Marcus.'

'Hi, honey, you OK?'

'Just delivering the tribe to their outside quarters, then I'm off to face the horror that is dress shopping.'

Her future husband laughed, 'You'll be fine. You're just a bit rusty, that's all.'

'Rusty! I haven't owned a dress since I went to parties as a small child. Thirty-odd years ago!'

'I don't understand why you don't go with Grace at the weekend. It would be easier together wouldn't it?'

Daisy sighed, 'I'd love to go with her, but I'll never get her away from her work more than once this month, and I've yet to arrange a date for her to buy a bridesmaid outfit.'

'Well, good luck, babe. I'm off to rob some bulls of their manhood.'

Daisy giggled. 'Have fun. Oh, why did you call by the way?'

'Just wanted to hear your voice, nothing else.'

'Oh, cute – ta!'

'Idiot! Enjoy shopping.'

As she clicked her battered blue mobile shut and slid it back into her working clothes, Daisy thought of Grace again. Perhaps she should accidentally invite loads of single men to the wedding to tempt her friend with. The trouble was, unless they wore Lincoln Green, and carried a bow and quiver of arrows, Daisy very much doubted whether Grace would even notice they were there.

Chapter Three

Mathilda thought she was used to darkness, but the dim candlelight of the comfortable small room she shared at home with her brothers was nothing like this. The sheer density of this darkness seemed to envelop her, physically gliding over Mathilda's clammy goose-pimpled skin. This was an extreme blackness that coated her, making her breathless, as if it was stealthfully compressing her lungs and squeezing the life from her.

Unable to see the floor, Mathilda presumed, as she pressed her naked foot against it and damp oozed between her toes, that the suspiciously soft surface she was sat on was moss, which in a room neglected for years had been allowed it to form a cushion on the stone floor. It was a theory backed up by the smell of mould and general filthiness which hung in the air.

Trying not to think about how long she was going to be left in this windowless cell, Mathilda stretched out her arms and bravely felt for the extent of the walls, hoping she wasn't about to touch something other than cold stone. The child's voice that lingered at the back of her mind, even though she was a woman of nineteen, was telling her – screaming at her – that there might be bodies in here, still clapped in irons, abandoned and rotting. Mathilda battled the voice down; knowing it that would do her no good at all. Her father had always congratulated Mathilda on her level headedness, and now it was being put to the test. She was determined not to let him down now.

Placing the very tips of her fingers against the wall behind her, she felt her way around. It was wet. Trickles of water had found a way in from somewhere, giving the walls the same slimy covering as the floor. Mathilda traced the outline of the rough stone wall, keeping her feet exactly where they were. In seconds her fingers came to a corner, and twisting at the waist, she managed to plot her prison from one side of the heavy wooden door to the other, without doing more than extending the span of her arms.

Mathilda decided the room could be no more than five feet square, although it must be about six foot tall. Her own five-foot frame had stumbled down a step when she'd been pushed into the cell, and her head was at least a foot clear of the ceiling. The bleak eerie silence was eating away at her determination to be brave, and the cold brought her suppressed fear to the fore. Suddenly the shivering Mathilda had stoically ignored overtook her, and there was nothing she could do but let it invade her small slim body.

Wrapping her thin arms around her chest, she pulled up her hood, hugged her grey woollen surcoat tighter about her shoulders, and sent an unspoken prayer of thanks up to Our Lady for the fact that her legs were covered.

She'd been helping her two brothers, Matthew and Oswin, to catch fish in the deeper water beyond the second of Twyford's fords when the men had come. Mathilda had been wearing an old pair of Matthew's hose, although no stockings or shoes. She thought of her warm footwear, discarded earlier with such merry abandon. A forgotten, neglected pile on the river bank, thrown haphazardly beneath a tree in her eagerness to get them off and join the boys in their work. It was one of the only tasks their father gave them that could have been considered fun.

Mathilda closed her eyes, angry as the tears she'd forbidden herself to shed defied her stubborn will and came anyway. With them came weariness. It consumed her, forcing her to sink onto the rotten floor. Water dripped into her long, lank red hair. The tussle of capture had loosened its neatly woven plait, and now it hung awkwardly, half in and half out of its bindings, like a badly strapped sheaf of strawberry corn.

She tried not to start blaming her father, but it was difficult not to. Why hadn't he told her he'd borrowed money from the Folvilles? It was an insane thing to do. Only the most desperate ... Mathilda stopped her thoughts in their tracks. They were disloyal and pointless.

They'd been relatively well-off when Mathilda was younger. They'd owned four horses, a few chickens, a cow, and a field for planting their own vegetables and a small amount of wheat. There was also the pottery shed and kiln where her father made his tableware and cooking pots, and a little orchard which backed onto the two-roomed house. Slowly, over the past few years, it had almost all been sold off. Only the workhouse, orchard, one horse and cart, and a single strip of the field remained.

Now she thought about it, Mathilda realised that they *had* been that desperate; she'd simply been so busy making the best of things that she hadn't had time to think about it. Since her mother had died four years ago, and the disastrous crop failure a few harvests back, combined with the decline in the demand for locally made pottery as ceramic tableware from Wales, the south, and even France flooded the markets, life had become steadily more difficult. Her father hadn't been able to compete, and each time he travelled the ten miles to the market at Leicester he seemed to come home more dejected than the time before, and with more and more unsold stock.

Last time her father had travelled to the city, he'd returned early, a desolate figure, with a cartload of shards behind him. A thief had struck in the market place, and in their unthinking eagerness to apprehend the villain the bailiff's men had run roughshod through the stalls, toppling her father's table as they went, leaving him with only broken stock and an increasingly broken faith.

'Our Lady,' Mathilda muttered in the gloom, her voiced hushed in fear, 'please deliver me from this place.' Then, guilty at having asked for something so boldly from someone she'd willingly begun to neglect of late, Mathilda added, 'I'm sorry, Our Lady, forgive me. I'm frightened, that's all. Perhaps though, you could look after my brothers and my father.'

Mathilda wasn't even sure that any of them were still

alive. The Folville family reputation made it more than possible that they'd all been killed.

As soon as she'd been taken, lifted bodily from the water as if she was as light as air, Mathilda had been bundled into a covered wagon and moved to the manor at Ashby Folville. A large man had sat with her, shoving a filthy rag between her lips to fend off the thousands of questions she had, and tying her hands behind her back.

The journey, although bumpy and bruising, was no longer than two miles, and soon Mathilda was untied and un-gagged and, having been thoroughly stared at from top to bottom by this impertinent man who seemed to have the ability to see through her clothes to the flesh beneath, was wordlessly bundled below stairs to her current lonely location. Her stomach growled at her, complaining at its emptiness. She felt cross with herself. How could she even consider food when her family was in danger?

'Just as well I don't want to eat,' she told herself sternly, 'as I probably won't ever see food again.' Then she collapsed to the ground, the terror and shock of the morning washing over her in a wave of misery.

Does Mathilda seem miserable and scared enough? Grace wasn't sure she'd laid the horror of the situation on thick enough. On the other hand, she didn't want to drown her potential readers in suffering-related adjectives.

No, on reflection it was fine; certainly good enough to leave and come back to on the next read through. She glanced at the clock at the corner of the computer screen. How the hell had it got to eight thirty already? Grace's stomach rumbled, making her think of poor Mathilda in her solitary prison.

Switching off her computer, Grace crammed all her notes into her bag so she could read over them at home, and headed out of her office. Walking down the Queen's Road, which led from the university to her small home in Leicester's Clarendon Park region, Grace decided it was way too hot, even at this time of the evening, to stand in the kitchen and attempt, and probably fail, to cook something edible, so she'd grab a takeaway.

Grateful it wasn't term time, so she didn't have to endure the banter of the students who were also waiting for associated plastic boxes of Chinese food, Grace speedily walked home, and without bothering to transfer her chicken chow mein to another dish, grabbed a fork, kicked off her shoes, and settled herself down with her manuscript.

The hall was foggy from a poorly-set fire, and it took Mathilda a few moments to take in her surroundings. The smoke stung her eyes, and even though the vast space was actually rather dark and dim, she blinked against the light, which was bright compared to the cell.

Her arms and feet hadn't been tied, but as a precaution against her potential escape the same surly man who'd deposited her in her prison earlier, dressed in the same dirty hose and capon, stood over her, his unusually tall frame giving off an unpleasant odour of sweat and fish.

As the fishy aroma assaulted Mathilda's nostrils, her mind flew to her brothers, and she opened her mouth to speak to the man sat at the table before her. The words never left her mouth though, as he raised his hand in a clear warning for her to remain silent.

Mathilda stared at him. He was finely dressed in a peacock blue cloak, with a green and brown tunic and matching hose. There was braiding around his collar, but this was not a man of high birth, nor was he the local sheriff or bailiff. His birth status was obviously somewhere in between high nobility and public servant. Mathilda swallowed nervously, and lowered her gaze to the floor in a natural response to before her betters – even if 'betters' was entirely the wrong description in this case. This man had to be a Folville. Mathilda began to shake with increased fear as a million possibilities of what might happen to her flew around her head. None of them were pleasant.

'I see you wish to ask questions,' His voice was husky but

soft, and without the harsh edge she'd been expecting, 'and yet wisely, and with a politeness I certainly appreciate considering the events of the day, you are waiting for permission. You will get your opportunity, but first I will ask *you* some questions.'

Mathilda kept her eyes firmly on the dusty floor, concentrating on her cold bare feet.

'What is your name, child, and how old are you?'

'Mathilda of Twyford. I'm nineteen, my Lord.'

'You appear much younger.' He looked harder into her face for a second before carrying on, 'Tell me, Mathilda, do you know the stories of Robyn Hode?'

Surprised by the question, Mathilda's head snapped up and for a second she found herself gazing directly into her captor's blue eyes. *Is he one of the Folville brothers after all?*

There was a grunt of derision from the man Mathilda had come to think of as her jailer as the possible Folville had asked his question.

Glaring over Mathilda's shoulder, straight at her escort, he dismissed him, 'I'm sure you must have parishioners to lead astray, Brother. I am sure I can attend to this girl alone.'

The religious brother, the rector of Teigh? Surely the man who'd dragged her here wasn't a man of the cloth? Mathilda had no time to speculate on this shocking revelation however, for the well-dressed man was repeating his question. 'Do you know the stories of Robyn Hode, child?'

'Why, yes, I do, my Lord.'

Catching the gleam in his eyes, Mathilda remembered herself, and hastily lowered her gaze again, frightened of his reaction to her infraction of class rules.

He seemed more amused than cross at her boldness, and Mathilda was sure she'd heard suppressed laughter in his voice as he continued, 'Well, Mathilda, can you tell me what Hode does?'

'He takes from rich people, sir, and helps those who he decides deserve it.'

'Very good. That's almost right. Although, if you listen to the balladeers carefully next time they are at the fair, you'll notice that he takes from those who are cruel or greedy; they weren't necessarily rich.' The man stood and came closer to the girl. She was filthy from the cell, and her shoulders shook, but he reflected, possibly more with hunger and thirst than straightforward fear. *Remarkable in one so young; especially a female.* 'You enjoy the stories?'

'Yes my Lord, my mother used to sing them, and I've heard them at the fair.'

'I like them too. I particularly like the bit when Robyn Hode takes a tax from those passing through Barnsdale, and how he punishes those who fail to discharge their debts.'

Bile rose in Mathilda's throat; so all this *was* about money. She wondered how much her father owed this man.

'Do you believe everyone should pay their debts, child?'

She tried to say 'Yes, my Lord,' but the words died in her throat as Mathilda imagined her father thrown into a cell like the one she'd occupied, and her brothers, dead or hurt. The horrific pictures rapidly growing within her mind suddenly swam together in an incoherent blur, and her legs began to buckle ...

Grace closed the notebook as she shovelled the final forkful of noodles into her mouth, reluctantly putting her novel notes away and turning her laptop on. She'd put off checking her emails all day, and knew that if she left them until tomorrow the messages that had already started to queue for her attention would have reached insurmountable proportions.

Scanning the list of forty-eight messages waiting in her inbox, she happily deleted twenty-one of them, all of which extolled the virtues of breast enlargements (Grace's Rubenesque size 16 figure would never need them), and penile extensions (for heaven's sake!). Then Grace skipped her eyes through the emails from her students, begging for deadline extensions for essays and projects that should have been handed in weeks before the summer break, along with their general gripes, groans, worries, and excuses.

Next she opened one from Professor Davis, who informed her he'd passed on her details to Dr Franks at Nottingham. Then she'd had an email from Franks himself.

Dear Dr Harper,

Many thanks for agreeing to step in 'cavalry-like' as the external examiner for my student – especially at such short notice.

Viva is a week on Friday at 2 p.m.

(Grace swore under her breath. Her boss had mentioned 'soon' but not 'instant')

Naturally I will take you out to lunch prior to the interview so we may discuss the thesis, its strengths, weaknesses, etc. A copy of the thesis has been sent to you via courier. You should get it tomorrow morning.

Perhaps you could meet me at 11.30 at the reception of the Lenton Grove building?

Looking forward to meeting a fellow medievalist.

Yours etc.

Rob (Franks)

'Creep.' Grace experienced an immediate dislike for this man she'd never met. 'Fellow medievalist' indeed! He made it sound like an exclusive club.

Finally Grace read an email from Daisy.

Hope you got my card. You WILL be my right-hand girl on this won't you? I couldn't possibly go through this wedding lark without your support.

Went to find a dress today – bloody disaster.

Have NO idea what suits me or what I want. I've even bought some wedding magazines in a desperate attempt to

get ideas. ME – WASTING MONEY ON MAGAZINES –
the world has gone mad!
   Anyway – when can we meet up to get your outfit?
Hope you ok. Give my love to RH!!
D xxx

Grace smiled; Daisy always sent Robin Hood her love, as
if he was a really was a tangible person in Grace's life. Her
smile died a little, however, as she thought of Daisy
buying magazines. That was not natural at all. And when
the hell was she going to find time to go dress hunting in
the next few weeks?

   She felt guilty. Grace knew she should offer to go with
Daisy to get her wedding dress as well as her own
bridesmaid's dress, but when? Shooting off an email,
Grace privately vowed to herself that writing, lecturing,
marking, and forthcoming viva notwithstanding, she
would find time for her best friend.

Of course I will be your bridesmaid. Looking forward to it.
   Will consult calendar first thing tomo morning re. dress
shopping, and we'll hit shops. (I won't whimper too much
if you promise I don't have to wear pink!!)
   RH says hi.
   G x

Chapter Four

Pulling back her curtains, Grace couldn't help but smile as the rain washed down the window. The hot sticky weather was all very well if you were comfortable wearing floaty skirts, or were happy to reveal your pasty legs for the critical observation of others. Grace wasn't. She never quite right unless she was wearing her trusty denims – black for work – blue for home.

There was something reliable and safe about pulling on a pair of jeans each morning. Grace knew they had become part of her identity over the years, and the last two weeks of sunshine-enforced thin linen trousers had made her feel wrong in a way she could never have explained to anyone else.

The view from her bedroom window was reassuringly the same as ever. Victorian terraced houses queued along the thin pavement opposite; parked cars lined up next to them in tight formation. Early morning dog walkers and paperboys and girls strode along the unexpectedly damp pavements of Howard Road.

Content with the scene, Grace reflected on how lucky she was to live in such a nice terrace within a stone's throw of work, and to be occupying one of the few homes in the area that wasn't neighboured by student accommodation on all sides.

It was only seven o'clock. Students usually cut through the street to the university from their residences at the top of Queen's Road, but at this time of year it was blissfully quiet.

Grace showered, pulled on her jeans and a long-sleeved T-shirt, shook out her shaggy mass of unruly brown hair, ignored the idea of breakfast, and, gathering her notes together headed into the muggy, warm Midlands air.

She felt strangely optimistic. Finally, Grace could see that all her work was beginning to pay off. Her novel was coming together, and the usual small voice of doubt at her superior's reaction at her prioritising of projects was, for once, happily lacking.

Determined to make the most of the day before her, Grace was already logged onto her office computer by eight o'clock, and was halfway through preparing a tutorial on the impact of the Black Death on the East Midlands for the MA students still in residence when, at ten o'clock, her stomach reminded her she hadn't eaten since her takeaway last night.

Saving her work, Grace grabbed the notes she'd written for the next chapter of her story and headed towards the senior common room, the prospect of a cuppa and suitably sticky muffin accelerating her speed.

Mathilda woke up disorientated by her surroundings. She had been laid upon a rough pallet stuffed with straw to make a mattress. A makeshift tapestry divider was drawn closed at her side, telling her that she was still in the main hall of the Folvilles' establishment, but had been moved to one of the servant's beds near the kitchen door to recover from her faint.

This consideration did not square with what she'd heard about the Folville family. Neither did the question about Robyn Hode, nor the amused demeanour of the man who'd asked it.

Mathilda had heard it said that Eustace de Folville would rip your head off with his bare hands if he so desired. There was no way that the man she had encountered could be Eustace. On the other hand, she wasn't finding it difficult to believe that her clergyman jailer had been a Folville. Richard, the rector of Teigh, fitted perfectly into an image of the family that rumour and gossip had spread all over the shire.

She'd heard stories about the family, of course, and although they always seemed to slip through the fingers of the law whenever a crime occurred, Mathilda knew with certainly that the family had been responsible for the organisation of thefts, kidnaps, assaults, and even the death of Baron Roger Belers three years earlier.[1] That murder of a Baron of Exchequer had been the stuff of local gossip ever since. Mathilda had been sixteen in that year, 1326, when the news that a gang led by the Folvilles had come together to dispose of the old man. She clearly remembered her father and brothers talking about Belers' death in hushed tones, more in awe and relief at the removal of such an unscrupulous man who, rumour said, had acquired much of his lands illegally, than in horror at the manner of his death. The gossip went further: that two men Mathilda had never heard of before, Henry de Heredwyk and Roger la Zouche, had paid the Folvilles to removal the baron from the face of the earth.

No one had ever been properly tried for the crime, but at the same time, everyone knew who was responsible, and enough suspicion had arisen for the Folville family to have their lands at Reresby taken from them; more as a warning than an official punishment.

Mathilda rubbed her forehead; it was hot and sticky despite the cool of the room, and she feared she might be feverish. Or perhaps it was sheer terror, as she contemplated the household's reputation. When she'd asked her eldest brother, Matthew, about Eustace after Beler's death, he'd simply said, 'he commits evils' and refused to be drawn further. It was a simple sentence, but it had been enough to make Mathilda want to keep well away from the Folville villages and manor.

The Folville family, from what Mathilda knew of them, had adopted crime as a way of making a living, alongside the maintenance of their lands and overseeing of the immediate area, although few would have been foolish enough to accuse them of such activities face to face. Thus, the family of brothers had made their presence felt beyond Ashby

Folville, across the Hundred of East Goscote and the county of Leicestershire as a whole.[2]

Mathilda sat up slowly on the bed. Her head thudded, but she no longer felt dizzy. She supposed she should try and escape, but realistically Mathilda knew that would be suicide, and might well endanger her family. She felt as helpless as she felt useless. Should she sit where she was until someone came to sell her to move? Should she announce that she was awake?

Aware of voices beyond the tapestry curtain, Mathilda could hear approaching footsteps. Someone was moving across the hall to where she'd been placed to recover ...

The sound of *Doctor Who's* TARDIS landing cut through Grace's concentration, forcing her to return to the present time-stream so she could answer her mobile.

'Hi, honey,' Daisy's interrupted thoughts of all the possible ways out of Mathilda's plight.

'Hello, everything OK?'

'Fine. Look, I'm really sorry to disturb you at work, but it's this bloody wedding stuff. It's only a small do but it's already taking over my life. Anyway, I need to hassle you about getting a bridesmaid dress.'

Hearing the stress in Daisy's voice, guilt stabbed at Grace; she'd totally forgotten about her emailed promise to sort out a shopping date that morning, 'Of course, no problem at all. Hang on ...' putting the phone down for a moment, Grace rummaged in her bag for her diary '... here we go. Now, when's good for you?'

'Any late afternoon in July, or any weekend apart from this coming one and the two before the wedding.'

Grace flicked through her calendar. That hardly left any time at all. She caught sight of the following Friday's appointment in Nottingham on her calendar. She supposed that once she was there she'd be on the way to Hathersage anyway, and if her Friday was being disturbed, she might as well lose the Saturday as well. 'I could head your way a week tomorrow. I have to be at Nottingham University all day, but I could come up to you from there and stay over, if you could stand it. Then we could shop on the Saturday.'

'That's fantastic,' Daisy failed to keep the surprise out of her tone.

'Why so shocked?'

'Well, come on, honey, you're not the easiest lass to drag away from work, even over a weekend.'

Grace blushed down the phone, 'I'm sorry, Daze, but I promise you, nothing is going to come between me and my best friend's wedding.'

'Not even a certain gentleman in green tights and his associated criminal rogues?'

'Not even them!' Grace was surprised by her determination, and was even more surprised by the fact that it was genuine. She wasn't going to let her need to work ruin Daisy's big day. 'I can't promise to find a dress I like though!'

'Well if it comes to that, neither can I. These magazines are useless unless you're stick-thin with fake boobs and perfect skin.'

'That's you and me out then.'

Daisy's sigh was audible down the line, 'I'm sure there must be a shop in Sheffield with exactly the sizes 14 and 16 we're searching for.'

'Of course there will be; let's hope they're not in pink frou-frou though, shall we!' Grace was relieved to hear Daisy chuckle down the line, and was suddenly reluctant to hang up. It was, she realised, a long time since she'd spared the time to have a proper chat with her friend. Still, if she was going to have a weekend off, she'd better crack on now, 'I'm sorry Daze, I have to go. I have scripts to mark and a viva to prepare for.'

'Sure thing. I'll see you in nine days!'

After she'd shut off her phone, Grace sat quite still. It had been years since she'd considered her outward appearance beyond the requirements of comfort and a gesture towards token smartness. She knew she didn't look too bad; she wasn't a fashion disaster or anything. She was just *ordinary*; jeans, T-shirts, jumpers, casual jackets, trainers – all the normal stuff. Nothing special; just normal. A feeling of inadequacy swept through Grace. How could she possibly do Daisy and Marcus justice? She didn't have a clue about how to be a bridesmaid, let alone what to wear.

The papers on her lap began to slip off, and the action of retrieving them brought Grace back to herself. For a split second she was shocked to find herself sat in the common room and not in her office.

'Ridiculous woman.' She murmured to herself, slugging back the remains of her cold tea, and heading back to work and the fourteen projects on the role of women in medieval society that awaited the judging scrawl of her red pen.

Chapter Five

The marking of the dissertations seemed to have taken forever. In three days' time Grace was due in Nottingham. The parcel that had been couriered over from Nottingham University containing the thesis lay untouched on her desk, and all the good intentions Grace had had about checking out some of the academic papers Dr Franks had produced to get a grasp of his field of study had come to nothing.

Taking a deep breath, Grace pulled the word-heavy doctorate out of its protective padded envelope and turned to its abstract.

This dissertation addresses the different manners in which lawlessness was dealt by those holding the office of Sheriff in the county of Nottinghamshire between 1300 and 1372. It will attempt to analyse this civil servant's role against a background of great historical change; the procession of three monarchs, Edward I, Edward II, and Edward III, the impact of the Black Death, and the subsequent economic boom that came in its wake, alongside the continual wars and the impact of the taxation needed to finance them.

An attitude of violence, fraud, and thuggery had become almost acceptable in the fourteenth century, and was certainly expected as a form of self-advancement for both the sheriff and his officials. This dissertation will look at this perception of behaviour in relation to the literary ballad evidence and political songs of the period which ...

Grace closed her eyes. She'd need some strong coffee if she was going to read all this today, or, better still, – she needed to hide. If she stayed in her office then she'd only be interrupted. Anyway, the Robin Hood posters on the walls were staring at her, telling Grace to get on with her novel. Ignoring the combined reproachful looks of the paper outlaws, thankful she had no teaching scheduled until the new term in October, Grace gathered up the thesis and headed to the library.

Heading down the steps that took her from her building, towards the ugly glass rectangle that held the university's supply of books, Grace consoled herself with the fact that at least the thesis should be an interesting read. *I might even learn something for my own book.* With that idea, Grace disappeared into the semi-tranquillity of the library basement, and sat amongst hundreds of unread PhDs, all lined up on the shelves, haunting the place with the ghosts of long-past students and their fleeting visits into the world of extended knowledge.

'Dr Harper?'

The voice was speaking with the forced calm that only library assistants and primary school teachers can manage. 'Dr Harper, I'm sorry to disturb you.'

Grace looked up in surprise, blinking slightly as her eyes adjusted to not staring at endless rows of neat Times New Roman.

'We're closing, I'm sorry.'

'Closing?'

'Yes, it's ten o'clock.'

'At night?'

'Yes.'

Grace felt stupid, and wasn't sure she believed the sensibly skirted young woman who hovered at the side of her table. She peered at her own watch. Ten o'clock. She'd been here, engrossed in her reading, since three o'clock.

'I'm sorry, yes, of course, I lost track of time.'

'Thank you, Dr Harper.'

'She must think I'm crackers,' Grace muttered to

herself as she closed the thesis. It had been much better than she'd expected it to be. In fact, it was excellent, and she had already, with only a mild pang of guilt, noted a few points for use in her own work, vowing to herself that the young writer would get a mention in her acknowledgements.

A list of possible questions and queries to ask at the viva were scribbled in her notebook, and even though she still had the final chapter and conclusion to examine, Grace felt on a firmer footing now she knew what the postgraduate had researched so thoroughly. It was important not to put herself in a position of potential ignorance next to the internal examiner. For an indefinable reason, which Grace was putting down to professional pride, she didn't want to appear an inferior historian compared to the apparently ultra-clever Dr Franks.

Her stomach growled at her as it always did when she walked home, as if it was calling out to the local takeaways all on its own. Never having mastered the art of being a domestic goddess, Grace rarely cooked, and it seemed cruel to her that although she hardly ever ate, yet she was a size sixteen – well, a fifteen really. Fourteens didn't quite fit, and sixteens were a bit big. Yet she wasn't worried about her body – or hadn't been worried until this wedding business had begun. It wasn't long now until she had to go shopping, and suddenly her unruly hair, ample bust, and padded hips, seemed even more unruly, increasingly ample, and more heavily-padded than before.

She could hear her mother's words echoing at the back of her head, telling her only child off for not looking after herself properly. Whenever Grace's mum phoned her, she conveyed how worried she was about her daughter's solitary lifestyle – which really meant, 'Why don't you get yourself married and give me grandchildren?' Grace always said she was fine thank you very much, and that she'd think about all that sort of thing after she'd finished her books.

The books. They had become her latest reason for not doing anything else with her days. In the odd occasional burst of honesty, usually at about three o'clock in the morning if she was having a sleepless night, Grace knew the books were merely the last in a long line of excuses. First there had been her degree, then her PhD, then building up her post-doctorate experience, followed by getting a good reputation as a junior lecturer; and in all that time the only interesting men she'd given any real quality time to had been dead for hundreds of years – if they'd even existed in the first place.

Ignoring the siren calls of the pizza place, Grace headed home to cook a quick dinner of pasta, eating it out of the saucepan while watching an old episode of *Robin of Sherwood* on DVD. Grace marvelled, as she always did, at how young all the actors looked. It may have been recorded over twenty years ago – but you only had to look at the once-gorgeous Ray Winstone … Grace chuckled to herself. Even Daisy hadn't understood her crush on the character of Will Scarlet. He was portrayed as the most violent, merciless, and unforgiving of the outlaws, and yet Grace always had the urge to give him a big cuddle. He was a bad boy you just had to love.

It was one o'clock in the morning before Grace finally put down the PhD thesis. There was no question in her mind: it was one of the best she'd ever read. She would have to watch this future academic carefully; he'd be stepping on her territory. 'Best make him an ally and not an enemy then,' Grace said to the framed poster of Basil Rathbone's Guy of Gisborne that was hanging on the upstairs landing wall, before she gave up on the day and went to bed.

Chapter Six

One of the household servants had been instructed to check on Mathilda every few minutes, and having found her awake and lucid, had followed his instructions to the letter and provided her with a hunk of reasonably fresh bread, some thin vegetable soup, and a cup of ale.

Mathilda had eaten and drunk hastily and gratefully. She thanked her new companion while chewing on a mouthful of bread in a manner which would have infuriated her father, who had strangely strict ideas on table manners compared to his easy-going nature in every other aspect of life. She knew his dinner table lecture by heart: 'You never know when important visitors might call. We should always be at our best and give a good impression at the table.'

She could hear her father's deep gravelly voice clearly, and see his grey-mottled bearded head. He'd been a tall man once, but since his forty-fifth year he'd seemed to dwindle, as if ill and fed up with the routine of daily existence without her mother.

The last drops of soup and ale gone, Mathilda brushed a few escaped breadcrumbs from her lap and whispered to her companion, 'What's your name? Can you tell me where I am?'

The boy, for he was no more than twelve years old, was edgy. 'They call me Allward.' He obviously hadn't been given direct permission to talk. On the other hand, he hadn't been forbidden to do so either, for after a moment's pause he whispered back, 'Ashby Folville hall, the home of his Lordship John Folville.'

'John? Not Eustace?'

Allward bowed his head, obviously uncomfortable, 'It is my Lord John's home, but he is rarely here, preferring instead to reside in Leicester or Huntingdon. Naturally his

33

whole family here in Ashby Folville too, on and off.'

'Was it my Lord John who bid me rest and eat?'

'No miss, it wasn't.' The boy stood up, 'I'm to take you back now, please follow me.'

'Back to where? To who?'

The boy didn't reply as he led her away from the small, closeted space into the main hall, but he threw her a look of apology that did nothing to calm Mathilda's quickly re-emerging fears.

'You are Mathilda of Twyford, daughter of Bertred of Twyford and sister to Matthew and Oswin?'

'Yes, my lord,' Mathilda stared at her feet as once again she stood back before the man in the blue cloak. She could feel the heat of his piercing eyes examining her closely.

'Do you remember what I asked you, Mathilda? Before you swooned.'

'Yes, my Lord,' Mathilda mumbled her reply, before remembering her manners. 'Thank you for looking after me, my Lord.'

'You are welcome.'

She risked a glance at her noble companion's face, but it gave away nothing. Mathilda judged him to be in his twentieth year, maybe a little older. His body was not as smooth as to indicate a wholly indoor life, but nor was it so tanned or calloused to indicate an existence labouring in the fields or at a craft. She placed him as one of the younger brothers, not quite having a role, unless to fight as a knight for the king, or to enter the church. Not that she could imagine him in the latter role.

'So what were we saying, Mathilda?'

'I agreed that debtors should pay their debts my Lord.'

'Good.' He stood and paced between her and the fire that now roared without excess smoke, but was remained rather too fierce for safety, causing him to gesture to Allward to come and tame it before the flames licked towards the house timbers. 'Sometimes debtors do not pay what they owe through sheer greed, and we, my brothers and I, have ways of sorting those situations out.'

Mathilda's spine tingled, and a chill ran through her as this calm stranger, a stranger who'd showed himself capable of kindness, implied threats and murder.

'On other occasions, a debtor, who is known to be otherwise honest, is unable to pay what's owed straight away. Or perhaps the debt is more complex than the mere owing of money. Chattels are used, sometimes crops or animals, or sometimes,' he paused again, his eyes assessing Mathilda shrewdly as he placed his hands on her shoulders, making her tense beneath his firm touch, '... with the loan or gift of servants or younger members of the family.'

Not giving Mathilda time to react to the import of what he'd said, the man continued, letting go of her and crashing without dignity into his seat with a sigh. 'These are turbulent times, Mathilda. King Edward II has been removed, and although his child sits upon the throne, he is but a puppet. It is his Queen Isabella and her lover Mortimer who pull the strings of this country. As the Despenser estates, and the lands and policies of Thomas of Lancaster, are continually argued over, and our fair country's honour over the matter of that cursed land of Scotland is debated, who has an eye on the small towns of England? No one. No, we must look to ourselves, Mathilda; we must take care of our shire and protect it against injustice. Don't you agree?'

Mathilda nodded. She hadn't understood a lot of what he'd said and, anyway, her mind was filling with the slow realisation that her father not only saw her as a mere chattel, but had exchanged her, like a cow or a carven chest, to pay his debt. The cold that seemed to have hung about her since her release from the small prison returned, and she had to fight to hide the shivers that were making her shoulders quake.

'I knew you were an intelligent woman.'

The nobleman appeared pleased, and Mathilda fought her confusion in order not to displease him, saying, 'You protect the area, like Robyn Hode would if he was really amongst us, my Lord, if you please.'

'Indeed, girl, just like Hode would if he were truly here.'

The Folville didn't say anything else for a moment, but seemed satisfied as he watched his quarry. She didn't shake now. He'd seen how hard she had fought within herself to still her external reactions to his news of her change in circumstance, and had admired her self-control. She had more of an offended dignity about her than terror. He wondered if she'd been taught her letters. Most families' didn't waste their time teaching their womenfolk such things, but this Mathilda was sharp and capable. With the mother gone, he imagined she'd run the household, and probably did the job well.

Breaking the silence that had stretched out between them he said, 'You have questions for me. I can see your mind jarring with them.'

'If I may, my Lord?'

'You may, although I should caution you, I may not always choose to offer a reply.'

Mathilda licked her lips and ran her clammy palms down her grubby belted dress, which largely hid the fact she was wearing boys' hose and flexed her cold numbed bare toes. 'Please, my Lord, who are you?'

This produced a bark of laughter, 'You don't know me, child? I apologise. You are well-mannered despite the indignity of being thrust, if only for a short while, into our cell, and have instantly spotted the flaw in my own behaviour, for I haven't introduced myself. I am Robert de Folville, youngest of the seven brothers of the manor.'

Mathilda curtsied, more out of natural impulse than any feelings of reverence to this man, who she now knew for certain had been party to at least one murder, 'You are brother to Eustace, my Lord?'

'Yes girl, I am.' He cocked his head to one side. 'That worries you?'

'He is a man I have been taught to fear, forgive my impudence, my Lord.'

He snorted, 'I would rather have honest impudence than bluff and lies. So, you have been instructed by your father to

36

be wary of us?'

'Not only my father, sir.' Abruptly worried that her boldness might place her family in more danger, Mathilda clamped her mouth shut. Seeing, however, that the younger Folville wasn't cross, but had a mild expression of acceptance on his face, Mathilda braved a further question.

'Where is my father, my Lord, and, Matthew and Oswin, my brothers?'

Robert paused, and after a moment's consideration, gestured for the servant boy to bring her a chair. Mathilda sat down gladly, confused at the equal status she was being afforded after her earlier abuse, as the Folville sat next to her, leaning in close to her slight, tensed frame.

'Your father and your brother Matthew are at home in Twyford working on ways to pay back our debt. As yet, I do not know all the details of Oswin's whereabouts. I am, after all, only one of the *younger* brothers.'

Mathilda heard the bitterness in him, and for the first time understood a little of this man. He would probably have made a good lord of the manor, but his lot was to be a minor son.

'You will have heard of the death of Belers three years hence?'

'Yes, my Lord.' Mathilda spoke softly, her mind going back to the day she'd heard about the murder on Brokesby Field. It may not have happened right on their doorstep, but the frisson of fear the crime had engendered had been felt even in Twyford; such was their closeness to the Folvilles manor house; and the waves the crime had created were still leaving ripples these many months later.

He must have read her mind, for Robert slammed his hand against the table, making Mathilda jump, 'Damn it all woman, Belers was a tyrant! An oppressive and rapacious man who had become a scourge on our county! We did what needed to be done. Robyn Hode would have done no less!'

Mathilda said nothing, but knew he meant what he said. Robert, and probably his brothers as well, evidently believed they were providing a public service, and took their fee for such a deed as wages, just as the sheriff did when he arrested a felon for the King.

Folville leant towards Mathilda earnestly, 'Did your father ever sing you "The Outlaw's Song of Trailbaston", child?'

'I've heard of it, my Lord, but no, I don't know it as I know the Robyn Hode tunes.'

'It contains much wisdom. I have no doubt that its great length influenced the author of the Hode stories.' Robert sat back in his seat, his long arms stretched behind his head as he began to quote a verse to his captive.

You who are indicted, I advise you, come to me,

To the green forest of Belregard, where there is no annoyance

But only the wild animal and the beautiful shade;

For the common law is too uncertain.[3]

What do you say, child?'

Mathilda swallowed again. The ale she'd drunk earlier had been stronger than she was used to, and had made her head ache and left her throat feeling sticky, producing a thirst worse than before. 'I believe there is wisdom within, my Lord. I have heard my elders say that the law is confusing. If we truly have been abandoned by the law, perhaps you are correct to take matters into your own hands – within reason, my Lord.'

Mathilda flinched, expecting her host to strike out. She shouldn't have said that last bit. Why couldn't she ever keep her opinions to herself and her tongue in check? Her directness had always been a bone of contention within the family, and now Mathilda was regretting sharing her opinion honestly, rather than telling Folville what he wanted to hear. She tensed, awaiting the call to the guard to come and throw her back into prison.

It did not come. Folville was peering at her quizzically, 'You are a curious creature, Mathilda of Twyford. You must have realised you have been used to pay off your father's debts, but you ask nothing of your own future, only theirs. My reverend brother placed you briefly in our cell, and you do not ask why, or make complaint about your hasty kidnap and enclosure.'

Mathilda bit her tongue, not wanting to say the wrong thing, despite her need for answers to the questions he'd posed.

'Your father told Eustace and the rector that you were headstrong and determined when they collected you, so Richard decreed a spell in our holding cell would soften you to our will.' Robert snorted into his mug of ale. 'He obviously never bothered to take the time to talk to you before he acted. A fact about my holy brother that surprises me not one jot.'

Mathilda looked back at the floor, the first glimmer of a smile since her removal from the river, trying to form at the corner of her mouth.

'Your father also said to Eustace that you have qualities more suited to the male gender than the gentler sex. It seems you are happier in the river or fields than the house or orchard, and only ran the home begrudgingly as it is your duty as a female.'

Mathilda said nothing, but was unable to prevent the crimson blush that came as she heard how her father had described her to a stranger. She felt indignant. Mathilda had worked hard to run the house, small garden, and orchard as successfully as her mother had done, even though it was a task she didn't enjoy and frequently resented.

'Well, Mathilda, I will tell you what Eustace has arranged with your father.'

Mathilda sat up straighter, her hands clasped in her lap as she listened.

'We have an adequate compliment of servants here, Mathilda, so exchanging you for payment of a debt was a rather unusual thing for Eustace to do.'

Mathilda felt sick. A thousand unpleasant uses for her swam through her mind.

'Eustace had considered selling you on, for servants and whores are always required.' Mathilda blanched at the easy, casual manner in which he spoke of her potential disposal, 'but your father told him you were intelligent, and so he had an idea of a more satisfying use for you – for all of us. Do you have letters?

'Some, my Lord, but only to read, not to write.'

'That is of no matter. Reading will be of help, and I'm sure you will learn more without too much trouble.'

Interest disturbed Mathilda's troubled features. Surely they were unlikely to be about to sell her as a slave to the highest bidder if they were interested in if she'd been educated.

'You are to be our assistant and my companion. Do you think you could do that, Mathilda of Twyford?'

Mathilda's jaw dropped open, but no words came out, and she gasped for air, as she took in the narrowness of her escape from the shame of prostitution. Yet she couldn't help wonder if her soul would end up being in even worse peril if she was to stay within these walls for too long.

'Mathilda?'

'My Lord, I will certainly do my best, but, if I may, sir, what sort of assistant?'

Chapter Seven

The triple knock on her office door could only have been from Agatha. The department secretary had her own special way of knocking, which she successfully employed so that the closeted academics would know it was her requiring attention and not a student; in which case, they shouldn't ignore the summons to answer the door.

'Morning, Aggie, how's tricks?' Grace liked the secretary, and unlike some of her colleagues didn't blame her personally for the piles of red tape they needed to wade through every week.

Agatha was the mother of two girls, stepmother to two boys, supporter of a million good causes, administrator of the local University of the Third Age, and multi-tasker extraordinaire. She was at least fifteen years older than Grace, maybe more, and yet Grace frequently wished she had half as much energy as the secretary did.

Pulling up a chair, Agatha slumped into it. 'You don't mind if I park my bum for a moment, do you? I'm shattered! I was up at five o'clock this morning trying to extract the mud Malcolm's rugby kit has plastered all over the insides of the washing machine, then I was in by six getting the marked exam papers sorted and put in the safe. I've been having an increasingly personal war with the undergraduate project results spreadsheets on my computer, only to have the damn thing crash on me. I may have lost the lot.'

'Oh, hell!' Grace winced, knowing exactly how much extra work that would mean, not just for Agatha, but for the staff in general.

'I.T. Ian is in my office dealing with it now. Heaven

knows if he'll manage to save it, but if the resident computer genius can't fix it then I'm stuffed.'

'Why on earth were you cleaning the washer at 5 a.m.? Surely your stepson's mess could have waited?'

Agatha sighed, 'He has football this evening, and has a habit of adding very muddy kit to *very* muddy kit, I've had to have the washing machine drum changed three times already. Two loads of mud will probably finish the machine off completely. Couldn't sleep, so I got up and dealt with it.'

'Oh.' Grace wanted to ask if she made Malcolm pay for it, after all he was a grownup, who earned his own wages, but she knew Agatha had a soft heart when it came to her children, step or otherwise, and didn't want to offend her by asking. Instead Grace asked, 'You want to come for a coffee? I was about to get one before I hit the road to Nottingham.'

'Ah.'

'Ah?'

'Well, um … yes. That's why I'm here really. You see, I've been meaning to talk to you about Nottingham.'

Grace was instantly suspicious, especially when she noticed how uncomfortable Agatha suddenly appeared. 'What is it?'

'Right, well it's like this.' The secretary hit her palms to her lap with a decisive slap, 'Remember, this is not coming from me; I am but a poorly paid messenger, OK?

'O-kay …'

'I have been told to ask you … no, I have been told to *tell* you that it is not considered acceptable for you to attend a viva inappropriately attired.'

Grace pulled a face. 'You mean I can't get away with wearing my black jeans and a posh blouse this afternoon.'

'You can't wear jeans.'

'Oh, bum.'

'I knew you'd say that.'

Grace madly began to gather everything required for the afternoon ahead into her bag, 'Look, I don't have much else to wear, as it is I've packed my only smart stuff to endure bridesmaid dress shopping in Sheffield tomorrow.' She pointed to the battered holdall stowed under her desk.

Agatha didn't bother trying to hide her smirk, 'You! A bridesmaid!'

'Yes, all right, I know,' Grace snapped, before smiling apologetically and sitting back heavily in her seat, 'So what does Professor Davis deem appropriate attire? I'm always smart, aren't I?'

'You are indeed, and to be fair, Davis doesn't give two hoots what you wear as long as you do your job properly. No, it's a new "directive,"' Agatha made speech marks in the air with her fingers and placed a resigned expression on her face, 'from the Vice Chancellor no less. Apparently we need to "promote the good name of Leicester University in other academic institutions".'

'You mean the old buffer is worried about how well De Montfort Uni is doing, and wants us to outshine them with our haute couture, even though our clothing has nothing to do with our brainpower.'

'That about sums it up.'

'Oh, hell! This is such a waste of time. So what do I wear?'

'Did you iron your shirt?'

'What do you think?'

'Do you own a suitable dress? A smart trouser suit?'

Grace grimaced and pointed to her holdall, 'I have a creased pair of linen trousers and a white blouse with a button missing to wear while shopping tomorrow.'

'Smart?'

'In a very casual way.'

'Not smart then.'

'Well, no.'

'When do you need to leave here?'

43

'My train is at 10.05.'

Agatha stood up, a determined expression on her face, 'Right, that gives us a whole hour and a half. Come on, Cinders, you shall go to the ball. Even though you don't want to!'

Ten minutes later Grace found herself back on Queen's Road out of breath, standing in a cramped Oxfam shop changing room. Agatha was passing her random skirts, tops and jackets, as Grace stood self-consciously in an un-matching bra and pants, and unsuitable black ankle socks and trainers.

Three skirts, four shirts, and two jackets later, Agatha declared Grace done, but insisted on fastening her own chunky silver necklace around Grace's neck, 'to add that "vital something."'

Having paid an amazingly cheap price for a complete outfit, Grace was hurried off to her home to put on tights and her one and only pair of court shoes.

As she stuffed her jeans and trainers into the top of her weekend bag, Grace swore at the Vice-Chancellor under her breath. About to meet the new historian on the block, and examine a whiz kid postgraduate in the most important interview of his life; she was supposed to feel relaxed, professional, and confident. Instead Grace felt conspicuous, and rather like an over-dressed Christmas tree.

Forcing herself to stand still for a second, Grace stared into her bedroom mirror and took some calming breaths. The creature gazing back at her seemed only vaguely familiar. A deep khaki, full length, but flattering shaped skirt was topped with a paler green V-necked top, which to Grace's mind made her boobs look enormous, but which Agatha assured her made them look shapely and attractive. The jacket they'd found almost matched the skirt, and was luckily plain and simple. Grace hadn't had the heart to tell

Agatha she only had navy blue shoes, but personally she didn't care, and was pleased by her minor flouting of fashion's bizarre rules.

She had twelve minutes to get to the station. Thank goodness Aggie had arranged a cab. Making sure she had the thesis, her own work, money, her iPod, a train ticket, and her overnight things for a stay at Daisy's, Grace let herself out of her house and onto the doorstep in the gentle sunshine as the taxi pulled up in front of her.

To Grace's immense relief, the train was five minutes late, and she managed to settle herself in one of the few vacant seats just in time for the East Midlands train to whisk her to Beeston station on the outskirts of Nottingham, which was only a stone's throw from the university.

Plugging her iPod into her ears, Grace rested her head against the seat and tried to relax, as the haunting tones of Clannad playing the *Robin of Sherwood* soundtrack soothed her. She briefly toyed with the idea of reading through some of her own manuscript, but it was only a twenty-five minute journey and she knew she'd be better employed re-reading the PhD abstract and conclusion.

Grace had just been re-impressed with the postgraduate's neatly tied together final paragraph when the train pulled into Beeston's small station. Five minutes later Grace was in another taxi, taking her to the nearby university campus.

She'd done about half a dozen vivas in her five-year stint as a lecturer, twice as a supervisor, and four times as the external examiner. Grace should have been calm and radiated confidence, and yet wearing these unfamiliar clothes, about to face a stranger she was slightly in awe of, Grace found herself questioning whether she really knew anything about her subject at all.

Usually when invited to attend such interviews, Grace already knew the other examiner fairly well, even if they'd never met she would have read their books and papers and probably heard them speak at a conference or two. The medieval England historians' circle was a small world, and everyone was aware of everyone else. This Rob Franks was new and therefore an unknown quantity. Was he young or old, black or white, straight or gay? Was he vastly published, or completely new and unpublished? Grace cursed herself for being too wrapped up in her own writing to research Franks as properly as she would normally have done. It was unprofessional, and she felt she'd let herself down.

Panic had a go at trying to claim Grace, but she quickly shrugged it off and attempted to be practical as she headed to the School of History, situated in a stunning Georgian building called Lenton Grove on the west side of the campus. Walking sedately, trying to get a grip on her nerves, Grace, not caring if anyone overheard and thought she was nuts, muttered under her breath, 'For goodness sake, this is Nottingham. If you're out there anywhere, Robin Hood, then help me get through this in one piece, and then I'll return to the novel, I promise.'

Chapter Eight

Determined not to appear as flustered as she felt, Grace took herself into the nearest cloakroom and washed her hands. Fluffing her mass of hair into a marginally less straggly state, she sternly told her reflection that she was clever, knew as much as anyone about medieval England, and that this Dr Franks would be friendly and it would all be fine. She didn't let herself think about after the viva. The idea of dress shopping with Daisy the following day made her palms sweat.

Picking up her belongings, Grace thought of her novel's protagonist, Mathilda, frightened but brave, sitting with a member of the infamous Folville family with no idea what fate was about to throw at her. 'And you think you've got problems!'

Having announced her arrival to the Humanities Department receptionist, and asking if he would mind storing her overnight bag until the viva was over, Grace took a seat and awaited Dr Franks. As she looked around at the inevitable Robin Hood motif and the associated posters you'd expect to see anywhere in Nottingham, her mind drifted once again to Mathilda. Aware she was in danger of getting bogged down in too much historical detail if she wasn't careful, she tried to work out how to move the story along a little faster.

Usually Mathilda bathed in the village ford, splashing around in an attempt to scrape off the flour, leaves, grass, and dust of daily life. Total immersion in a bath was a completely new experience for her.

When the austere female servant had been instructed to take her to bathe, Mathilda had been frightened, not really understanding what was about to happen. Everything was changing so fast. Only a little while ago she'd been catching fish in the river, then she'd been taken and imprisoned, and now she was being told to strip off all her dirty but familiar clothes, and get into the water that steamed before the fire in a small room off the main hall.

Her fears, in this case a least, were unfounded. Plunged into the lightly lavender-fragranced tub, the blissfully warm water soothed her undernourished body and un-knotted her tense muscles. Mathilda sighed with the feeling of a temporary reprieve, for while she immersed in that pool there was nothing she could do about anything except get clean, and she found herself unexpectedly grateful for a period of forced inactivity, where she could neither receive instructions nor fruitfully plot to run away.

I'm alive, she mused, and if, as Robert de Folville himself had told her she'd been exchanged for a debt, then her family should also be alive and well, so that could work on paying it off.

As the tight-lipped housekeeper undid the remaining ties of her hair, and washed out its knotted tresses Mathilda resolved to believe that her new master was basically kind. It was less frightening that way. If the opportunity arose for her to ask about her family again, then she would do just that.

'Dr Harper?'

A tall, fair-haired man, who she'd guess was probably in his late thirties, towered over Grace.

Rising with a start, Grace dropped her manuscript into her bag as she stood. 'I'm sorry, I was miles away.'

'Was it nice there?'

'Sorry?'

'Forget it, I was being silly.' He extended a perfectly clean and pleasantly warm hand, the remnants of a tan faintly discernible, 'I'm Robert Franks. Everyone calls me Rob.'

'Grace.'

'Good journey?' Dr Franks went into the usual routine of small talk as he led Grace towards the staff common room, and the chance of lunch and a more serious conversation about the forthcoming viva interview.

After ordering a baked potato and cup of coffee apiece, they settled themselves by a window overlooking the expanse of parkland beyond the university. Grace stared out across the green landscape, her eyes mentally removing the lampposts, litterbins, and students, to see it with medieval eyes.

'It's a nice view, isn't it? Dr Franks was watching Grace intently, 'They tell me the grounds run to about 330 acres.'

Grace found herself blushing under the intensity of his stare, and was furious with herself for letting his piercing blue gaze affect her.

'That's a lot of walking.' Her voice sounded rather brusque as she attempted to regain her composure, wishing that Dr Franks wasn't quite so attractive, and then tacitly rebuked herself for being so superficial.

Mellowing her tone, Grace added, 'I've never been up here for food before.'

'I'm surprised; I assumed you'd have been an examiner here before.'

'Not here, no. I had your department head come to Leicester last year though.'

'So, this is the return match?'

She smiled; her preconception that Dr Franks was going to be stuffy and without a proper dry British sense of humour already dissolving, 'Indeed.'

'I should apologise,' Rob said as he picked up a thin paper serviette and flapped it carefully over his lap, 'I wanted to ask you to be the external examiner in the first place, but some politics became involved.'

'As usual,' Grace chipped in.

'As usual! And I had to ask a bod up in Durham first.

'David? He's a nice chap. Damn clever.'

'I've not met him. Excellent reputation of course, but not exactly right for the subject in this case, although I'm sure he'd have coped brilliantly.'

'He would have. No question.'

'You sound very sure. You know him well?'

'He was the external at my own viva.'

'No way! How did you get on?'

'Well, I failed, obviously!'

'Oh, ha ha!'

Grace's memory filled with the full horror of the occasion. She'd never been so nervous before or since. As she'd sat before her examiners, knowing that the next few hours would determine the course of her career, she'd been almost paralyzed with fear until her examiner, who she now knew on first name terms, had smiled at her and asked her a question about how the stories of Robin Hood had influenced criminal activity in the later middle ages. From that moment it had been a breeze – well, it had been as good as a nightmare can get.

'So,' Grace asked, 'what happened to stop David facing the train trip south?'

'He got a better offer.'

'Makes sense,' Grace chewed thoughtfully, 'and so, here I am, saving you at the last minute.'

'Like Robin Hood himself.'

Grace tried to ignore the effect the mischievous twinkle that had appeared at the corner of her companions eyes was having on her. 'Tell me about the student, what was it, Christopher something?'

'Christopher Ledger; he came over from Houston with me.'

'Really?'

'It's not as dodgy as it sounds. His Dad works in the oil industry. For Texaco or BP – I never was sure which. He was over there for four years before coming back to live in

Aberdeen. The contract in Houston was almost up, so as I was coming home, Chris got a room in halls here for six months and came too. His family are back in Scotland now.'

'So he'll head back up there once we're done here today?'

'He will, although I can't imagine it'll be long before he gets an academic post in a university somewhere. Chris really knows his subject.'

Grace smiled, 'Let's go and put that claim to the test, shall we, Dr Franks?'

The PhD exam was flawless. Grace had never been to one that ran so smoothly. The candidate was confident without arrogance, and the strategy of questions she and Rob had agreed upon beforehand had worked well.

Sitting back in a padded armchair in Dr Franks' office, Grace waited for him to return from privately congratulating his student in the main reception. Looking around her, Grace saw a smaller book-lined study than her own, but very similar, albeit without the added Robin Hood paraphernalia. While surveying the space, her eyes caught a glimpse of her skirt, and Grace started in surprise at not seeing her jeans covering her legs, and privately pleased that she'd performed so well without wearing trousers, and therefore operating outside of her comfort zone. Then she told herself off for thinking such idiotic psycho-babble.

The door opened, 'Well, that was fantastic,' Rob crashed into his chair, his face glowing with pleasure and pride, 'I've never had a viva go so well. Chris is over the moon.'

'So he deserves to be.' They'd had no need to confer. This unique student had so obviously deserved his PhD, and the distinction that went with it, that further discussion hadn't been necessary.

'Now,' Rob sat back up, 'this leaves us with a dilemma.'

'It does?'

'Yes. We were supposed to have an hour of heavy debate as to whether he'd pass and what rewrites were required. Naturally this is not needed, so, shall I take you for a coffee, or shall we go for a walk in the park? Wollaton Hall and its grounds are within walkable distance if you fancy it.'

Grace had made noises about leaving to catch an earlier train than planned, but Dr Franks had managed to persuade her against it, and in the end Grace had agreed on a short walk; after all, the grounds were beautiful and the sun was shining.

'I have an ulterior motive for holding on to you a bit longer. I wanted to ask you something.' Rob looked at Grace with a quizzical expression as they strolled away from Lenton Grove, 'If that's OK?'

'Depends what it is,' Grace was amazed at how at ease she felt in this man's company. This wasn't like her at all.

'Tell me about Robin Hood. Tell me why him, and how your book is progressing. Professor Davis obviously has high hopes of you. I've also heard you're something of an obsessive when it comes to outlaws.'

Abruptly, the feeling of being comfortable disintegrated, and Grace blushed at hearing herself described in such a way. She knew she was an obsessive, Daisy had told her often enough. But Daisy was a friend. This man was a relative stranger, and had no right to tease her.

Grace could feel herself becoming defensive and prickly, 'I've always been interested in the legend. Since I was a kid; and the book is fine, thank you.'

Aware that Rob was privately laughing at her, Grace looked away quickly. It was like being a teenager again, the subject of bemusement and private jokes. It had hurt then and it hurt now – some feelings never disappear. Grace snapped, 'No need to be so damn superior. You are obviously as obsessed with your work as I am, or you wouldn't be here.'

'OK, OK.' He put up his hands in a placating gesture, 'I was only teasing.'

'Well, don't'

'Right. Sorry.'

They walked on through the park, the lack of conversation less companionable than it had been only a short while ago, until they reached the lake. Standing, staring into its depths, the two medievalists saw how the last few days' rain had swelled its volume so it lapped at its banks. The gentle sun made the surface water sparkle, highlighting the orange flash of the goldfish which darted to and fro, before they became abruptly motionless for a few seconds, and then flitted off again.

Never one for an uneasy silence, Grace sighed and launched into her well-rehearsed and often repeated justification of her Robin Hood fascination.

'The Robin Hood legend is so resilient, so utterly lasting. We all know the stories from childhood, whether we enjoy them or not. They have engendered countless films and television shows, and taught generations of people how brutal the consequences of our less-advised actions can be. The story is more widely known than Shakespeare, for its language has adapted with us over the centuries. I believe, or at least, I'm working on the hypothesis, that the tales themselves held a strong influence over the genuine outlaw bands or lawless groups of the fourteenth century and beyond. So much so, that some families used the Robin Hood ballads and accompanying stories and songs of the day as examples of the justice they aspired to and hoped for. Maybe they even used them as justification for their criminal activities.'

Dr Franks continued to peer into the lake water as he

listened to Grace's passionate declaration. 'You may well be right about using the ballads as tales to live by. Damn tricky theory to prove though.'

Grace smiled wanly. 'Completely impossible.'

Rob tilted his head towards Grace, but refrained from looking at her as he replied, 'Not completely, surely, what about Folville's law?'

Grace's head snapped up so quickly that she almost lost her footing in her unaccustomed footwear, and had to catch hold of Dr Frank's linen-clad arm for a split second to steady herself so she didn't examine the lake at soggily close quarters, 'You know about Folville's law?!'

'Of course. I am, as you have pointed out, an obsessed medievalist.'

'But you've been in America.'

'Incredible as it is to believe, they do have books in America.'

Grace scuffed her shoes against the banks, embarrassed at being teased again, but knowing that this time she deserved it, 'Sorry, it's just I've not met many people who've heard of Folville's Law.'

Rob stared at Grace levelly and quoted directly from William Langland's medieval epic *Piers the Plowman*,

'"*And some ryde and to recovere that unrightfully was wonne:*

He wised hem wynne it ayein wightnesses of handes,

And fecchen it from false men with Folvyles lawes."*[4]

In other words, Folville's Law said it was OK to redress a wrong with violence.'

Grace stood open-mouthed, staring at her companion, disbelief etched on her face as Rob continued, 'I think you may be on to something. How are you going to write it up though? Will you truly be able to get the idea across, and can you quantify it?'

She had an uncharacteristic urge to tell him about the novel, but just as Grace was about to, the usual unease she experienced about sharing the idea in academic circles claimed her. She really didn't want to be teased on a professional level as well as for fun, so she simply said, 'It's proving a challenge, and taking far longer than I had planned.' Which was the truth – almost.

'It always does.' Rob started to walk them back towards the less attractive square buildings that formed most of the Nottingham campus. After a few steps he added, 'You haven't told me about why you like him personally, or your views on Robin Hood as a figurehead for justice, though.'

'I know,' Grace spoke bluntly, keeping her gaze firmly on the path before her, 'but I have to get going. I have to endure the horror that is dress shopping in Sheffield tomorrow.'

'A horror? Surely not? You wear your clothes so well.'

Grace's cheeks reddened at the unaccustomed compliment, while wishing Agatha hadn't made her wear such a low-cut top, and mentally admonished herself for allowing him to turn her face to crimson twice in one afternoon. 'Thank you,' she squeaked, 'but I confess, this is not my usual attire.'

He tilted his head to one side, 'Jeans and T-shirts?'

'Yup,' Grace laughed despite herself, letting some of the tension that had built up between them slip away.

'Me too.' He looked down at his crumpled suit with an unsavoury grimace.

'Really?'

'Yes, but there's been this stupid three-line whip about what clothes we can wear during interviews. They actually sent me home to change into a suit this morning! Can you believe that?'

Grace's mouth dropped open in surprise for the second time in ten minutes, and burst out laughing, before telling him about her own similar start to the day.

Chapter Nine

A strong black coffee in a double layer of cardboard cups to protect her from the heat of its contents sat on the lap table fastened to the back of the train seat before Grace.

The journey to Sheffield wouldn't take long, but Grace decided to do some writing before Daisy picked her up from the station. It would prevent her mind from replaying the viva she'd just experienced (or more accurately, the walk with Dr Franks she'd had afterwards), and keep the prospect of dress shopping tomorrow at bay.

Flicking her way to the correct place in her notebook before fishing out a red pen from her ancient Tom Baker *Doctor Who* pencil case, Grace found herself wondering what Rob Franks would make of her ownership of that. He'd probably wonder why, if she must own a child's pencil case rather than a sensible boring adult one, why she didn't have a Robin Hood one.

The lecturer been a lot nicer than she'd expected really. OK, he had teased her a bit, but she'd probably asked for it. She knew she got a bit touchy about her work sometimes. Despite her determination for it not to, Grace's mind drifted to when they'd stood by the lake together and she'd had to steady herself against him, albeit briefly. His crumpled linen jacket had been rough beneath her touch, and yet warm from the sunshine. The slim muscular arm beneath had suggested that maybe he worked out …

The conductor came into the carriage and broke Grace's unsolicited daydream by asking for her ticket. She admonished herself firmly; she'd just wasted a good ten minutes writing time with pointless reminiscences and fruitless wishful thinking.

'Mathilda.'

Robert de Folville spoke sternly, and at once Mathilda could see why it would be unwise to argue with his man unless you were very sure of yourself. It was as if he had two sides to him. A side that was never to be questioned, that was ruthless and determined. And a kinder, more gentle side, considerate of the individual and the locality. It was how these two halves mixed and intertwined that intrigued Mathilda as she stood shyly in only her chemise before him.

The housekeeper who'd bathed her had produced new clothes for Mathilda, and despite all her experience and sharp temper, had been unable to persuade this new girl to put them on, claiming she favoured her own familiar, if rather dirty, clothes. Eventually the older woman threatened to get his lordship, whether Mathilda was naked or not. Mathilda had said she wouldn't dare, but the housekeeper had dared, and grinning knowingly went to fetch Robert.

Mathilda had only had time to pull on the long kirtle before Robert came striding in, a look of annoyed impatience across his face. 'You will dress in these,' he pointed to the pile of semi-new clothes. 'I can't waste my time with things like this, girl.'

Shaking her head firmly, Mathilda braced herself as she risked provoking his temper. The housekeeper was looking expectantly at Folville, and Mathilda wondered if she was disappointed when Robert steadied his temper and took a deep breath before speaking with deliberate clarity.

'Mathilda, it is important that you temper that natural directness of yours, not to mention your boldness. Those are valuable skills, but I need you to hide them under style and grace.' He pointed again to the garments laid out before them. 'These clothes will help you give the impression we require you to portray. Your own clothes will be cleaned and returned to you when the job is done.'

'You see my directness as a skill, my Lord?'

Robert almost smiled as he replied with exasperation, 'Boldness, intelligence, directness, and an uncanny knack of knowing what's going on when you shouldn't may well get

57

you out of here alive. But overconfidence won't.'

Indigent, Mathilda's face flushed, 'I'm no gossip, my Lord.'

'Indeed not, but as you have proved to me once again, you *are* bold.' He turned to the housekeeper, treating her to the edge of his simmering anger, 'Now, for the Lord's sake, Sarah, get some clothes on her, she looks like a whore,' and he stalked out of the room.

Bright red with embarrassment, Mathilda allowed the disgruntled maid to help her into fresh clothes.

Over the chemise, Mathilda wore a tightly sleeved dress of light brown, and on top of that came a longer sleeveless surcoat in a fine blue wool, a little paler in shade than her temporary master's cloak. Finally, a wide simple leather belt, with a plain circular clasp, was used to pull in and girdle her tiny waist, and a pair of practical leather boots adorned her bruised feet.

Clothes such as these, Mathilda knew, placed her in the arena of those who worked for the rising gentry, rather than those who traded for a living. For the daughter of a potter who only just kept his family alive on his own tiny stretch of land, and his skill with clay, it was a major transformation.

Describing Mathilda's new clothes wrenched Grace out of her concentration and filled her head with images of the potential bridesmaid dress which was just out there, waiting to be found. Putting on such a garment would feel as strange to Grace as her unexpected new outfit would have done to Mathilda.

At least, Grace thought, *Daisy is unlikely to force anything I hate upon me, and the choice of colour will probably be my own*. Unplugging her music, Grace laid down her pen and watched the grottier parts of Sheffield's outskirts come into view though the carriage window.

Daisy was waiting beside her battered old Land Rover, a wide beam on her freckled face. Her dungarees had some white paint smeared across one leg, and her mad shoulder-length curly hair was stuffed behind her head in a red scrunchy that clashed alarmingly with her ginger colouring.

When she caught sight of Grace, she had to do a double-take. It looked like Grace, but in a skirt and jacket? And no trainers either? Surely not?

'What the hell is this?' Daisy pointed in amused disbelief at her as Grace dropped her bag into the Land-Rover.

'Don't ask! Just get me to a decent Ladies' cloakroom so I can put my jeans back on.'

'I am going to ask, but I guess it can wait. How about I find us a Pizza Hut, a couple of glasses of wine, and, as you wish, a nice clean cloakroom, and then you can tell me why you're dressed like a business assistant for an IT company?'

Grace enveloped her friend in a hug, 'Daze, you're a star!'

Grace couldn't actually describe the relief she felt when she slipped her jeans and trainers back on. They didn't even look that bad with the charity shop's blouse and jacket. She studied her reflection in the washroom mirror. It seemed even odder to Grace, now she thought about it, that she'd been comfortable during the interview despite her unfamiliar clothing. That wasn't like her at all. She normally fidgeted and shuffled non-stop outside of her regular attire. Perhaps it had been because Rob had made her so welcome, and had obviously respected her work and her opinion. *Maybe I should have told him about both of my books? No.* Even as the notion entered her head, Grace knew she didn't want to risk a fellow historian laughing at her. Or worse, losing the respect Rob had for her work before he'd really got to know how good she was at what she did.

'Is that better?' Daisy was already studying the menu as

Grace returned, appearing far more like her old self, but with fewer creases than usual.

'Tons, thanks,' Grace grabbed her menu, 'what are you having?'

'Well, despite what I said earlier, I'd better skip the wine and have a Pepsi as I'm driving, but I'll definitely have a Hawaiian pizza. Marcus hates pineapple so I don't get to have it any more.'

'Why not?'

'We buy a big pizza and share it.'

'Cute!'

Daisy blushed slightly, but smiled anyway, 'Stop it. It's not cute, it's economical.'

'If you say so, Daze.'

'Stop teasing me, and tell me about the viva, and more importantly, about the internal examiner. Was he ninety years old, crusty and dull, or twenty, and scarily brilliant, but disappointingly plain and as wet as a lettuce?'

'Actually, he was neither.' Grace paused in her account of Dr Franks to relay her order of a pepperoni pizza and cola to the hovering waitress. 'I guess he was probably a bit younger than us, mid-thirties probably, intelligent and interesting. He's newly arrived from teaching in America.'

Daisy's eyes shone with mischief as she listened, 'And is this young interesting man single?'

Seeing where Daisy was heading, Grace said, 'Oh for Heaven's sake, Daze! I only said he was almost our age, I didn't declare a secret crush or anything, and I'm sure he's probably been living happily ever after with some American airhead for years.'

Daisy pounced, 'So you do have a crush on him.'

'I said I didn't!'

'No, you didn't! You said you hadn't *declared* a secret crush – that implies you have one to declare. And you were mean about a girlfriend he probably doesn't have.'

'Oh hell, Daisy, you're impossible now you're all

loved-up.'

'I only want you to be as happy as me, babe,' Daisy smiled as she leant towards her friend, wagging her finger in mock admonishment, 'and anyway, you're the one who's supposed to be good with words. I'm only playing you at your own game!'

'Honestly, Daze, Rob was just a nice guy, that's all, and our research covers similar areas.'

Daisy put her newly delivered drink down with a thump. 'Rob? The intelligent, interesting, nice guy is called Rob?' Daisy looked directly at Grace, 'I mean, he's working in Nottingham, he's a medieval historian, and his name is Rob – as in Robert – as in Robin. Do I have to paint a picture here?'

Grace, who was beginning to wish she'd had a glass of wine after all, gave Daisy one of her Paddington Bear stares; the sort she used on students who were persistently late with their coursework. 'You can stop your match-making right there, thank you, Daisy Marks. Dr Franks will be unlikely to re-enter the framework of my life again anytime soon, and if he does it will be because we work in the same field of study. OK?'

'Yes, miss.' Daisy giggled as her pizza arrived.

'Right then!' Grace began to laugh as well.

'Seriously though,' Daisy wiped away her giggles along with some honey and mustard dressing she'd accidentally trickled over the table, 'you don't normally say these people are interesting. The subject, yes, but rarely the people that go alongside her studies.'

Grace thought as she chewed at a particularly well-stuffed cheesy crust. Daisy was right in a way. Dr Franks had been more interesting and easier to talk to than the typical medievalists she met at meetings and conferences. 'It's probably because he's my age, and even more important, he's heard of Folville's Law.'

'Of course he has. He's obviously as much of a

61

crackpot as you are.'

'No, honestly, Daisy, I use Folville's Law as a sort of test. You'd be surprised how many historians haven't heard of it.'

'Criminal!'

'Oh, ha ha ha. Now, will you stop teasing me please?'

'Only if you stop behaving like an idiot. Fancy testing a person's level of interestingness with the knowledge of one obscure quote from hundreds of years ago. Only you could be that mad.'

Grace felt defensive. She knew it was silly, but it wasn't like Daisy to get at her like this, 'Let's drop it, OK? So, what's the plan for tonight, tomorrow's shopping bonanza, and beyond?'

Unsure why Grace wasn't being her usual easy-going self, Daisy changed the subject, but privately vowed to get more information about Dr Franks at a later date, 'I hope you won't mind sharing a room with a couple of guinea pigs tonight, we're a bit stacked-up at the moment.'

Grace relaxed. This was more like Daisy. She could imagine the state of the little guest room. It was only really big enough for the single bed that was squashed along its far wall beneath the window, and the small matching dressing table and chair squeezed opposite it. Grace however, had never seen it without empty, or sometimes full, hutches stacked across every square inch of the floor. She knew the walls were magnolia, but as she had never seen the carpet through the homes of the furry incumbents, she couldn't even begin to guess at its colour. Yet it was always comfortable at Daisy's place, even if it did have a faint aroma of clean straw and fur.

Grateful for the change of subject, Grace said she wouldn't mind sharing with the four-legged guests, and deciding she'd better act on her good intention to be a decent bridesmaid, said, 'Break it to me gently Daisy. What colour do I have to wear to this wedding of yours? I should warn you, though, that if you say Lincoln Green I may empty this salad bowl all over your lap!'

'Actually, that hadn't entered my head,' Daisy replied untruthfully, 'I thought we'd see what suited you. You're the only bridesmaid, so it doesn't matter that much.'

'Not pink.'

'Definitely not pink, and perhaps not a colour that will clash with my ginger locks.'

'Good point,' Grace stabbed some lettuce around her salad bowl to dab up the last few bacon bits, 'so that's orange and bright red out.'

'Yuck! I'm doing the traditional ivory bit, so at least that will go with anything.'

'Not wearing white then?'

Daisy stuck her tongue out.

'Have you got a dress sorted out?'

'Sort of,' Daisy grimaced at the memory of her second attempt at trawling around every wedding dress shop and boutique in South Yorkshire and Derbyshire, 'I've narrowed it down to three. I hoped you could help me narrow it down to "the one" tomorrow. I've found a friendly little wedding shop that doesn't make you feel like you're gate-crashing a society event just by walking through the door.'

'Well done! I bet that took some doing.'

'You have no idea!' Daisy took a sustaining gulp of Pepsi, as if trying to rinse away her memory of a parade of bored wafer-thin bridal shop assistants, 'It has a great selection of stuff for you as well as me, so fingers crossed we can get it all there and have the rest of the weekend to ourselves.'

'Sounds good to me,' Grace lifted up her hands so Daisy could see that she'd crossed all her fingers, 'here's hoping.'

Chapter Ten

Grace sat up in bed, her manuscript resting on a large book about breeding rabbits that she'd found propped up in the corner of the room. Why anyone would need such a book Grace couldn't imagine. Didn't rabbits just breed? Surely a book about stopping them breeding would be far more useful?

Attempting to focus on the last paragraph of Mathilda's story she'd written, Grace found her mind drifting off to Rob Franks again. What would he think of her for spending time on this novel when she was supposed to be working on a textbook? Would he respect her for it? Grace shook her head, 'Daisy's putting ideas in your head, girl. Stop it.' She fished a red pen from the depths of her bag and began to update her work so far.

Mathilda curtseyed to each brother in turn, starting with the one at the head of the table, who she assumed was John, the elder brother and Lord of Ashby Folville. The row of candles on the table flickered in the draught of the hall, and obscured the shadows, making it difficult to accurately assess all the men's features.

'You appear much improved, Mathilda.' Robert nodded encouragingly at her, but Mathilda had spotted the furrow on his brow, which didn't quite match his warm tone, 'Let me introduce you to some of my family.'

Robert gestured to the head of the table. 'This is my second-eldest brother, Eustace de Folville.'

Mathilda curtseyed again, reappraising the man she'd incorrectly taken to be the lord of the manor. She judged he was about thirty-five years of age. His stature and build matched that of his younger brothers, and his well-tailored attire was in the latest European styles. His face was smooth and his hair cropped short as pertained to the French fashion. Mathilda recalled how she'd heard her father telling Matthew some time ago how the Folville family had originally come over to England with William the Bastard from Picardy in France, and had been entrusted with Ashby Folville as a reward for their services.

Robert moved his attention to the next chair. 'This is my cousin Laurence, and next to him is Richard, rector of Teigh, who you met briefly earlier.'

Again Mathilda reflected that, even though he'd lost the fishy aroma picked up from when he's captured her, Richard de Folville couldn't have looked less like a rector if he tried. In fact Mathilda couldn't imagine a less pious-looking man existing, yet she bowed with sensible grace, and acknowledged his religious status, 'Greetings, Father.'

'This is Thomas,' Robert gestured to the clergyman's neighbour, 'and finally we have Walter.'

Mathilda bowed and curtseyed again. Not entirely sure which gesture was expected of her, so adopting a generally submissive position somewhere between the two.

Returning to his seat, Robert left Mathilda hovering, small and vulnerable, before the panel of blue eyes, square jaws and muscular frames. As she observed them studying her through the dim light, Mathilda has no problem imagining them delivering their own brand of justice; and in some cases, relishing doing so.

'You wish to know where our brother the Lord John de Folville is?'

In fact Mathilda had been wondering why Eustace, more than any other brother, seemed to exude a controlled menace from a disconcertingly blank expression 'Yes, my Lord,' she answered Robert clearly, but lowered her eyes further, suddenly unsure if she had actually been supposed to reply.

Eustace roared with laughter, and gestured to Robert, 'You are right, brother. The chit is a bold one.'

Mathilda's cheeks coloured brightly as she continued to

concentrate on the dirty patch of ground between her feet. The other brothers, with the exception of Robert, joined in the thunderous laugh, but, Mathilda suspected, they laughed more out of duty then any genuine stirrings of amusement.

'I believe she is what we need, Eustace.' Robert spoke firmly. 'She is bold, bright, and has some letters.'

Eustace chewed at the inside of his cheek, 'Quick-witted as well, I'll warrant.'

'Indeed.'

'Your age, child?' The rector broke his silence, and asked the question as a demand.

'I am nineteen, Father,' Mathilda already hated him. The others she was wary of, and Eustace, she might always be afraid of, but the rector oozed coldness and a lack of compassion. She vowed that she would keep as far away from him as possible.

Richard said no more, but his hawk-like eyes never left her.

'Tell me, girl,' Eustace re-took the mantle of questioning, 'do you know why it was necessary to place you in the cell for a while?'

Mathilda glanced at Robert, checking if she was supposed to reply this time. His almost imperceptible bow of his head reassured her. She swallowed, thinking quickly, 'I may be wrong, my Lord, and I beg your pardon if I offend, but I imagine it was to keep me out of the way while you decided what to do with me. To remind me of my place, and to use my suffering to punish my father,' Mathilda hastily added another, 'my Lord,' and then returned her gaze to the floor.

The sinister air at the table lasted an uncomfortably long time. Continuing to examine the rough floor Mathilda felt the fear which she had so carefully controlled and suppressed, creep up her spine and prickle the skin beneath her tightly harnessed hair. She didn't look up. She didn't want to see the sullen angry expressions her answer may have given them.

What would they do to her? Mathilda hadn't needed Robert to confirm for her that the Folvilles administered their own take on the law. There would be no sheriff or bailiff to intercede for her here. They might imprison her again, wound her, cut out her tongue for her boldness, or leave her in the hands of the rector ...

As Mathilda's imaginings became wilder and more painful, the gruff tones of Eustace de Folville cut through the expectant hush of the hall. Rather than comment on her statement, he took her by surprise, 'Your father and brother Matthew are safe.'

Mathilda opened her mouth to ask about her younger brother, Oswin, but closed it again on seeing a warning glance from Robert.

'They are back at home, toiling to earn enough money to discharge their debt, and have you returned to them.' Eustace's eyes seemed to bore even further into her soul as Mathilda choked back all the questions she was desperate to ask, but had the common sense not to.

The eldest Folville present continued, 'Your father has made himself our debtor by his own free-will, and debts must be paid. So,' Eustace took an unpleasant sounding guttural breath as he stared the newly scrubbed girl, 'you are our prize for as long as it takes for your family to discharge their payment.'

Eustace walked towards the fire, warming his palms against the approaching chill of the summer evening. 'My brother Robert speaks well of you. I see a liking there.'

Mathilda wasn't sure if he was teasing her or scolding his brother, and daren't glance towards Robert to see how he responded to such a comment. The rector sniggered quietly into his wooden mug of ale.

Robert said nothing however, as Eustace continued, 'You know something of us, Mathilda, from living life long in these parts. And I have no doubt, my dear brother has explained to you our beliefs on looking after our lands and beyond, keeping a weather eye on the dealings of all men in this Hundred of East Goscote.'

Mathilda bit her tongue in an effort to remain demurely mute, trying hard to concentrate on what Eustace was saying and not on the unknown fate of her younger brother.

'He has also, I believe, told you of his fascination with stories,' Eustace gave Robert a blunt stare; leaving Mathilda to wonder whether it was Robert's passion for the tales of the minstrels, or the fact he'd shared that belief and interest with a mere chattel such as her, that he disapproved of.

'The balladeers have become obsessed of late with the injustices of this land, and often rightly so. Naturally the fabled Robyn Hode has become a hero. An ordinary man who breaks the law and yet somehow remains good and faithful in the eyes of the Church. In years past the sheer vastness of such a character's popularity would have been unthinkable, but these days, well ...' Eustace begun to pace in front of the fire, reminding Mathilda of how his brother had moved earlier, '... now we are empowered by the young King, the Earl of Huntingdon, and Sheriff Ingram, to keep these lands safe and well run, and by God and Our Lady we'll do it, even if we have to sweep some capricious damned souls to an earlier hell than they were expecting along the way.'

Eustace was shouting now, but not at her. His voice had adopted a determined hectoring passion, and Mathilda resolved that she would never willingly disappoint this man; it would be too dangerous.

'Many of the complaints of crimes and infringements that reach my family's ears are not accurate. I am sure that more felonies are alleged out of spite or personal grievance than are ever actually committed. We need more eyes and ears, girl. Accurate, unbiased eyes and ears. The sheriff of this county is not a bad man. Well, he is no worse than the rest, but Ingram is sorely stretched. He has not only this shire, but that of Nottinghamshire and Derbyshire within his writ. The man cannot be everywhere at once. No man can.

'We are believed to have a band of criminals under our control, Mathilda. This is not true. I'm no Hode, although I am lucky to have the respect of the local population, and although I know that respect is because they go in fear of me, I'd rather have that than no respect at all. Hode's principles I embrace, as I do other outlaw heroes' who have flouted a law more corrupt than they are. Those such as Gamelyn can also give a man a good example to follow. What was it he declared to the justice at his false trial, Robert?'

Moving into the light of the table, Robert thought for a second before reeling off a verse he'd probably known by heart since childhood,

'Come from the seat of justice: all too oft
Hast thou polluted law's clear stream with wrong;
Too oft hast taken reward against the poor;
Too oft hast lent thine aid to villainy,
And given judgment 'gainst the innocent.
Come down and meet thine own meed at the bar,
While I, in thy place, give more rightful doom
And see that justice dwells in law for once.' [5]

Eustace nodded thanks to his brother, who had already shrunk back into the shadows of the nearest wall, 'I do not have such a band at my beck and call, Mathilda. When I need help I have to pay for it.'

All the time Eustace spoke the other members of his family pointedly stared at Mathilda as they drank their ale, which was frequently topped up by the same servant boy who'd provided her with food earlier.

Sitting on a seat with a sigh, Eustace gestured to Allward to add more candles to the room, for the approach of the dark of evening was filling the place with a ghostly chill and an encroaching gloom. 'To answer the question you didn't actually ask, girl, my eldest brother, the Lord John de Folville, is currently in Huntingdon. We are enfeoffed to them and the connection is strong. He is often there. This manor is run, on a practical level, by Lord Robert, who acts as steward, with additional assistance from Richard, rector of Teigh.' [6]

Mathilda shivered, refraining from meeting the expression of the harsh eyed man who'd dragged her from prison, making sure he touched as much of her flesh as possible, as he snorted with ill-concealed contempt from his seat on the far side of the table.

'I am telling you this, Mathilda, because it will be important in your task. You are to appear to the world to be Robert's woman.'

Mathilda couldn't disguise her intake of breath at that news, and ignored the smattering of smirks on the faces of the daunting panel of solidly muscular brothers before her. She hadn't really believed Robert when he'd suggested that would be her role earlier.

'In reality you will be an information gatherer and deliverer of messages. My brother, Lord John, commands a reasonable estate which demands constant attention. I – we – need to know what is happening across its villages, holdings, and beyond. I need someone I can trust to liaise with our colleagues in other counties, and who better than someone innocent of appearance, and whose very devotion is wrapped up in the safety of her family.'

Mathilda blinked in the face of guttering candle smoke, her throat drier than it had ever been. She was to be a spy. A professional gossip. This was hazardous work which held brutal, legally enforced punishments she didn't even want to think about. Mathilda forced herself to hold back her unease at Eustace's veiled threat towards her family if she refused him, and listened.

'You will be the eyes and ears I speak of Mathilda, and our representative. What say you, girl?'

'Of course, my Lord.' There was nothing else she could say.

Chapter Eleven

'Are you OK, Grace? You look tired.'

Grace, who'd been writing until about midnight, and then hadn't been able to sleep due to a combination of squeaking guinea pigs, the inability to stop her brain rehashing the previous day's viva and the subsequent walk with Dr Franks by the lake yet again, not to mention her fears about buying a dress today, yawned as if on cue. 'I'm fine; it's been a busy week, that's all.'

'Sorry we had to get up so early, but parking in Sheffield on a Saturday is hell if you don't get there first thing.'

Daisy had woken Grace up at seven o'clock with hot coffee and two rounds of toast and marmalade. Now, at only a few minutes past eight, they were bouncing out of the driveway towards the city for a day of trying things on.

Grace was staring blindly out of the window, when a thought struck her. It had been a week last Tuesday since she'd last bothered to shave her legs and under her arms. What on earth would they be like now!? Cursing herself for not thinking to check on the status of her stubble last night, Grace groaned. Her legs were bound to be on show again today. The idea made her feel a bit sick. When it came to imparting knowledge on medieval England Grace could stand and talk to hundred people without more than a few butterflies, but showing even her best friend any part of her anatomy, or being the centre of attention in any other way, made Grace want to run away and hide.

'Are you sure you're all right Grace?' Daisy glanced at her passenger anxiously as she negotiated a left turn, 'you've gone a funny colour.'

'Well, um,' Grace knew she'd have to come clean, she didn't want to ruin the day for Daisy by appearing to be miserable, 'I have a bit of a confession to make.'

'Oh my God! Is it about this Robert Franks bloke? You didn't sneak off and have sex in his office after the viva, did you?'

'Daisy!' Grace's sickly complexion went scarlet. 'Of course not!'

'I was only joking. Well, half-joking.' Pulling the Land Rover into a convenient lay-by, Daisy turned to Grace. 'What is it? You've gone as white as a sheet.'

'All right,' Grace fiddled with her seat belt as she confessed, 'I'm scared I guess.'

'Scared? Of what?'

'Letting you down. Trying on clothes with people looking at me.'

'You're kidding!'

'Not kidding,' Grace grimaced but with a smile to indicate to Daisy she knew she was being ridiculous, but couldn't help it. 'I'm even sat here remembering how stubbly my legs are. I didn't even remember to check if my underwear matches. I'm being a crap bridesmaid and I haven't even got the dress yet.'

Fighting the urge to laugh, Daisy took hold of Grace's hand, 'I don't give two hoots at the state of your stubble or your underwear, and I don't believe for a minute that you'll let me down. I know you don't like people looking at you, but you're beautiful, and it's about time you realised that. Stop hiding behind your work and your jeans.'

'I am too fat, my hair is too straggly, and my boobs are too big,' Grace held up her hand to stop Daisy arguing with her, and added, 'and anyway, you wear jeans all the time too!'

'Of course I do, I have little creatures pooping down me all day. When Marcus and I go out I put something else

73

on, though. I'm not always hiding behind denim.'

'Oh.'

'Honey, this isn't meant to be a torture session; it's meant to be fun. Let's be two silly people playing with posh dresses and take it from there shall we? To be honest, I'm pretty nervous as well. I don't actually like dress shopping myself, do I?' Daisy spoke as though she was encouraging a small child.

'I'm sorry, Daze, thanks. I really don't want to let you down.'

'You won't.' Daisy spoke with finality as she screeched the Land Rover back into gear and headed towards the city, 'Now, let's forget dresses for a second. Are you OK to stay with me the night before the wedding? I've reserved a couple of rooms at the hotel nearest Hardwick Hall, but I need to confirm the booking really soon. Is that all right?'

'That's a good idea. I'd like to be able to help you out before the off.'

'Thanks, I'd appreciate that. It's called the Partridge Hotel. Marcus won't be staying there, his folks live nearby, and so he'll be with them. I'll confirm tonight.'

'Thanks Daze, you're a star.'

'True,' Daisy risked a glance at her friend, and was relieved to see that she no longer giving the impression that she was about to throw up, 'It's a double room – just in case!'

Reclining on the cream leather sofa, Grace sipped her freshly squeezed orange juice. The shop was unbearably warm, probably due to the almost permanent state of undress of most its clients, Grace thought it wasn't unlike sitting in a greenhouse on a hot day.

Daisy had already tried on the first of the three dresses she'd reserved, but on this second try had decided against it. A decision Grace had to agree with. Lovely though it was, it wasn't low-cut enough, and squashed Daisy's boobs, giving her a figure that resembled a cottage loaf.

Grace could hear Daisy muttering happily to the assistant. She was supposed to be searching through the row of size 16 bridesmaid dresses the assistant has sorted out for her while she was waiting, but so far all Grace had done was run her eyes over them from the safety of the sofa, mentally discarding certain colours and shades. She was just considering if something in a rich plum colour would suit her, when the changing room curtain was drawn back and Daisy, a little flushed, but grinning broadly, was helped out.

One minute later Daisy was stood on an upturned box so that the assistant could pin up the hem to the required length. She looked incredible. The happy radiance to future bride's eyes told Grace that she'd fallen in love with the dress she had on already.

Ivory, but inlaid discreetly with a spattering of delicate beads within an occasional silver leaf and butterfly pattern, it flattered Daisy's figure perfectly. Little tank-style sleeves covered the very tops of her arms, and a crossover asymmetrical draping of the slightly dropped torso slimmed her rounded stomach. An A-line skirt completed the effect, slimming her even further.

Grace gasped as she got up and circled her friend. At the back of the dress a V-shaped panel was laced securely to help produce the required line, which then flared out at the back to form a neat chapel-length train. 'I love it Daisy. I totally love it. You look incredible.'

Daisy glowed as the assistant, who after an hour of seeing her in her underwear, had introduced herself as Ashley, added to the compliments.

'I have to have this one, don't I Grace?'

'Damn right you do. God, I never knew you had a waist beneath those dungarees, you cow!'

Daisy laughed, 'I haven't, this hidden corset business is

holding in a multitude of sins.' She paused. 'Do you think I should try on the last one I reserved as well?'

'That's up to you,' Grace said, privately hoping she would, thus keeping her out of the limelight for a little longer, 'but you do look totally incredible in that one.'

Trapped by indecision, Daisy appealed to Ashley, the assistant, who said, 'Well, to be truthful, I think you should go with the one you have on. The other dress is lovely, but of the three this is the one that suits you best. Of course, that's only my opinion.'

'And as you see women in these things all the time, you should know,' said Daisy decisively, a huge smile still plastered to her face. 'Right then, this is the one! Do you think Marcus will like it, Grace?'

'He'll love it. Trust me, I'm a doctor!' Grace couldn't help but beam back at her friend, who was positively alight with happiness, but experienced an unexpected wave of envy, which took her totally by surprise. Grace swallowed it back with a dose of self-disgust.

'Now then,' said Daisy firmly, 'it'll take me at least ten minutes to get out of this; you look at those bridesmaid dresses. I bet you haven't even peeked at them, have you?' One glimpse of Grace's sheepish face confirmed Daisy's suspicions. 'We don't have to get one here, but it's a good place to start hunting. So hunt!'

Nodding meekly, Grace did as she was told, hoping there would be something she liked, and they would therefore be spared traipsing all around the city looking in other shops. Besides, she was getting hungry.

After ten minutes of baffled staring Grace appealed to Ashley. 'I'm sorry, but I haven't the first clue what will suit me. Can you help?'

Ashley smiled. 'No problem. First things first. We need to see what styles suit your figure, and then we'll see what colour would be best. You'll need a dress made up, so don't worry about size as such. All the dresses are made way too big, and then we alter them to fit you once you're wearing them.'

'Blimey,' Grace gave a nervy laugh, 'really?'

'Yup,' Ashley, seeing how apprehensive Grace was, gave her another bolstering smile, 'I tell you what, I'll pull out three that I think could work for you style wise, and we'll go from there. OK? If you don't like any of them, don't worry, we'll chose three more, and so on.'

Thirty minutes later Grace and Daisy had swapped positions. Daisy was relaxing on the sofa with a much-needed cold drink and Grace was standing on the box having a chocolate brown dress pinned around her. She was trying to stand as statue-like as possible, as she had a childish fear of being pricked with a pin.

The first two dresses she tried on had already been declared, 'OK if we can't find anything else'. This third one however had felt right even before it was pulled into place. Grace was a little embarrassed as the urge to grin at her own reflection consumed her, and could tell from Daisy's face that she liked it too.

The wide-scooped halter neck ran down to a midriff sash and a laced-up back panel, which helped pull in her waist and show off her chest to its best advantage, while stopping short of being indecent. Grace instantly compared it to the emergency top she'd bought from the charity shop yesterday. Perhaps Aggie had been right to insist on a lower neckline, it did seem to suit her. And remembering the brief but admiring glance that Rob Franks had given her, perhaps he liked that style on her too. The thought made Grace's cheeks colour as she admired the sleek A-line skirt which matched the form of Daisy's dress. It was plain and simple, and suited her perfectly.

'Now,' Ashley put her hands on her hips, a fresh wave of determination on her young face, 'the dress is you – but the colour isn't.'

'Why not?' Grace loved it. The rich mocha fabric felt

familiar and therefore safe.

'Because, I bet you wear blue, brown, or black all the time. This is supposed to be different, special, and because, to be brutal, it would be good for you to wear a colour that complements your hair rather than one that matches it exactly.'

'Dead right,' added Daisy, but on seeing Grace's distraught expression quickly added, 'we're not saying brown doesn't suit you, honey, but I want you to be different, just for one day.'

'OK,' Grace muttered sounding far from convinced.

'What colour do you suggest, Ashley?' Daisy asked, 'I don't mind as long as it goes with my ginger hair, and makes Grace look even more incredible than she does already.'

'Well, the best colour really would be this one,' Ashley pulled a dress off the rack, 'it would suit each of your colourings, and the rich shade would enhance your figure Grace.'

The friends burst out laughing, but on seeing Ashley's worried face, Daisy did her best to stifle her giggles, 'Don't worry, we're not laughing at you.'

'Is it the colour? I know some people can be funny about it, but honestly, it isn't unlucky at all, and it really is the ideal shade for each of you.'

Forcing herself to be more composed, jiggling about as she laughed had already caused a pin to jab her, Grace asked, 'So, what colour do you actually call that shade then, Ashley?'

'Bottle sage.'

'Not Lincoln Green then?' Daisy and Grace burst into renewed fits of giggles.

Chapter Twelve

Lincoln Green! She'd never hear the last of it. Grace sat at her little desk in the converted bedroom that operated as her home study, and experienced a flutter of excitement. The dress had made her feel different. Special somehow, and although the irony of the colour wouldn't go unnoticed by Daisy's family at the wedding, it felt gratifyingly right that that particular shade of green suited her so well.

Grace's study was her favourite room in her two-bedroomed terraced home. Although it would have been a squash to use the second bedroom for anyone bigger than a very small child, it was just big enough for three rows of bookshelves, a filing cabinet of research notes, and her desk. The walls, unlike in her work office, were not bedecked with posters of Robin Hood and medieval landmarks, but held a myriad of photographs from various periods of Grace's life, stuffed into a variety of different-sized frameless frames.

Her childhood friends, birthdays, her parents, her family home, and her pets, all now long gone. The students she'd known, some briefly, some that she stayed in touch with via email and the odd letter in a Christmas card. Daisy was there in numerous guises, captured forever at various points in their lives over the past twenty years. Now, Grace thought as she swivelled on her chair, there would be wedding snaps to add to the collection.

Grace was still amazed that there would be. Daisy had been so adamant about not getting married, and here she was, neck-deep in arranging a wedding, honeymoon, and recruiting a band of helpers to feed and care for her animals while she was away. Grace hadn't ever made such a negative decision about marriage, though in fact she'd never really considered her future in that way at all. She'd wanted a career, and she'd got one. Exactly the one she desired. Grace had simply supposed she'd meet someone when the time was right, but suddenly, without it feeling as if any time had actually passed, she was almost thirty-nine, with forty looming at her from around the corner, single, and about to be the world's oldest bridesmaid.

Daisy had booked her a double room at the hotel, and somehow it seemed a waste of bed space that was there to mock her. It had been three years since Grace's last date, which had been such a non-event that she hadn't been in a hurry to repeat the experience. 'Which is just as well,' she told a photograph of herself standing in front of Exeter cathedral with Daisy at the tender age of 19, 'as there's no one I'd like to date out there anyway.'

Her mind drifted back to Rob Franks. He was the nicest man she'd met for ages. But he was so nice she couldn't believe he was single, and anyway, he was a handsome man. He could have any slim young student he wanted. 'There's no way he'd settle for a sad, plump-ish, outlaw-obsessed almost forty-something, even if we do have work in common.'

Sighing with a hint of self pity, Grace switched on her email. She hadn't checked it since her return from Sheffield the night before, and now, early on Monday morning she faced the list of contacts with a feeling that life had rather defeated her.

Running her eyes down the list, searching for anything she could delete or legitimately leave until she got into work, she saw a message from Rob Franks.

Her heart jumped a little as she saw his name. 'Oh for Christ's sake, girl, get a grip. You are too old for a teenage crush.'

Opening the message, Grace read,

Hi Grace, thanks again for a great viva. Christopher

has already been on to York Uni with reference to a post-doc research post; which I am damn sure he'll get.

I've been thinking. We should write something together. A paper on 'Official criminology during the Black Death' or something???

What you think? I'll be honest – a joint paper with a respected historian such as yourself would help consolidate my post at Nottingham – plus, I think it could be fun to work together.

Have you got time over what remains of the summer vacation?

Hope shopping was a success.

Best, Rob

Reading the email through for a second time, Grace was touched that he'd remembered about her shopping trip, flattered that he believed her worth collaborating on a paper with, but alarmed by the thought of such a paper taking up the rest of the summer holidays. She had planned to finish compiling the draft of her novel over the student break, and then finally get back to her textbook in the autumn term before Professor Davis despaired of her.

Her fingers hovered over the keyboard while she wondered how to reply. It had been a while since Grace had written an academic paper, and such things were very important for keeping your name known and respected in university circles. And if her novel ever got out there, she'd need all the respect she could get. But how could she possibly find time to do anything extra? She had to finish the novel and edit it; the textbook needed a serious sort out and a proper draft compiling – and on top of all that, she'd promised to give as much help as she could towards Daisy's wedding.

Grace hit the reply button and settled for hedging her bets. Ignoring the voice at the back of her head which screamed at her to arrange to see Rob again as soon as possible, and telling her that working together would give

her a chance to see if she really did fancy him, or if it was
Daisy putting ideas in her head, she typed,

Thanks for inviting me. It was a great viva.

*Christopher will go far. You and I had better look out
for our jobs in a few years!*

*Would like to do paper – summer tricky as have book
and wedding to sort.*

Grace re-read it, and then added,

*But would like to do a paper though. The Christmas or
spring break would be better for me time wise. Are those
times any good for you?*

Best

G

Hitting 'Send', Grace watched the email disappear into the
technological ether and pulled herself off the chair. It was
high time she had a shower and headed off to work.

From where she was sat at the edge of the hall, Mathilda
considered her situation. She didn't really understand what
she was supposed to do, but she knew it could be dangerous
if she wasn't careful. As she waited to hear details of her
first task, Mathilda thought about how she'd always been
good at finding things out simply by virtue of being a good
listener. But gossiping could get you into serious trouble.
Not only was it frowned upon within the local towns and
villages, it could led to being arrested and punished. How
would she be able to gain information of the sort the
Folvilles were alluding to, without endangering herself and
those innocent informers that she spoke to?[7]

'You seem pensive, Mathilda,' Robert had finally emerged
from the main hall, where he had been addressing the finer
points of Mathilda's first task with Eustace, 'positively
demure, even.'

'Thank you, my Lord.'

'I am not fooled, however; what were you thinking

about?'

He sat beside her on the long wooden settle which backed onto the wall dividing the hall from the kitchen. 'I was wondering how I'd get the information you require safely, my Lord.'

'You're only our messenger Mathilda; there is no reason for you to worry about your safety.'

'Forgive me, my Lord,' Mathilda choose her words carefully, 'but I must have misunderstood. I took it that I was to be an informer for you – a spy.'

Folville almost blurted out a denial, but thought better of it. This child was no child. At nineteen she was past the earliest marriageable age, and due to the loss of her mother had been used to the ways of adulthood for some years now. She was also no fool. 'Mathilda, if you are sensible, then this is not a perilous job. Eustace laced the task ahead of you with an exaggeration of the danger involved. It is the thing he enjoys most; making a theatre of a situation and revelling in the anxiety it causes in others.'

Not at all surprised by his description of Eustace, but feeling far from relaxed about what lay ahead, Mathilda asked, 'Do you have other messengers, my Lord?'

Robert looked uncomfortable for a second, but answered her squarely, 'Not at the moment, although there have been, and will be again.'

Mathilda decided not to ask of the fate of the previous messenger. She has no choice in her position, and the detailed knowledge of her predecessor's death or imprisonment would not help. Anyway she was too busy trying to work out how to tackle the other issues which preyed heavily on her mind. 'My I ask something more, my Lord?'

'You seem to have developed the taste for questioning me, Mathilda.' A smile played at the corner of Robert's lips, but Mathilda remained cautious.

'I dared not ask before my Lord Eustace, but no mention was made of my younger brother, Oswin.'

Robert spoke candidly. 'We don't know where he is, and

that's the truth of it.'

'How so, my Lord?' Hope rose in Mathilda's chest, but she was afraid to show it too openly.

'Richard tells me Oswin slipped through his fingers by the river, gone towards Lincolnshire we think. I can reassure you that he is not in the river. We checked for drowned victims.'

Relieved to know Oswin wasn't lost to the water, but still worried, Mathilda asked, 'Will you pursue him?'

'No, girl, you were our prize. Although without Oswin's help in the pottery, it will take your father longer to buy you back.'

While she digested the information, another idea drifted to her mind.

'My Lord Eustace, sir,' Mathilda couldn't look at Robert now, a blush of embarrassed uncertainty on her face, 'said I was to appear as your, well, your um ... companion.'

Robert sat back down, 'You fear for your reputation girl, your virtue, when you are already held here, when gossip has probably already spread and placed you as a group concubine.' Robert sighed as Mathilda's green eyes focused on his, not as meek in his company as she had been, 'It is but subterfuge for your safety, Mathilda, it might cost you your blushes and some whispered remarks, but it could save your life. After all, only a desperate fool would attack the girl of a Folville brother.'

Mathilda had to acknowledge the truth of this, even if it was a truth she didn't like. In that one statement he'd as much as admitted she was open to attack after all. And yet, for all that, she still felt he wasn't telling her everything.

'To that end, I have something for you.'

'My Lord?'

Reaching into the leather bag he'd been carrying, Robert unrolled a delicate leather belted girdle. It was unlike anything Mathilda had ever seen, and as he passed it into her hands, she ran its length through her fingers, admiring the intricacy of the work. The leather had been punched into a latticework pattern of diagonal lines and tiny butterflies, and ended with a wide rectangular buckle, engraved to match the strap.

'You are supposed, in the eyes of the world at least, to be my woman. It is fitting for our purposes that you wear a token from me that proves our link.'

'It's beautiful, thank you, my Lord.'

'Put it on, I want to see if it suits you.'

With reverence, and fumbling fingers, Mathilda undid her belt, and fastened the new girdle around her waist. 'It will be hard to return this, my Lord, when my task is complete.'

Roberts face blackened in anger. The abrupt change in his appearance made Mathilda start in fear, 'It is a gift, girl, do not insult me by suggesting it will need returning.'

Mathilda spoke hastily, 'My Lord, I'm so sorry. I assumed, well … the subterfuge and everything my Lord. I never meant to offend, I'm truly sorry.'

He gave an almost guttural grunt, as he looked at her ashen upturned face, and spoke with the manner of a man not used to curtailing his anger so quickly. 'I suppose your assumption is not strange in the circumstances. Come, you need food and rest. Tomorrow will be a long day.'

Having eaten a meal of stew and bread alone near the fire, Mathilda wasn't sure what she was supposed to do next. It was late, and only the boy servant, Allward, was bustling about at the other end of the hall, preparing the room for the coming of the new day, before bedding down behind the far screens for a night on his own straw mattress. Robert hadn't told Mathilda where to sleep, nor if she was to wait for him after she'd finished eating.

Pulling her cloak closer around her shoulders, Mathilda shuffled a few inches nearer to the fire place. Her finger ran along the length of the new girdle. It really was beautiful, a work of art, and she wondered where it had come from. She'd been worried for a while that it had been stolen, but Robert had implied it had been made especially for her, and Mathilda choose to believe that was the case.

Watching the dying flames, Mathilda decided that if

Robert didn't turn up in the next few moments, she'd go and ask Allward where she should bed down for the night. While she waited, she prayed to Our Lady with every inch of her being, something, Mathilda hadn't done in earnest since the famine of a few years ago had so cruelly taken her mother from her.

Chapter Thirteen

He found Mathilda on her knees before the fire. Her lips were moving so fast that he could hear the rush of silent words she offered gallop straight from her mouth to heaven. Robert marvelled at how the girl could still have faith after all that had happened to her. The crop failures that had cost the whole country so dear, and many, including Mathilda, the loss of parents and children; the growing failure of her father's business; her missing brother; and now, her own kidnap and enforced service; surely any one of those events alone were enough to end any faith.

Robert shook himself. Of course she believed. Everyone believed; it was safer that way. Yet, the ferventness of her prayer had surprised him. Perhaps this girl wasn't so different from the rest. Folville waited for her to finish, before helping Mathilda rise from the cold floor. 'I was surprised to see you appealing to the Almighty.'

'My Lord?'

'You have not exactly had it easy, child. Praying has obviously not helped you in the past.'

'You speak blasphemy, my Lord.' Mathilda lowered her eyes from him.

'And you think blasphemy, girl, I have seen it in your face.'

Indignant, Mathilda pulled her body to its utmost height, 'Did not Robyn Hode, despite his defamed state, still risk capture, arrest, death even, to reach the shrine of Our Lady in *Robyn Hode and the Monk*, my Lord?' [8]

Robert couldn't contain his grin 'I forgot your memory for a tale, child. You are right, he did indeed.'

'And I think, my Lord,' Mathilda spoke almost haughtily, the realisation that, at least for now, the Folvilles needed her so were unlikely to dispose of her at this stage of their plans, making her braver, 'if I may be as bold as you say I am, and say that our charade as a couple would be more successful if you were to stop referring to me as a child.'

Folville studied Mathilda carefully, and inclined his head. What was it about her that made her so brave in the face of her own peril? He didn't for a second think it was because she was foolhardy.

Gesturing for her to follow him, Robert escorted Mathilda into the side room where she'd been bathed earlier. It already seemed a lifetime ago. 'Sit down, Mathilda, we have much to discuss, and we need privacy to do so.'

Wiping a bench clear of the damp clothes that had been laid out to dry, a wary Mathilda waited for her master to speak.

'You are going on a short journey to Bakewell, stopping at Derby on the way. Do you know the road to Derby?'

Mathilda gasped; going to Derby wasn't a short journey. It was many miles away. 'I know of it, my Lord, but I've never travelled that far.'

'You surely didn't think your message would need delivery within Ashby Folville? I could have taken such a missive myself.' He surveyed at her with an expression of amused derision, which Mathilda found unsettling, 'The debt your family has to reply involves more than money, and therefore is going to take more than a quick trip or two into a local town or even Leicester.'

Avoiding the mocking look in his eyes, Mathilda asked, 'And once I'm on the road to Derby, my Lord?'

'You are to head to Bakewell. There you will ask for audience with Nicholas Coterel.'[9]

Mathilda's face went white, and her palms clenched together. 'I see you know the name, Mathilda. Tell me, how does a potter's daughter know of such a man?'

Mathilda swallowed, trying to ease the sudden dryness of her throat, 'I heard the name in the spring, my Lord. I was in Leicester with my father. It was a name spoken of in hushed tones, in awe, my Lord, and with fear.'

'Nicholas Coterel and his brother John are not men to

trifle with, Mathilda. Nor, however, are they men to fear –
unless you have particular cause to do so.'

Mathilda boldly fixed her gaze upon Robert's face, fear
making her forget her position of inferiority in the hope of
receiving more information about her task. 'I see, my Lord.'

'They are like us; my brothers and I. The Coterel family
see the disintegration of our country and counties, and have
taken steps to curb the worst excesses of those who abuse
their positions of power too widely.'

Mathilda didn't respond to his statement, and as Robert
stared at her tiny frame and delicate features, he seemed
unsure for the first time, 'I admit that John Coterel appears
to have developed a taste for violence beyond the necessary.
Even more so than Eustace and Richard have. That worries
me. But, I tell you that in confidence. Do you understand,
Mathilda? I am trusting you to keep my confidence.'

'I am honoured, my Lord,' Mathilda was anything but
honoured. With each word Robert spoke her shaky bravery
was knocked away, and fear at what was being asked of her
began to knock louder at the surface of her mind.

'To you I can admit I am wary about Eustace's plan to
work with the Coterel brothers, but I think he is right in
one important respect.'

'My Lord?'

'Look at yourself, girl. Who would take you for anything
but an honest worker, a highly placed servant of the family,
doing her master's bidding? You are the perfect candidate to
carry this message.'

Mathilda looked down at her unfamiliar clothes. He
probably had a point. 'What must I say, my Lord, when I
reach the Coterel home?'

'You'll be told in good time. Once you get there, all you
have to do is pass the information on, and await a reply.
Then you bring it back here.'

'And then I can go home?'

'If you're successful, and if the debt has been repaid, then
yes.' Mathilda tried not to read anything into the fact that
Robert coloured slightly, and didn't look at her while he

replied.

'May I ask a further question, my Lord?'

'Indeed.'

'How will I travel, my Lord? On foot the journey will take days, and yet unaccompanied on horseback it'll appear suspicious, a girl of my status out on her own.'

Robert studied her shrewdly and with satisfaction. 'Eustace was right. You are perfect for this assignment, and your question is a good one.'

Standing and stretching out his long legs as if restless, Robert added, 'I will ride with you as far as Derby, we have friends there. They will accommodate us overnight, and then, the following day, I will arrange for you to be taken on a cart with Master Hugo, an associate of mine who fought loyally by my side in the last Scottish war, to Bakewell, where they hold a weekly market. Hugo has a stall there selling leather wares. You will slip away from the stall to the Coterels' hall, deliver the message, obtain the reply, and then return to the market. When you are back with Hugo you will help him sell his goods until the end of the day. Once you have been returned to Hugo's workshop, I will bring you back here.'

Relieved not to be travelling alone, Mathilda was sure the task wasn't going to be as simple as Robert was making it sound. 'Please, my Lord, why cannot you or your brothers deliver the message?'

Robert sighed, 'How would you react, Mathilda, if you witnessed a member of the Folville family and the Coterel family meeting?'

'Of course. I understand, my Lord,' and she did, very well indeed.

Part of what Robert de Folville had told her the night before had seemed unimportant as she'd listened to her instructions. During a long, lonely, wakeful night on a cot at the edge of the main hall , Mathilda hadn't been able to stop thinking about the sentence, 'The debt your family owes involves more than money.' She'd just given up trying to decide what Robert had meant by that, and fallen asleep, when Mathilda was woken at dawn by Sarah the housekeeper. Even as she blinked her eyes into wakefulness, a mixture of the images that had plagued Mathilda's night time mind, her father, her brothers, and her own situation as a spy, continued to haunt her.

Led through to the kitchens, she found Robert already booted and cloaked, ripping off some hunks of bread and placing them in a saddle bag for the journey.

'There are things you need to know, Mathilda. Come on girl, get some bread and ale in you, and follow me down to the stables. We have to make an early start.' Striding away, Robert called over his shoulder, 'the groom has your horse ready, don't be long.'

Mathilda gulped down some liquid and tried to chew the crusty bread, but it seemed to grow in her mouth, and it took a huge act of will to swallow it down. She hadn't dared tell Robert that she hadn't ridden a horse since she was a small child, but had always travelled in the back of her father's cart with the pots, keeping them safe from the perils of breakage on the uneven road to Leicester market.

Hastily following her new master's retreating steps, Mathilda carried the remaining bread with her, and was soon being hoisted into the saddle of a chestnut palfrey, which she was relieved to see was shorter than she'd feared, with kind, docile eyes. A saddle roll hung off its harness, and she stuffed the bread inside in case hunger overtook her anxiety on the ride. As they trotted briskly out of the courtyard and onto the quiet road west, Robert drew in close to Mathilda's side. She was hanging onto the reins and her mount's mane for all she was worth. Robert raised his eyebrows as he observed her discomfort, but said nothing on the matter.

'Before we arrive, you must know that my family's collaboration with the Coterels is at best a necessity, usually a financially rewarding one, but it is not, generally speaking, an alliance based on friendship. Money does the talking when it comes to John and Nicholas Coterel, perhaps even more than it does with Eustace. They afford us harbour within the Peak District sometimes, and we return the favour when required. Now and again we both agree that a local issue needs addressing and we work together to do just that.

'Then there is the small matter of your position. You are supposed to be my close acquaintance, and it will be assumed that you will be aware of the details of Belers' death and its consequences. There are always consequences, Mathilda.'

She risked a glance away from her palfrey's neck to look at Robert. His face was handsome, and if it wasn't for the cruel streak that could flare up in him with no warning, she could, perhaps, truly like this man. The prospect unnerved her, and Mathilda quickly pushed it to one side. 'Indeed, my Lord.'

'That my family was involved in Belers' death is widely known. That it was Eustace that arranged it, you have probably guessed. But you should also know that I helped with the planning, as did Walter.'

Feeling his hot gaze on her, Mathilda carefully concealed her reaction, but her insides clenched as she waited for him to continue.

'Belers had been a thorn in the side of the gentry in the region for some time. You need not know how the breaking point for action was reached, but you should be aware that we were paid to do the job by De Herdwyk and La Zouche. Remember their names, Mathilda, you will be asked for them by Coterel as proof that you come from me.'

'De Herdwyk and La Zouche.' Mathilda repeated the names back at him.

'The hunt for Belers' killers was widespread, for he was an important man. Leicestershire's sheriff at the time had no choice but to pursue us.'

'Edmund de Ashby, my Lord?'[10]

Folville was surprised, 'You know his name?'

'Of course, my Lord, he was the sheriff.'

'Again you prove your worth, Mathilda.' Robert pulled his

impressive jet-black mount closer to her more ladylike palfrey, and examined her more carefully as they proceeded at a slower pace, while the sun rose to its daytime position.

'Thank you, my Lord.' Mathilda, feeling as if she was less likely to fall and hit the ground now they were proceeding at a walking pace, began to survey the landscape around her. This was unknown territory to her, and the world was beginning to stir, getting ready for the working day ahead.

Whispering, keeping a watchful eye on the wakeful villagers they passed by, Robert made sure they could not be overheard as he continued his account of the events of two years ago. 'The authorities couldn't catch us, but they had to do something to illustrate their attempts to do so, however futile. A trailbaston was held in our absence and they took our lands in Reresby in punishment for conspiracy. And then we were outlawed.'[11]

Mathilda drew in a sharp breath. This she hadn't known to be true. She'd heard rumours, of course, but had dismissed them. In this case, at least, it now appeared she'd been wrong to do so. He'd been outlawed! That meant even being seen talking to him could put her in danger.

Seeing her fearful reaction, Robert continued, 'Fear not, you are not vulnerable with me, for our outlawry was lifted with a pardon a year later. My brothers and I left the region for a while during its application, making contacts in Lincolnshire. We considered an arrest and payment for a quick pardon, followed by a short time in the service of the King, worthwhile for ridding the world of a scoundrel like Belers.'

Mathilda hadn't heard the last part of what Robert had said. Her breath had snagged in her throat. An outlaw! The balladeers songs of Robyn Hode she'd heard at the annual horse fair last year swam in her head. Robert was more like the hero of folklore with each new revelation.

'There is more,' Robert's chin was thrust forward in defiance, 'My family supported Thomas of Lancaster, a sturdy voice during the times of chaos.'

Mathilda said nothing, and in truth, knew nothing of this

name beyond its connection to power.

'His supporters are no longer welcome in this *new* England, and I have charges hanging over me on that score, although I've never been arrested over them, nor will I be!'

Robert sped to a trot now they'd passed through the last village for a while, having reached Charnwood Forest. 'That is enough for now,' he called across to Mathilda, whose palfrey was bouncing her up and down mercilessly in the saddle, 'keep close to me through the forest. Not too fast though, or we will draw too much attention to ourselves.'

Grace got up from her office desk to find a map of medieval Leicestershire. She wanted to plot Mathilda and Robert's route, and so add some colour to her description of their journey for her potential readers.

She was a little concerned that anyone of a non-historical bent would be either bored or confused by the last conversation between her lead characters, but it was essential to the plot. Or was it? She'd keep it as it was for now, but had the feeling her red pen would be crossing the mention of Lancaster out.

Grace was also worried about the fact she was now well outside of her proved fact zone. Mathilda was purely fictitious, and therefore so was the trip she was now on. Grace knew that the Folvilles and Coterels had both employed spies and messengers, and hoped that her desire to tell a good story wouldn't be ruined by the historical purists.

The Folville and Coterel families really had collaborated with each other on occasion, so the trip itself between their establishments must have been undertaken, possibly even by Robert de Folville himself.

Finding the relevant map, Grace traced the route from Ashby Folville to Bakewell that she imagined Robert and Mathilda would travel, and began to sketch in the details for her novel. Grace had finished what she was doing when her computer beeped at her impatiently, announcing the arrival of an email.

Totally understand about book. Is it all RH or Folvilles or something else?

Would like to meet and talk shop – maybe we could agree on subject for paper and aim to write it in the spring?

What you think?

I'm theoretically available every afternoon until Oct.

Best

Rob x

Chapter Fourteen

Daisy ran an eye over her notes. Guinea pigs, rabbits, gerbils, mice; all their feeding times and cleaning out requirements were listed neatly on the paper before her. As she flicked through the pages of information she'd written, all the relevant instructions seemed to be there, but Daisy had a nagging feeling she'd forgotten something. The three willing helpers recruited to look after her menagerie for the two days before the wedding, and for the duration of the honeymoon, would arrive soon to learn the ropes. Daisy wanted everything written down as a back-up, so that they didn't have to call her with a query while she was away.

Somehow time seemed to have speeded up to an impossible pace over the last few weeks, and the wedding, about which she'd been so laid back, was now causing her the occasional bout of butterflies.

Marcus, as calm and steady as ever, had told Daisy to chill, and that all was in hand. The hotel accommodation was sorted, the venue was booked, the officiant was arranged, the photographer booked, the reception menu had been agreed, altered, and agreed again, the cake was ordered, and the wedding organiser Marcus had insisted on was the type of woman who forgot nothing. Marcus's suit was ready at the hire shop, as was his brother's and best man Simon's, and apart from the final fitting the bridesmaid's and bride's dresses were ready.

All Daisy had left to do was find some shoes and her outfit was complete. Yet she couldn't help worrying as the final days of her independence slipped away.

Not that she was regretting her decision to marry

Marcus. Not at all. But Daisy had managed alone for such a long time, and it all seemed to have happened so fast; it was going to be a learning curve, albeit a very exciting one, having to share every bit of her life with someone else. From nowhere unaccustomed tears pricked at the corners of Daisy's eyes. Wiping them away angrily, Daisy decided to phone Grace; she'd talk some sense into her.

'Grace? Is this a good time?' Daisy had picked up the mobile without considering the time, or where Grace might be.

'Sure, what's up? You sound weird.'

'Sorry, Grace, I'm having a mini panic about the wedding. I am doing the right thing, aren't I?'

Grace, who theoretically had been working on her novel, but had in fact been mulling ideas over for the paper she might write with Rob, was glad of an interruption to her time-wasting, 'Of course you are.'

'It's just, well ... I've managed alone so long.'

'I know, Daze, but you love Marcus.'

Daisy sniffed down the phone, rummaging about in her dungarees pocket for a tissue, 'I loved Daniel Harcourt, but I didn't marry him.'

Grace laughed, 'Daniel Harcourt was a git. And anyway, you were only nineteen at the time. Thank goodness you didn't marry him!' An image of Mathilda popped into Grace's mind as she spoke. She was nineteen as well. *I wonder ...*

Daisy relaxed and began to giggle, 'You're right ... I guess.'

'Come on, Daze,' Grace closed her eyes, temporarily shutting out the sheer Robin Hood-ness of her office, 'Marcus loves you. You love Marcus. Your lives fit perfectly. He adores animals, and so do you. He works shifts, so you'll have the luxury of time apart as well as time together. You're a lucky woman, so sit back and enjoy it all.'

'Thanks, Grace. You're right. I knew you'd sort me out.'

'By telling you what you knew already?'

'Yup!' Daisy, her irrational outburst already swept aside, carried on, 'By the way, have you heard from the nice, intelligent, interesting Dr Franks again?'

Now it was Grace's turn to sigh, 'Sometimes, Daisy, I think you're a mind reader.'

'Ah. So he is on your mind then?'

Grace quickly explained about the paper proposal before her friend's imagination galloped off at a romantic tangent. 'What should I do, Daze? I'd like to do it, but I'm so short of time.'

'Right.' Daisy sounded sharp and abruptly businesslike. 'Are you listening to me properly, Dr Harper? Are you sitting down?'

'Y-e-s ...' Grace answered hesitantly, 'I'm working from the study at home today.'

'Now look, honey, I'm going to take hideous advantage of being your best friend and hope that that's enough to stop you getting all offended by what I'm about to say. OK?'

'O-K ...'

'To start with, press the pause button on the novel. Don't ditch it, you've come too far, but leave it for a while,' Daisy could hear Grace mustering herself to protest, so she began to speak faster, 'concentrate on the textbook between nine and one every day throughout the summer hols, just get the damn thing over with. You say you've done the research. Well, use it and write it up. If you don't do it soon, then you know as well as I do that someone else will come along and beat you to it. Next ...' Daisy was in her stride now, 'you need to get a life. One that's outside Robin Hood, the Folvilles, and the students. So get yourself over to Nottingham, meet that Rob Franks bloke again, sort out the paper, arrange to work on it in the afternoons or something. Give him first authorship and then he'll have to do most of the work, and you'll have the chance to get to know him. And, before you start arguing, don't you dare tell me you don't fancy him, because I don't believe you!'

Grace felt like she'd been running in a race, but had somehow taken the wrong road and missed the finish line. A lot of what Daisy had said made sense, although contacting Rob Franks about a paper was hardly leaving everything else behind, was it? And could she really put the novel aside so easily?

She had to admit that the volume of daydreams about Rob had been increasing, and if she was honest, at two or three o'clock in the morning, when her rational, sensible, rather boring self was absent, he was far more to Grace than just a fellow historian she'd only met once.

The trouble was, now she'd admitted as much to herself, she knew she'd blush like an overripe tomato the very next time she saw him.

As yet Grace hadn't replied to Rob's latest email, even though she knew it gave her the perfect opportunity to meet him again. Taking a deep breath, Grace decided to take half of Daisy's advice, by clicking on the email Reply icon. At least, she thought as she typed, seeing him again on a purely professional basis will let me see if I do actually like him, or if Daisy has been putting ideas in my head. I'll probably find he's married or not remotely interested in me beyond my mind. Or I'll discover that I was totally wrong about him being that nice in the first place.

Hi Rob, would be good to meet soon to discuss a paper.
Also free 'in theory' most afternoons.
Fancy a coffee and a planning session next week?
Hectic with wedding plans after that.

Do you want to come here, or shall I head up to Nottingham?
Best,
Grace.

The speed of his reply back took Grace by surprise, and filled her mind with unwanted hope, just as she'd convinced herself he'd never be interested in her in a thousand years.

Sorry. Been bullied into doing an adult education thing next week.
I'm free tomo about 2pm?
Is that ok? Or too short notice? I'll come to you if you can fit me in.
Hope you can make it – I have lots of ideas ...
Let me know a.s.a.p. so I can book train ticket.
Best
Rob x

Grace's mouth went dry, as she turned to the nearest photograph from the filming of *Robin of Sherwood* for support. It was her favourite one of Jason Connery, with all his merry men lined up beside him. 'Tomorrow afternoon! Oh hell, guys, I'll never have got myself together by tomorrow!'

Swallowing her nerves, thinking of Daisy's advice, Grace emailed back an agreement, giving Rob details of where to meet her the following day, and then, ignoring the remainder of Daisy's lecture, decided to stop herself worrying about her forthcoming non-date by picking up her manuscript.

She was so stiff from the journey that Mathilda had to be bodily lifted from her palfrey by the waiting groom. Flexing her arms and legs, she tried to ease the ache in her limbs without drawing attention to herself.

Hanging back from Robert and the steward, who'd quickly approached him on their arrival; Mathilda examined the scene around her.

The courtyard was not large, and from its centre Mathilda could see a narrow alleyway running off to its right that presumably led to the stables. Directly before her was the main house, a fine gabled building, modest in size, but obviously a cut above the standard tradesman's dwelling. Attached to the house was a workshop, behind which Mathilda could just see some strips of land sloping gently upwards, which were obviously in productive use for the household and, assuming this was a demesne property, to provide food as part of the local landlord's taxes.

An overpowering scent of leather filled the air, and Mathilda remembered that Robert had told her the man they were to stay with was a successful trader; a merchant who dealt his wares far beyond the local community. Mathilda looked around, comparing her current whereabouts to her own home.

Mathilda's father was an excellent potter, but due to the readily available quantities of clay in the region, there were many other potters in Leicestershire. It wasn't enough to be the best any more, especially with the added pressure of foreign imports. You needed to have a head for business, and her father had never had that. Although it would never have been openly admitted, it had been her mother who'd quietly got on with that side of things, and since her death, the difference in their fortunes had been staggering.

Mathilda's contemplation was cut short as Robert turned to her, 'Come, Mathilda, Master Hugo is expecting us within.'

It was strange and yet reassuring to be escorted on Robert's arm into the square room which formed the main centre of activity for the house. *So*, thought Mathilda, *our fake courtship has begun, even though we are in the home of a trusted ally*. Her heart thumped in her throat as she walked demurely next to Robert, her eyes taking in the detailed tapestry that hung against the wall opposite the fire place, its rich colours reflecting heat back into the room.

Practically furnished, the house spoke of sensible expenditure. The few luxuries that were evident all had a worthwhile nature; hangings to maintain warmth, and pots and cups that had been made to last, rather than to show off with.

Master Hugo entered the room in a flurry of bustle, a servant at his side, armed with a tray holding a pitcher and, rather tellingly to Mathilda, only two pewter mugs.

Mathilda's mind had conjured up the expectation of this Master Hugo being a large, powerfully built, jovial man with thick red hair and huge hands. The reality of his appearance was in stark contrast to this imagined image. Dressed simply, but in quality cloth, Master Hugo was small of stature and slim, with thin fingers and hands that seemed to hang off the arms which were now wrapped around Robert, embracing him in a friendly greeting that seemed to last for an uncomfortably long time to the waiting Mathilda. She didn't feel exactly threatened by Hugo's presence, as she had done when she'd met the rector of Teigh, nor was she in wary awe as with Eustace, but she still found she'd taken an instant dislike to the man, although she had no idea why.

Robert regarded Hugo with respect, but said nothing. The atmosphere in the room changed as they faced each other, and Mathilda felt as if she was intruding, and dipped her eyes further.

The spell was broken by the clatter of a dropped cup. The servant muttered his apologies, which were irritably brushed away by Master Hugo, as he picked up the dropped vessel, and began to pour out two portions of ale.

'So Folville, this is your temporary prize from the Twyford debt?'

Mathilda flinched inwardly at being referred to in this way, but wisely held her tongue. She realised with some shame that she had relaxed in Robert's company, and for a few precious moments, had forgotten the reality of her situation. Under her breath, Mathilda swore there and then that she must never again forget that she was a mere object to these people. A tool; something to be used while they could, and if she perished in the process – well, there were plenty more where she came from ...

'Yes, Hugo, this is Mathilda de Twyford. A fine young woman.'

'I'm sure,' Hugo's smile didn't quite meet his eyes as he accepted her curtsy with a dismissive curl of his lips.

'Mathilda knows the plan. It only remains for me to pass on my family's message to her, and then you'll be able to borrow her help to sell on the stall until the end of the day with no problem.'

'Without problem you say, Robert. Are you sure?' Hugo's doubts were plain. Mathilda could almost feel the words roaming around his head. *A mere female. She'll be useless.*

'Do not be mistaken by her appearance, Hugo. Mathilda is a sharp, intelligent young woman who is older than she appears to be. She also has a lot to lose if things don't go as we desire. She would be a fool to let us down, and I can assure you, Mathilda is no fool.'

Mathilda's palms had begun to prickle with sweat. Robert spoke with a confidence that should have flattered her, and perhaps it would have done, if it hadn't been accompanied with such a strong hint of menace at the prospect of her failure. All along their journey through the midland county roads, Mathilda had convinced herself that she'd be fine, and all would be well soon. Now she was here, at this house in Derby, the confidence she'd forced herself to portray was wavering. Tomorrow she would have to travel a considerable distance with this Master Hugo, and he obviously didn't trust her; he didn't even like her. A feeling that was entirely mutual.

She could tell that Robert did trust him however; this was the most relaxed Mathilda had seen him during their short yet eventful acquaintance.

Hugo pointedly passed a cup to Robert, dismissing Mathilda with a barked request which sounded very much like an order, 'Mathilda, you will go to the workshop and find Mary. Until the morning, you can assist her as she wishes. There is a good deal to do before we go to market.'

Mathilda wordlessly curtseyed again, and followed the inclination of Master Hugo's head, hoping it would lead her where she was bidden. Glancing back as she reached the door, she saw the men were already engrossed in conversation, and were paying no attention to her at all.

The workshop was small, but warm, and felt much more familiar and welcoming than the main house. Mary, an able woman, of about two score years, was hard at work piling belts into a wooden crate, her sleeves firmly rolled up . She came forward to welcome the visitor.

'I've been sent to help.' Mathilda spoke shyly, but was already glad to be away from the unsettling atmosphere of the main house.

'You must be the girl from Twyford. I'm Mary, and any help you could give would be very gratefully received.'

'I'm Mathilda.' It was a genuine welcome, and Mathilda took to her companion straight away.

Mary turned to the only other occupant of the room. 'This is Roger, Master Hugo's apprentice.'

Mathilda greeted him politely, but the lad, no more than fourteen years old, only nodded curtly in response as she passed him on her way to the far end of the workshop to help Mary with the boxes of stock. It was obvious he was learning his manners from his master as well as his trade, for he offered no further words to the two females.

Deciding to concentrate her attentions on Mary and the task she required help with, Mathilda asked, 'Master Hugo works leather?'

'Yes,' Mary pointed to Mathilda's girdle, 'that's one of his.'

Mathilda stroked the fine belt she wore in wonder, stunned that such an obnoxious little man could have made something so beautiful. As she searched about her, she saw an array of equally detailed pieces of work, many of which held the same intricate pattern of lines and butterflies. Passing each separate item to Mary to pack in soft barley straw, Mathilda caressed them with the reverence such works of art were due.

'They're beautiful.'

Mary smiled, 'Indeed, my master has the gift, sure enough.'

Mathilda was surprised, 'Master? Forgive me, I assumed you to be his wife.'

Mary let out a short laugh that contained no trace of humour, 'Master Hugo wants no wife.'

Chapter Fifteen

As Grace waited, sat at her usual table in the window of the Mrs Beeton's tea shop, she began to think that perhaps this hadn't been such a good place to arrange to meet Rob. A cafe tucked away in St Martin's Square at the far side of the city wasn't the easiest place to find if you didn't know Leicester very well. And it was a good twenty-minute walk from the train station, even at speed.

Unwilling to witness his reaction to its Robin Hood-esque décor, Grace had experienced a strong desire to keep him out of her office. Not only could she not have coped with any derisory comments he might be compelled to make, it seemed too private a place to share with him yet, although she wasn't sure why she felt that way. The result had been suggesting somewhere to meet that was some distance from work.

Four times she'd got dressed that morning. Four times, for heaven's sake! This was not normal behaviour. In the end Grace had plumped for the top and jacket she'd worn to the viva, and some clean jeans. Smart but flattering. Or so she hoped. She'd worried for a moment that he'd only think she had one set of clothes, but then told herself not to be so damn stupid, and had marched to work before she started staring at her limited wardrobe of clothes, and found herself getting changed all over again.

Flicking to a clean page in her notebook, Grace tried to concentrate on formulating a plan for the paper Rob had suggested. It was no good though. Fidgety and uncomfortable, Grace found herself glancing out of the window so often that forming any cohesive outline was nigh-on impossible. Sustaining herself with a large cappuccino rather than her usual pot of tea, Grace blew through the circling steam and stared into the liquid, attempting to focus her thoughts.

'Praying to the god of caffeine?'

So caught up in her thoughts, Rob's sudden arrival made Grace jump, causing her to slop coffee into her saucer. Realising that despite her determination not to, she was already blushing, and embarrassed to be caught looking vacant, she mumbled, 'Something like that,' before pulling herself together. 'Coffee?'

Damn. He looks even better in jeans and that old rugby shirt than he had in his linen suit. Rats.

Grace tried to pay attention on what Rob was saying from his position sat opposite her, but her mind was too busy trying to convince itself that she really didn't find him attractive at all. On failing that particular task, Grace worked on telling herself firmly that Rob wouldn't be either interested in her or available anyway.

'Are you with me, Grace?'

'What? Oh, sorry,' Grace's cheeks coloured again, and she began to bluster, 'I've not been sleeping well, lots on my mind, you know how it is …'

'Indeed.' Rob was studying at her with a curious mixture of concern, puzzlement and regret, 'So, do you fancy having a crack at this paper for the *English Historical Review* then, we could aim for next Easter instead of October?

'Yes, sure. "*The Fourteenth-Century English Crown Needed Criminals*" sounds a feasible title with all the research we've already done. Are you sure you don't mind doing the bulk of the writing?'

'No problem. As long as you are sure you don't mind me stealing your research notes.'

'I've done the work; it might as well be used. I'll need it for the textbook, but not for a while yet.'

They continued to sip their coffees in silence before

Rob said, 'But you said you were intending to start writing up your book over the student holidays?'

'Well, yes,' Grace thought quickly, 'but most of my notes are on the computer, I can attach them and send them over to you, without losing out myself. Anything else can be photocopied.'

'Right,' Rob sat back, his eyes twinkling slightly, making Grace feel uncomfortable.

Turning her gaze away from his, Grace forced herself to steer her mind to the paper again; *after all*, she told herself sternly, *that's the only reason why he's come here*. 'We could use the examples of Nicholas Coterel and Eustace de Folville to illustrate our argument.'

Robert was looking at her in a rather strange way, so Grace rambled on. 'They were career criminals in the "lesser gentry" class, and they were both pardoned for serious crimes. Murder, rape, kidnap, and so on, so that they could fight in the King's wars.

'Nicholas Coterel was even made the Queen's Bailiff in the High Peak of Derbyshire in 1335, and he continued to commit serious crimes. Eustace was knighted by the king for services in the wars, and yet within six years he'd received three further pardons for murder, rape, and armed robbery.

'Crime was simply a way to make a living for these people, to give them the luxurious life they wanted, and as long as they fought for the Crown when required to do so, they got away with it.'[12]

'I think that's the longest sentence I've ever heard you utter!'

'You've only known me for a few days!'

'Sorry, I was being flippant.' Rob rubbed his hands down his jeans, 'that sounds like a good basis to start from. Those two characters alone have enough ammunition to show that the hiring of criminals by the Crown was not anti-propaganda, but a frequently practised past time when they needed soldiers for their never ending wars.'

'Then of course, there's the result of the fighting.'

'How do you mean?' Rob nodded, encouraging her to explain.

'When these men were in between wars, they had nothing else to do but commit crimes again, so then they'd need another pardon, and therefore go back into service to pay for it. And each time they went to war they got closer to perfecting the art of killing.'

'A self-fulfilling felonious prophecy.'

'Exactly.' Grace didn't know what else to say, so hid behind drinking her now cold coffee.

Rob just sat there, watching her. Grace found herself beginning to feel paranoid. 'Do I have food on my face or something? Why are you looking at me like that?'

'What? Oh sorry, I was thinking about your textbook.'

Grace picked up the cafe menu and pretended to read it, 'Oh, really?'

'Yes, really.' His eyes seemed to be laughing at her again, 'Did you know that whenever I ask about the textbook, you don't look at me when you reply, or you avoid replying altogether?'

'Do I?'

'It's almost as if you're hiding something. Or stranger still, like you're ashamed of it.'

Grace put down the menu and began to fidget with a paper napkin instead, not quite daring to meet Rob's eyes, but determined not to satisfy him by looking completely away either.

'I haven't known you for long, but I can't see, even if you were the most private person on the planet, why you'd be embarrassed by your work. Not when you are obviously very good at it.'

'Oh well, you know how it is, I never think anything I produce is good enough.'

'Hmm …' Rob wasn't sounding at all convinced.

'And to be honest, I'm not sure I'll get as much done as I hoped, not with the wedding and everything.'

Rob stopped smiling, and picked up his own cup. 'When is the happy event?'

'Eighth of August.'

'Is that a special date for you, or a Saturday picked out at random?'

'It's a Friday, actually,' Grace wondered why he'd turned so prickly, 'and I'm simply doing what I'm told.'

Rob's eyebrows shot up, 'I can't imagine you ever doing what you are told.'

'Charming!' This was weird, one minute he was flirting, the next he was surly, and then he was flirting again.

'He must be one hell of a bloke to achieve that.'

Grace frowned, 'Well, to tell you the truth, I've only seen him a few times. It's all happened rather fast.'

'A whirlwind romance then.'

'Yes. Marcus seems nice enough though.'

'Nice enough! Good grief, woman, you're way too young to be settling for "nice enough."'

Rob had gone a funny colour and finally, Grace understood why, 'You've got it all wrong! I'm not the one getting married. I'm the bridesmaid. It's my best friend's wedding.'

Now it was Rob's turn to appear uncomfortable. He put his cup down with a clatter. 'Ah, I see.' Then, with a confidence Grace could only envy, he put his hand over hers. 'Good.'

Grace didn't say anything; she was too busy feeling shocked, and unexpectedly happy.

Half an hour later, unable to take any more caffeine, they elected to walk back to the university so Rob could collect some of Grace's primary evidence for the paper, before heading back to Nottingham.

Funny how different everything suddenly looks. Grace smiled to herself as they walked up New Walk, past the museum and the rows of eighteenth-century houses. Rob hadn't let go of her hand since he'd grasped it in the café, and rather than feeling suffocated as she had with boyfriends in the past, Grace felt warm and safe. She also seemed totally incapable of stopping smiling. Neither of them spoke as they walked, but somehow that didn't matter.

Rob had told her while they were in Mrs Beeton's that he'd hoped to see her again from the first moment he'd clapped eyes on her huddled in the Reception armchair before the viva. When she'd mentioned a forthcoming wedding, Rob had assumed it was her own, and resigned himself to having missed out on a possible relationship again.

Grace had protested, entirely on autopilot, 'Who the hell would marry an insane person like me?' When Rob had told her to stop being daft and shut up. Grace had blushed again, but this time she hadn't cared.

It wasn't until they reached the wrought iron gateway of the university's main entrance that Grace began to feel self-conscious, and let go of Rob's hand.

Apologising as she freed herself, she was unsure why she wasn't prepared to go into work looking as if she was part of a couple. If that's what they were?

'It's OK, this is work,' Rob winked, 'and your colleagues aren't used to seeing you with someone.'

'Thanks,' Grace grinned at his understanding, 'they're not the only ones. I need to get used to the idea myself.'

'Me too, if it comes to that.'

Grace gazed at Rob's face; an expression of mild amazement was etched on his features. 'Are you sure you haven't got someone tucked away at home?'

'Idiot. Now,' Rob began to stride towards the main cluster of the campus buildings, 'which of these hideous edifices do you hide in all day?'

'Bloody hell!' Rob stood in the middle of Grace's office and circled slowly on the spot. 'I see you have opted away from the subtle approach to décor.'

'Cheek.'

'Well, at least no one could ever be in any doubt as to your historical interests.'

Rummaging around in the nearest filing cabinet for the crime statistics she had unearthed from the Patent and Court Rolls for 1327, but as yet hadn't committed to her computer, Grace eventually produced a stapled together set of sheets, and passed them to her fellow historian.

Rob sat down in her swivel chair, 'So, tell me the truth, Dr Harper, why the uneasy looks whenever I mention the textbook?'

Grace sighed, she'd have to tell him, he'd only keep asking her, and anyway, hiding the novel all the time was being tiring and tedious.

'Come on,' Rob tapped his knees invitingly and, with a quick glance to make sure the office door was shut properly, Grace sat on his lap, feeling like a loved-up teenager.

Rob wrapped his arms around her, 'Now Grace, I badly want to kiss you. In fact, I have badly wanted to kiss you for the past three hours, not to mention do a hell of a lot more with you besides, but I am willing to torture myself further and withhold that kiss, until you tell me the truth.'

'You're a hard man, Dr Franks.'

'I sure am with you on my lap!'

Grace coloured crimson, even though she was privately thrilled at his body's response to her presence, 'Honestly!'

'Go on, tell me.' He began to tickle her waist, at which point, Grace pulled away and faced him properly.

She told him about the novel, about not wanting to just produce some dry old handbook to history that no one will read. And then, as Rob had neither looked disapproving, or burst out laughing, she told him about how, as the book progressed, she'd become increasingly worried that it had journeyed too far away from factual history. It was becoming far more of a saga than she'd anticipated.

'Is it about Robin Hood?'

'Indirectly. It is more about the ideals his tales promoted in the fourteenth century. It's based loosely on the Folvilles. I'm working on the assumption that the ballads were already well known, although I realise that is a bone of historical contention.'

Rob didn't argue with her assumption, 'I'd like to read it – if I may?'

'Well, I … it isn't finished yet.'

'Even so. I could give you my opinion of it so far. If you want it.'

Surprised that she did, Grace readily accepted the offer. 'I know I've become obsessed with finishing it, when I should be doing the textbook, but I just *need* to do it.'

'I don't understand your reluctance to make it an easy-read novel, rather than a perfectly historically accurate novel. Surely if it's a good read that happens to teach the reader something as they go along, than that's enough in itself.'

'Well I …'

'And why not make it a romance? They are very popular. You're a romantic, after all.'

'I am not!' Grace sounded so indignant that Rob couldn't help but laugh.

'How can you say you're not romantic? Look around you, woman. If Robin Hood isn't a romantic ideal, then I don't know what is. Let me read the novel draft so far while you hurry up and write the rest. Meanwhile I'll write the paper, and then you can get the textbook started properly, and get on with the rest of your life.'

Grace was about to issue a whole stream of sensible

objections, but she didn't get the chance, because Rob kissed her.

Chapter Sixteen

It had been with great reluctance, armed with as much of Grace's novel as she'd typed up, along with the primary evidence for the forthcoming paper, that Rob had left Grace's office and headed back to Nottingham.

Without his presence the office felt very empty, and Grace was torn between feeling lost in the space, sad at his departure, and excited by the prospect of future meetings. Not that he'd mentioned seeing her again.

'What do you think, boys?' Grace addressed the posters on the walls, 'is he the one for me, or is he going to disappear now, never to be heard from again, or worse – will he stay in touch until he's got me to bed and then break my heart? Or worse even than that, turn into a tedious historian from hell, and bore me to death?'

Conscious that her euphoria was already beginning to be eclipsed by doubts, Grace was determined to claw it back, and picked up her mobile to call Daisy. Her friend's rather muffled grunted greeting surprised Grace. 'Daze, what are you doing? I haven't interrupted you and Marcus at a vital moment, have I?'

'I wish! No, I was unloading the Land Rover. I had a packet of pet food between my teeth. I've been to the wholesalers. What's up? You hardly ever call during in the day.'

'Oh well, just fancied a chat, you know.'

Picking up on Grace's unusually breezy tone, Daisy asked, 'Hey, are you all right?'

'Totally all right. Well, I think I am.'

'Something's happened?'

Grace heard Daisy open the Land Rover's side door,

118

and sit down on the squeaky drivers' seat, ready to listen to her friend, 'You've seen Dr Franks again, haven't you?'

'Yes.'

'I knew it. I knew you liked him. So?'

'Calm down Daisy, he only came to talk about the paper.'

'"Only" my arse!'

'Daisy!'

'And? Come on, enough of the suspense!'

'He kissed me.'

'Yes!' Daisy mentally punched the air before becoming sensible, 'is he accompanying you to the wedding then?'

'Hold on! It was only a kiss. Well, a kiss and some hand-holding, and a cuddle.'

'Sounds damn good to me.'

'But, the thing is Daisy; now he's gone ... it's odd but ...'

'Everything feels a bit flat.'

'Yes. How did you know that?'

'Been there, done that, getting married to him.'

'Bloody hell.'

'Quite.'

'There's something else. I've given him my novel so far to read.'

'Wow. You really do like this guy.'

Grace could feel her face flushing all over again. 'He thinks I should forget about being historically accurate and just write a good story; add some extra romance and stuff, then do the textbook.'

'Sounds a sensible chap. I'll try not to be offended that you'll take that advice from him and not from me!'

'Oh Daze, it's not that. He's a historian as well and ...'

'I was only joking, honey.'

'Oh, of course. Sorry, I feel a bit all over the place. Anyway, I think he might help me out with it a bit over the summer.'

'Which one, the novel or the textbook?'

'Both, I think.'

Daisy clapped her hands in delight, 'Excellent. Right, now I have to go, the animals need feeding, but I want to hear more very soon. Don't forget, we have another dress fitting on Saturday.'

Having managed to calm herself with some coffee and a bar of chocolate, Grace had just started some work, when her email beeped. It was Rob.

Wanted to check I'm not dreaming. We did kiss didn't we? Rxx

With her smile instantly back on her face, Grace fired off a reply.

We Did Gxx

Can we do it again? Rxx

We can Gxx

You free on Saturday? R xx

In evening yes – dress fitting in Sheffield all day. G xx

Come 2 dinner with me – please!! Do you like Chinese food? Rxx

Seeing as you asked so nicely – I'd love 2 – Chinese great Gxx

Fantastic. Will pick u up from Nottingham station when u ready. I'll email u my mobile no. later so u can text me when finished dress shopping. Must go now – work demanding my attention. R xx

Whether it was sheer fatigue from the previous day's early start, the travelling, or the work she'd shared with Mary and the uncommunicative Roger, Mathilda had slept soundly in her allotted corner of the room above the workhouse. Her body felt jolted and confused as she was a woken by Mary, who shook her to consciousness before even the crack of dawn.

'I'm sorry, Mathilda, but it's a long ride to Bakewell, and you need to get there to set up before trading starts.'

Instantly alert to what was expected of her that day, Mathilda sat up and tried to conquer the panic that threatened to overtake her and rule out all sensible thought.

She had expected Robert to come and find her yesterday, but he hadn't. In fact she'd seen nothing of either him or Master Hugo all day. On the other hand, she had learnt a lot about the leather trade from Mary, how the market stall was operated, how much they charged for each item, and so on. It was important that she appeared to know what she was doing once she was at the market. Thankfully, the leatherworker's sales procedures were not very different from her father's, although the quality of his goods was far higher; as were the prices.

Mathilda barely registered the breakfast Mary forced upon her, nor did she recall, when she looked back later, putting her clothes on or helping Mary to dress her hair into a practical style. All Mathilda remembered, as she sat behind a quiet Master Hugo, her cloak wrapped tightly around her against the early morning chill, were the words Robert had spoken to her, having appeared on the scene just before she'd left the security of the workshop.

'You will listen to the directions Master Hugo gives you on the journey. He will tell you exactly how to get from the market to the Coterels' manor.' Robert gently shook her shoulder, 'Are you listening, Mathilda?'

She nodded, wiping the sleep from her eyes as she swallowed some moisture down her nervously dry throat.

'Good. Once you're at the manor house, you will ask to be taken to the steward. To him and him alone, you will say the names La Zouche and De Heredwyk. That is all he'll need to hear to grant you an audience with either John or Nicholas Coterel. Once you have been admitted, you will give whichever of the brothers you see Eustace's message. Are you ready to hear that message, Mathilda?'

'Yes my Lord.'

'OK, it is, "De Vere has agreed". That's all. It is an easy sentence to relay.'

Mathilda repeated the words back to him and curtsied.

'Well done, Mathilda.' Robert looked down at her slight presence. 'There's something else.'

'My Lord?'

'I want you to have this. Just for your protection, you understand. I'm sure you won't have the need of it, but these are uncertain times.' He pulled a short, sheathed dagger from the folds of his cloak and passed it to a stunned Mathilda.

'But my Lord, I can't carry this. If I'm found with it, you know what they'll do ...'

'Keep it hidden beneath your cloak.'

'But, my Lord, it'll be visible when I bend over.' With her milky skin growing even paler, Mathilda asked, 'Do you honestly think I'll need this, my Lord?'

'Keep it with you, Mathilda. For the unexpected. Not that they'll be anything like that, but ...'

'It's an uncertain time my Lord, yes, you said.' Mathilda took the short blade, and weighed the handle in her palm. It was a beautifully made piece, carved and patterned across the handle, with a single blue stone placed between the blade and the hilt. 'I'll conceal it beneath my outer dress, if I put another belt there, it can be slotted away safely, and it'll be placed further out of sight.'

'Again Mathilda, you are wise ...'

'For someone so young, my Lord? You keep speaking of me as though I am a child, yet I am nineteen, not twelve. And you are sending me into the lair of some of the most notorious men in this Hundred, on a mission you, I hope, would not lay upon a child.'

Robert smiled in rueful acknowledgement of her words, before taking Mathilda totally by surprise and drawing her close, hugging her briefly, 'Be careful, my girl. Follow your orders, listen to Master Hugo, and then come back to me. I'll take you home to Ashby Folville.'

'Thank you, my Lord,' Mathilda muttered, her cheeks burning, astonished at such a gesture from the man who was essentially her gaoler. If it was meant to assure her, it had failed, for it just reinforced the perils of the mission to her. *Maybe that had been his way of saying goodbye, just in case that mission turned out to be one of no return?*

'You must go now; Hugo is ready to leave.'

'My Lord,' Mathilda bowed briefly, and turned to go, but one more question burned in her throat, that she had to ask, 'Forgive me, but Master Hugo? Do you trust him?'

Roberts's face flushed with a flash of anger, and for a second Mathilda flinched in readiness for an explosion of his temper, but he caught himself, and in a sharp, controlled voice said, 'I'd trust him with my life, something that I have in fact done on the battlefield on more than one occasion.'

She bowed again and left without another word, wondering though if Master Hugo could be trusted as generously with her life.

An hour had passed since they'd left the boundary of Derby, and although dawn was still breaking, the roads were busy with wagons and carts on their way to Bakewell for the fair. Feeling Robert's knife pressing against her thigh, Mathilda wriggled into a more comfortable position in the back of the cart, pulling the thick brown travelling cloak she'd borrowed from Mary closer around her shoulders. The day promised sunshine, but the early mists had yet to clear, and the chill in the air was trying to burrow between the layers of her clothes.

Mathilda was glad of the presence of the other traders travelling the same road, for she had dreaded being alone with Master Hugo. Greetings were called and exchanged as those heading to Bakewell recognised each other from other markets and fairs. Yet Mathilda kept her own mouth shut, just in case she was spotted by someone from the markets she had frequented with her father. She didn't want to have to answer questions as to why she was there.

Sat in the back of the cart amongst the leather wares, Mathilda closed her eyes. This spare time was dangerous – it allowed her to think. She needed to stay busy to drive away the worries that beset her about her family. Was her brother Oswin home now, or lost in Lincolnshire? Or somewhere else entirely? Were Matthew and her father working all the hours of daylight they could to get her home, while still managing to support themselves and keep the home going?

If she jumped off the cart now, Mathilda knew she could easily disappear into the woodland that currently bordered the road. It would take several days to get home, but she could do it, and then ... no, that wouldn't help. The debt would still require payment, and the Folville brothers wouldn't be likely to stop at kidnap next time.

Banishing plans of potential escape, Mathilda bought her mind back to the matter in hand. So far she had avoided having to talk to Master Hugo, but as they drew closer to their destination, she knew that would have to change.

Mathilda was still unsure why she disliked Hugo so much. Although he hadn't gone as far as being friendly, he had been courteous, had treated her well in his home, and was helping her to carry out her allotted task. Yet there was something about the way he appraised her, with a sort of resentment about his features, which made Mathilda feel vulnerable and uncertain. He was a successful merchant, he was free of many of the worries the majority of the trading and lower classes had to endure; surely it was she that should have been resentful of him?

Her thoughts ceased with their abrupt arrival at the gates of Bakewell. The carts before them had started to queue up, as stewards and other assorted officials directed the traders, entertainers, and merchants to their allotted stalls. As they crept slowly forward in the queue, Master Hugo called to Mathilda. Clambering down from the cart, she went around and took hold of the horse's bridle to lead them into the market place.

Speaking in a low mumble, Hugo said, 'Once we are set up, and the earliest customers arrive, that will be your best chance to slip away. But don't be long, child, by noon business will be brisk and I shall need your help.'

'What if I can't get back on time? I wouldn't want your business to suffer because of me.'

Hugo stared at her shrewdly as he explained that there was a local lad that helped him out sometimes, and that they'd manage until she returned. If they had to.

Mathilda nodded, 'The directions, my Lord?'

'I am not your lord, girl, nor anyone's,' He spat his bitterness.

'I'm sorry, Master Hugo; I simply meant to show respect.'

'Indeed.' He seemed far from convinced, but after a few uncomfortable moments said, 'From my stall you must head left and walk the length of the fair; once you reach the final stand in the row you'll see two roads. Take the second, on the right-hand side, and follow it for about a mile. The manor you seek will be there. It is an easy route, but not an easy task. I confess I am surprised at Folville's choice of mate and confidante.'

Mathilda bit back the retort that came to her throat, saying instead 'Thank you. I shall return as soon as I am able. I do not wish to linger with the Coterel family for any longer than I have to.'

Chapter Seventeen

Thanks to Mary's instructions, and the time they'd spent in Roger's dour company sorting the plain practical belts and aprons from Master Hugo's intricate girdles, delicate butterfly-patterned belts, and dagger sheaths, the market stall was soon set up.

The crisp morning air remained cool, but the earlier promising hint of sunshine was starting to break through, and the buzz of happy expectation from her fellow traders was infectious. The first customers of the day began to descend on the scene as jugglers and other street players started to ply their light-hearted entertainment alongside the merchants of the county and beyond.

Set out in a series of rows that ran from one side of the square to the other, every possible commodity was available, providing you had the money to pay for it. From Master Hugo's finest luxury leatherware stall at the far end of the second row, there were others displaying goods as far ranging as intricately worked pieces of silver and gold jewellery, wicker baskets, combs and skeins of wool, and rolls of fabric, to food of all varieties, from the local to the exotic.

Time seemed to be passing incredibly fast to Mathilda, and before she'd had time to think about planning her exit properly, the local boy, Tom, had arrived to help Master Hugo, and she bid them a temporary farewell, slipping away to complete her allotted task.

With a racing heart, Mathilda raised her hood, and hugged her cloak around her, afraid that the knife would be spotted despite being hidden beneath several layers of clothing. Glancing around to make sure no one was looking at her in particular, but at the market in general, Mathilda edged closer to the last stall in the row. She could just make out the gateway she needed to get to over the crowd's heads.

Passing stalls displaying apples, freshly baked bread, and roasting pigs, nothing registered beyond her duty. Soon only two stands remained to be passed. Mathilda could now clearly see the slim walkway ahead, between a fenced off garden and the back wall of a workshop. She had just increased her pace, when Mathilda spotted a familiar face behind the final stall of the row.

She froze on the spot. There were plenty of people about. Surely she wouldn't be easily singled out from them, but Mathilda pulled her hood further forward anyway, covering as much as her face as possible as she watched Geoffrey of Reresby selling his pots with comfortable ease on the final stall in the row.

A jealous, angry bile rising in her throat as her eyes ran over the mass of ceramicware he could afford to offer. He may have appeared welcoming and friendly, but Mathilda knew differently. Reresby had beaten her father to the best pitches at markets and fairs for the past few years, often cheating or bribing his way into favour with the local lords so that they would buy from him and no one else.

She was only partially surprised to see him so far from home; this was a popular market after all. Mathilda also knew of her own father's shortcomings. It would never have crossed his mind to travel so far to make money.

Making sure she stayed shrouded behind a group of women chatting about the goods on offer, Mathilda moved slowly with them, until at last she was close enough to the alleyway to slip away from the stall without Geoffrey seeing her. Suppressing the idea of turning back and throwing one of the small stones which littered the edges of the road at the stall, and smashing as many of his pots as possible, Mathilda left the bustle behind her; wondering if it was her presence with the Folvilles was what had caused this abrupt, uncharacteristically violent urge.

Just as Master Hugo had said, there was a choice of roads. She took the right-hand one as instructed, and walked purposefully, trying to give the air of someone who knew where they were going, and had a perfect right to be there.

She'd travelled about a mile and was sure she should have arrived by now. She had passed the final dwelling and yet there was no manor house in sight, just a stretch of land strips to the right and a cluster of coppiced wood to the left. Mathilda dare not ask anyone for help. Anyway, the market had drawn most of the population away from their daily labours for a few precious hours, and the side street before her lay deserted.

Slipping between the trees Mathilda came to a standstill, her mind racing. Somehow she must have gone wrong. Thinking fast, she reran her instructions in her head. *Go on the right path, and keep going.* She had done exactly that. Childish tears sprang to the corners of her eyes as Mathilda took in her situation. She scrubbed them away, angry at herself, but angrier with Robert. He'd trusted Master Hugo, even though she hadn't. There was no other conclusion to reach. The leatherworker had given her the wrong directions on purpose.

A vision of her father and brothers flashed through Mathilda's head. She wouldn't let them down. For that matter, she didn't want to let Robert down either. Not because she cared about him, she told herself, but because she wanted to prove she wasn't the little girl he thought she was, and was worthy of the expectations his family held of her. Although the Folvilles' methods worried her, they were effective, and the fear they engendered was at least smeared with respect.

'What would Robyn Hode do?' Mathilda whispered to herself as she crouched between the spindly trees, watching for any other sign of life. 'He'd make a plan and stick to it. I have to find the manor, so I'll have to ask someone, I have no choice. But I need a plausible reason for asking.' This was less easy to think up. She had no money on her, so she couldn't buy a gift to pretend to take to the Coterel's home, she only had her message. Would that be enough? Or was she supposed to keep the fact that she was delivering a message a secret, along with the message itself?

It had to be the gift idea. A present from a master to Coterel perhaps? A master she would have to make up, so if she was forced to give more details, she at least sounded plausible. How about Master Hugo? She owed him some trouble after all.

Mathilda felt the knife against her side, thankful now that Robert had forced it upon her, and with a heavy sigh strode back the way she'd come. There was only one thing she could claim was a gift to the Coterels from Master Hugo, and with a heavy heart, she undid her girdle and laid it across her palms. With any luck she wouldn't have to part with it once she'd reached the manor. She really didn't want to face Robert's fury if she lost the girdle, even if it was through no fault of her own. She ran her fingers over the pattern, and was struck with the idea that she'd seen it somewhere else as she began to walk faster, her heart thudding in her chest.

Retracing her steps, Mathilda mused as to Master Hugo's motives. Why send her the wrong way? She was convinced he hadn't done it by mistake. Was he really on the Folvilles' side? Or was his friendship to Robert fake on his part for some reason, the bond they forged on the battlefield merely convenient for his own plans? Mathilda resolved to be even more wary, and also to say nothing to him of his success in misleading her when she got back to his stall. There was no way she'd give him the satisfaction, and was determined to frustrate Master Hugo by somehow succeeding in her mission.

On reaching the first holding on the edge of the town, Mathilda called out, trying to keep the nerves from her voice, 'Excuse me.'

She was relieved when it was a child who ran to meet her hail, 'Can I help you, my Lady?'

My Lady? Mathilda was momentarily stunned by the address, until she remembered her new attire, and quickly adopted what she hoped would be the mannerisms to go with her assumed social status.

'I have taken a wrong turn, I think. My father has instructed me to take this gift to the manor of the Lords Coterel, do you know the way?'

The boy, who she guessed was no more than ten years old, shrank back a little, 'The Coterel manor, you say?'

'Please. They are expecting this, I bought it from the market,' she showed the boy the girdle, 'and I fear it would be unwise to delay in its delivery.'

'You are right there, my Lady, my father says the Coterels are not patient men.' He bit his lips, suddenly, as he wondered if he'd spoken out of turn.

Mathilda smiled to reassure him, 'You can direct me?'

'I can, my Lady; you are two miles adrift. Go towards the market place, and just as you reach it, there are two further paths, one to the market, and one to the left. Take the left road. A mile or so down there and you'll reach the house.'

'Thank you,' said Mathilda with all the authority she could muster.

'Please, my Lady,' said the boy as she turned to go, 'where are your horse and attendant?'

Mathilda hadn't been ready for this question; her cheeks flush in betrayal of her role, 'My maid is helping at the market, and my horse is lame.'

She hastened away, uneasy at leaving the boy staring after her in disbelief, but glad that she now knew where she was going. She strode as quickly as was seemly, aware that she was already well behind time if she was to return to Hugo's stall by midday.

A sound behind her made her turn. It was the boy on a pony and cart. 'May I assist you; I can give you a lift as far as the market, if you don't mind travelling in the cart. I apologise, I should have offered before, but I wasn't thinking straight.'

Mathilda only hesitated for a second, before agreeing and thanking her helper.

The boy chatted away as they rode, 'I wouldn't want anyone to get any trouble from the Coterels, my Lady. I have seen them at work. No, I wouldn't want a pretty lady like you in trouble with them!'

Mathilda almost asked him what he'd seen, but then decided she didn't want to know. As they reached the crossroads she'd been at earlier, she alighted, 'Our Lady's blessings on you, child.'

'Thank you, my Lady. Good luck.'

This time the directions were correct, and it wasn't long before Mathilda could see the manor house ahead of her, at the end of a rough driveway. Re-securing the girdle around her waist, relieved that she hadn't needed to bargain with it after all, Mathilda lowered her hood and, hovering behind an oak at the roadside, took a moment to decide what to do next.

She was close to her destination now, and nerves swam haphazardly in her stomach. These were men to be cautious of, but, she thought with a stab of pride, she'd already survived being kidnapped and put in the Folvilles' holding cell, so she could survive this. She had stood before the Folville family, and was now being trusted with a task which, Robert had told her, was vital to both them, and the second felonious family she was about to encounter. She could do this. She must.

Judging that it must already be about an hour until noon, Mathilda knew it was unlikely she would be back before the specified time. That was a shame; she would love to have seen the look on Master Hugo's face if she had.

Wasting no more time, and with a quick stroke of Robert's dagger for luck, she went cautiously forward. The driveway wasn't long, and Mathilda soon found herself in a neat courtyard.

A boy hurried up to her, 'May I help you, mistress?'

'I am instructed by my master to see the steward.'

Thankfully unfazed by her request, the boy ran towards what Mathilda took to be a workshop of some sort in the far corner of the yard.

She had barely time to examine her surroundings, when a gruff barrel of a man strode impatiently towards her. She'd obviously disturbed him from his labours, and he

131

wasn't too impressed by that fact.

Mathilda spoke quickly, 'My apologies for the disturbance. I have a message. La Zouche and De Heredwyk.'

The solid man's eyebrows knotted together in a frown of disapproval as he stared at her with disdain. Mathilda raised her head in response, copying the expression of haughty annoyance she had seen on Sarah the housekeeper when she'd struggled to bathe her two days ago.

Grunting, the steward set off towards the main house, 'Come on then.'

Following him, Mathilda resisted the temptation to run to keep up. She repeated the message over and over in her head, hoping that her welcome would be well received, and that this visit would be swift.

'Wait here.' The steward left her in a narrow corridor between the main door and the hall. It was a larger house than the Ashby Folville residence, but no warmer or lighter, and as Mathilda peered around her, she saw it was in more need of care than the Folvilles home.

'In here.' The steward spoke abruptly, pointing his way forward with a calloused hand.

Mathilda went were she was directed, into a hall busy with servants at one end, and a long table near the fire place at the other.

A stocky man with tamed curly black hair and a clipped beard was looking at her expectantly. His fine clothes told her he was a Coterel, but not which one.

'My Lord,' Mathilda curtseyed, 'I have a message.'

'Give it, child.'

'Please, my Lord, I have been instructed to ask whom I am addressing first.'

The man smiled, not a friendly smile, but a knowing smile, one that told her that he would have instructed a messenger of his own in the same way should the roles have been reversed.

'I'm Nicholas Coterel. The message?'

'De Vere has agreed.'

Coterel's shrewd face gave little away, but his dark eyes

shone with what Mathilda hoped was satisfaction. He stood for a moment and then said, 'You may give the Folvilles my reply. Tell them, "The message is well received. Three days. Midnight."'

Mathilda copied the message back, 'The message is well received. Three Days. Midnight.'

'Exactly right,' Coterel gestured to Mathilda to sit down as he took a draft of ale, 'I am curious at Folvilles choice of envoy. Who are you, child?'

Mathilda sat down, swallowing nervously, wishing that everyone would stop referring to her as a child, 'I am companion to Robert de Folville, my Lord. My name is Mathilda, and I'm from Twyford.'

Coterel choked on his drink and sent a fine spray across the table, 'Are you? Are you indeed? Now that is interesting ...' His voice trailed off, but his eyes never left his visitor.

Mathilda stiffened, unsure how to respond, so simply said, 'If you'll forgive me, my Lord, I must return to my duties, I have another errand to run.' She flicked her eyes around the hall; Mathilda had an increasing feeling that Nicholas wasn't the only one watching her.

'Of course, but have a drink first; you have travelled far and must be tired. I confess I am curious to know how you got here, as my steward tells me you have no horse.'

Mathilda inclined her head with gratitude as she was presented with a cup of honeyed ale.

'I should advise you to tell me the truth, Mathilda of Twyford. I'm sure you will have been told all about me by your young man, although I find myself believing that you would never be so stupid as to lie to me anyway.'

133

Chapter Eighteen

Doing her best to ignore the fact that all the hairs on the back of her neck had stood up, and her conviction that she was being surveyed from some hidden location in the smoky hall, Mathilda had seen the sense in telling Nicholas Coterel everything about her day so far when he'd asked, although how she came to be in the company of the Folvilles in the first place she kept to herself.

Nicholas had not appeared surprised by Hugo's behaviour; although he didn't venture an opinion as why the leatherworker had acted in the way he had, beyond saying 'Master Hugo is an odd one and no mistake. I can see why you wish to get back to him on schedule. He'd hate that!'

'I can't possibly manage that now, my Lord. I'm weary from walking, and it's another two miles back to the market place.'

Coterel regarded her with open curiosity, 'Were you not scared, girl, to walk into this notorious den of thieves?'

Mathilda again chose honesty as the best course, 'I was terrified, my Lord, but it was important to Robert that I succeed in my task.' She did not add that it was even more important to her father and her brothers.

'You genuinely like Robert, don't you?'

Mathilda found herself blushing at the suggestion, but determined to keep up the companion pretence said, 'He is a good man, my Lord.'

'Despite his deeds?' Coterel cocked his head to one side, a mischievous curve playing at the side of his lips.

'His deeds are for the general good, my Lord.'

'Not always, child.'

'No, I suppose not; but often they are.' Folding her palms in her lap, it came as a surprise to Mathilda to realise that she really did like Robert, and was now only beginning to see that fact clearly.

Nicholas broke away from his piercing appraisal of the messenger, 'I have a proposal for you. A way to dissatisfy that upstart Hugo. Are you interested?'

Mathilda leaned forward conspiratorially. 'Yes, my Lord.'

'I will lend you a mount and lad. If you gallop hard the first mile and trot the second through the town's outskirts, you'll make it on time, and Hugo will be dumbfounded.'

'You'd do that for me, my Lord? I'm only a messenger.'

'You are a polite and efficient emissary from the closet thing this family can call an ally in these treacherous times, besides,' Nicholas stood up decisively, 'I can't stand that Hugo, even if his craftsmanship is second to none.' He gestured to her girdle with his head as they walked, 'That was a present from Robert?'

'Yes, my Lord.'

'Makes sense. He won't have a word said against the belt-maker; I believe Hugo saved his life when they were in arms. My advice to you, therefore, is to keep Hugo's betrayal secret if you can.'

Nicholas strode through the hall, forcing Mathilda to jog after him. She'd been bursting to tell Robert about Master Hugo's lack of worth, and felt disappointed that she'd been advised against it. While she considered what Coterel had said, she peered from side to side, trying to catch a glimpse of the set of eyes she'd felt boring into the back of her neck since she'd set foot in the hall, but saw nothing.

As they reached the courtyard, Coterel called for his steward to make swift arrangements to ferry Mathilda to the town. 'Do you ride well, Mathilda?'

'No, my Lord, I'm afraid not.'

'Then it'll be best if you share a horse.'

He turned to a slim young man who'd emerged from the workshop. 'You will take the Lady Mathilda to the edge of town. Leave her at the market crossroads, before riding directly back here.'

The young man inclined his head in a surly manner that reminded Mathilda of Hugo's apprentice, Roger.

Coterel himself helped a surprised Mathilda into the saddle before the lad came up behind her. It was strange having a male body pressed up against her back, and stranger still when he wrapped his arms around her to reach the reins.

'Good luck, Mathilda of Twyford, I shall enjoy hearing all about the look on Master Hugo's face when next we meet.'

Mathilda smiled down at him from the horse, and found she hoped that she did meet again. 'Thank you, my Lord. I much appreciate your kindness.' As she spoke, Mathilda suddenly remembered that Nicholas Coterel was a murderer and, some said, a rapist, and yet she still wasn't afraid of him like she was of Master Hugo the leatherworker.

The lad swung the horse around and was steering them towards the gateway, when Coterel called after them. He ran back to her, and put a restraining hand on her stirrup. 'Mathilda, do you have a weapon? Did Robert give you his dagger?'

Mathilda was confused, 'Why, yes, my Lord, he did.'

'While you remain with Hugo, keep it close. He has no humour, and may not take kindly to being thwarted, however much it might amuse you and I. Take care, child.'

Calling back her thanks, Mathilda held on for all she was worth as the lad spurred the horse forward from a gentle walk to a full gallop in only seconds.

It took very little time to reach a stream of people moving away from the market, and as the horse slowed to a trot, Mathilda surveyed at the myriad of wares the local populace were carrying home from the market. Her eye fell on a young serving girl carrying a large grey pitcher. She was walking gingerly, as though her very existence depended on her getting the vessel back in one piece, and she supposed that it very well might. It had a familiar pattern on it. Diagonal lines and the occasional butterfly.

The lad pulled to the side of the road and helped Mathilda down.

Ignoring the curious glances of the passers-by, (they could think what they liked, she didn't live around here after all), Mathilda thanked her companion.

'My Lady,' He nodded and returned the way he'd come, leaving Mathilda free to stride through the thick crowds. Hugo had been correct; things were much busier now the sun was at its height.

Even if she lived for a hundred years, Mathilda would never forget Master Hugo's expression. She took a secret delight in watching as he struggled to place an expression of relieved pleasure onto his weasel face, as Mathilda weaved through the stalls towards him just as the church bells chimed twelve. It was the sweetest feeling. A tiny victory against a man she suspected had the capacity for more danger and deception than all the Coterels and Folvilles put together.

'I hope I haven't kept you too long, Master Hugo,' Mathilda kept her voice demure and, without giving him time to comment, she joined the leatherworker behind the stall and began serving customers.

The dress fitted.

Ashley had been proved right, the bottle sage colour (or Lincoln Green as it would forever be to Grace and Daisy), suited Grace's skin tone perfectly. Daisy too, was relieved to find that no more alterations were required to her dress, and that the shop had a range of neat, unfussy tiaras in stock that would complement both her outfit and mass of curls. They also had a selection of almost plain veils that could perform their function well without Daisy having to start the next chapter of her life feeling as though she was peering through an over-patterned net curtain.

Grace had a grin on her face that she couldn't shift. Her mind constantly flickered between her meeting with Rob at Mrs Beeton's, their walk to her office, how intoxicating his presence had felt in that small space, and the meal she was looking forward to enjoying with him later that day.

Daisy had been pumping her for information about Rob from the second she'd stepped off the train into Sheffield at ten o'clock that morning, and Grace knew it wouldn't be long before she'd have to give her friend some answers.

'Right then,' Daisy handed over her credit card with only a slight wince at the price as she paid for the dresses.

'I was going to pay for mine, Daze.' Grace protested as she was dragged back to reality by the shock of hearing how much her friend was spending on two outfits that would only ever be worn once.

'No way. That's how this wedding lark works. You can buy me a stupendous wedding present instead.'

'And Marcus!'

'Of course, and Marcus.'

'Family pack of guinea pig nuggets fit the bill?'

Daisy poked Grace in the ribs as they walked outside, leaving the dresses hanging in the shop to be steam-cleaned before collection two days before the wedding. 'OK, so that's my big day sorted, let's get you sorted out now.'

'Me?'

'Yep. What you going to wear tonight?'

Grace pointed at her smart jeans and linen blouse, 'This.'

'Oh hell, honey, come on.' Daisy grabbed her friends elbow and doing an almost perfect imitation of Aggie, frog-marched her to the nearest charity shop. 'Let's sort you out once and for all.'

Never mind butterflies; Grace felt as if a whole shoal of fish was swimming in her stomach, as she waited for the train to pull into Nottingham station. Feeling rather strange in a pair of brown suede trousers and a new (ish) black, low-cut shirt, along with a chunky but smart black woollen jacket, she sat, leaning slightly forward in her seat, as if she was about to be interviewed for a job she really wanted but had no idea if she could actually do.

She had been so excited, so high about meeting

someone so much on her wavelength, and actually getting asked out by them for her first proper date in years, that the practicality of the evening ahead hadn't occurred to her. It was already six o'clock, which meant that by the time they'd had their meal it would be late, and Grace didn't fancy getting the train back to Leicester alone in the dark. She also didn't relish the embarrassment of going back to Rob's place. She was not ready for that – well, she was, but didn't think she should. *Perhaps I'd better book into a hotel or something?*

All of a sudden Grace wanted to run and hide; all her exuberance had evaporated in an instant. This was too hard. She'd been fine on her own for ages, doing what she liked when she liked. Why was she putting herself through all this angst anyway? It was only a kiss and a hug. It meant nothing; she'd been letting her imagination run away with her as usual. That's what happened when you spent all your time writing stories and living in the past.

And that was another thing! What if Rob had read her manuscript? What if he hated it? She really wasn't brave enough to have her first real date in years and her work analysed all in one go.

The train shuddered to a halt. Fighting the cowardly option of staying in her seat and letting the train take her home to Leicester, Grace stepped down onto the busy concrete platform.

She couldn't see Rob at first, and was surprised by how disappointed she felt despite her own inclinations to flee the scene. That's a good sign, Grace decided as she eased her way through the commuters; it proves I really do want to be here after all.

Rob was elbowing his way through the mass of oncoming passengers in the opposite direction when she eventually spotted him. He looked mildly flustered, and for the first time it occurred to Grace that he was probably anxious as well.

139

Chapter Nineteen

To Grace's relief, once they'd negotiated their way out of the crowded station her initial nervousness had dissipated.

Leaving the depressing grey environment of the station behind them, they headed towards Nottingham city centre. Scooping Grace's hand in his as they strolled towards the main street, Rob asked, 'So how was the nightmare that is dress shopping? All over now?'

'More or less. I need to get shoes and book a haircut, then I won't have to think about getting all dolled up until Daisy's big day.'

'It can't be as bad as that surely? I thought women liked having the chance to get all dressed up every now and again.'

'Bit of a generalisation there, I think! That's like saying that all men like football.'

'Millions of them do.'

'And millions of them don't.' Grace laughed at the image that had popped into her head, 'I can't imagine you perched on the edge of the sofa, a bottle of lager to hand, shouting at the referee, and worrying about the consequences of a man who failed all his exams at school not getting a ball between two posts.'

'Bit of a generalisation there yourself!' Rob held her hand a little tighter, 'I'm sure not all footballers failed at school.'

'Probably not. I was only being silly.'

'I know, but you're right. I don't like football. In fact, I don't really "do" sport. I take it from your rather jaundiced description that you aren't a football fan either.'

'No, but I do understand why people do like it.'

'You do?' Rob raised his eyebrows, 'For most people football is a Marmite situation. They love it or hate it. I've never really understood why folk like watching overpaid men running around a field showing off.'

'I think it's all about passion.' Grace's words had come out with far more force than she'd intended, and as soon as the sentence had left her lips she went bright pink.

Wiggling his eyebrows mischievously, Rob said, 'Tell me more!'

'Oh, you know what I mean! I wasn't talking about ...' Grace broke off her sentence as Rob pointed to the restaurant doorway to their left hand side.

'I thought we'd try here if that's OK with you.'

Grace stared through the glass next to the door into a tastefully decorated Chinese restaurant.

'I'm afraid I don't know what it's like food-wise as it hasn't been here long, but I've heard good things, and I've been dying to give it a go. What do you think? Shall we?'

'Definitely.'

Grace found she rather enjoyed allowing herself to be escorted by the elbow into a restaurant by a handsome, intelligent man, and happily let the aromas of crispy duck and fried rice assail her nostrils as her coat was taken and they were shown to their table.

Hung with Chinese paper lanterns in discreet streamers along the walls, the red and gold decor was traditionally Oriental, and yet the place managed to remain far more understated than many similar restaurants she'd visited over the years. It was completely devoid of aquariums containing oversized carp, and there wasn't a single waving lucky cat in sight.

This place was not only new, but unlike its comrades along Nottingham's High Street; it was definitely not aimed at the student market. One glance at the menu once they'd been seated by a most helpful waitress confirmed to Grace that this was 'properly posh' as her grandmother would have said. She privately decided that when it was time to pay the bill they would be going Dutch.

The wine they'd ordered arrived quickly, and Rob raised a glass, 'To Grace, the reluctant bridesmaid!'

'I'll drink to that!' Grace took a draught of wine, enjoying the perfectly chilled liquid as it slid down her throat like silk. 'Daisy is absolutely the only person on this planet I would put myself through this for.'

Rob looked at her thoughtfully for a second before asking, 'So what does Daisy do? Is she another history buff?'

'Not these days. She cares for stray and injured animals. It started on a small scale as a hobby, but now her home is a mini animal sanctuary.'

'So, you'd say she was *passionate* about animals then, like some people are *passionate* about football but not about wearing posh frocks?' His eyes twinkled as he peered at Grace over the top of his menu.

'And there I was thinking you'd let me off the hook with that one.'

'No way, Dr Harper. I'd like you to choose what you'd like to eat, and then I'd want to hear your views on passion. Preferably in detail.'

Grace had been only half-listening when she'd agreed with Rob that she should order a heap of noodles, rice, chicken, duck, and beef dishes. She was far more concerned with how to phrase her point of view about being passionate about things without it inevitably leading to a discussion about bedroom preferences. Not that she minded that, but not in the middle of busy restaurant on a first date. Grace wasn't ready for any conversation that might ultimately lead to revealing her cellulite.

In fact, now she'd seen the sheen in Rob's eyes when she'd mentioned passion, albeit in a totally non-sexual context, the reality of what that meant hit Grace, right in the middle of her inadequacy button. Her body had been kept under wraps for years. It had more lumps and bumps than the local landscape. If Rob saw it naked he'd run a mile! It was all very well him liking her mind, but Grace couldn't help suspecting he'd change his views about the benefits of intelligent conversation if he ever witnessed how disappointing the body that went with the brain was.

'Grace? Are you with me? You did say you liked noodles, didn't you?'

The waitress was looking at Grace expectantly, her pencil hovering over her pad.

'What? Oh yes, I'm sorry, I'd phased out. Tired after all that shopping. Yes, I love noodles, thank you.'

Telling herself she was being ridiculous, vowing to leave the over-thinking until later and just enjoy the meal, Grace gestured encouragingly toward the waitress. After all, she thought, Rob had only been teasing her. He wasn't to know that she'd never coped well with teasing. *Just relax, woman, you're out of practice with men, that's all.*

'You OK?' Rob reached a hand across the table and rested it on top of Grace's.

'Fine. Sorry.' Flipping her palm around, Grace held his hand properly, 'I was thinking about how to explain what I meant about football.'

'Oh, yes! The passion theory. Go on then. Tell me all.'

'No need to look so hopeful, Dr Franks, this is not about that sort of passion!'

Fluttering his eyelashes like a schoolgirl, Rob said, 'I don't know what you mean!'

Rolling her own eyes Grace laughed, 'All I meant was, and this is going to sound so flat now, that I can understand why people get passionate about things, whether it's football, or climbing, or skydiving or whatever they love to do. And although I'd never want to do any of those things, I wouldn't knock people for loving them. I hate it when people do that to me, although I admit my passion hobby-wise isn't that usual. But you only have

143

to hear people expound about their favourite sports team, or the highest mountain they've climbed, or the rush of the air as they fall from insane heights out of a plane, to see that it lights them up. To recognise actual passion. Just a glance at their eyes while they talk will show you that it makes them feel alive.'

The smile at the corner of Rob's lips widened. 'That's how you feel about your work, isn't it? Robin Hood and the fourteenth century is your passion.'

'Yes. I'm very lucky. To be able to work with the feeling that I'm doing what I love every day of my life is a privilege,' Grace took another sip of wine, 'and although there are down days, when it doesn't work, it's still good.'

'You mean, even when your football team fails to score, they're still your team, and you still love them.'

'Exactly.'

'You're an unusual woman, Dr Harper.'

'You mean I'm odd.'

'Well of course you're odd, but on the whole, I think that's a good thing. And I like that you're odd.'

Grace picked a prawn cracker out of the basket that had discreetly been placed on the end of their table, 'Well, you know what they say; takes one to know one!'

Rob gave a mock bow in agreement, before asking, 'And would you say that people who are creative are more passionate than those who aren't?'

Grace considered for a moment, 'I think so, although perhaps it's a different sort of passion. Artists and writers put so much of themselves into their work, it has to feel like a personal affront if anyone puts it down, and a total triumph when they have success. I think all creatives are a bit obsessive.'

Rob laughed, 'Are you talking about all creative types, or just yourself?'

'Both, I think.' Grace looked down at her hands with a sigh, 'I should warn you, Rob, I am a dreadful workaholic,

I am obsessive about people who've been dead forever, and very probably didn't ever exist in the first place, and paranoid about how people see that obsession.' She looked up sharply, as if challenging him. 'So, now I've warned you what I'm like, do you want to leg it?'

Shaking his head as if he couldn't quite believe this woman sat over from him, Rob's grin widened, 'You are talking to a man who used to be exactly the same. OK, for me medieval England is an interest that I've made into my career, and not a complete lifestyle, but it was once. I was a terrible workaholic. There was nothing else. That's one of the reasons I came back to the UK. I was making myself ill over there in Houston. The work was non-stop. It felt as if what I loved to do was swallowing me whole. Then I realised that it wasn't the university or the students that were making me feel like that. It was me. I was doing it to myself.'

Grave swallowed slowly against the lump that had formed in her throat. What Rob was saying rang horribly true. Abruptly she moved the subject along, 'So you came home? Where is home anyway?'

'Bath. My parents run a bookshop there.'

'Oh, how wonderful! You lucky thing!' Grace leant back in her chair as the waitress arrived at their table with two hot trays, and began to distribute enough food to deal with world famine. 'That looks amazing!' The food smelt incredible. As the waitress departed, Grace picked up her chopsticks, 'Did we really order all this?'

'We did! Although if I'd realised how big the portions were then I'd have ordered less. Hope you're hungry. It does look incredible, though, and I guess we'll know to order less next time won't we?'

'Next time?' Grace looped some noodles around her chopsticks, 'You're prepared to be seen out with me again then, despite me being an oddly passionate obsessive?'

'Maybe. It will all depend on how well you behave!'

'In that case I'd better skip flippancy and ask you a serious question, Dr Franks. So, you came back here to escape the rat race in the States, is that right?'

Rob sighed, 'It was great to start with. I loved working in Houston, but I began to miss fresh air. So much of Houston is trapped under air conditioning. I also missed English rain that smells of farmyards, a decent cup of tea, and chocolate that tastes of chocolate. And don't even get me started on cheese in a can.'

'Hang on. Rain that smells of farmyards?'

'I told you, I grew up near Bath. Lots of farms. Everything in Somerset has a slightly appealing edge of silage to it.'

'Lovely!' Grace wrinkled her nose, but couldn't help the smile that crossed her face. This guy was every bit as odd as she was.

'And the Nottingham post was there, so I applied for it.'

'And you got the job!'

'I was lucky.'

'No, Rob. No one gets a lectureship by luck; not these days. You got it because you're good at your job. Professor Davis told me you were well respected, and he was right.'

'You flatter me.'

'Simply stating a fact.' Grace cheeks flushed.

Rob didn't seem to have noticed her pink face as he ladled a heap of fried rice into his bowl. 'So, I read your novel.'

Grace's chopstick dropped to the table, spattering shards of rice across the neat red cloth. She'd been trying to forget that he had a copy of her manuscript. 'Oh God, I'm sorry.' Fussing around the cloth, picking up all her spilt food, Grace felt flustered.

Taking no notice of the mess, Rob fixed her eyes with his, sending a shot of unaccustomed lust direct to Grace's

146

soul.

'It's good. It's really good. Stop worrying about it. Finish it. Get it out of your head. Send the first three chapters and a synopsis to a publisher now, before you've finished it. It will spur you on. Do it. Do not argue with me. Then finish that textbook afterwards.'

Grace's mouth dropped open, 'But what about Professor Davis, and work and the wedding, and …'

Taking no notice of the fact that Grace had spoken, Rob carried on talking, 'Obviously you'll need a pen name so you can keep your professional credibility. But that's cool; loads of people have *noms de plume*. Could be fun choosing one. And don't get hung up on the history to much. The story's the thing and all that.'

Squeezing her eyes shut for a split second, Grace felt a weight lift from her shoulders. Not for the first time she cursed her ability to understand everything there was to know about life in the fourteenth century, but not see the obvious in the here and now. 'A pen name? Good idea. I hadn't thought of that.'

Suddenly feeling the need to offload all her worries about her writing, Grace stared into her noodles, twiddling a chopstick between her fingers, 'And do you think it sounds historical enough? I deliberately haven't gone overboard on the period dialogue, but now I'm wondering if perhaps I've gone too modern?'

Rob stabbed a stray water chestnut thoughtfully. 'I'd leave it as it is at this stage. At the moment it's a nice middle ground between modern and historical language. You can always change things when you edit it later. So what will you call it?'

'That is a very good question, and if you come up with an answer I'd love to know! I thought maybe *Folville's Girl*, but I'm not completely sold on it.'

'It's a good working title, and that's all you need for now I should think.'

'I'll need something better if I get it published.' Grace sighed wistfully, unable to stop herself wondering if she was simply wasting her time. 'Do you really think anyone will actually want to publish it?'

'Honestly, Grace, I haven't a clue. It's a tough world out there in book land, but you need to try, otherwise it'll eat you up. Now, talking of eating, let's eat this.' Rob manoeuvred a chopstick balanced with sweet and sour chicken into his mouth, 'And stop looking so worried – if I didn't think it was any good, I'd have said so. I think writing this novel, even if it doesn't get out into the world, will help teach you the trade. After all, writing fact is very different from writing fiction. I haven't known you long, but I know this is too important to you to lie about. Now, tell me what happens next. How is Mathilda getting on with Robert? Good choice of name for your hero, by the way.'

Grace playfully stabbed at the back of his hand with a chopstick. 'Behave, or I'll kill Robert off and make Walter Folville Mathilda's keeper instead!'

Chapter Twenty

Robert hadn't said a word as he watched the largely empty cart arrive back at the workshop in Derby. Mathilda hadn't expected a major display of gratitude, but the lack of a 'well done' on seeing her return to him on time, and in one piece, or a quick glance to make sure she was well, hurt more than Mathilda liked to admit.

As Hugo's apprentice Roger tugged Mathilda from the cart and hoisted her directly onto her pony for the ride back to Leicestershire, Robert disappeared into the workshop with the leatherworker. Then minutes later, his expression thunderous, he mounted his own horse, and mutely gestured for Mathilda to follow him in an agitated trot out of the courtyard.

The evening's journey from Bakewell back to Derby after the market had been frosty enough. Master Hugo had sat morosely at the reins of the cart, despite having had a most successful day's trading. Mathilda had been glad of his silence, and had kept Nicholas Coterel's warning words in mind, her hand as near as she possible to Robert's secreted dagger.

Robert's silence as they returned to Ashby Folville, on the other hand, was unnerving and felt ungrateful. Mulling the reply she'd been given by Coterel over in her mind, Mathilda wondered if she should ask Robert if he wanted to hear what it was straight away. However, his sullen nature was making her nervous, and she began to consider the possibility that Master Hugo's account of her behaviour while working on his stall had been less than accurate.

A dab hand at selling, Mathilda had quickly endeared herself to the customers, and managed to persuade several of the merchants who came to the stand, whose fine clothing indicated they could well afford it, to purchase rather finer and more expensive goods than those they had originally come for.

Only once had Mathilda had to shy away from a sale, and that was when Geoffrey of Reresby had hovered near the stall for a few moments His hawk-like gaze had surveyed Hugo's goods with an avaricious gleam that Mathilda suspected had nothing to do with working out how he could profit from another trader's success. Unfortunately, Hugo had spotted Mathilda moving back from a customer in order to avoid Geoffrey seeing her, and he had not been pleased.

Mathilda had tried to explain the reason for her action to Master Hugo, indicating how it would not be in Robert's favour for Geoffrey to see her there, but her pleas had fallen on deaf ears. He had been far too delighted at having an excuse to admonish and belittle her in public to listen to reason.

Now she supposed Hugo must have focused on that one moment of dissatisfaction, rather than reporting to Robert how much profit Mathilda had made for him today. With her bottom bruised from bouncing out of sync with the movement of the mount, and her palms dry from a day of dealing with leather, Mathilda ached all over. She'd survived her task with the Coterels and a day with the obnoxious leatherworker. Now all she had to do was go home.

It didn't help that it was getting darker, and Mathilda couldn't stop herself from peering into the trees on either side of them, constantly expecting someone to leap out at them. The dagger's hilt dug into her side, the stone in the hilt bruising her thigh as she clung onto the palfrey's mane, leaning forward to help her keep her balance. Mathilda began to wonder how fast she could pull the weapon from its hiding place if they were assailed by outlaws. Then again, not even an outlaw would be stupid enough or desperate enough to attack a Folville. Mathilda wasn't sure if that thought gave her comfort or not.

Forcing herself to concentrate on watching Robert's back through her windblown fringe instead of looking from left to right all the time, Mathilda reflected on how different their return journey was. On the way Robert had stayed by her side. He'd made sure she was safe, that she was comfortable, and that she was prepared for the task ahead. Now she'd completed that task it seemed his solicitousness was a thing of the past. Perhaps it had never existed in the first place, but was just a Folville acting in a way that would ensure he got what he wanted.

When they finally rode through the gates of the Folville manor house, the stable boy helped Mathilda's stiff body down from her short steed, his brow furrowing as he held her shivering frame against his. 'Are you all right?'

'Thank you, but I'm a little cold, and it has been some time since I ate.' Mathilda glanced around her. Robert had disappeared.

Unsure where to go, and feeling unsteady on her feet, she held onto the horse, unwilling to let go of its reins least she fall to the floor. Mathilda was about to ask the boy where she should wait, when he gestured towards the back door of the kitchen, 'I think Sarah wants you.'

Mathilda turned to see the housekeeper looking at her impatiently.

'Come on, girl!' Sarah snapped under her breath, 'the men are waiting for you!'

Passing the reins to the stable lad Mathilda headed toward the housekeeper. Each step was an effort. Her stomach growled in protest at its lack of sustenance, and the cold shivers that had engulfed her on the journey home were joined by streaks of heat, and before Mathilda could call out in distress, her legs gave out from under her, and she sank with no grace whatsoever onto the damp hay-strewn gravel.

There had been a brief sensation of falling, that the world was spinning, and darts of a sickly green had flashed behind her eyes. Mathilda thought she'd heard a woman shouting, and she knew male hands had lifted her from the ground and carried her into the kitchen, but she wasn't sure whose they had been.

Now, with one of the horse's blankets swathing her, Mathilda's eyes slowly came back into focus. She didn't seem to be able to stop the quiver in her legs, and her head thudded. Doing her best to pull herself together, angry with herself at having swooned like some sort a feeble princess in front of members of the Folville household for a second time, Mathilda was about to apologise when the housekeeper let fly.

'What in heaven's name do you think you're playing at, girl? Sarah rolled up her sleeves as she spoke, and for one second Mathilda had the impression that she was going to hit her.

Sarah merely grunted and she shook her head in clear disapproval. Her hair hung loose around the shoulders as if she'd been preparing to turn in for the night when the returning party from Derby had disturbed her, 'Come on! They are waiting!'

'Who is waiting?' Mathilda's head swam and dots of perspiration had appeared on her forehead. Wiping dust and small shards of gravel from her palms, Mathilda struggled to concentrate.

It didn't matter that she'd survived a meeting with Nicholas Coterel; Sarah the housekeeper, as she stood there like a disgruntled matriarch, with her hands on her ample hips, made Mathilda feel as though she was as welcome as an infestation of mice in a bakehouse, and every bit as inconvenient.

'My Lord Eustace and his brothers, of course!' Sarah stamped her foot impatiently, 'Heaven help us; don't say your fall has knocked the wits from your head.' Then, in a tone that was more concerned than annoyed she added in a whisper, 'You haven't forgotten the message have you?'

The unexpected concern on Sarah's face brought Mathilda up short. 'You know of my mission?'

'Of course. The brothers trust me. Now,' Sarah passed Mathilda a cup of ale, 'drink this and I will take you through.'

Taking her time, Mathilda stood for a minute or two,

letting gravity plant her feet firmly on the ground before she attempted to move. 'I'm very sorry. I am not given to fainting. I am quite all right now. Thank you for taking care of me.'

Sarah raised an eyebrow, but said nothing as Mathilda pushed her shoulders back and began to walk; giving the world the firm impression that she was a young woman very much in control of herself.

Feeling far from in control however, Mathilda hoped that the brothers would not keep her long, for she feared that if she didn't sleep soon, she would disgrace herself further.

'You haven't eaten much.'

Rob pointed a chopstick towards Grace's half-full bowl. Although the food was delicious, Grace had been so busy talking through how she imagined Mathilda had got back to Ashby Folville from the market that she hadn't taken more than a few mouthfuls.

Using her story-telling as her excuse, Grace smiled, covering up that in reality she hadn't been able to stamp out the persistent mutterings at the back of her head telling her she had to lose two stone, miraculously vanish away her cellulite, and tone her stomach, all preferably by the time she left this restaurant.

As the evening went on, and the realisation that she'd enjoyed herself (and the company) more than she had in years grew stronger, and the smile on Rob's face got wider, Grace experienced an overwhelming need to escape. To get home, to get away before he suggested they go back to his place.

Not that Grace didn't want to go back to his place. She did. The idea of being somewhere alone with Rob, where they could experience a great deal more kissing and perhaps a lot more besides, was deliciously appealing. But what if she disappointed him? What if Rob took one look at her 'lived-in' frame and ran the other way? It had been so long since anyone but Grace had seen her body. In fact the only other person who'd seen Grace in nothing but underwear for three years was Ashley when she had manoeuvred Grace into her bridesmaid dress; a feat which Grace had no doubt had involved a fair amount of professional blindness on Ashley's part.

When the waitress took away the plates, and placed a steaming pot of China tea on the table, Grace, determined to remember she was an in control career woman and not an insecure love struck teenager, picked up her handbag and dug out a railway timetable. 'That was a lovely meal, and I've had a great time, but I guess I ought to be sensible and check the train times; I don't want to miss the last one back.'

Grateful that Rob had the good manners not to mention the disappointment that she wouldn't be staying overnight that flashed across his face for a nano-second, while being perversely pleased to have seen it there, Grace scanned the timetable.

'There's one at 11.30, do you think we'd make it?'

Rob checked his wristwatch, 'No problem, it's only 11.' He gestured for the bill to arrive. 'You know, I do have a spare bedroom. You are very welcome to use it. I can assure you I would be the perfect host and leave you undisturbed – unless you didn't want me to, of course. Then I think it's safe to say I would enjoy giving you a fairly sleepless night.'

Grace turned the colour of beetroot, 'Well I ... it isn't that I don't want to, but ...'

Placing a hand on hers once more, Rob spoke gently, 'But it's been a while, and you haven't known me long, and you're an old-fashioned lass at heart. Fourteenth century, even!'

As her cheeks shaded from beetroot to the hue of a bright red radish, Grace didn't know what to say.

'Well luckily for you, Dr Harper, I'm a bit of a gentleman on the quiet, and as I have a feeling that you're a woman who is worth waiting for, then I'll spare you my protests.'

Still speechless, Grace allowed her gentleman to pass her coat and escort her from the restaurant, all her good intentions of paying half the bill wiped from her head.

As they walked out into the night air, Rob wrapped an arm around Grace's waist, 'I think it only fair to warn you, Dr Harper, I may be a gentleman, but I'm not going to be able to wait long. And the only way I am letting you get on that train tonight, is if you promise we can meet up again very soon.'

The blatant lust in his eyes made Grace gulp as she said, 'I'd love that. Can you come over to Leicester on Friday night? I'll cook.'

Rob's expression told Grace the answer to that question was a definite yes, saying as he met her dry lips with one fast, hard kiss, 'I think you'd better quickly tell me what happens to Mathilda next, or I might forget my resolve and whisk you into the nearest taxi and back to my place anyway!'

Chapter Twenty-one

'Why the hell did I say I'll cook?' Grace muttered to herself as the largely deserted train pulled into Leicester station. She couldn't stop herself remembering a sitcom she'd once seen, where the female lead had explained to a friend that telling a man you'd cook for them was the same as saying, 'Let's have sex and I'll cater!'

Now she was away from the Chinese restaurant and her nerves began to calm, Grace realised she was hungry after all, and regretted not having eaten more of the delicious food they'd been served. Guilt stabbed her. It had been so lovely, and so much had been wasted. She tried not to think about the inevitable homeless hungry people she'd have to go past once she got off the train and walked through Leicester's railway station, or about how much the meal must have cost Rob.

Telling herself that her rumbling stomach was her own fault, and that it was a small price to pay for her wastefulness, and might even have the added benefit of not adding to the calories that seem to love living on her hips, Grace wrestled the carriage door open and got off the train.

Grace had never been hung up on her size before. Always in proportion, her eye-catching smile and ample chest had always seemed to cheat any male admirer's brains into thinking she was slim. Walking through the spookily hushed station, and deciding not to risk walking across Victoria Park on her own so late at night, Grace hailed a taxi with the words, *but you've never really liked them back before, have you? You've never cared if they liked what they saw or not. Until now …* running through her head.

The irony of it wasn't lost on Grace. For the first time she was genuinely interested in a bloke beyond having someone convenient to go to the cinema with, or the occasional bout of sex to break up her general 'celibate but for her vibrator' lifestyle. Someone who not only seemed to 'get' her, but loved Robin Hood stories, and didn't seem to think she was weird or borderline insane. But rather than feel excited and thrilled, Grace just felt self-conscious, frumpy, and nervous.

Damn it, woman, you're a grown up! You're a professional. So what if you've invited him to your home. That doesn't mean you have to sleep with him!

But I want to ... Oh hell, how big an idiot can I possibly be? I ... Grace stopped her internal argument with herself as she slid the key into her front door and collapsed upon her sofa. Then her thoughts careered off in a totally different direction. 'Oh my God! How did this place get into such a mess?'

'I mean, Daze, how on earth have I lived in this muddle for so long?' Grace flicked a duster at the television, wondering if she'd be able to reach the cobwebs that hadn't so much set up home in the corner of her living room ceiling, as had built a small town, complete with high rise blocks and outbuildings.

'Hang on a minute.' Daisy was trying not to laugh down the telephone. 'You are Grace Harper, aren't you? No one's come along and replaced you with a doppelganger in the night?'

'Oh, very funny! I'm not that bad.'

'Grace, honey, you're a domestic disaster, but fear not, I love you anyway.' Daisy did laugh out loud this time, 'I had hoped that when I called to see how the date went, you wouldn't answer due to being confined to a duvet somewhere in the Nottingham area.'

Deciding that at least the spiders kept the flies away,

Grace left them to it, and took the call from Daisy as a chance to sit down, 'It was only the first proper date, Daze!'

'So?'

'Oh come on, I'm not like that.'

'We're all like that, honey, which means something happened to stop you going back with him. And don't tell me he didn't want you to, because I won't believe you.'

'How can you possibly know that? You've never even met Rob.'

'I know because I know you, and because against all the laws of the universe you actually like this man. This is not something that happens every day. Also it is fate.'

'Fate?' Grace sounded incredulous, 'I don't believe in fate.'

'But does fate believe in you?'

'Don't go all Freudian on me, Daisy Marks. What do you mean?'

A steady squeaking sound could be heard coming down the line, telling Grace that Daisy hadn't stopped work for this conversation. She could picture her sitting on the grass in the middle of the guinea pig pen with the little creatures running all over her, pinching grass cuttings from between her fingers.

'I mean, his name is Robert, for crying out loud! What more do you want?'

'Thousands of men are called Robert. That doesn't mean they are perfect for me. That's like saying you love Marcus because he looks like a guinea pig, which he doesn't by the way, but you know what I mean.'

Ignoring Grace's off-kilter comparison, Daisy continued to push her point home. 'And he's a history man, and his speciality is the fourteenth century, *and* he lives in Nottingham! I mean, woman! How perfect do you want it? Added cream and a cherry on top, I suppose?'

Grace's eyes landed on the bookshelf opposite her. It

was crammed from floor to ceiling with Robin Hood DVDs, books, pamphlets, souvenirs, and even a limited edition Lego set of Robin and his Merry Men in a plastic brick-built tree house. She'd been so hung up on her new irrationality about being too big and her house not being fit for any visitors, that it hadn't occurred to her that she might not actually like Rob for himself at all. Perhaps it was the fact that he was about as close a human being she was ever going to meet to her historical (or not) hero that was the big attraction.

'Oh hell, Daze, you don't think I only like him because of the Robin Hood thing do you? What if that's what it is? That would be awful.'

Daisy rolled her eyes and groaned. Scooping the handful of squeaky fur off her lap, she scrambled to her feet. 'I was joking, Grace. Come on, you said he was fun, attractive, and you enjoyed his company. *That's* why you like Rob. The rest is merely the aforementioned cherry and cream.'

'But what if he thinks that's why I like him. And worse than that, what if this is all just a burst of hormones from an obsessed woman who can see forty on the horizon, and whose clock is ticking.'

Striding across the grass to her house, Daisy ran a hand through her hair in exasperation. 'Right, that's it. I'm getting on the next train to Leicester. Do not go out.'

By the time Daisy arrived at her house Grace had built up a mini-mountain of newspapers to take for recycling, shoved as many of the books she was in the process of reading onto the bookshelves as possible, and had removed a grey sheen of dust from the skirting boards. In fact Grace had been quite surprised to find they were painted white, and not the cracked cream they'd appeared to be for years.

'Good heavens, what have you been doing?' Daisy lifted a hand to wipe a smear of dust from Grace's cheek.

'I told you, I've been clearing up.' Grace sank onto her sofa with a sigh. 'I don't think I've looked at this place through the eyes of a visitor for years. I hadn't realised how tatty it had become.'

Sitting next to her best friend, Daisy scanned the living room. It was tidier than she'd ever seen it, but with the best will in the world she couldn't declare it wasn't tatty. 'It needs a lick of paint, that's all.'

Grace frowned, 'Do you think I have time to do that by Friday?'

'Only if you don't go to work?'

'I suppose I could work part-time this week; that would do it. It does need doing.'

Daisy regarded her in disbelief. 'I came all this way to talk some sense into you when I could have been mucking out the chickens, and you don't need me to at all.'

'What do you mean?' Grace's forehead creased in confusion. She had a horrible feeling that her life had blown completely off track, and wasn't sure whether she liked the sensation or not.

'Never have I heard you volunteering to sacrifice work time to do something to impress *anyone*, let alone a bloke.' Daisy's face broke into a wide smile, 'Don't you see, Grace. This is your chance. I had no plans to meet anyone and live happily ever after, and then it happened. Now it's your turn.'

'But weren't you terrified?' Grace's voice was very small, and she found herself thinking about Mathilda and how frightened she had made her as she faced the Folville brothers. That was a very different situation, but …

'Of course I was. But it's an excited sort of terrified.' Daisy looked more closely at her friends face, 'Have you slept?'

'Not really, I couldn't stop thinking.'

'About your book or about Rob?'

Grace found a smile creeping across her face despite

herself, 'Well, Rob actually.'

Daisy clapped her hands in delight. 'Oh my God, you're Olivia de Havilland!'

'What?'

'You know, when she played the role of Maid Marian opposite Errol Flynn's Robin Hood. The bit when she's talking to her lady-in-waiting after she has met Robin for the first time.'

Beaming, Grace said, 'Oh yes! She talks about not being able to sleep as "a nice kind of not sleeping," because she can't stop thinking about the man she loves.'

'Exactly.' Daisy stood up, 'My Lord, the case for the defence rests. Now, as I'm here, and this place is no more going to get decorated than Kevin Costner will ever make a convincing Robin Hood, we might as well make use of my visit and go and get the dreaded wedding shoe shop over with.'

Reluctant to buy footwear she'd only wear once, but thrilled to have her best friend to talk to, Grace stood up, 'OK, but on one condition.'

'Yes, we can go to the cafe and grab a cup of tea first.'

'Thanks, Daze, you're a star!'

Collapsing in a heap, holding a shoebox bag each, Daisy and Grace didn't stop giggling as the waiter laid two menus onto their table.

'I can't believe you did that, Daze!' Grace dropped her new shoes to the floor, and picked a menu. 'You're shameless!'

'Well, honestly!' Daisy laughed through her indigence, 'How thick are some people? How on earth can she have thought that Aberdeen was in Saudi Arabia? I mean; honestly!'

'I can't even remember why we were talking about Scotland now anyway.'

'It was that set of matching tartan shoes and handbag

you spotted.' Daisy picked up her own menu. 'I think after the double nightmare of shoe shopping and being hit on the head with such startling ignorance I need a glass of wine!'

'Good plan!'

Having ordered two hefty-sized glasses of Pinot, Grace said, 'You know, it isn't funny really. She was only young. Maybe she never did geography at school?'

'Don't you go making excuses for her! It was a clear case of all that peroxide leaking into her brain and a diet of reality TV, *Geordie Shore* and *Made in Chelsea*. Even if she doesn't know where in Scotland Aberdeen is, she should have known it is *in* Scotland, for heaven's sake. Whatever happened to general knowledge?'

'Take a swig of that wine, Daze, quick, before you fall off your high horse!' Grace shook her head, 'She was happy in her work, that's all that matters.'

'Oh, stop being so nice!' Daisy picked up her menu, and started to giggle again, 'Perhaps I shouldn't have given her a quick lecture on the layout of the British Isles though.'

'I'm not sure if she looked more confused than shocked, or more shocked than confused.'

Opening her new box of shoes on her lap, Daisy shook her head ruefully, 'I'll say this for her, though, she knows her shoes.'

'And we don't! Maybe we should count ourselves lucky she didn't give us a Jimmy Choo lecture in revenge!'

'Who?' Daisy creased her forehead.

Grace pointed her menu at her best friend, 'See, you don't know everything either! He's a shoe designer. Very expensive.'

'How on earth did you know that? Don't tell me you're a secret shoe buff?'

'Hardly. I've heard my students discussing them.'

Grace nodded towards to two ivory satin-covered shoes in Daisy's lap. 'They are lovely. What will you do with them afterwards? Seems a shame to only use them once.'

'I was thinking that. I'll probably dye them black. How about yours?'

'I'm not sure. I can't imagine I'll need anything with heels again.'

'Your own wedding perhaps?' Daisy wriggled her eyebrows mischievously.

'I am going to ignore that! Now, what are you eating?'

Daisy sighed as she ran her eyes down the menu of tempting choice of pizzas and pasta, 'I suppose I ought to be careful. I really don't want to grow out of my wedding dress now that I've bought it.'

'Oh, not you as well!' Grace groaned, 'I was hoping you'd talk some sense into me about that, and here I am finding you're as bad as I am.'

'What are you talking about?'

As Grace, talking barely above a whisper so only Daisy and not the other customers could hear, launched into her whole worried about Rob seeing her naked confession, her cheeks prickled with dots of embarrassed heat.

Daisy listened carefully until Grace had finished speaking, before saying, 'So that was why you came home alone. You wanted to stay the night with him, didn't you?'

'Oh course I did, he's lovely, and I would be lying if I said I wasn't more than a little curious to see what he's like stripped, but ... Oh Daze, what if he sees me naked and runs a mile? Petite I'm not!'

'I tell you what, Grace, let's meet food halfway until after the wedding. I can't afford to buy new dresses for either of us. And while neither of us will ever conform to a size 10, I know for a fact that research shows that the majority of men like women with curves rather than stick women, and the best thing we can do is maintain who we are now, rather than getting any bigger or any smaller.

After all, the size you are now is the same size you were when Rob first set eyes on you a few weeks ago.'

Grace narrowed her eyes suspiciously, 'You sound like you're reciting a speech.'

'I am quoting Marcus verbatim. I had an almost identical meltdown when I made similar excuses not to sleep with him the first opportunity I had.'

Grace shook her head in despair at the both of them and raised her wine glass, 'Here's to good old-fashioned female paranoia! Where would we be without it?'

'Happy?'

'Good point!' Grace grinned, 'Shall we order a couple of chicken and bacon salads then?'

'Perfect. With maybe just one side order of chips?'

Chapter Twenty-two

Mathilda swallowed the bile that swam at the base of her throat as she was stood before the long table in the main hall, at which sat all the Folville brothers, including the previously absent John.

There was no doubt that the pecking order had changed now that the older brother was in residence. Eustace's disgruntled expression said as much, even without the corroborating evidence of the uneasy atmosphere and the generally hostile body language. Mathilda, wasn't sure if this was being directed towards her, or if it was a show of bravado from the younger brothers to the head of their household, which was a position only achieved by accident of birth.

Mathilda had other things to worry about though. Like staying upright, not swaying, or showing any weakness in front of the assembled men.

'My brothers have informed me of the reason for your presence in my home.' John was even less pleased with this than he sounded, and as his tone was so sharp Mathilda could almost feel it cutting into her. 'I would be obliged if you would prove to me that the risks taken in sending out a hostage to relay a vital message have been worthwhile. Frankly, I was surprised you returned.'

Mathilda was vaguely aware of Robert staring at her. The expression of displeasure on his face made John's evident annoyance seem insignificant, and made her wonder why she hadn't run away as well.

'So,' John tapped his dagger on the table impatiently, and Mathilda noticed that it was almost identical to the one she had hidden beneath her tunic, but for the colour of the stone, 'the message from the Coterels? I assume you got it?'

'I did, my Lord. I spoke to Nicholas Coterel as instructed.'

Mathilda clenched her toes inside her boots, and concentrated on not letting her eyes swim out of focus.

'And? Come on, girl, what was the response?'

'He said, "The message is well received. Three days. Midnight."' The glow of the fire behind the table was making Mathilda's eye's water, and now her mission was fully complete, and the message delivered, she could feel her body shutting down, as if it was refusing to take the instructions from her brain telling her to stay on her feet. Luckily, an arm came to her elbow however, before the ground had the chance to reclaim her.

'Forgive the interruption, my Lords,' Sarah bowed with her usual sharp respect, 'but if you have finished with this girl, I require help in the kitchen.'

Without giving the household time to respond, Sarah steered Mathilda to the side of the hall behind the servants' dividing tapestry, and sat her onto the straw cot she'd been allowed to rest on before.

Frowning with confused gratitude, Mathilda opened her mouth to say thank you, when the housekeeper put a finger to her lips, and spoke in a guarded whisper, 'Nothing you can say to them tonight will please them. When was the last time you ate?'

'But ...'

Sarah shook her head sharply, and shoved a hunk of fatted bread into Mathilda's shivering hands, and placed a cup of hot broth on the floor next to her. 'Don't you get it, girl? It is not safe to talk now. Eat that and then sleep.'

The housekeeper disappeared back into the hall, and Mathilda dug her teeth into her supper, surprised that Sarah had not only taken the trouble to rescue her from the brothers' suspicious eyes, but had also kept some of the servants' supper warm for her.

As Mathilda chewed, she could hear Sarah's boots crossing the stone floor and then the sound of her offering ale to the brothers. The dig of the dagger's handle in her ribs alerted Mathilda to the weapon she still carried. Not wanting to sleep with it on her person for fear of stabbing herself in the night, she pulled it from its hiding place and hid it carefully under her cot, ready to return it to Robert as soon as she had the chance.

The uncomfortable stillness from the hall was abruptly broken by John, who either didn't realise Mathilda could hear him, or simply didn't care. 'Do we trust that this is a genuine message? What was to stop the girl making up a message so that she didn't have to face Coterel and could worm her way to freedom, and secure the safety of her family?'

Behind the tapestry, Mathilda blanched. It had never occurred to her that they wouldn't believe she had delivered an honest response.

'What say you, Robert? Eustace tells me you are soft on the girl. A fact that comes a relief to us all, I have to say!'

Mathilda's body tensed as she waited for Robert's response. She'd thought he liked her. Or at least that he understood her need to please him to ensure her family's safety, but Robert's behaviour after their meeting with Master Hugo had given Mathilda serious second thoughts about his motives for being kind to her earlier on. His response to John, however, was at least partly positive.

'The girl is a brave one. I am sure she went to Coterel as instructed. After all, the risk involved with the discovery of feeding us misinformation would be high indeed. However, we would be wise to remain cautious. The chit is unusually clever.'

Eustace spoke up for the first time, 'You think that she may have sided with Coterel?'

'That is not what I am saying,' Robert snapped, 'I am merely reminding everyone present that we should never completely trust *anyone* involved in this venture.'

A tiny flutter of hope stirred inside Mathilda. Had Robert realised where she was, and that she could hear him? Was it him that had instructed Sarah to get her out of the brother's presence as quickly as possible? She was convinced he was addressing her as much as his family as she listened.

'While we must bear in mind that Mathilda wants to

secure the freedom of her family, I am sure she fully understands that there are no shortcuts to that goal. If however, she does double-cross us, then she'd be extremely unwise. A fact I am sure she understands.'

Mathilda almost chocked on her mouthful of bread. He *did* know she was listening. All her doubts on that score were gone.

John virtually growled at Robert in exasperation. 'So, do you trust her in this or don't you!'

Mathilda held her breath as she waited for Robert's answer.

Robert however, did not get the chance to answer, for Eustace cut across his elder brother. 'Forget the girl. She got the message, and as it is pretty much the response I expected. I think we can assume it to be genuine. The real questions here are not if the girl is to be trusted, but are we ready to proceed in three nights' time with planning this necessary enterprise, and what are we going to do with the girl now?'

If Mathilda had been listening hard before, now her ears positively strained. She'd done what they wanted; surely they were going to send her home to help her father earn enough to pay off his debt now?

Wishing she could see what was going on, Mathilda was perturbed by the ominous peace from behind the thick curtain. She hadn't heard any footfalls, so the men must all still be there. She imagined Robert shushing them all, reminding his brothers that she was in the room. Or perhaps they weren't speaking because the answer to Eustace's question was so obvious to them that it only needed the hand signal indicating that her throat should be cut?

Despite her hunger, Mathilda found she could no longer swallow the bread, and not wanting to hear anything else, good or bad, she lay down on the straw cot and pulled the thin blanket up over her head, trying to drown out all thoughts of her immediate future.

Grace read back through the last paragraph before clicking the 'save' button and turning off her computer for the night.

Now she'd given up referring back to the original historical texts each time she wrote something, the process of writing Mathilda's story was not only easier, but actually more fun. Rob had been right. There was no need to keep things accurate down to the last degree. Although Grace found herself in two minds whether she should get Mathilda to ask more questions about the meeting that was obviously being set up between the two families or not. She'd made Mathilda naturally curious – but she'd also made her sensible, and no sensible person in that position would ask such questions. Too much knowledge would be too dangerous. No, Mathilda would ask nothing.

Grace also realised that her book had begun to exhibit all the hallmarks of a budding romance, but she was having doubts about keeping things that way. 'Besides,' Grace told her computer, with a determination she hoped Mathilda would have been proud of sweeping through her, 'this isn't really going to be a romantic tale. Time I let Mathilda decide what happens to her, I'm just her outlet, after all.'

Climbing the stairs of her little home to her bathroom, Grace ran a deep bubble bath. Easing herself into the blissfully warm water, she laid her head against the ceramic surface, not caring if her hair got wet as it bobbed around her shoulders. Having started the day in a fluster, Grace now felt surprisingly calm. Not only had she written another section of her novel, but Daisy had managed to talk a great deal of sense into her before taking the train back to Sheffield, and returning to her ever-demanding menagerie.

If Rob wasn't interested in her then he wouldn't have made it so clear that he wanted her to stay with him. If her rounded figure was a problem, then that was his issue, not hers, and while she agreed with Daisy that it was a good idea not to change size either up or down until after the wedding in case this instigated a dress adjustment-related emergency, Grace decided that she might try to eat a healthier diet. Not because of Rob, but because she knew, now she'd forced herself to think about it, that she'd been relying on fast food and snacks as her main diet for far too long.

Rippling her hands through the bubbles floating on top of the water, Grace began to think about Friday night. What should she cook? Should she rely on Marks & Spencer's prepared food, or should she make the effort not to burn something in her oven? Silly question really. She'd pop to M&S after work on Thursday. There was no good fooling the man into thinking she could cook. Some lies were too difficult to pull off, and she really didn't fancy spending their second proper date in Accident and Emergency, holding his hand while his stomach was pumped.

Grace had also dismissed decorating her house by Friday as a stupid idea. Even if she found the time to do it, or paid someone else to do it, the house would still stink of paint fumes when Rob arrived. Gagging on whiffs of tacky emulsion wouldn't exactly make for a romantic evening, although she had resolved that painting the house was a task that needed doing sooner rather than later, Rob or no Rob.

'He'll just have to take me for what I am.' Grace spoke to the clump of bubbles that clustered around her toes, before her brain went off at a far more delicious tangent. 'I wonder what else he might feel like taking.'

Luxuriating in the water, Grace lost herself in fantasies that had firmly knocked all thoughts of possible colour schemes right out of her head.

Chapter Twenty-three

Mathilda woke with a start, her insides contracting in alarm to find Robert looming over her, shaking her to consciousness, a finger planted firmly on her lips to make sure she didn't cry out.

Without giving her time to decide if he was about to silence her forever or draw her into his confidence, Mathilda found herself tugged bodily from her cot and manoeuvred into the kitchen, dressed in only her shift.

Taking one glimpse at Mathilda's dishevelled state, Sarah tutted loudly. 'Honestly, my Lord Robert. You can't bring the girl in undressed. What will people think?"

'I thought that was the point!' Robert looked cross and uncomfortable as he pushed Mathilda towards Sarah, 'She's supposed to be my woman, isn't she? You said it would be a good idea.'

'It is a good idea!' Ignoring his petulant tone, Sarah took off her shawl and wrapped it around Mathilda's shoulders, 'but you are a brother of the lord of the manor! You have to be seen to do these things with at least some level of propriety!'

Mathilda's mind raced. What the hell was going on? Why was Sarah talking to Robert as if she was an equal and not his housekeeper? And why had Robert manhandled her here in the first place?

Before she could ask, Sarah called across the room to the lad who seemed to do every odd job about the place. 'Allward!'

Everything that was happening seemed to be going on without there having been any need to drag her from her bed.

'Allward, go and fetch Mathilda's clothes. Quick, boy!' Having sent the boy on his errand, Sarah turned her attention away from the occupants of the kitchen and began busying herself with getting breakfast ready for the household.

Sitting next to Mathilda on the bench by the door, Robert laid a hand on her knee, only to be surprised and affronted as Mathilda hastily shoved it away.

Shocked at herself, Mathilda opened her mouth to apologise, knowing that if she'd pulled away from him in company then she'd have been in for a mouthful of admonishment. 'I'm so sorry my Lord, I ...'

'No Mathilda, I'm the one who should be sorry.' Robert glanced towards Sarah's turned back, knowing she was listening even if she wasn't watching. 'There is much to explain, and little time to explain it in.'

The early morning chill of the kitchen was making Mathilda shiver, and she was cross with herself for doing so, even though it had nothing to do with any weakness on her part, but with the fact that she'd been continually cold, hungry, or tired since she'd been deposited into the Folville home. Rather than comment and risk saying the wrong thing, Mathilda bit her tongue as she waited for Robert's explanation.

'First, I must apologise for not being able to congratulate you for your bravery in meeting with Coterel. Time was of the essence, and for reasons I am unable to divulge, it was important that I was not seen to be pleased with you.'

Frowning, Mathilda wondered if perhaps Robert distrusted Master Hugo as much as she did after all. Even as she thought about it though, she found that didn't ring true. There was something about the way the men were together that was too comfortable to have any level of distrust within it, and yet ...

Mathilda's musings were interrupted by Allward returning with her borrowed dress, belt, and an extra shawl, which Mathilda assumed Sarah had instructed him to find for her. She expected Robert to avert his eyes while she dressed, but as Sarah rather curtly pointed out; he'd been sitting next to her in her shift for ten minutes, so there was little reason left for decorum now.

Dressing as fast as she could, more in her keenness to be warm than to hide the outline of her figure, Mathilda lifted the belt Robert had entrusted to her, and weighed it in her hands, aware of Robert's green eyes on her as she fastened it around her waist.

'You like that belt, don't you.'

'It is most beautiful. I will be sad to give it up when I leave.' Hoping that Robert would pick up on her mention of leaving, Mathilda smoothed out her dress and sat back down.

Robert didn't rise to the opening, but continued with his previous discourse, 'My brothers were pleased with the message but ...' he looked about him as if checking that no one but those already in the kitchen could hear them, '... they are cautious. You are the hostage for a debt. They have no reason to trust you.'

'Surely the fact that I am a debt hostage means they should trust me. I love my family, and I want them to be safe.'

'I know, but not all hostages care about the people who have put them into danger in the first place.'

Mathilda only just managed to stop herself from snapping out her response, instead speaking with controlled calm, 'Well, I am not most people, and now that I've done as requested I'd like to go home so I can help my father make back the money he owes you.'

Robert's expression was one of pure disbelief, 'You didn't think you'd be allowed to leave before the debt was repaid, did you?'

Feeling foolish, Mathilda's eyes flicked from Sarah to Allward, who was busy pouring ale into flagons, and back to Robert. She sounded small and quiet when she finally managed to speak, 'But you said ...'

'I told you what I was supposed to tell you. Come on, Mathilda, you're cleverer than that. You didn't think you'd get out of here so easily, did you?'

'Easily?' Mathilda felt the injustice of her situation fill her up from her toes, until it was forcing itself up her throat and out of her mouth in a torrent of unwisely spoken words, 'You think it was *easy* going into one of the most notorious family's houses in Derbyshire? Especially when Master Hugo deliberately gave me the wrong directions to the Coterel's manor.'

'I beg your pardon?' Robert's placating voice turned to ice.

Sarah swung around from her work, and gave Mathilda a warning stare from her shrewd eyes, but Mathilda had had enough. 'He told me to take the wrong road. It was bad enough trying to dodge being seen by that Judas, Geoffrey of Reresby, but if my Lord Coterel hadn't helped me out, I'd never have got back to Master Hugo's stall. Where, I might add, I made him a fortune selling his trinkets!'

Out of breath, regretted her outburst, the moment she finished speaking. Hanging her head, Mathilda muttered, 'I'm sorry, I forgot myself, I ...'

The grip of Robert's hand as it thrust forward and grabbed her chin jarred Mathilda's whole body, 'How dare you speak about one of my most trusted allies like that!'

'I tell you the truth, my Lord!'

'You forget who you are talking to!'

'And you forget that you told me you liked my directness. How can my father possibly raise enough money with two of his children missing? How ...'

Mathilda, her jaw aching from the pressure of Robert's firm fingers, took a ragged breath as realisation dawned. 'You don't intend for them to be able to pay you back, do you? I am too useful to you, and it suits your family to keep mine in debt to them.'

Sarah crashed down the jug she held in her hand, 'Foolish woman! You are so sharp you might cut yourself!'

'I can handle this, thank you, Sarah.' Robert dropped Mathilda's chin, and took a tight grip of her hand, 'It seems our guest does not wish to be updated on the current situation, or receive our words of help and advice to get her through this. She apparently knows better.'

'My Lord, no, I ...'

Again Mathilda was cut off mid-sentence, as she realised exactly how unwise she'd been. Coterel had warned her not to reveal Hugo's deception to Robert, and now she wished she'd listened to him.

A gloating laugh cut through the argument as Father Richard entered the kitchen, demanding a drink from a taciturn Sarah, before, with an expression on his face that made it look as if he was delighted to have witnessed such ire towards Mathilda, disappeared as fast as he'd arrived.

Robert shot the view of his retreating brother a black look, before rounding on Mathilda once more, 'Not another word, girl. Not one. Just you listen to me. Master Hugo is a loyal friend. He had no pleasure informing me that you had shirked your duties, that you'd made him a loss rather than a profit, and had been over two hours late in starting work on his stall. He has nothing to gain from lying to me. Therefore he did not lie.'

'Of course he did!' Mathilda knew she'd gone too far, pushed her luck too much, but it was too late now, 'Of course he did, he's a clever man! It suits him to lie to you. Coterel himself claimed Master Hugo to be untrustworthy and yet you believe him over me! Me, who has put her life at risk for you in order to save the people I love. You claim to follow the example of Robyn Hode – well, you're not doing that this time!'

She hadn't cried since she'd first left the Folvilles' small cell. Now, as Mathilda found herself back in the tiny stone prison, she let all the held in grief and fear escape. Tears cascaded down her cheeks in torrents, and her cheek stung from the slap of Robert's palm that had met her face with so much power that if she hadn't been sitting down, it would have floored her.

Why hadn't she held her tongue? Her father had told Mathilda many times that her quick retorts would be the death of her. For the first time she considered he might be right. Literally.

Mathilda couldn't see how she would ever leave this household alive now. She knew the Coterels were planning to work with the Folvilles, and if the amount of planning they were putting into whatever task it was they intended to undertake, she was sure it would involve a felony of some sort. She knew that Master Hugo was jealous of her, but she hadn't a clue why, and she knew her anger at Robert was as much to do with the fact that she wanted him to think better of her than a liar like Hugo. Mathilda cradled her head in her hands. She knew too much – even if she didn't understand any of it.

Mathilda wasn't sure how long she'd been locked back in the shadows. She hadn't moved from her crouched position on the floor since Robert had left her with the parting words, 'It seems John was right; I was foolish to trust you after all.'

In spite of the truth of her ill-advised outburst in the kitchen, Mathilda was stung by Robert's words, and the expression of disappointment on his face, which was far worse than the anger that it had replaced. Her head whirled. Why was Robert confiding in her one minute, and then blasting her with mistrust the next?

The more she thought about her situation, the less if made sense.

Thinking back, Mathilda saw how wrong she'd been to think she'd be able to leave once she'd delivered that one message. Eustace himself had told her that she was to be their eyes and ears, their messenger. He hadn't said that there would only be one message. She'd been so relieved to have survived her trip to Bakewell that she'd jumped to conclusions.

Weary from her early awakening, Mathilda decided to escape from reality for a while and take solace in sleep. Not even attempting to get comfortable, she rested her head against the mossy stone wall, and closed her eyes.

Her semi sleep-like doze had been littered with nightmares and faded hopes for the fate of her family, and Mathilda felt a sense of relief when she fully came back to consciousness. With her tears dried against her face, Mathilda blinked. The shadows cast over the four walls loomed over each other as if the slime on the walls was illuminating the space, but then, and her eyes roamed the confided space, she saw a glitter of light just inside the door.

Cautiously reaching out, Mathilda caressed the unmistakeable length of a dagger. The same dagger Robert had lent her the day before. How had Robert come to find it under her bed where she'd stashed it awaiting a chance to return it to him? Had Sarah or Allward found it and, recognising the colour of the stone to name the weapon as Robert's, returned it to him and forgotten to tell her? And why had he snuck back her and left the dagger for her? Had it been him? She must have been far more deeply asleep than she'd imagined. Anyone could have opened the heavy wooden door and slid the dagger into her prison.

The only fact that Mathilda knew for sure was that it hadn't been there before she'd gone to sleep.

Grace got up from her desk and hit the start button on her coffee machine. Stretching her back, she closed her eyes and inhaled the delicious aroma of brewing coffee as it filled the air.

It was no longer just Mathilda who didn't know what was happening in the Folville manor. Grace had a feeling that the plot was getting away from her; and that fairly soon someone was going to have to die to keep the plot on track. The trouble was, Grace was unable to decide how that death might happen.

Although she was very clear on who was destined to meet a premature end, and why.

Chapter Twenty-four

With the scrape of the gaol door opening, Mathilda hastily slid the dagger out of sight up her sleeve. Her heart thudded harder as she waited to see who was coming to see her.

Sarah, her jaw set firmer than ever, grey shadows around her eyes suggesting that she hadn't slept too well either, beckoned urgently to Mathilda to follow her.

Bunching her right hand into a fist so that the hidden weapon didn't slide from her sleeve, Mathilda scrambled out of the cell and went with the housekeeper, not to the kitchen as she'd expected, but to a bedroom.

Only when the door had been shut behind them, did Sarah speak. 'This is my Lord Robert's room. You will assist me in making up his bed and collecting his dirty linen for washing. And more importantly, you will keep your mouth shut and listen. We don't have long.'

Hoping that her compliance would lead to Sarah telling her what was going on; Mathilda tucked and smoothed the rough sheet. The hems and backside of her clothes were soiled from the damp and slime of the cell, and stuck to her legs. Mathilda was thankful for the warmth from the dying embers of the fire that had been warming Robert's room during the night.

Moving around the bed, flapping linen into place, Sarah spoke. 'All of the brothers are out, but there is no knowing when they'll be back.' Sarah moved to the fire and carefully laid a couple of slim twigs onto its embers, ready to coax a stronger flame from the ashes. She sighed heavily. 'Despite the impression my Lord Robert gave you, he knows you did well, Mathilda, but don't think that one success has given you the right to any favours here. In truth, your position is now more perilous than it was before.'

Thinking this was something of an understatement

considering where she'd just been delivered from, Mathilda asked, 'Please, Sarah, I know I spoke out of turn, and I'm truly sorry for that. But I did exactly what I was ordered to, despite being double-crossed by Master Hugo.'

Sensing that Sarah was having a battle with herself as to whether to say more or not, Mathilda added, 'I was left a dagger in the cell. Did you put it there?'

'A dagger?' Sarah's faced grew pale. 'Show me.'

Easing the short-bladed weapon from her sleeve, Mathilda passed it over to the housekeeper, who sat down heavily on the edge of the bed, something Mathilda was sure she'd never normally allow herself to do, especially just after she'd finished making it.

'It's my Lord Robert's, isn't it?' A sense of foreboding ran down Mathilda's spine as Sarah's eyes met hers. 'Something bad has happened, hasn't it?'

Grace swore under her breath. If she didn't stop writing now she'd never get to work on time. She had a group tutorial with her research students in two hours that she hadn't even started preparing for. Reluctantly leaving Mathilda in suspense, she headed off, checking her emails on her phone as went.

Amongst all the offers for penile enhancements and cut-price insurance was an email from Daisy. Then Grace's stomach did a back flip when she spotted that the email beneath it was from Rob.

Reading Rob's email first, Grace found herself smiling at her phone screen. He was offering to take her out tomorrow night if she didn't fancy cooking for him. Grace surprised herself by replying that cooking was no problem as long as he didn't mind cuisine a la M&S, and that she was looking forward to seeing him.

As soon as she'd pressed 'send' on the email, Grace felt silly for her previous panic about Rob coming to her place. Daisy had been right. He was a nice guy. If he was the right nice guy then he'd have to accept her, warts and all.

And that meant all her messy clutter and lack of domestic skills inclusive.

Flicking onto Daisy's email, Grace looked up to check she wasn't about to walk into a tree as she crossed the park, and scanned the message which seemed to be a list of all the jobs that needed doing before the wedding.

Vowing to give this her full attention, but knowing she'd need a cuppa and a sit down in which to do so first, Grace pocketed her phone and began to walk faster towards her office.

After a brief knock on the door, Agatha elbowed her way into Grace's room, her arms laden with folders. As soon as she saw the lecturer properly, her face creased into an approving smile. 'You feeling all right, Grace? Only you appear to be wearing smart clothes.'

'I'm fine, thank you.' Having prepared herself from some mild teasing, Grace returned the secretary's smile, and smoothed out the outfit she'd worn to the viva. 'I assumed with the wedding coming up, I should try and get used to wearing better clothes, so it isn't so much of a culture shock parading about in a bridesmaid's dress for the day.'

'How long it is until wedding now? You got your shoes broken in and stuff?'

Grace hooked her feet out from under her desk and flashed her brand new dark green suede heels under Agatha's expert gaze.

'Oh, I like!'

'It would be nice if you didn't sound quite so surprised that I can have decent shoes, Aggie!'

Not fooled for a second, Agatha laughed, 'You didn't choose them, did you?'

'Nope. Daisy did. They're higher than I'm used to so I'm going to wear them at home and in the office so I get used to walking in them without breaking an ankle.'

Approving of this uncharacteristically smart and sensible Grace, Agatha asked, 'What are you buying the happy couple as a wedding gift?

'Oh my God!' Grace felt like her determination to be a far more organised person had failed at the first hurdle. 'I have no idea! I'd forgotten all about it.'

'Well, no need to look so alarmed; I'm sure they'll have a gift list or something.'

'Apparently not. Daisy doesn't want people to feel obliged to get them anything. It's so difficult finding something for a couple who already have everything they could possibly need house wise after years of having separate homes.'

Placing two folders of completed essays ready for making on Grace's desk, Agatha looked thoughtful. 'You really should get them a gift though, Grace. You're the bridesmaid! How about a time cheque?'

'What the hell's a time cheque?' Grace opened the top folder, and grimaced. She already knew the first essay on the pile wasn't going to be worth reading; well, not unless the student in question had learnt to cherry pick his answers from the internet with rather more care than he had in the past.

'A time cheque is a sort of IOU. An offer to house-sit the animals so that Daisy and Marcus can have a weekend away in future. You know, once they've been married for six months, and are dying to get away from reality again for a while.'

'That's a great idea! Thanks, Aggie.'

The secretary headed for the door, pausing as she pushed it open, 'Who are you taking with you, anyway? You can't go to a wedding alone. And I assume you aren't seeing anyone right now?'

Flustered, and not wanting to jinx things with Rob, Grace said, 'Oh, course I'm not, but I'll be fine just with Daisy.'

Agatha shook her head sharply, 'Of course you won't! You'll need someone to balance you up on the wedding photographs. I tell you what, I'll get my stepson Malcolm to come with you for moral support, I'm sure he'd oblige.'

Before Grace could protest, Agatha had disappeared along the corridor, ready to deliver the next batch of essays to the lecturer in the next office.

'Damn!' Grace stared up at the face of Errol Flynn on the back of the door, 'Now what do I do!'

Feeling it was far too early in their friendship to assume too much with Rob, Grace hadn't mentioned their previous or forthcoming dates to anyone but Daisy. She desperately didn't want to spark any gossip around the office; especially via Aggie who, for all her kindness, loved a juicy rumour.

Grace had heard a fair bit about the secretary's stepson Malcolm, and it always seemed to be along the lines of him being a really nice guy, but rather thoughtless. Knowing she had to act fast to stem Aggie's well-meaning matchmaking, Grace got up and wobbled on her new heels to the secretary's office.

More tottering than walking, Grace made it to the office without breaking her leg, and put her head around the door, preparing to decline Aggie's offer. On arrival however she found that the secretary was already on the phone. Grace's heart sank as she listened to the conversation in process.

'You'll love Grace, Malc, she's pretty, bright, and totally lovely. Shall we say coffee this afternoon?'

Sensing she was being watched, Agatha twirled her swivel chair around, and beamed at Grace, 'and here's the woman in question!' She held up a hand to indicate to Grace that Malcolm was still talking, before she finally hung up the phone.

'Four thirty today, in the New Walk Museum cafe. OK, Grace?'

What else could Grace do but say, 'Sure. Why not?'

Running after Sarah back to the little prison, Mathilda's blood pounded in her throat. She didn't know why she was being hurried back into confinement; the housekeeper's worried expression made it clear that it was for her own safety, not out for some malicious intent.

Once Mathilda was back inside, Sarah crouched at the door, glancing behind her nervously, her ears alert from any sound.

'Please, Sarah ...'

Shaking her head urgently, Sarah spoke fast, 'Father Richard might be back soon, and if he learns I let you out, or indeed have done more than bought you some bread and ale, then he'd have my hide. He's been waiting for an excuse to get me out of here for years.'

'Why?'

'Because his brothers trust me. They haven't always done the right thing, but they believe what they are doing is the best thing. The rector just believes blindly, and his brand of justice is frankly frightening.'

'Why do the others trust you?'

'Because I'm merely their housekeeper, you mean?'

'Forgive me, but yes.'

'I brought them up, raised them from pups. All but for Richard, who was carted off to a monastery at the age of five. He never grew to know or trust me like his brothers did, and has always held the fact he was sent away against me, although his departure was none of my doing.' Sarah was getting more agitated, and Mathilda could tell the housekeeper was thinking fast. 'Give me the dagger. It is best it was never here.'

'What do you mean? Robert obviously thought I might need it.'

'If the dagger wasn't here when you first arrived in the cell, then it wasn't Robert who left it. He went back to Derbyshire the moment you were imprisoned.'

Mathilda drew in a sharp breathe, 'Do you think he

believed me about Master Hugo lying about me after all?
Has he gone to quiz the leatherworker?'

'No. But I believed you, and that made Robert think.'
Sarah took the dagger and wrapped it in her apron, 'It is
very important you do *not* have this dagger when they come
to release you.'

'Why?'

'Because word has not long come from Derby. Robert
didn't get to ask Hugo if he was telling the truth or not.'

'Why not? What word? Who from?'

'From Hugo's apprentice, Roger. Master Hugo was found
dead just after Vespers last night.'

Grace paused, flexed her fingers, and gave in to the
nagging doubts in her head about what time of day
Vespers actually was. She knew that the church clock was
something of a moveable feast depending on the time of
year, but for the life of her she couldn't remember what
time of year she'd decided to set her story; if she'd ever
really thought about it in the first place.

Quickly googling the monastic calendar to check that
she was right in thinking that it was about 7 o'clock in the
evening. Grace told herself off for not having kept any sort
of continuity notes, and promising herself she'd check to
make sure that all her characters had the same colour eyes
and hair at the being of her story as at the end, she read
through the information on the screen.

Vespers was at seven in the evening, although that was
only the case during midsummer. If her story was based in
mid-winter, Vespers would be nearer 3 p.m. 'Why the hell
can't I remember what time of year I've set all this stuff
in?!'

Cursing the fact she had to keep stopping and starting
her story because of work, Grace became increasingly
worried that her novel would read as disjointedly as it has
been written.

Catching sight of the time, she reluctantly turned off

the computer with a sigh. If she was going to see Malcolm, she'd have to go now. She really didn't want to offend Agatha.

Chapter Twenty-five

Grace had already counted every vertebrae of the skeleton of the Rutland Dinosaur, a *Cetiosaurus,* which majestically lorded it over the other residents of the New Walk Museum's dinosaur gallery. She'd observed the woman behind the cafe counter serve thirteen other coffees and four teas since they'd sat down an hour ago, along with three slices of carrot cake and two packets of assorted biscuits. While Grace had witnessed all of this, she had also been nodding and smiling in all the right places, as Malcolm regaled her of tales of sporting triumphs and his marketing coups at work.

It wasn't that he was boring, and with his stylish short blond hair and his classically fit physique, he was certainly an enjoyable eyeful, it was just that every sentence began with, 'I did this' or 'I did that' or 'You'd never guess what I did?' Grace idly wondered if he would notice if she got up and another person sat in her seat instead.

Malcolm was also making very sure that she understood that he was a good ten years younger than she was. As Grace listened with only one ear to a blow-by-blow account of how his latest rugby match had ended in him successfully tackling someone twice his size, she vowed that if she heard one more 'cougar' joke, then her phone was going to bring her an emergency she had to go and address straight away.

Aggie's stepson had already been sat in the cafe when Grace arrived at the museum, two minutes late due to having to change out of her wedding shoes and into her more practical flatties, so she wasn't sure how tall Malcolm was. Grace was prepared to put money on him being taller than she was. About six foot, maybe six two? As she laughed at a joke that wasn't remotely funny, Grace began to wonder if perhaps Malcolm's physique might be a good one to model the character of one of the Folville brothers around …

'Grace? Do you?' Malcolm was looking at her as if perhaps she wasn't quite as intelligent as his stepmother had led him to believe.

'I'm sorry Malcolm, I missed that. Do I?'

'Want another cup of tea?'

Grace sensing her chance to escape, and eager to get back to Mathilda, she stared at her watch and sighed dramatically, 'I'm so sorry, I hadn't realised the time. I ought to get back to work.'

'Work? But it's nearly six o'clock? Surely you finish at five?'

Grace couldn't help but snort. 'We don't really ever finish work, we keep going until starvation drives us from the office; and I really do need to get back to my marking and editing. Thanks for a lovely tea break, though.'

The concept of working outside of regulated office hours seemed to leave Malcolm temporarily flummoxed, but he had the good manners to escort Grace to the door of the museum. As they walked, with Malcolm cradling her elbow, Grace wasn't immune to noticing the admiring glances they got as a couple. Malcolm was getting looks of unsubtle and unadulterated lust from the women, while she found herself on the receiving end of glares of the 'you lucky cow' nature from the same quarter.

Unsure if she was flattered or offended by the 'how did she pull someone as good-looking as him' implication as Malcolm kissed her cheek by way of a goodbye, that when he asked Grace out to dinner the following Wednesday, she found herself saying yes, just to show the gawping onlookers that she wasn't batting out of her range. It was only when she was walking back to the university on her own that Grace realised that she'd just agreed to go on a date with a man she didn't like very much.

Daisy was furious, 'For goodness' sake, Grace, you're with Rob now. And I mean – Malcolm! He sounds like a homicidal king from a Shakespeare play.'

Feeling the guilt that she'd been ignoring simmer under the surface of her skin, Grace explained how Agatha had backed her into the situation, and that, as she hadn't wanted to tell anyone about Rob in case it jinxed things, she'd gone along with it.

Calmer, Daisy said, 'I get that, but why on earth did you agree to go on a dinner date with him? I mean, you did your duty, you haven't offended Agatha. You have a date at your place with Rob tomorrow night!'

'I know. I didn't mean to.' Grace sighed, 'Malcolm's a nice bloke and everything, but he was a bit dull. Did you know there were almost two hundred bones in a complete Cetiosaurus skeleton?'

Daisy shook her head in exasperation, 'Are you seriously telling me that you are jeopardising the chance of a proper relationship with Rob, a man with whom you have a heap of stuff in common, and who makes you laugh, for a guy who is so dull that you ended up counting random dinosaur bones to pass the time?'

Feeling defensive as well as guilty now, Grace said, 'It's not like I'm cheating on Rob, is it? I mean, he hasn't actually told me how we stand, or asked me out properly or anything, and anyway, I was thinking of you.'

'Me?' Daisy was completely nonplussed as she listened in bewilderment.

'You should have seen the looks Malcolm got from the women sat nearby. He may be a bit self-centred, but he is extremely easy on the eye.'

'Grace, what the hell are you talking about? And what about the looks you got from the men? I bet there were loads.'

'Not that I noticed.'

'Were you looking?'

'Well, no. But think about it, Daisy. Malcolm would look great in your wedding photos. Should I ask him to come with me? I must admit, I'm a bit nervous about coming on my own.'

'What on earth are you talking about now?' Daisy clattered down the cup she'd been drinking from, and spoke very clearly down the line. 'It's *my* wedding, you're *my* best friend Grace, and I want you to be there with someone you actually like. And you don't like Malcolm, do you?'

'He's all right.'

'Grace?'

'OK, he's a self-obsessed ego manic – but he is a very handsome one. Your photos would be …'

'I don't care if he's a dead ringer for Ryan Reynolds! I don't want to look back at my wedding album in ten years' time to remember the only day you ever got to be gorgeous in Lincoln Green with the wrong man stood next to you. Why isn't Rob coming with you?'

'I haven't asked him,' Grace knew she as being ridiculous, and that it was all due to feeling guilty for having coffee with Malcolm, and not being sensible enough to back out of the dinner date the second it had been made. 'But like I said, I don't really know where Rob and I stand.'

'Oh for goodness' sake, Grace! You aren't half thick for a clever person.'

Slipping her new heels back onto her feet, Grace sat at her office desk, pleased the shoes didn't feel quite as alien as they had when she'd first put them on.

She'd already poked her head around the administrators' office door to ask Aggie for Malcolm's phone number so she could cry off their non-date, but the secretary had gone home. Cursing herself for always trying to please all of the people all of the time, and usually messing everything up in the process, Grace looked up at the reassuring presence of her Robin Hood paraphernalia all over the walls and bookshelves. Why was she bothering with this dating lark? She already had someone who'd never cheat on her, would always be there at the touch of her DVD player, and could therefore never let her down.

Trying to drown out the contradictory voice at the back of her head, which was sternly telling her that mythical men wouldn't ever keep her warm at night, and a feeling of a resignation that her desire not to offend Aggie might have already messed up any chance she'd had with Rob, Grace decided to lose herself in fourteenth-century England. After all, no one could hurt her there.

Mathilda's heart was racing as she thought over everything Sarah had told her before she'd relocked the cell door and rushed back to her kitchen duties. If she'd believed herself to be in a dangerous situation before, that was nothing compared to the position Mathilda found herself in now.

The information the leatherworker's lad had imparted to the Folville's stable boy was sparse.

Master Hugo of Derby had been found stabbed in the wooded ditch that ran to the north side of Twyford, only a short distance from the workshop that belonged to Mathilda's father, just as the bells for the call to Vespers had rung across the countryside.

Sarah had kept talking, but there had been no need for her to spell out the situation. Mathilda's head was already buzzing with the implications, not to mention the conclusions the sheriff and his bailiff would jump to.

Hugo was a known associate of the Folvilles. Her father, Bertred, not only owed the Folvilles money, but owned the workshop nearest to the place where the body was discovered. On top of that, both she and her brother Oswin of Twyford had not been seen around the family home for a few days, instantly making them suspects.

To make things even worse, someone had left a dagger in her prison. A dagger that Mathilda now had no doubt had been placed there to implicate her.

She wondered what Sarah had done with the weapon she'd hurriedly removed from the cell, and what she'd say if questioned by the authorities. Sarah had promised Mathilda that she would not mention she'd been let out of her prison to help with making the beds; but Mathilda knew well that if a heavy handed method of inquisition was used against the housekeeper, she might not be able to keep that promise, however genuine it had been at the time.

It seemed odd to recall how hostile Sarah had been to her on arrival in the Folville home only days ago. Forcing herself to drink the broth that Sarah had bought her, Mathilda took comfort from the one piece of welcome news Sarah had also given her alongside all the extra worry.

As soon as word of the murder had reached her ears, Sarah had experienced similar fears to Mathilda's, and had sent her kitchen hand Allward to creep carefully up to Mathilda's Twyford home in order to check on the wellbeing of her father and Matthew.

Yet, although relieved that she'd soon have word of her kin, Mathilda was concerned for the boy. If Allward was spotted spying around Twyford, without being able to give a good reason for being there ... she reined in her imagination. There was no point in stewing over things she couldn't control. Wrapping her arms around her crouched legs, Mathilda wished that Robert would hurry up and come home so she could talk to him.

For the first time since she'd got to Folville manor, Mathilda was grateful to be locked in a cell so that there was no way she could be believed to be the killer ... although someone obviously wanted her to be accused ... otherwise why put the dagger there?

Mathilda heard the shouting even through the thick wooden door of her captivity. There were at least two male voices, and the pleading, placating tones of a woman, who Mathilda was sure was Sarah. Frustrated at not being able to pick out what was actually being said, Mathilda could tell that slowly the tones had changed from outrage, to the lower pitch of someone doing their best to keep their feelings under control.

After another ten minutes of waiting, the door to her prison swung open. Eustace had a preventative hand on Robert's chest as he attempted to push past into the cell.

'Mathilda, I would like you to follow me, please.' Eustace gave his younger brother a warning glare, which clearly declared that although he'd dropped his hand, he could move it back at any time, possibly with his sword in it.

Following the small group meekly, Mathilda found herself back in the main hall, standing next to Sarah, and facing Eustace, Robert, and to Mathilda's dismay, a smug Richard, rector of Teigh, who managed to look as un-priestlike as ever. If he hadn't been there Mathilda would have spoken unguardedly, however his presence made her wary. He seemed far too pleased by recent events.

'First,' Eustace paid no heed to either of his siblings and addressed the women, 'Allward has returned safely from Twyford.'

Mathilda failed to contain her sigh of relief.

'I see you are pleased, young woman.'

'My Lord, I would have hated anything to happen to the boy.'

'Indeed.' Eustace glanced at Sarah, 'you told the girl of Allward's mission?'

The housekeeper bowed in respect, 'When I took her some broth, my Lord. The girl was troubled about her family, and I saw no harm. I apologise if I did wrong.'

Eustace didn't respond to this, addressing Mathilda instead, 'Your father and elder brother are well, although the sheriff's men may well be sniffing around them by the morning. A natural development, as the body of Master Hugo was found so close to your family home and workshop.' He shot another unreadable expression toward

196

Sarah, 'Our housekeeper has told you of the grisly finding around Vespers.'

'Yes, my Lord.' Mathilda added, 'Thank you for letting me know my family are safe.'

'Safe for now, Mathilda. You know as well as I do that unless something is done the sheriff will want a criminal to go with the crime. I hope he doesn't decide to pick one based on convenience rather than guilt.'

Mathilda opened her mouth to protest at how unfair that would be, but closed it again quickly. Such statements were pointless folly.

'Richard and I are going to prepare for our meeting with the Coterels. This matter I am leaving to Robert. Making sure the right man is accused is after all his passion, thanks to his love of stories. I trust his Robyn Hode will bring you comfort and suggest a few solutions. That is, of course,' Eustace gave his brother a stare, 'if his common sense has kicked in and he has stopped blaming you.'

Mathilda blanched, forcing herself to keep her eyes on Eustace and not swing around to face Robert. 'Me, my Lord. But I've been in your cell for hours?'

'True. But the rector tells me when he checked on you while you slept, there was a dagger by your feet, and yet when we collected you just now there wasn't. Can you explain that, Mathilda?'

Dread gripped Mathilda. All she could do was repeat herself. 'I have no dagger, my Lord, and I've been a prisoner since long before the hour of Vespers.'

'And yet, Mathilda, why would a man of the church lie to his brother?'

Eustace and a smirking Richard looked at Robert, who in turn, stared at Mathilda with a face as creased with grief and resentment.

The rector gestured a lazy arm towards Sarah. 'Get that woman to search the waif. The dagger was there, and so if it wasn't on the cell floor, it must be about her person.'

Mathilda stiffened, 'My Lord, I really don't have ...'

Eustace raised a hand to silence her, 'Sarah, if you would

please do as my brother requests?'

Tight-lipped, Sarah inclined her head in agreement and went to steer Mathilda towards the curtained bedded area.

'No.' The rector's words were already edged with triumph, 'here, before all of us. I do not trust our housekeeper as much as you do, dear brother.'

'But, sir,' Sarah appealed directly to Eustace, 'I cannot strip the girl before you all.'

The rector however, was adamant. 'I insist. My word has been doubted by a servant. You will do as you're told.'

An imperceptible affirmation toward Sarah from Eustace, and Mathilda found herself turned so that she was facing away from the men sat around the table, and her shawl, surcoat, belt, and dress were removed, so that once again she found herself before Robert in only her chemise and undergarments.

As Sarah ran her palms up and down Mathilda's arms making it clear to the onlookers that nothing was hidden beneath, Richard positively bristled with rage. 'She must have it. Take her shift off!'

'My Lord, I must protest!' Sarah's disapproval was joined by the previously silent Robert.

'Brother, that is hardly a seemly request for a man of the cloth. I think it is more than clear that there is nowhere on Mathilda's person where a dagger could be secreted. You must have been mistaken.'

'I was not mistaken!' The rector's face burned red in vehemence. 'You are all in this together!' The churchman stormed from the room, his fists clenched, blaspheming in a way that would make a whore blush.

Chapter Twenty-six

'I've tried to call Agatha to cry off the dinner date with Malcolm, but she isn't answering her phone.'

As she listened, Daisy crossed 'check hay store supply' off her lengthy 'Things to do before the wedding list', before speaking into the phone tucked under her chin. 'Well, at least you have the sense to know you need to cancel it. Honestly, Grace, I was beginning to think you'd taken leave of your senses.'

'All right, I know.' Grace ticked three boxes on the student development form in front of her. 'I was trying not to offend and it all went wrong.'

'More importantly, are you ready for tonight's date with Rob? I take it you have dived into M&S and swept the contents of the latest £10 meal deal off the shelves?'

'Of course I have. Who wouldn't?'

'Quite! Are you nervous?'

'I am a bit.' Grace glanced up from her desk, and scanned her unnaturally tidy living room. Despite her determination that Rob should take her as she was, a fear that the extent of her usual untidiness would be a little too much in one go had forced her to tidy up just a little bit more. She'd decided it was kinder to inflict the extent of her chaotic muddled-ness up on him in small doses.

'And you are wearing?'

'Clean blue jeans, black vest, and semi-open black shirt. Any good?'

'Sounds spot on.' Daisy smiled as she added, 'check no guinea pigs due to give birth over honeymoon' to her list.

'How about you Daze, no more last-minute nerves or anything?'

'Not really last minute yet. There's two weeks to go. I have far too much left to sort before August 8th to consider this being last minute. Did you get my email?'

'Yes. When do you want me up there? I know you've sorted the overnight room for me, but did you want me to come to your place the night before we head toward Hardwick to help sort things out? Make sure flowers are there, that the guest list is up to date, get the seating plan sorted and stuff, or does the wedding planner do all that?'

The sigh that came from Daisy was one of utter relief. 'Oh, honey, would you? Come early I mean?'

'Of course! You only had to ask.'

'I didn't like to. What with books, and students, and Rob, and work and things.'

'I know I'm an obsessive with my work, Daze, but if I can't put things on hold for my best friend's wedding, then I'm not much of a friend, am I? And don't forget the undergraduates have broken up now. It's only the post grads I'm tutoring at the moment, so there is much more time for research and a bit of flexible time management.'

'Talking of which, how is the paper going with Rob?'

'Oh, hell!'

'You hadn't forgotten about that had you?' Grace's silence down the line told Daisy all she needed to know. 'Grace!'

'I hadn't forgotten. I just haven't done anything about it. I've been so wrapped up in Mathilda.' Grace paused, before speaking more quietly, 'I'm doing it again, aren't I?'

'Doing what again?'

'Getting lost in the past. Losing myself in my writing so I can avoid thinking about the scarier aspects if seeing Rob, and the wedding, and trying to think how to let down Malcolm without upsetting Agatha, and …'

'Woah!' Daisy spoke with her puppy training voice, 'Don't you see. You aren't doing it, not this time. You

201

aren't lost in the fourteenth century any more. I mean, a bit of you is. You wouldn't be you if a part of your soul wasn't off climbing trees in Sherwood with Robin Hood while giving Will Scarlet the eye. And the novel has to happen or you'll never forgive yourself, but its *real* life that is consuming you right now. My wedding, not upsetting Agatha, and spending time with the lovely Rob. Not the mess that was medieval England. I think you may finally have joined the twenty-first century!'

'God, that's a scary thought.'

'No it isn't; it is real though.' Bringing the conversation back to her wedding before Grace disappeared into paranoia, Daisy said, 'Do you really think you could come up a bit before the wedding? I was going to ask if you'd come here on the 6th, then help me at the Hall on the 7th before the kick off the next day.'

'No problem at all. We need to go and collect the dresses anyway. We could go on into Sheffield on the Wednesday, that way if we've lost too much or put on too much weight since we last tried the dresses on, Ashley can wave her magic wand and fix them for us.'

'You don't think you've lost weight, do you?' Grace detected a veiled horror in Daisy's question.

'I wish! I just meant it would be good to try the dresses on once more in the place where adjustments can be made if required. Sorry, Daze, I didn't mean to worry you.'

Daisy dropped her pen and ran a hand through her mass of curls, 'You didn't really. There's so much to do, and it's so daft. We'll be exactly the same people after the wedding as we were before. Seems a lot of paraphernalia for a piece of paper.'

Grace frowned; it wasn't like her friend to be dismal. 'It's rather more than that, Daze! You're showing the world that you're in love. It's a celebration. It'll all be incredible, I promise.'

'Thanks, Grace. I'll make up the spare room bed ready

for you today, and then I can write it on the list of things to do, and then enjoy crossing it off straight away!'

'Why not have a rest now, and then I'll make up my bed when I get there. In fact, why not leave anything we can tackle together until I arrive. It'll be fun!'

'Thanks, Grace. Now, you'd better go and peel back the lids and shove things in the microwave.'

Grace glanced at the clock she'd been keeping half an eye on ever since she'd first started talking to Daisy. There was half an hour until Rob's train was due to arrive at Leicester station. 'It's a shove in the oven job, actually. I thought I ought to make half an effort! I think I'll go and pop it all in the oven, and then brush my hair and stuff.'

'Don't tell me you haven't brushed it already?'

'Of course I have, but I'm nervous. It'll give me something to do!'

'Call me tomorrow! Good luck.'

Grace ran the brush through her hair for a third time and stared at her reflection in the circular mirror that hung on the hall wall. She was conscious of a faint sheen of nervous perspiration that had coated her palms and the back of her neck. 'Oh don't be so ridiculous, Grace!'

Heading to the bathroom to wash her hands under the tap, Grace gave herself a mini lecture. 'It's bad enough to give him a pre-prepared meal, and introduce him to your muddle; you can't expect him to have to hold a clammy hand as well.' *Assuming he wants to hold your hand of course.*

Niggling doubts about her blossoming relationship with Rob began to whisper at the back of Grace's head. *Why haven't I heard from him much this week? One email isn't exactly the sign of keenness, is it?*

Grace looked out of the kitchen window, peering as far as she could see down the street. If Rob intended to take a taxi from the station then he'd be here very soon now. If he walked, he'd be another half an hour yet.

Deciding to be sensible, having already arranged and rearranged the table with cutlery, wine glasses, and plates, and with the freshly cooked chicken and ham in cheese sauce plus potato gratin staying warm in the oven, Grace knew there was nothing to be gained from staring out of the window.

Her nerves would only get worse if she hovered around without doing anything. So sitting back at her desk, Grace shuffled through her notebooks and found where she'd scribbled the proposed title for the paper she and Rob had decided to write together, wondering how he'd got on sorting through all the primary evidence she'd lent him.

Thinking that discussing the paper would at least give them something to talk about if the conversation ran dry and became awkward, Grace began to compile a list of possible points to cover; even though as Rob had volunteered to write most of it, he'd probably done that himself already.

Grace had six ideas scribbled down when the front door bell rang, making her jump. Her heart immediately thudded faster in her chest, and she felt excitedly queasy. *Oh for goodness sake, woman. Get a grip!* Taking a long exhalation of air, Grace went to let Rob into her home.

Passing her a bottle of wine and a bunch of flowers, Rob seemed vaguely embarrassed, 'I know these are clichéd, but well, I wanted to get you something, and I have to confess I chickened out of anything that there was a danger of you hating.'

Grace laughed and found herself relaxing in the face of his anxiety, 'The flowers are beautiful.' She buried her face into the bunch of sunshine yellow roses. 'I love them, and they are extra special, because no one has ever bought me roses before.'

'You're kidding.' Rob put the wine down on the table, and smiled broadly as he surveyed her living room. 'I can't believe that's true.'

Grace braced herself as she watched him look around her living room, 'Do you want to run a mile now you've seen what sort of organised chaos I live in?' She ran her own eyes over the piles of books, folders, and newspapers, that had never got put away properly, and saw through a stranger's eyes how old and worn the sofa and armchair were, and how badly the threadbare carpet needed replacing.

'Not at all. It is precisely as I imaged it; a glorious hotchpotch of clean clutter.' Rob took hold of Grace's hand, 'It is rather similar to my own home, but obviously you have the edge when it comes to pictures of outlaws on the walls.'

Feeling the warmth of his palm flow through her, Grace smiled back at him, 'At least they are tastefully framed.'

'This is true.'

Coming back to her senses, and going into hostess mode, Grace pulled away from Rob and carried her flowers into the kitchen. Calling over shoulder to see if he wanted a drink, Grace found herself yelling straight at him, as Rob had followed her into the tiny cooking space. 'Blimey, you made me jump.'

'Something I seem to be in the habit of doing.' He took hold of both her hands this time, and Grace's insides did a back flip as Rob drew her against him.

As Rob's lips came to hers, Grace had vague thoughts that she ought to turn the oven down before the chicken burnt, but they dissolved as his right hand transferred itself from her palm to her rear, and sent mini electric shots of desire through her denims and down her legs.

He didn't speak, and Grace didn't want to break the tantalising new tension in the room. It hung heavy with a desire she hadn't felt for years, and without knowing how he did it, Grace found herself backed against the closed kitchen door, with a hand cupping her groin and Rob's steel blue eyes fixed into hers.

Grace sighed into his renewed kisses, as her hips moved forward to meet his firm caress, reassuring Rob without words that she welcomed his touch. As Grace reached up, and felt the broad curve of Rob's shoulders as he moved his palms to her waist.

The warmth of Rob's touch seemed to burn straight through Grace's clothes, and sent flickers of bliss shooting from her toes to the pit of her stomach, and onwards, racing from her throat in a gentle mewl of pleasure.

'Hello, you.' He removed her hand, making Grace sigh softly into his shoulder, as he cradled her close. 'Nice?'

'Mild understatement, Dr Franks.' Grace took a few moments to recover herself, before she double-checked her approval of his kisses by rising up on her tiptoes and testing that she liked them all over again.

It was the smell of burning that bought her out of her unexpectedly aroused state.

'Oh, hell!' Hurrying to the oven Grace pulled open the door, only to be greeted by a waft of charred steam, and confronted by two very dried-out chicken breasts and some rather caramelised potatoes.

Grace wanted to burst into tears. Seconds ago she'd been riding on an emotional and physical high, and now she couldn't even give the man who'd made her feel so incredible an edible dinner.

Turning off the oven, Rob shut its door. 'Fish and chips cuddled up on the sofa?'

Smiling at him gratefully, Grace nodded. 'Come on. There's a great takeaway around the corner.'

Eating the last chip from the greasy paper spread out on the coffee table before them, Grace said, 'I've made a few notes about the paper you suggested writing,' as she snuggled in further under Rob's arm and rested her head on his shoulder, 'you want to see them?'

'Yes, but not now. I'm more interested in you telling me about how Mathilda is getting on.'

'Really? Well, she's in a bit of a pickle right now. Someone's been killed, and she is looking like the chief suspect.'

Rob laughed, 'Grace, you are adorable. Only you could call being accused of murder as being "in a bit of a pickle." Most people would add at least a handful of expletives into that statement.'

'I don't like swearing. Old fashioned, but I can't help thinking there are far more interesting adjectives out there than offensive ones.'

'Not so much a fourteenth girl as a Victorian one then?' He kissed the top of her head as he spoke.

'Oh I don't know; some of those Victorian gals could be pretty risqué, you know.'

'Is that so?' Rob returned his attention to her lips, and Grace decided he tasted as good flavoured with salt and vinegar from the fish and chips as he did without.

They'd kissed, chatted, and kissed all evening, and although Grace had enjoyed every second, her body kept nagging at her. If he could make her feel that good with just his kisses, how on earth would he make her feel if he stayed the night?

Unsure how to ask if he was planning to stay, Grace took a deep breath and was about to speak when Rob beat her to it.

'The last train is in half an hour, love. Do I take it, or do I stay? It has to be your choice. I will respect either decision.'

Grace giggled, 'But you'd prefer one answer over the other, I suspect?'

'You've become very sure of yourself since our time in the kitchen.'

Blushing, Grace said, 'Well, actually, you're giving

yourself away.' She said no more, but allowed her eyes to flash towards his obviously enlarged crotch, that was pushing none too subtly against his jeans.

'Which is why I need to go now if I'm going; I can't vouch for my good behaviour if I stay much longer.'

'Then stay.' Grace didn't even hesitate, all her qualms about being alone with this man had gone. All she wanted was for him to ravish her right there, right now, and then do the same thing all over again once they'd reached her bedroom.

'Thank God!' Rob turned around, and half tickled, half cuddled a giggling Grace until she was laying full length on her sofa. He moved her like she weighed nothing, and somehow, under the intensity of his desire driven gaze, Grace stopped laughing. All of a sudden she felt as if she was the most attractive woman in the world. What the hell had she being doing even having coffee with Malcolm? Daisy had been right again. In that moment, Grace found she wanted Rob by her side for at the wedding. It wouldn't be right without him now.

'Rob? Will you come to Daisy's wedding with me?'

'And see you in a posh frock and tottering in heels?'

'And nice underwear ...'

He groaned slightly, 'How could a man resist? When is it again?'

'8th August, It's a Friday.' Grace whispered into his ear, suddenly feeling that her shirt was far too tight, and life would be a hell of a lot better when she could take it off.

Rob drew back a fraction, regret etched across his face, 'Oh hell. I knew that date meant something, but I couldn't remember. Damn!'

'What's the matter?'

'I can't come. I'm in Houston the week before for a conference I planned before I came home. The 8th is the day I fly home. Damn. I'd have loved to come with you.'

Grace was amazed at how let down she felt, even

though she knew it wasn't Rob's fault he was busy. After all, only a few hours ago she had seriously considered asking someone else to the wedding. Trying to hide her disappointment, Grace brushed it away, 'Well I'll just have to take my toyboy then, won't I!'

Rob's eyes narrowed, 'You have a toyboy, Dr Harper?'

'Not really, it was only the department secretary's stepson. He took me out for coffee, and then he ...'

'What?' Rob stood up, leaving Grace feeling alone and vulnerable on the sofa, 'you've been seeing someone else?'

'Of course not! Well, not on purpose.'

'Not on purpose?' The smile in Rob's eyes died and turned to stone, 'How can you go on a date not on purpose?'

Panic crept through Grace as she saw the pain in the face before her, 'It wasn't a date. Honestly. I was sort of cornered into it by Agatha, and then ...'

'Save it!' Rob was already striding towards her front door.

Hurrying after him, Grace didn't know what to say, her mouth opened, but everything she wanted to say sounded like feeble excuses.

He spun on the soles of his shoes as he opened the door. 'Enjoy the wedding. I wish I wasn't able to imagine how incredible you've going to look as a bridesmaid. Goodbye, Grace.'

'But ... Rob, it was only coffee. I don't even ... What about the paper?'

'You can kiss goodbye to the paper, Grace. And trust me, that is the only thing you'll be kissing in the future if you two-time the first man you've dated in years this early on in a relationship!'

Chapter Twenty-seven

Grace felt as though she'd been dropped from a great height.

Slumped on her desk chair, she stared across at the sofa. If didn't seem right to sit on it somehow. Even though he'd gone, Rob's presence continued to fill the room like a confused spectre.

How had they gone from being happily snuggled together, feeding each other chips like a couple of loved up teenagers, to him storming out of her home and accusing her of seeing someone else.

What made it worse was that Grace knew that technically he was right. She *had* seen someone else, but she hadn't been given a lot of choice. And she had actively been trying to get out of the dinner date all day.

Grace had tried to call Rob's mobile twice, but his phone was switched off. Now as she sat staring at her phone, longing for it to ring, and for Rob to give her the chance to explain properly, despair overtook her.

She knew could send Rob a text or an email for him to find when he was ready, but Grace didn't think he'd believe a single word she wrote – if he even bothered to read them before pressing 'delete'.

'I have to face it, boys, it's pointless.' Grace spoke to the neatly framed posters that lined the wall behind the sofa, 'Daisy was wrong. Rob can't be the one for me. I know I should have told him about Malcolm straight away, but if he overreacts like that, and can't even be bothered to give me the chance to explain before he stormed out, then he can't be Mr Right. The fact we have interests in common is merely a coincidence.'

Grace closed her eyes to the disapproval she was sure she could see on the faces of all the celluloid Robin Hoods. The last thing she needed was her imagination making them disagree with her as well. She had to face facts; she'd missed the boat where men were concerned. She'd been on her own too long, and had been independent for too many years to understand the rules of the game any more.

Unable to sleep, Grace gave up the unequal struggle to stop her overactive brain from rehashing the previous evening over and over again. She wasn't sure she'd be able to go into her kitchen ever again. It would forever be the place where Rob brought her body to life with his kiss and the gleam in his beautiful round blue eyes.

Wrapping her duvet around her shoulders, Grace looked around her tidy bedroom. It seemed to be mocking her somehow, as if the fact she'd tidied this room more than any other in the hope that Rob might see it had somehow jinxed the whole affair.

Rubbing the sleep from her eyes, Grace took herself downstairs, and braved a glimpse at the clock. She winced. It was only four thirty in the morning.

Flipping open her laptop, Grace sighed. 'Looks like it's just you and me now, Mathilda.'

Reading back through the last few pages of her story, Grace pushed her mind into fourteenth-century mode, and concentrated on asking and answering all the question she knew must be simmering in Mathilda's head as she stood, half-undressed and vulnerable, in front of Robert in the Folville brothers' draughty manor house hall.

Mathilda tried to think. Why would the rector lie about the dagger? The obvious answer would be that he was the one who'd placed it in her cell ready to be discovered, but why would he do that? His reputation as the most ruthless brother, apart from Eustace, was well deserved if you

211

believed the local rumours of rape and murder, although Mathilda was sure that he'd never been caught or tried for any of his crimes.

Robert's chair scraped against the dirty stone floor as he stood up, his feet still booted for riding, and his cloak grimy from so long in the saddle.

Mathilda studied him properly for the first time that morning. He appeared sallow and strained, but then, she realised, he had just lost a friend. Although she couldn't understand why Robert was friendly with such an unpleasant man. After only one day in his company, Mathilda had no problem with imagining Hugo upsetting someone enough for them to kill him, but she could see the situation had clearly rattled Robert more than he would ever be likely to admit.

'Get dressed, Mathilda.' Robert broke off each word as though he was snapping twigs with his voice. 'Sarah, bring the girl to the kitchen. It is time we bought her up to date. Then we have a new mission for her.'

The way he spoke, as if she wasn't even there, sent shivers up Mathilda's spine. He seemed a far cry from the Robert who had given her the fine girdle belt she now hung back around her waist. She felt his eyes on her, or rather on the leather belt, as she dressed, her fingers struggling not to fumble over the exquisite fastening.

The kitchen was welcomingly warm compared to the open space of the hall. Allward was busily sorting out vegetables ready for Sarah cook up some broth for tomorrow, but when he saw the trio come into the room, he immediately stopped what he was doing, bowed to his master, and offered him some ale.

'Thank you,' Robert took the pottery cup. Mathilda immediately recognised it as one of Geoffrey of Reresby's, and felt a stab of resentment. The Folvilles were expecting to receive the repayment of her father's ill-advised loan, and yet they hadn't even been bothered to buy his pottery to help him reach that aim.

'Sit down, Mathilda. And you, Allward. We must keep this brief, for there is much to do.'

Mathilda realised she didn't understand this man at all. Robert may only have been the youngest son of a noble family, but it wasn't usual for someone of his status to sit at the same table as the household servants, and yet he did it freely; although not when his brothers were around. Perhaps his Robyn Hode-inspired principles ran as deeply as he'd proclaimed after all.

'Allward, explain quickly to Mathilda where you were after the noon bell yesterday.'

The boy shifted uncomfortably, obviously as unused to being treated as an equal as Mathilda was.

'Come on, boy, time is short.'

'Sorry, my Lord.' Allward sat up straight and turned his small round face towards Mathilda. 'Acting on instruction from my Lord Robert I secretly rode to the household of your father, Bertred of Twyford, to observe their condition.'

Mathilda gasped and turned to Robert, 'My Lord, you did?'

Robert concurred, 'I thought you would be happier in your mind if you knew that your family were still safe and well. Besides, I owed you an apology, and this seemed a good way. However, in the light of recent events it seems my sending of Allward on this mission was timely. You understand the significance of Master Hugo being found so close to your family home, I am sure.'

Mathilda inclined her head.

With a nudge in the ribs from Sarah, Allward carried on his commentary. 'I kept to the outskirts of the workshop and house. I did not wish to be seen.'

'They looked well? Were they all there? Oswin, as well as my father and Matthew?'

'Your father was in the workshop. He was, if the sounds travelling from the window could be trusted, stacking the kiln with fresh pots for firing. He was also talking to someone, but beyond being able to tell you that his companion was male, I know nothing more. I saw no one, and I did not hear him reply. Your brother Matthew could be seen through the kitchen window, and from his grumbles about having to do women's work, I suspect he had taken on your duties. I saw no sign of Oswin.'

Mathilda was silent for a second, and then addressed Robert, 'Thank you, my Lord. I am indeed easier in my mind for knowing they are well, and that my father hasn't given up hope, and is still working to pay his debts.'

'But you wish you knew where Oswin was.'

Mathilda didn't ask how Robert had guessed this. It was obvious. 'I do. May I ask, what time did you leave them, Allward? Long before the death of Master Hugo?'

'By at least two hours, if not more. I'm not good at timekeeping. I saw no sign of the leatherworker or any of his household in the area.'

'And you saw no one else nearby?'

'There was a horse tethered in the orchard, but I assumed that to belong to whoever was in the workshop with your father. There was no one else around until I got back to the heart of the village, and then it was just locals going about their business. Nor were there any about when I returned to Twyford this evening, after news of Master Hugo's attack had reached us.'

Robert was grave, 'Thank you, Allward, you may get on now, two such trips in one day will have made you behind with your work.'

Evidently relived to be able to excuse himself, the boy disappeared out of the kitchen.

'You are wondering who was with your father in the workshop around noon?' Robert's thoughtful gaze landed on Mathilda. 'Do you recall if any clients were due to visit him this week?'

'There were none expected when I was last there, my Lord, but of course, that doesn't mean new orders couldn't have come in.' Although, even as she said it, Mathilda knew that to be unlikely. If there had been money coming in soon, she was sure that her father would have pledged it to the Folvilles when he was informed that his daughter had been taken in lieu of repayment of debts, as so Robert would have been aware of it already.

'And you can think of no one it could have been?'

Mathilda shook her head dumbly.

'Then perhaps I should tell you what I think, Mathilda.' Robert banged his cup upon the table. 'I believe that after only a day in your company one of my friends is dead. And this came only hours after he reported to me of how badly you behaved while you worked for him. How you were late to your duties, and how you refused to serve one of his most important customers.'

Sarah put a restraining hand on Mathilda's arm as the girl opened her mouth to protest, and somehow she swallowed her words as Robert went on.

'I have sworn to my brothers that you can be trusted, and here I am in an impossible position. Richard is convinced you had a dagger with you in the cell. My dagger, I assume? Where is it now?'

Mathilda swallowed. 'It was in my cot. I put it under my mattress when I got back from Bakewell ready to return it to you. When I awoke after falling asleep in the cell it was by my feet. I swear upon Our Lady herself that I did not have it with me when I went in.'

'That does not answer my question, Mathilda. No one knew I had given you the dagger, unless you told them about it.'

'Only Sarah knew, and only because she saw it in the cell when she bought me some broth.'

'This is the truth, my Lord.' Sarah rose from her seat and went to the cutlery store. Checking around her to make sure no one else was watching, she reached a hand to the very back of the cupboard, and pulled out a rag-covered bundle, which she passed then to Robert.

Unwrapping his dagger, examining it for signs of flesh and blood, of which there were none, he spoke more quietly. 'And you truly did not have this with you when we returned you to the cell?'

'I swear.'

Robert was quiet for a moment. 'I am grateful to you, Sarah, for stowing this.' He picked up the blade. 'I will return it to its rightful place.'

No one spoke for a while, and Mathilda began to fidget in her seat. She was thinking harder than she ever had before. Who could have put the dagger in the cell? And why? 'May I speak, my Lord?'

'Go on.' Robert positively oozed suspicion, but he held his tongue while she spoke.

'Perhaps whoever put the dagger in the cell wanted to add credence to your belief that I did wrong by Master Hugo. It could suit whoever that person is to paint a black picture of my character.'

'Master Hugo has never had cause to lie to me, Mathilda. I suggest you tread very carefully with what you say next.'

Sweat was gathering on Mathilda's forehead as she ploughed on with her desperate theory, 'Perhaps it was an act meant to add to the suffering of my family. It does seem as if someone is trying to blacken my family's name and reputation. I am here, my father is in debt, and my brother is missing, and now a body has been found near my home.'

'There is another possibility, of course.' Sarah stared meaningfully at Robert while gathering the vegetables prepared by Allward to peel. 'Someone could be out to blacken a name all right, but not yours, Mathilda.'

Robert stared at the housekeeper carefully, 'Go on.'

'My Lord, it was you who proclaimed a trust of Mathilda to your brothers – a trust you have been made to think was broken. I know it was not. Also, it is *your* friend who has died. A man who, if you will forgive me saying so, was not held in high esteem by many. He was an excellent craftsman, without doubt, but his personal habits were often rumoured to be questionable. I wonder if it was not Mathilda who is being framed as the target for unpalatable attention, but you, my Lord.'

Mathilda could feel her pulse race as she added, 'Our Lady save us, my Lord! It was *your* dagger planted in my cell.'

'Tell me, Mathilda, on your soul, and that is not a threat I make lightly, did you tell me the truth? Did Master Hugo send you the wrong way as you claim? Did Coterel help you return to spite the man?'

'I promise my Lord. I promise you that is the truth.'

Chapter Twenty-eight

'We have another pressing issue aside from Master Hugo's death. More pressing perhaps.'

The following morning Mathilda found herself standing, once again, across the table from Eustace and Robert in the main hall, but this time without the reassuring back up of the housekeeper, who was catching up with her work. She couldn't begin to imagine what could possibly be more important than clearing her family name of murder. Or at least establishing if it was threatened in the first place.

The set expression on Eustace's face however told her he was in deadly earnest. Robert and Eustace were joined by the younger brother Walter, whose expression was carefully blank. The tension, which always radiated throughout the hall, seemed heightened somehow as Eustace continued, 'The message you collected from Coterel, Mathilda, means that the time for action is almost upon us. In the light of recent events however, it would be foolish for myself or any of my family to be seen in the region intended.'

Wary of asking questions she'd be better off not knowing the answers to, Mathilda decided to not enquire what that message had meant beyond the obvious arranging of a meeting, Mathilda placed her hands over her belt in an attempt to be calmed by its beauty. For the first time she wished she still had the dagger Robert had loaned her. She had an unpleasant premonition that she was going to need it.

Glancing briefly at his brothers, Eustace continued, 'This means that we require your assistance once more. Mathilda, Robert has assured the three of us that you did act as you claimed during your last visit to Derby after all, and so we are inclined to trust you again.'

The three of us. Did that mean that the absent brothers,

John and Richard, did not trust her? Where was the rector anyway? Mathilda wasn't sure if his absence was more or less disturbing than his presence. Aware that she really didn't want to find out, Mathilda listened anyway, in the hope that further explanation would be forthcoming, along with news of her family and the hunt for Master Hugo's murderer that must surely underway by now.

For every second of the past twelve hours Mathilda had expected the sheriff's men to come knocking at the Folvilles' front door; but so far there had been nothing. Were the brothers expecting a visit from the authorities as well? Is that why they wanted to be seen to be here, rather than roaming the countryside with messages they shouldn't be replaying? There was certainly an air of unease that had taken the edge off their usual self-assured arrogance.

'At midnight tonight I am due to meet Coterel myself to speak of future matters. This is no longer possible. I wish you to go in my place, and meet him to present a gesture of my trust, and rearrange a new time and place to marshal our plan and make sure of each other's intentions.'

The way Eustace chewed at his words, his fists clenched against the table, made it all too clear how angry he was at having to reschedule whatever he'd been plotting. The blood drained from Mathilda's face as she realised she was going to have to represent the most feared Folville. 'Me? How, my Lord?'

Robert took over from Eustace, while all the time the eyes of Walter remained fixed on Mathilda, making her wonder if the man ever blinked. 'There is to be an exchange. A gesture to show that we each understand and agree to this frustrating need for delay. It will be a show of good faith on both sides. Nicholas Coterel will give us a signal or an item we desire to see, and in return we will give him something. Something you will carry to them for us.'

'But ...' her forehead furrowed with confusion.

'Mathilda, there has been a murder.' Robert snapped through her sentence, 'The victim can be connected to this household, and at least one member of this household has made no secret of his dislike of Master Hugo.'

'Father Richard, my lord?' Mathilda whispered the words, not quite sure if she was permitted to speak or not; but every instinct in her telling her she was right.

'Indeed.' Robert's brow darkened as he spoke, 'And although Hugo was a loyal friend to me, my Godly brother felt unable to exercise the forgiveness men of the cloth are so often spouting, deciding instead to damn him to hell for his inclinations. Inclinations he never actually had. He was fiercely loyal, and coveted exclusiveness to his friendships, but that was all.'

'Inclinations?' Mathilda searched the faces of the men sat before her. Each one was carefully blank.

Ignoring her enquiry, Robert continued, 'you will be escorted, but from the shadows. To all intents and purposes you will appear to be alone.'

There was a silence, and Mathilda took her chance, 'The item I am to deliver?'

'It is a package. Only small. You'll easily be able to conceal it about your person.'

As nothing was to be achieved by arguing, Mathilda decided to be practical, 'But surely I am to be accompanied by someone else as well as my hidden escort? A woman out on her own so late at night will cause suspicion.'

'It will be me alone.' Robert walked towards the fire to warm his hands, 'I will be keeping to the trees. You won't see me, but I will be there at all times. The route you need to take is wooded on either side. My concealment will not be difficult.'

'And what of the concealment of others? Outlaws are not unknown between here and Bakewell, I could be taken by them, or by the sheriff's men if they identify me as my father's daughter. I have no doubt they will suspect him of having a hand in Master Hugo's death.'

Robert bristled. 'I have given my word that you'll be kept safe. That should be enough for you.'

Mathilda said nothing else, hoping that his Hode-style surveillance would be enough to keep her safe. Unconvinced that Robert had completely stopped believing all the poison fed to him by Master Hugo prior to his death, she couldn't help thinking that she'd be safer if Eustace was shadowing her.

'May I ask what I might expect to transport back in return?'

'I will tell you as we travel.' Robert nodded to his brothers for confirmation, inviting them to add anything he may have missed to Mathilda's instructions.

Addressing Mathilda, Eustace said, 'Be careful, girl. It isn't only your safety wrapped up in this mission. Your family owes me. Money, it is becoming increasingly clear, as each day goes by, isn't something they can easily repay. Your services are becoming a more permanent form of payment. If harm comes to you, and you are no longer able to provide those services, then I will need to extract another form of payment from you father. I am sure that is not something you want.'

'No, my Lord.' Mathilda looked at her feet. The threatening tone of Eustace's voice was replaced by Robert talking again, but she no longer heard what was being said, as she attempted to marshal her thoughts, and get a grip on the thought that was beginning to nag in the back of her head.

Allward had reported that her father had been in the workshop talking with someone before Hugo's death. So, who was the visitor? A new customer? It had to have been. Their regular customers had all but disappeared thanks to Geoffrey of Reresby and his fellow importers.

And where was Oswin? Was he out trying to acquire more money to pay off the debt quicker? There weren't many ways to earn enough extra income that were worth leaving the family business for; and none she could think of that were legal. Mathilda's blood chilled as she considered some of the risks Oswin might be taking to help the family. If he was still alive? She closed her eyes. That was an idea she didn't want to consider.

Oswin might have been two years older than her, but

Mathilda had always looked after him. A large, gentle soul, Oswin always did what he was told; without necessarily spending a lot of time thinking about consequences.

'Mathilda?'

Aware of a pair of startling blue eyes staring into hers, Mathilda came back to earth, shocked to find she was still standing in the hall, with everyone was staring at her.

Robert placed one of his large hands on her shoulder, 'Did you understand that? Do you know what you need to do?'

'I need to save my family.' She spoke slowly, more to herself than to the Folville before her. Then, forgetting her servile status, she stared back at Robert, pushing her shoulders back as she addressed him, 'and if that means I have to stay here and spy or send messages for you and then so be it; although the logic in keeping me here when I could be at home helping them earn money to get you what you are due escapes me, my Lord.' She paused, and placed her hands on her hips. They needed her, so for now at least she could risk a little impertinence. 'But please could you tell me exactly how indebted my father is? If I know how much we owe then perhaps I can help them reach the goal.'

Robert gestured to his seated brothers as if asking how much he should say.

Eustace, with a confirming nod from the ever-mute Walter, said 'The debt your father owes is only partly financial. We have been informed by a reliable source that he did some damage that needs paying for. Money will not make that better. Only his inconvenience will do. His punishment is to find the money he owes without your help. Without his right hand. Since the death of your mother, Mathilda, you are that right hand.'

Thinking furiously, trying to remember a time in which her father had defamed or inconvenienced her captors, Mathilda was about to ask the nature of this inconvenience, when Eustace and Walter rose to their feet, 'Robert, the girl knows enough. Too much for her own safety, perhaps. Any more would be unwise for us and dangerous for her. I suggest you repeat the instructions she plainly didn't hear, and then hand her over to Sarah. She might as well make herself useful and work in the kitchen until it is time to go.'

The brothers swept around the table and stood before Mathilda like a solid wall of intimidation. Eustace, his hand resting on the hilt of his sword, spoke with a final deliberation. 'Some advice, young woman; don't ask questions. Do what you are told, and perhaps one day you'll get to go home.'

Grace pulled back from the laptop. There was water falling on the keyboard, and for a moment she wasn't sure where it was coming from.

Angrily wiping her tears away, Grace resigned herself to leaving Mathilda's fate hanging in the balance, and ran to the bathroom.

Stripping off her pyjamas she turned on the shower, and leapt under the water before it had had the chance to warm up. Shivering beneath the cool spray Grace worked a bar of lemon-scented soap between her palms. As the temperature climbed, and steam began to fill the small cubicle, Grace scrubbed at her flesh, giving her tears of loss free range to fall down her face, without a single sound escaping from her lips.

Trying to blank out the hurt that had been etched on Rob's face by focusing on Mathilda's story, and concentrate on where she was going to take her medieval captive next, Grace found the face of Robert de Folville merging with Rob's as he'd lent in to kiss her. She shook her head hard, but the face of Mathilda began to blur, taking on her own form, and Malcolm (or possibly Nicholas), had started to shout in the background. He was telling her she was late for coffee and she should just sit down and listen to him tell her about how he'd come first in an archery competition, and …

Grace slammed her hand against the shower's off button, and grabbing a towel from its hook scrubbed at her wet body. Her mind felt as if it was about to explode from an insane mixture of past and present, fact and fiction, and suddenly she didn't want to be at home any more. She didn't want to be in the house where she had so *almost* been happy, with her only friends bar Daisy captured inside lifeless glass frames on her walls.

Not sure what time it was, Grace moved around her home without seeing anything but what was directly before her, and without thinking of anything but escape. Glad it was the summer, and that she had no further student commitments beyond those that could be sorted via email until September, Grace only experienced a minor pang of guilt as she stuffed handfuls of underwear into her old student-hood holdall.

Piling some tops, spare jeans, jumpers, and a spare pair of trainers on top of her screwed up lingerie; Grace took a separate smaller bag, and more carefully placed in it the shoes she'd bought for Daisy's wedding, her toiletries, and a hair brush, before returning to the living room.

Turning the computer back on, she printed out the last two chapters of her novel, picked up her notebook and a selection of pens, and making sure her phone charger and purse were in her handbag, Grace shrugged on her leather jacket and boots, and slamming the front door behind her, fished her mobile from her pocket. Without a backward glance, Grace rang her most frequently dialled number.

'Daisy, I know it's a bit earlier than planned, but can I come and stay?'

Chapter Twenty-nine

As the taxi pulled up outside the house, Daisy yanked her front door open. Grace appeared tired and drawn. There were faint traces of streaks on her face where tears had run recently. Daisy couldn't remember the last time she'd seen Grace cry – if she ever had. Normally any boyfriend-related upset or unsuitable brief encounter was brushed aside with an 'I'm OK' smile, or tackled head-on with a pizza, a bottle of wine, and a Robin Hood film. If that tried and tested strategy hadn't worked, then this was serious.

Hiding her concern behind the genuine relief that she was going to have another pair of hands helping get everything ready for her fast approaching nuptials, Daisy took the largest bag from Grace's hands. 'I can't believe you still have that old holdall! I haven't seen it since we went backpacking around the country after our second year at Uni!'

'Oh you know me, Daze. If it isn't worn out to the point of disintegration then I'll get some use out of it.' Glad she could rely on Daisy not to drown her in a wave of unhelpful sympathy; Grace followed her friend through the cosy cottage. 'As I am now officially student-free until 6th October, and all my work can be done wherever I happen to be via the marvel of those twin inventions, the pen and paper, I thought I'd arrive early to help out. So, here I am, ready to muck in.'

'Or muck out more like!' Daisy pointed to the bucket and shovel propped against the back door, 'The stable is in use at the moment. I was about to clean it out, but the prospect of a coffee with you first is rather more appealing! Cuppa?'

'Tea would be good if you're sure the stable can wait? I had an obscene about of coffee on the train, and although it has done its job and kept me awake, it's all I can taste now.'

Sitting down at the oak table in the centre of the kitchen, Grace stretched out her legs and let the tension drain from her shoulders. As she observed Daisy sorting out drinks, she knew she'd come to the right place. And if she could help her friend with the preparation for the most important day of her life; then at least the irrational abandonment of her home couldn't be classed as running away.

Only when they were sat with steaming mugs of builder's tea did Daisy address the real reason for the nature of Grace's welcome, but sudden, arrival.

'Go on then. What happened that was so bad an episode of *Robin of Sherwood* failed to fix it?'

Grace sighed as she blew across the surface of her drink, causing it to ripple perilously across the top of the mug, 'Believe it or not, that didn't even cross my mind, to sit and lose myself in Robin Hood stuff I mean.'

Cradling her depressingly appropriate 'Keep Calm and Carry On' mug, Grace was rather shocked at herself. Not only hadn't she taken her oft-practised self-defensive route of hiding in a past she'd never experienced, together with an accompanying excess of calories, it hadn't even occurred to her to do so. 'I know, it's all my fault. Rob arrived on time. He bought me a gift and he was so lovely. I burnt the dinner, but that wasn't a problem because the reason why I burnt the dinner was so ...' Grace trailed off as she squeezed her eyes closed for a split second trying to block out the memory of how delicious their time in the kitchen had been before forcing herself to carry on, 'so we ended up having fish and chips instead. After that, I'm not sure what happened.'

Fixing her eyes on her mug of tea, Grace kept talking,

trying to make sense of the situation for herself as well as for Daisy, 'I asked Rob if he wanted to come to your wedding with me, and he said he couldn't because he was travelling back to Houston that day. I was really disappointed, and made some flippant joke about having to take my toyboy to hide the fact that I minded. That's when I told him about Malcolm, and Rob went sort of distant. His face went all dark.' Grace spoke faster and faster, as if trying to get the explanation of the confusion of his reactions out of the way as quickly as possible. 'But I wasn't allowed to explain, you see, and then he was gone. I've never felt alone like that before. I love my own space, and being in my little house by myself. This morning though, Daze, I didn't want to be on my own any more, and ...' She sighed sadly, 'I suppose I've run away.'

Daisy's face was etched with curious concerned, 'You seem to have given me the edited highlights and not the whole story.' She reached out and laid a hand over her friend's wrist to still her manic stirring of her tea. 'How about leaving the "all by myself" stuff for a minute, and telling me *exactly* what happened.'

'Everything?'

'The lot. From start to finish. Especially the bit that contains the reason why the dinner burnt. I can only help if I know *everything*.'

'It's not that you're being nosy or anything?'

'Well, of course I am, but I want to help, so spill the beans, Dr Harper, or I'll put you on solo stable-cleaning duty all week!'

Daisy had made a second mug of tea each and broken open an emergency packet of chocolate chip cookies before she'd got to grips with what Grace was telling her.

'OK,' Daisy dunked her cookie, 'the situation is this. One; Rob walked out after giving you a mind-blowing snog session because you told him about seeing Malcolm, probably not explaining yourself very well. Two; before you were given the chance to explain properly that you'd been Shanghaied into the coffee date, he'd already run for the hills. Three; you tried to call him but Rob's mobile was off. Four; you haven't left any texts or emails for fear of deletion, and he hasn't sent you any. Then five; meanwhile, you have realised you've fallen in love with him and haven't a clue what to do. Does that sound about right?'

Grace gave Daisy a weak smile. 'I think this wedding has turned you into a serial list-maker.' She wasn't sure what else to say for a moment; she hadn't allowed herself to address the "L" word, not even in her subconscious; and now of course there was no point.

Pushing away the tea she didn't really want, Grace understood for the first time the true feeling behind the phrase 'a heavy heart'.

'You should have seen his face, Daze. It was as if I'd struck him, or something. He looked angry but sort of crushed at the same time.'

Thinking to herself that it sounded very much as if Rob had fallen for Grace as well, and that pride had reared its ugly head and messed everything up for both of them, Daisy got up, 'Come on, let's go and do that stable. The horse in situ at the moment is going home tonight, and I want him and his quarters to be at their best when the owners collect him so they'll use me as a horse holiday home again. Anyway, a bit of physical activity will do you the power of good. It'll clear that addled brain of yours.'

Pleased that her sense of humour hadn't completely died, albeit in a self-deprecating way, Grace said, 'I thought I'd be getting some physical activity this morning, but not from mucking out horses!'

They'd been cleaning and re-spreading hay for half an hour before Grace said, 'Do you think I should call Aggie and ask her to tell Malcolm I won't be there for dinner tonight?'

'Nope. It'll do him good to be stood up. This Malcolm sounds as though his ego could use some bruising.'

'It isn't his fault though; it's mine, I should have turned him down from the off.'

'But you tried and no one was listening.'

Grace dragged an unused hay bale to the doorway, 'I think I will call Aggie though. She was only trying to help, and she'll be wondering where I am.'

'I thought you were allowed to work anywhere you wanted to out of term-time?'

'I am, but I never stray far from my office. She'll think I'm ill.'

'OK, but for goodness sake don't let her persuade you that inviting Malcolm to my wedding would be a good idea!'

'As if I would!'

Watching as her friend left the stable to make her call, Daisy was sure if Grace would explain to Rob what had gone on with Malcolm – which was nothing at all really – they'd be all right. But Grace had decided it was pointless, and when Grace had made that sort of decision experience told Daisy, that it would be difficult budge her opinion.

Ten minutes later, with the stable's temporary resident happily reinstalled, Grace reported back to Daisy. 'Aggie was fine. I told her you needed wedding help and I was here. Hope that's OK? I don't like lying really.'

'Honey, that isn't a lie. I really do need help. You were right about me and making lists at the moment. Every time I cross something off, there is something else to add to it. And Marcus's mother is being ...'

Grace found herself on the edge of a genuine laugh, 'Deep breath, Daze. Tell me what's next to clean out, and you can have a proper panic while we work.'

'Well I could, but to be honest, I'd rather just get on with it. Tell me about the book instead. How is Mathilda

getting on in Folville-land right now? I hope you're
sticking to your guns and making it more story than
historical textbook.'

Mathilda was kneading the dough for the day's bread so
roughly that Sarah was beginning to think it would only be
fit for the pigs. 'Have you never made bread before?'

'Sorry, Sarah.' Mathilda stopped her elbows pumping, but
kept her hands moving over the mixture. 'I was thinking
about tonight.'

Continuing to work at a far more sedate place, lightening
her touch so she aerated the dough properly, Mathilda was
aware that the housekeeper was watching her. 'Do you know
what they want me to do, Sarah?'

'Yes.'

'Oh.' Mathilda didn't know what else to say, the tone of
Sarah's single word response had seemed final, and was
obviously not going to be elaborated on.

Knocking the bread into shape before leaving it to rest,
Mathilda went to a pail of clean water Allward had provided,
and washed the flour from her hands. All the time she
scrubbed at her skin, Mathilda ran the instructions Robert
had given her through her mind. They seemed
straightforward. Too straightforward.

The meeting with the Coterels was to be at midnight
that night. As the sun began to go down, she and Robert
would ride to a midpoint between Ashby Folville and Derby.
When they were about a mile from the meeting place, they
would split up, and she would continue alone until she met
one of the Coterels. Probably Nicholas. While Robert kept as
close to her as possible, but in the shadows. Keeping a
sensible distance, he assured her, not from the Coterel
brothers, who knew he'd be there, but from the law and
unwanted questioning should the sheriff's men be lurking in
the area after Hugo's death. Mathilda had to concede that,
although she didn't want to go alone, this was a sensible
move in the current climate.

Once she'd located the Coterels, Mathilda wouldn't have

to say anything. There was no message to verbally recall. All that was asked of her would be the handing over of the package Robert would entrust to her when they were ready to go. Then an item would be given to her in return, and she would proceed back along the path she'd come from, before Robert returned her to the safety of the Folville manor.

Pointing to a pile of apples that needed peeling, Sarah nodded with satisfaction as Mathilda set to work without complaint. 'I hope you don't mind that I persuaded Robert to let you help me today. As you're here, providing I keep an eye on you, I told him you are of more use around the house than trapped in a cell.'

Not knowing what else to say, Mathilda said, 'Thank you, Sarah.'

'He needed reminding that now, more than ever, it is vital to give the local community the impression that he is interested in you as a future wife. Robert can hardly do that if you are in a cell, and helping with the domestic chores will support the subterfuge.'

Mathilda was shocked for a second. With all that had happened in the last forty-eight hours she'd forgotten about the front she and Robert were supposed to be presenting to the world. She was about to ask why it was it was even more important now, but Sarah had changed the subject. 'I see you must have been a good housekeeper for your family when you're not being distracted by darker issues.'

Mathilda looked up from her work, 'Thank you, Sarah. I hope I was. My mother was very efficient; I try to be like her.'

Heading to the door to check they wouldn't be overheard, Sarah moved to Mathilda's side. 'Don't react, just in case we are watched. I'm about to tell you something that I don't think the brothers know about.'

With a prickle of perspiration dotting the back of her neck, Mathilda exhaled softly, 'Yes, Sarah.'

'I was concerned for your safety in tonight's mission. It all seems too easy somehow. So I sent the stable boy to look at another location yesterday.'

Mathilda's knife slipped, nicking her finger, causing her to drop the fruit. Sucking at the tiny cut, she said, 'Please Sarah, is there news of Oswin?'

'I believe so. The lad rode to the Coterel manor. He entered the stable block and asked for directions he didn't really need so he could look around a little. He spied a young man answering to your brother's description working as a servant in the Coterel household.'

'Oswin is with the Coterels! Are you sure?'

'No, Mathilda, I'm not sure, but it is likely.'

Mathilda suddenly remembered the feeling of being watched she'd had when she was talking to Nicholas Coterel. It had been merely a feeling of being observed, not a sinister sensation that being observed by a stranger can give you. It had to have been Oswin!

'And you don't think the Folvilles know about this?'

'As I said, I don't know for sure. If they do, then I can't think why they haven't told you.'

Mathilda suspected they probably did know, and it was likely that they hadn't told her because it suited them to keep her worried about Oswin. If she had more than one family member to be concerned for it would make doubly sure of her obedience to them.

Keeping this theory to herself, Mathilda said, 'Sarah, please don't think me ungrateful, but why are you helping me like this? It's such a risk for you and Allward, not to mention the stable lad.'

Sarah's usual austere countenance broke into a hitherto unseen gentle concern. 'I told you that I raised almost all the brothers.' She peered around her, alert and wary even in her more soften state, 'and I know it's wrong to have a favourite, but I do.'

'Robert?'

Inclining her head, Sarah's tone was full of regret, 'I have tried to keep him safe. Tried to look after him and his family, but they walk into trouble, those men.'

'Their intentions are good.'

Sarah's expression reverted to its usual shrewd state. 'You really believe that, Mathilda?'

'I wasn't sure, not at first. But, now, I think we can assume that the sheriff's men will be sniffing around my family; and knowing full well how the sheriff likes to find a perpetrator for the crimes in his jurisdiction, even if it isn't the right one – well, some justice seems better than none.'

'Have you heard of Folville's Law, Mathilda?'

'No.'

'What you're doing here, that's Folville's Law. The meeting tonight, that's Folville's Law as well. Just as, if my suspicions are correct, the killer of Master Hugo will be found using Folville's Law.'

'You mean this family takes the law into their own hands and administers its own justice. A more direct form of justice.'

'I mean exactly that.'

'Like in the Robyn Hode stories.'

Sarah smiled. 'You've heard the travelling players sing the Robyn Hode stories?'

'Yes, at the fair last year. I'd heard a few before then as well though. My mother used to sing them to me.'

'They are complex tales, you remember them well?'

'I've always had a good memory for words.'

'Is that so?' The housekeeper picked up some firewood and gestured to Mathilda to follow suit.

Moving into the deserted hall, Sarah knelt to the grate, and tapped the floor for Mathilda to sit with her. 'My grandfather taught me many such songs. Not the Hode ones of course, they're too modern; but the lines he sang with his fellow soldiers after the failure of De Montfort's revolt were fairly similar in sentiment.'

Mathilda gasped; even now, over six decades since Simon de Montfort and his barons had failed in their rebellion against the excesses of King Henry III, it wasn't sensible to mention any sympathies towards them. Mathilda felt oddly flattered that the initially hostile housekeeper was confiding in her in such a way.

'There's one verse that has stayed with me. It's from a song I used to sing to the Folville boys when they were children. Sometimes I wonder if that was such a wise thing to do when they were so impressionable, still ...' Then, much to the younger woman's surprise, Sarah began to sing.

Right and wrong march nearly on equal footing;
there is now scarcely one who is ashamed of doing what is unlawful;
the man is held dear who knows how to flatter;
and he enjoys a singular privilege ...[13]

There was a moment's quiet, and then Mathilda said, 'Things haven't changed much, have they?'

'Sadly, child, they have. It's worse now, much worse.' With a final placing of the cut wood on the fire, Sarah added, 'I think it's time to answer the question you haven't asked me.'

'Which one? I have a great many questions.'

Sarah grinned, 'I am referring to the question that is most important at this moment in the light of Master Hugo's death. Why it is you need to be seen to be Robert's companion at this time, more than ever?'

'Are you ready?'

Robert, dressed from head to toe in brown and grey to aid in his shadowy concealment, reined in his horse as the same bleary-eyed stable lad who'd located Oswin for her hoisted Mathilda into her saddle.

'I am.' Mathilda didn't feel at all ready, but with a new resolve engendered by Sarah, and the knowledge that Oswin was very probably alive, even if he wasn't free to go home, she sat with all the confidence of a woman who fully expected to be Robert's future wife. A concept she was surprised to find didn't repulse her as she'd assumed it would; especially now she knew precisely why it was so vital to her survival, her father's success in paying his debt, and Robert de Folville's very life to appear convincing in the role.

Chapter Thirty

'I can't possibly be in love with him. I barely know him.'

Grace stood at the little bedroom window staring out across Daisy's massive garden, stroking a baby guinea pig who'd been squeaking for attention from the second she had woken up.

Believing being busy was the best cure for the blues, Daisy had barely let up on the hard graft since she'd arrived, and Grace felt physically refreshed after a proper sleep bought on by sheer exhaustion.

Mentally however, she remained bruised and a little bit lost as once again she tried to reason the situation into a more coherent mess by adopting Daisy's newfound list-making skills.

Settling the guinea pig, which she'd decided to call Chutney in honour of his pickle-coloured coat, onto her lap, Grace tore a piece of paper from her notebook. 'OK Chutney, I've proved that I am hopeless at explaining myself out loud, let's see if I can do a bit better with the written word. If I can't, then I might as well give up working on Mathilda's story right now!'

Writing the number 1 on the top left-hand corner of the piece of lined paper, Grace rested her pen next to it and sighed, 'Come on, Chutney, help me out here. I don't know where to start. What should I put first?'

Understanding why the healing powers of stroking animals was considered so beneficial, Grace decided to forget working in a logical order and simply hammer out every feeling and thought she had concerning Rob. She could put them into some sort of sensible order later on.

1. I have lots in common with Rob
2. We get on – at least, I thought we did
3. Conversation is easy
4. He doesn't treat me like I'm weird
5. I feel good when I see his name in my inbox – well, I used to
6. I need to tell him about Malcolm – he may still hate me, but he <u>has</u> to know I didn't do anything wrong. In fact I was bored out of my mind with Malcolm!
7. No one has ever made me so sad that I didn't want to watch a RH film before!
8. He has nice eyes and smile
9. He makes me laugh
10. Our kiss in kitchen

Grace couldn't bring herself to write about exactly how she'd felt in the kitchen. After all, nothing had really happened; but there could be no denying that the air between them had been charged with so much sexual tension and promise (dashed promise now), that she wasn't sure she would ever feel the same cooking in there again. 'Oh, crikey!' Grace lifted Chutney up to her face, 'I've just remembered – the burnt dinner we abandoned is sat in the cold oven!'

Groaning, knowing that her kitchen was going to stink when she eventually faced going home again, Grace took a steadying breath and picked up the mobile she'd turned off the minute she'd arrived in Hathersage.

Switching it back on, she closed her eyes, preparing herself for the disappointment of not seeing any text messages or email alerts from Rob. She had to check though, and was able to stop herself from hoping that there was something from him, even if it was a negative. The familiar hum of *Doctor Who's* TARDIS told Grace she did have a text.

'It probably isn't from Rob, though,' she told the

guinea pig as, with her eyes still closed, she bought the phone closer to her face. Then, stealing herself for a second dose of rejection, Grace looked at the screen.

The text was from her mother.

Cross with herself at her level of disappointment that Rob hadn't contacted her, she ran an eye down her emails instead, of which there were many demanding her workday attention, but none from Rob. Grace balled up the list she'd just written and threw it on her bed in a fit of frustration. Returning Chutney to his hut with his noisy friends, she shrugged sadly, 'If he can't even face sending me an angry message, then that tells me all I need to know, doesn't it?'

Although it was only six o'clock in the morning Grace headed downstairs to see if Daisy had got up yet. When she reached the kitchen Daisy was nowhere to be seen, but it was clear that she was about somewhere. The kettle was warm and her wellington boots were missing.

Knowing her friend could literally be anywhere in the grounds, Grace sat at the table, and began to think through the end of Mathilda's story. One way or another, events were closing in on her fourteenth-century girl.

As she considered her options for Mathilda, Grace realised she'd finally stopped feeling guilty about romanticising the period from which she was convinced the stories of her beloved Robin Hood had come. She knew she'd strayed from the reality of the historical facts of the time, and Mathilda and her family were her own creation; and yet still every string of the tale had echoes of fact running through it. Having made herself a cup of tea, Grace sat at the old kitchen table and, grabbing an old brown paper bag that used to contain rabbit feed, began to write some notes on it to type up later.

As they rode through the subdued evening light, Robert said nothing; his concentration taken up entirely by his surveillance of the landscape around them.

For once the quiet didn't make Mathilda feel uncomfortable. She welcomed more time to think back over the conversation she'd had with the housekeeper that afternoon.

After Sarah had confided in her while they'd made up the hall fire, they'd gone on to discuss more about the troubles in London. She'd told Mathilda that a merchant had been adding to the buzz of gossip that had been circulating the weekly market for some months now. Unwisely telling anyone who'd listen, rather too loudly, about the latest liberties taken by King Edward II's wife Isabella and her lover Mortimer, who had stolen power from the King almost two years ago, and how the violence and corruption which had become commonplace in London were spreading fast in every direction across England as its population remained unsure who was actually in charge.

The conversations that Mathilda's father and brothers had about the way the country was being run when they knew they were alone, and out of ear shot of anyone who might report them, had given her the impression that the local sheriff, Sir Robert Ingram, and his bailiff were already corrupt and that there was very little they'd refrain from doing if the money was right.

While Sarah had been talking to her about events in the south, the thoughts that had been vying for attention in Mathilda's head had begun to crystallise. The fog of fear for her own safety had lifted, and she was beginning to see the reality of the situation more clearly.

Although undeniably tough and uncompromising, the Folvilles, and quite probably the Coterels as well, had decided that the law was failing them. That was why they did what they did. They weren't the good guys, and Mathilda certainly disapproved of many of their more extreme actions, but compared to the avaricious excesses of the authorities, they were the lesser of two evils. In Mathilda's eyes they became more like Robyn Hode and his outlaws every day. After all, the merry men were fictional characters who weren't exactly saints, but compared to those in power within their stories, they were principled indeed.

Breaking the silence as they left Ashby Folville far behind them, Robert pointed the horses towards a path that would take them deep into Charnwood Forest. 'Are you scared of the dark, Mathilda?'

'No.' Mathilda spoke honestly. 'But I am afraid of what may lurk in the dark.'

'Very wise.' Robert smiled, reminding Mathilda of how handsome he could look. 'In ten miles the path will split and I will go one way, and you the other. For a few moments you will be alone, but after that the path sweeps around and I will be riding parallel to you.'

Not allowing her hands to tremble with the nerves that had been slowly bubbling back up in her stomach, Mathilda pushed her shoulders further back and sat bolt upright in the saddle. 'And the package?'

'You already have it.'

'No my Lord, I don't.' Mathilda's voice gave away a little of her uncertainty. Had Sarah been meant to give her something before they left the manor?

'I'm afraid you do.' Robert reined his horse in next to Mathilda's, bringing them to a halt for a moment.

Reaching out a hand, he gently flipped her cloak to one side to reveal the finery of her leather girdle belt. He smoothed it with a single finger of his gloved hand. 'That is their prize, Mathilda.'

'My belt?'

'Sadly, yes.'

'But ...'

Robert nodded, 'I regret I told you it was for you. It was my honest intension for you to keep it once you left us. However, with the death of Hugo ...' He lapsed into a silence that seemed to spread out into the grey night as the tress thickened around them.

The horses moved forward again. Mathilda shivered as Robert spoke in a more guarded fashion, 'The belt is needed to prove our goodwill to Coterel. It is a valuable object, and now Hugo has gone, is worth more still.'

She nodded with sad understanding, stroking one hand over the intricate lattice work, 'I shall miss it. I've never owned an object of such beauty before, even if only for a little while.'

'I almost did, but I fear I may have ruined my chances.'

Mathilda turned her head toward Robert's face sharply, 'My Lord?'

Robert said no more on the subject, pointing instead to a fork in the path. They were getting close to their undisclosed destination.

The texture of the air seemed to change the second Robert was out of sight. Despite her resolve to be brave and see this through, spurred on by the hope that if Nicholas Coterel was in receptive mood, she would take the chance to ask him about Oswin, Mathilda was even more frightened than she'd expected to be. The trees felt as if they were closing in on either side of her, and that the light of the moon was being physically snuffed out by the close-knit overhanging branches.

Suddenly all the jolly outlaw stories she had ever heard the mummers sing and watched being acted out in fairs and markets seemed to take on a sinister edge. Forgotten were all the verses about getting the better of a corrupt authority. Now all Mathilda could recall were the verses of violence. How the outlaws had skulked in the forest, how they had waylaid travellers and demanded a tax to pass by. The words, *'To invite a man to dinner, and then him to beat and bind. It is our manner,'* drowned out the lull of her usual happier recalled line, *'For he was a good outlaw, and did poor men much good ...'* [14]

Her ears alert for every rustle of leaves and every possible crack of a twig under foot or hoof, Mathilda's mind merged and muddled her thoughts, entwining them into the ballads she held so dear. From the depths of her mind she remembered the devious potter who'd double crossed Robin. *'... The potter, with a cowards stroke, smot the shield out of Robin's hand ...'* [15]

'The potter!' Mathilda more breathed the words than

spoke them. The gloom surrounding her became more suffocating, and her eyes flitted from one side of the path to the other as her mind forced another line of verse out of her murmuring lips. '*I have spyed the false felon, As he stondis at his masse ...*'[16]

She wasn't sure why the random utterance of this line from *Robyn Hode and the Monk* made all the hairs on the back of her neck stand up, but with a feeling that a ghost had crossed her path, Mathilda tried even harder to spot the shadow of Robert through the trees. Although she knew that being unable to see him didn't mean he wasn't there, she wished she could see him just a little bit.

Feeling cold and alone, Mathilda's common sense seemed unable to unlatch itself from her overactive imagination. Her thoughts flew to Master Hugo and the terror he must have experienced as he realised what was happening to him as the dagger got closer and closer ... a shadow fell across the ever-narrowing path, and Mathilda started as her horse snorted into the stagnant air. Pulling the reins hard, she came to a stop and looked behind her.

Mathilda was convinced she was being watched, and not just by Robert.

Was it Robert, a Coterel, soldiers, men out on the hue and cry, or outlaws who were observing her? Mathilda pressed on again, her unease making her grip her leather reins so tight that they were in danger of cutting her palms.

Despite her fear about what she might find around the next turn of the thinning path, the image of Hugo wracked with pain continued to take prime position in Mathilda's imagination – a vision which abruptly contorted into the mocking face of Richard Folville, the rector of Teigh ...

Daisy pushed open Grace's bedroom door to collect the hutch of baby guinea pigs, to give them their first taste of grass and the great outdoors, when her eyes fell upon the screwed up ball of paper on the bed.

Opening it to make sure it wasn't anything important before she threw it in the bin, Daisy smiled as she read. 'I think that Rob should see this list, guys? What about you?'

Receiving a cacophony of positive sounding guinea pig squeaks in reply, Daisy slipped the paper into her pocket. 'I wouldn't normally spy on Grace, boys, but right now she's all heartbroken. This means that I need to take charge, and if that means being sneaky, then so be it!'

Glancing around the bedroom, feeling like a benevolent spy, Daisy said, 'Now, do any of you boys remember if Grace took her mobile with her, or if she left it in here somewhere?'

Chapter Thirty-one

'Have you been ill, Grace?' Ashley pulled the sage bridesmaid's dress in an extra inch at the waist, 'You've lost weight.'

'No, I ...' Grace turned to Daisy, 'I'm so sorry, Daze!'

Sensing the concern in Grace's voice, Ashley quickly calmed the waters. 'Don't worry. I can easily fix this. That's the beauty of choosing a dress with lace ties at the back.'

Grace sighed with relief, 'Thanks. I'd have felt awful if I'd ruined things.'

'Daft woman, of course you won't ruin things.' Daisy smiled at her bridesmaid as Ashley indicated that Grace should take off her outfit so she could make a few instant adjustments.

It had been over a week since Grace had come to stay with Daisy, and although she had been a great help, had mucked in, mucked out, made up the guest room for the pet-sitters due to arrive later that day, and had re-written and edited her story in every given spare moment, at no point had Daisy seen Grace check her email or glance at her mobile phone.

No mention had been made of Rob at all, and although Grace seemed to have got her smile back over the past couple of days, Daisy had noticed that her friend had pushed food around her plate at mealtimes rather than eating it. It was the fact that Grace was more or less existing on biscuits dunked into mugs of tea that had spurred Daisy on to bring the dress fittings forward a day earlier than planned, for she had suspected that Grace was losing weight. Daisy would have been jealous if her friend hadn't been so obviously unhappy.

More worryingly, Grace hadn't made any reference to Robin Hood. Not one. This was seriously odd. Daisy had never known Grace to have any lengthy conversation without bringing in at least one outlaw reference. She hadn't even taken her habitual walk from Daisy's home to the alleged burial site of Robin Hood's right-hand man, Little John. Legend had it that the giant man was entombed in a stone casket not more than three miles from Daisy's backdoor. Even though whenever she got to the grave Grace talked for ages about the gullibility of tourists and how John could no more be buried there than the Queen of Sheba could, she always made time to take the short pilgrimage. But not this time.

Daisy had the feeling that Grace was acting her socks off, playing the role of the woman who was 'determined to be all right without a man.' Any day now her brave-face mask was going to crack. Privately cursing Rob for not having had the courtesy to at least let Grace explain about Malcolm, and cursing Grace for being too stubborn to email or call him, Daisy took off her wedding dress, allowing bubbles of excitement at the thought of her forthcoming nuptials to overtake her sympathy for her friend as she lovingly hung the only dress she'd ever loved on its hanger.

'Only two days of being Miss Daisy Marks left then!'

With Daisy's Land Rover packed to the rafters, and the pet sitters installed in the small holding with so many lists of instructions they could have been bound and made into a substantial book, Grace raised her glass of lemonade in a toast to her friend, as they took temporary refuge in the local pub.

'This ought to be a glass of wine, really, to see you on your way to becoming Mrs Daisy Stevens!'

'I promise we'll have a glass as soon as we get there!'

'You're on!' Grace ate half a chip and put her fork down again. 'You feel OK though, don't you? Not sorry you're not out getting drunk on a hen night rather than sat with your history-obsessed friend munching fried potatoes?'

Daisy laughed, 'Can you really see me tottering around Sheffield in high heels and a tiny dress, with a learner sign on my back, a sloganned sash, and a pink cowboy hat?'

'Thankfully, no I can't! I'm actually surprised you knew that the pink cowboy hat was a hen night essential these days!'

'I'm surprised you do!'

'Leicester has its fair share of drunken young women on Friday nights, you know. I always feel a bit sorry for the hen. I can't imagine that many of them want that sort of launch into marriage, but it's sort of expected these days.'

'Well, this does me just fine.' Daisy shovelled up a portion of jacket potato. 'Thanks for your help this week. I honestly don't think I'd have been ready without you.'

'Marcus would have come to your rescue.'

'Well, yes, but you being here meant he could concentrate on getting the practice safe to leave.'

'You must have missed him, though?'

'Yes, but I'll have the rest of my days to catch up on what I've missed, and not having seen him for a while will make it extra-special when I see him on Friday.'

The content expression on Daisy's face made Grace's insides contract. Not for anything would she ruin the most important few days of her best friend's life by sharing her own regrets.

Surely she should be feeling less heartbroken by now? But somehow, now Grace had finally admitted to herself that she had fallen in love with Rob, she felt worse and not better.

'What's the plan of action when we get to the hotel,

then?' Grace slugged back her drink and put down her cutlery.

'Check in, grab that glass of wine, and go to bed. Tomorrow we'll get going on the wedding planning. Tonight we'll rest. I have a feeling we are going to need it!'

Daisy fished the keys for her Land Rover from her pocket, 'Come on, last one to spot the hotel's front door buys the wine!'

The setting was perfect. Built under the instruction of the formidable Bess of Hardwick in the 1590s, Hardwick Hall was a stunning Elizabethan mansion, hidden away in the Derbyshire countryside. As Daisy was introduced to the resident wedding organiser, Grace took her chance to walk around the magnificent entrance hall, unusually devoid of its usual horde of tourists. Hung with beautiful sixteenth-century tapestries, the air of the space hung with echoes of the past. Grace had no trouble picturing men and women from history meeting, greeting, plotting, and planning in that very space, while Bess of Hardwick herself showed off her latest wall hangings to everyone who passed through her doors.

It was a dream wedding location. Fifty or so chairs were already in position for the ceremony the following day, and in Grace's mind, she could see herself walking down the aisle space left between the chairs behind Daisy and her father. On her own. Not that Rob would have actually walked with her, but for a short while she had dared to imagine herself with a proud onlooker in a seat to one side.

She swallowed down her sigh. Grace was beginning to get cross with herself about the sighing. She seemed to be doing an awful lot of feeling sorry for herself lately. It would have to stop. Heartbreak might help the waistline, but it played havoc with her self-confidence, which, beyond the medieval, was pretty shaky anyway. *Five more hours*, Grace told herself as she examined the unicorns so intricately woven into the tapestry nearest to her, *I can have five more hours moping and that is enough. Then it's new start time. You never know, there might be someone nice coming to the wedding tomorrow who may have a thing about spinster historians dressed in Lincoln Green.*

'Grace, what do you think?' Daisy was pointing up to a balcony where no doubt Bess had once ordered minstrels to serenade her. 'Marcus and I were going to have a recording of the 'Wedding March' and stuff, but apparently the string quartet that plays here when they have special functions is available tomorrow. Should we have them?'

'Definitely!'

'You don't think Marcus will mind?' Daisy peered over her shoulder towards the main door, 'He's supposed to be here by now to go through the order of service and have a mini-rehearsal.'

'Of course he won't mind. Anyway, you could get all modern and ask him.' Grace mimed using her phone.

Daisy grimaced and held up her mobile. 'No reception, and we need to decide now or they'll get offered to someone else.'

'Why not use mine, oh ...' Grace hooked her phone from her pocket to find she had the same problem.

'Sorry, ladies,' the wedding planner whose badge announced she was called Wendy, smiled, 'No reception anywhere up here. I'm really sorry to have to put you on the spot, but I only just heard they had a cancellation, and it is a bit now or never.'

Grace looked up at the gallery. She could already see the musicians guiding Daisy up the aisle. 'Go for it Daze. It'll be so romantic; in perfect keeping with this place.'

'Oh why not.' Grace turned to Wendy, 'we'll have them. Can they play the music we'd asked for?'

'They can play anything you want!'

Beaming, Daisy thanked Wendy, who instantly headed to her office to make arrangements via the landline, calling after her, 'If you're worried about Marcus, feel free to come and use the office phone.'

'Thanks, I will if you don't mind,' Daisy turned to Grace, 'you be OK a minute? I won't be long, then I'll show you the East Colonnade, where we'll have the drinks reception before the meal.'

'It's OK, I've been here a few times, I know where it is. I'll head out there, and you can join me when you've spoken to Marcus.'

Sitting on a bench in the East Colonnade, Grace stared out at the panoramic view of the gardens, the early August sun shone down on her face. She hoped this summer weather would hold out for the actual wedding. Although they had the use of the Long Gallery and High Great Chamber for photographs after the ceremony, Daisy had wanted her wedding pictures taken outside in the gardens.

Grace couldn't stop visualising her own wedding here one day.

She sat bolt upright.

That thought had to be dismissed right now. Deciding that Daisy would probably be a lot longer than she imagined, and not wanting to allow any more time for unproductive thinking, Grace pulled her ever-present notebook from her bag. 'After all,' she told a nearby statue, 'if this isn't the ideal place to write a spot of historical fiction, then where is?'

The woodland surrounding Hardwick Hall had been there for centuries, and in her mind's eye Grace saw the medieval landscape mapped out before her. Without a single pylon, cable, or motor vehicle to spoil the view, it wasn't difficult to picture Mathilda and Robert pushing through the trees before her. In fact, right at that moment she wasn't that far from where the imagined encounter she was currently plotting would have taken place. In reality she doubted the Folville brothers would have bothered indulging in such midnight subterfuge, but this was her story, so if she wanted it to be more cloak and dagger, then it would be.

Right now Grace's writing felt as though it was the only thing she had control of in her life – and she was going to take as much refuge in it as she could.

The voice came out of the night, its hollow echo bouncing off the trunks of the closely packed trees. Mathilda tugged her palfrey to an abrupt halt and strained her eyes and ears. The words she was sure she'd heard could have come from any direction, and although she felt the presence of another person – no, other people, there was more than one set of eyes trained on her, she was sure of that – she couldn't work out where they were concealed. Would they appear in front of her, or would they creep up on her from behind?

Hoping that Robert was as close as he'd promised to be, the voice came again, clearer this time. 'Mathilda of Twyford?'

It was more of a question than a statement, and hoping that the fact they knew her name meant that they were expecting her, and must therefore be the Coterels and not the sheriff's men, she summoned up her courage, 'Yes, my Lord, I am Mathilda of Twyford.'

There was a faint rustle of leaves to her right and the stately figure of Nicholas Coterel came striding through the trees. Mathilda was surprised he was on foot, and immediately supposed that the other person she'd sensed in the area a probably a groom, and would have his stallion held at a safe distance.

'I'm pleased to see you looking well, Mathilda. I feared Master Hugo might mistreat you after our prank at his expense.'

Having taken comfort in the reassurance from Robert that she wouldn't have to say anything during the exchange, Mathilda found herself unprepared for pleasantries, and gabbled 'Thank you, my Lord, I am well.'

'Good. Not that it matters now that leech has been hurried to hell. Tell me, was he surprised by your prompt return to the market after our last encounter?'

Mathilda felt a surge of hope in her chest. If Coterel was saying Hugo had double-crossed her, then maybe Robert would finally believe the truth of it. 'He was my Lord, thank you.'

'So, to business.' Nicholas gestured towards the girdle Mathilda wore around her waist, before calling out, 'Robert, you may as well come forth; we have scoured the area, a hue and cry has not been mustered to hunt Hugo's killer this deep into Charnwood tonight, and there isn't a soldier for miles.'

Robert stepped from the shelter of the trees. He was without his horse as well. Inclining his head to his Derbyshire neighbour, Robert held out a hand, helping Mathilda from her mount so she could remove the girdle.

Keeping her face as neutral as possible, not wanting either of the men to see how much she disliked handing over the belt, Mathilda wordlessly passed it to Nicholas.

Holding it up to what little moonlight there was, Nicholas then closed his eyes and ran the tips of his fingers over the lattice pattern. 'I believe I was informed correctly.' Then, calling into the trees behind him he said, 'Tell me, Oswin, what do you think?'

Mathilda's heart soared as her youngest brother strode into the small clearing. Although slimmer than when she'd last seen him, his face was its usual circle of good-naturedness, and she couldn't prevent herself from running into his outstretched arms.

'If I could have your attention, Master Twyford!' Coterel clipped his words out, and Oswin, his face a shock of embarrassed red, came to his lord's side.

'Is this as we suspected?'

Oswin's chunky fingers stroked the carved leather as if it was of the finest ceramics. 'No question, my Lord.'

Coterel's brow creased, 'You're sure?'

'Positive, my Lord.' Oswin went to give the girdle back to Nicholas, but Coterel waved it back in Mathilda's direction.

'Never let it be said that I deprived the beautiful woman of an ally of her finery.'

Robert's face darkened, but he made no comment on the subject as Mathilda clipped the belt back in place. 'Perhaps you'd like to tell me what you are both talking about? I was under the impression that you wanted the finery as a token of trust. Why did you wish to see the belt up close only to return it? '

'I will tell you on one condition.'

'Only one?' Robert's sarcasm was as thick as honey, but Coterel ignored him.

'I will share what we suspect if you will agree to assist in the matter we were going to discuss before that damn leatherworker got up enough people's noses to get himself murdered and delay our clearing-up of the judicial corruption in this area.'

It was clear from Robert's expression how difficult he was finding it to not to mention how much the corrupt nature of the legal system often worked to their benefit, 'My brothers and I are in total agreement. Our families will act together on that matter. Eustace suggests a gap of three to six months for planning and to let the dust settle on Hugo's death.'

'Four months maximum.'

Robert paused before saying, 'Agreed.'

Obviously satisfied with whatever agreement had been made, Nicholas then addressed Oswin. 'You may return to Ashby Folville with your sister as discussed and share our thoughts about the murder with her and her current household. However, if you do not return to me by dusk the day after tomorrow as agreed, there will be consequences. Yes?'

Mathilda turned to Robert, her face full of wonder, 'Oswin is the item we are to collect?'

'Your brothers are obviously as important to you as mine are to me.'

253

Speechless, unable to keep up with Robert's changeable nature where she was concerned, Mathilda turned her attention back to the two men who'd travelled from the Peak District.

Giving his sister a look which told her plainly to ask no questions for the time being, Oswin took hold of Mathilda's bridle, and made ready to lead her palfrey back along the forest path.

'You may tell them everything once you are in the safety of the Folville manor, Oswin.' Then disappearing into the forest, Nicholas called over his shoulder 'I'd make that girl yours fast, Robert, before I'm tempted to steal her from you.'

Chapter Thirty-two

Mathilda's head buzzed with dozens of questions, which swarmed in her brain like an angry hive of bewildered bees.

Her need to ask Oswin why he was working with the Coterels was losing out to her desire to ask Robert precisely what his intentions towards her were. On the other hand, she was desperate to find out more about the significance of Oswin and Nicholas's examination of her girdle, not to mention wanting to share her own mounting suspicions about the leatherworker's murder.

Mathilda was convinced that the dagger had been placed in her cell by the rector, and the more she thought about it, the more convinced Mathilda was that the holy Folville brother must be mixed up in Hugo's death. Yet it seemed ridiculous to think Richard would kill Hugo. For a start, he was a cleric, albeit one with a history of violence behind him. But an attack on Hugo was an attack on Robert, and why would he want to hurt his brother? It made no sense. Mathilda had a feeling Robert would scoff at her idea, and probably be furious with her for even having it in the first place. And she really didn't want to upset him after his recent act of extreme kindness in ensuring Oswin was returned to her, if only briefly. And yet she couldn't shift the notion that the rector had something to hide.

As they'd travelled the weary miles back, Oswin had said nothing, but every so often he'd give his sister the familiar comforting smile he used whenever he was telling her everything was going to be all right. It wasn't until he helped her dismount, tired and dusty from the road and the earliness of the hour, that Mathilda finally took her chance. Speaking under her breath, not sure if Oswin would want to share his answer publicly, she said, 'Why are you working for the Coterels?'

Dealing with the removal of her palfrey's saddle, without looking at her, Oswin murmured softly into his task, 'Rumour is rife that the Folvilles and Coterels are planning something together. Something big. My sister was kidnapped by the Folvilles, so where else would I go to learn all I needed to know about your safety than to their main rivals and now, it would seem, confederates? I wanted to make sure you couldn't be implicated in whatever they are planning. When they heard I was your kin, they didn't hesitate to appoint me.'

Impressed by this unusually sharp thinking by her brother, Mathilda had no time to ask further of him. Robert was ushering them towards a plainly impatient Eustace and a taciturn Walter.

Consoling herself with the fact that Oswin had headed to the Coterel manor of his own free will, and had not been forced into service as she had herself, Mathilda followed her new owners, employers, or kidnappers. She wasn't sure who they were to her, or who she was to them any more beyond a bargaining counter; a fact, Mathilda realised, that made her no different from most of the women born into the families of the gentry, be they lesser ladies or princesses of the realm.

'Off to bed with you, Mathilda.'

'What?' In her surprise and indignance she forgot her manners, squarely facing Eustace, 'But I went all that way in the dark and ...'

'And now we don't need you. You did a good job, but you must be tired. You will be allowed to see your brother before he returns to Bakewell. You were up all night walking the paths of Charnwood Forest, Mathilda; sleep now, while you can.'

Without the presence of Sarah to back her up, Mathilda felt fatigue grip her, making her as tired as Eustace had suggested she was, and rather than wasting energy protesting, she headed to her cot hidden away in the corner of the hall. Privately, however, she vowed to stay awake as long as she could listen to the family's conversation.

Mathilda wrapped herself in her blanket to wait, alert for any sign of trouble, from either inside or outside the hall. It was of growing concern to her that not one soldier had come calling, and that the hue and cry had never been out hunting for Hugo's killer. Why not? Had someone stopped them from hunting the murderer down, or was he so disliked that everyone was pleased the leatherworker was gone?

Sat unmoving, so as not to giveaway the fact she was eavesdropping, Mathilda continued to speculate about the lack of effort being taken by the law towards finding Hugo's murderer. It was so foreign to the usual pattern. The sheriff was generally overzealous in his keenness to wrap up a case and get the 'guilty' party parcelled up for judgement before the day of the crime was over. The fact that she had neither seen nor heard a soldier or a man asking questions made Mathilda wonder if any measures had been taken by the law at all. And if it hadn't, then why not? There was a scrape of chairs, so Mathilda knew that at least some of the men had sat down; then at last, the sound of Eustace's voice travelled across the hall.

'Master Twyford, Robert tells me that you were the offering of surety from Nicholas Coterel, and that you have leave to stay with your sister until early tomorrow, when you must return.'

'Yes, my Lord.' Oswin bowed, his large frame making rather clumsy work of the respectful gesture.

'And I am given to believe by Robert that in an unprecedented gesture of compassion, Coterel didn't take the girdle belt from Mathilda, but merely examined it. Can you explain to me why this was, Master Twyford, or am I to assume that Nicholas has merely taken a liking to your sister?'

Mathilda could feel an embarrassed glow fill her cheeks as he caught the look of displeasure that this suggestion sent over Robert's face.

'My Lord Coterel felt it was enough that the gesture of the gift was made, he had no intension of doing more than examine it. Naturally he is more preoccupied with the nature of your forthcoming stratagem.'

Eustace grunted, 'And so he should be. This business with Hugo is poorly timed. Still, at least he is keen to carry on at a later date. Four months did he say, Robert?'

Inclining his head, Robert said, 'I'm sure that De Vere, La Zouche, and De Heredwyk will all be agreeable to the change in date.'

'As long as it happens!' Eustace banged a fist upon the table, 'Never did I think this land would be at the mercy of a justice worse than Belers, yet this ...'

'Brother!' Robert shouted the warning, gesturing to both Oswin and Mathilda, 'we agreed to keep his name quiet did we not, to protect those who do not need to know?' Turning his attention back to Oswin, Robert said, 'The Lord Coterel gave you leave to tell me why he was keen to see the belt Mathilda wears. Will you please do so?'

The belt again? Mathilda leaned forward, and pressed her ear as close to the dividing tapestry hanging as she could.

'My Lord, on market day, one of the kitchen staff was instructed to purchase a new pitcher for the kitchens. When the girl served ale from it to my Lord Nicholas, he recognised the similarity of the pattern on it to one he'd seen before. To the design he had noticed on the girdle that surrounds my sister's waist.'

Mathilda sucked in a low breath. Of course! She knew she'd seen the pattern before, but hadn't been able to recall where. It was on the pitcher being carried so carefully by the girl she'd seen walking away from the market when she'd been hunting for the Coterel manor.

Obviously bored with the conversation now he'd heard Coterel's response to his message, Eustace barked, 'I fail to see why this concerns us.'

Robert, held up his hand. 'Go on, Oswin. What do you and Coterel suspect?'

'It occurred to my master that if Geoffrey of Reresby suspected that Master Hugo had been stealing his signature pattern, it made sense that he should have been hovering around the pottery stall to examine the ceramics for himself. It also gives him a motive for attacking Hugo.'

The men were talking again, but Mathilda was unable to hear them properly. Pulling her blanket tighter around her shoulders, she tugged off her boots, her heart thumping so loud that she thought it would be heard and give her away. Creeping to the edge of the tapestry divider on her stocking feet, hoping her shadow wouldn't cast across the hall and give her away, Mathilda could see the outline of Eustace's back through the frayed needlework as he addressed Oswin, 'You have other news on this matter?'

'I do, my Lord. The pottery merchant Reresby has long been a plague in my family's side. He has been undercutting my father's prices for some time.'

Eustace had run out of patience, and swooping around the table, he picked Oswin up by the neck, and rammed him back against the nearest stone pillar. 'We agreed you would be returned to Coterel, we didn't say in how many pieces. Now spit out whatever it is you are finding so difficult to trip off your tongue!'

Forcing herself not run to her brother's side, Mathilda watched as Robert unpeeled his older brother's hand from Oswin's throat. 'He can't tell us anything if you have your hand at his neck.'

The glare Eustace gave his brother would have quelled a lesser man, but Robert held his stare. 'We need to hear him speak!'

With a sharp nod of encouragement from Robert, Oswin went on, 'After Mathilda came to work for you, I ran. I knew the only way to find out what had happened to her while in your care was to disappear and grab information where I could. When I heard rumour of your future plans to work with the Coterels, I decided to get temporary employment with them.'

'They took you just like that?

'No, my Lord, they took me because I told them the truth. It pays them to know what you are up to as much as it pays you to know as much as you can about them.'

259

Walter snorted, 'Well said. And ...'

'I saw Mathilda come to the manor to report to Nicholas before she went to help at the market. My Lord Coterel does not trust Master Hugo, and bid me follow my sister on the return to the market in case he treated her badly. Nicholas Coterel feared that Hugo would hold a grudge of jealousy against her for being held in my Lord Robert's affection.'

Walter snorted louder than before, reminding Mathilda of a disgruntled pig.

Ignoring Walter's derision, Robert pulled out a chair and bid their visitor to sit down. 'What did you see or hear, Oswin? Don't miss out anything.'

'Are you sure, my Lord?' Oswin spoke directly to Robert, whose face furrowed as he looked from Eustace to Walter and back again.

Speaking frustratingly quietly, forcing Mathilda to risk taking another few steps from the curtains so she could hear, hoping that the men would be far too concentrated on each other and their conversation to turn around. 'I know what is said behind cupped hands about me and Hugo, Master Twyford. As do my brothers. However, I would keep it from your sister if I am able, so please keep your voice down in case she is not yet asleep.'

Mathilda took one noiseless step backwards, touched that he cared enough to want to shield her from the gossip that surrounded him, and glad that she hadn't told him that Sarah had already confided to her what vile words were said about him and his fallen friend.

Oswin still appeared uncomfortable, but he kept going, addressing Eustace directly, 'May I ask, my Lord, which of your brothers decided that my father should pay for his slander with the kidnap of his only daughter? Was it the same brother who suggested to my father that your family could lend him some money to help his business recover from the damage Geoffrey of Reresby has done in the first place?'

Robert froze to the spot, while Walter and Eustace stared at each other.

After what felt like an eternity Robert finally asked Eustace, 'Was it his idea?'

Mathilda didn't need to hear Eustace's reply. Although no name had been accused, suddenly all the pieces fell into place in Mathilda's head.

The dagger appearing in her cell while she'd slept. The rumours about Robert that Sarah had shared with her. The finding of Hugo's body so close to her father's home. All of it. Everything was beginning to make sense – except for the lack of sheriff's men hammering on the door asking questions.

'Was it him?' Robert spat the words this time.

As the tension in the hall trebled Mathilda knew she had to act now; tell the brothers right away what she suspected. If she didn't, she had the feeling that there would be another murder very much closer to home.

'Grace? Grace, are you with me?' Daisy was sat on the opposite side of the table squinting into the sunlight. 'Sorry I was so long, it took ages to track down Marcus. He's got stuck delivering a calf that got halfway into the world and then decided to go back.'

'Sensible calf! I don't blame it!'

'Grace?'

'Sorry! I was about to catch a murderer, and to be honest, I think I have the plot a bit muddled; plotting a murder is a bit like doing a jigsaw without the benefit of seeing the picture on the box and having lost three corner pieces.' She lay her pen down and massaged her wrist. She'd been writing so fast that Grace hadn't noticed how much it throbbed until the pen hit the table. 'I'm out of practise with a biro! Obviously more used to the keyboard these days than I thought.'

'If you were about to proclaim that the butler did it, then does that mean I've interrupted you at the vital moment?'

Grace smiled up at her friend, 'Daft woman! I was only

distracting myself while I waited. The whole thing will need rewriting once it's all drafted anyway. Plus I can't remember if slander was a crime back then or not. I don't suppose you can?'

Daisy laughed, 'I doubt if I ever knew in the first place.'

'Rob would know.' A cloud passed over Grace's face. It was the first time she'd said his name out loud for days.

Speaking softly, taking her friend's arm as they walked along the gravel path back towards the house, Daisy said, 'Why don't you ask him? It would be a question you genuinely need an answer to. It might help break the ice.'

'I don't think so. You didn't see his face when he left me. For him I am a closed subject. Anyway,' walking faster, sticking a smile onto her increasingly sun freckled face, Grace said, 'let's forget about Rob and Mathilda and everything for now, you're getting married tomorrow! So, tell me, how's Wendy getting on in there? Has she organised you to within to an inch of your life yet?'

'She is a bit daunting!' Daisy steered Grace back towards the hall, 'On the other hand, she is very good at her job, knows exactly what she is doing, and best of all, has just opened a bottle of *vino* for you and I to share while we decide where to put the flowers, and wait for my parents and Marcus's brother to turn up for the rehearsal.'

Glad that she had Daisy's wedding to occupy her mind fully for the next few hours, Grace obediently turned the corners of her mouth up at the edges, and even managed to make her laugh sound convincing when Daisy joked about her getting together with the best man.

'It's traditional you know, Grace! Best man and bridesmaid. And in this case it would be so cool.' Daisy looped her arm through Grace's, 'because then we'd be sister in-laws!'

Chapter Thirty-three

As every new hour of the day before her wedding passed, Daisy looked more radiant. Gone were the nervous bubbles of tension that had burst out every now and again over the past week. A calm confidence that everything would be all right had taken over, partly from the effects of the wine and the sheer efficiency of Wendy, but not only that. Grace noticed that each time Marcus was mentioned Daisy glowed a little rosier, and her eyes shone a little brighter.

When he'd eventually made it to Hardwick Hall, Marcus was rather more bedraggled than he'd intended to be after a lengthy fight with a stubborn calf and a frighten heifer. As he'd scooped his future wife up in his arms, the love between them had been so blatant that Grace had felt she could reach out and touch it.

Now, tucked up in her own comfortable hotel room at six o'clock on the morning of the wedding, with her bridesmaid dress hanging in its protective cover on the wardrobe door, Grace gave up hope of settling back into sleep.

Her dreams had been full of pseudo-medieval images of her and Rob sat either side of a vast oak tree in the middle of Sherwood Forest, with him chivalrously apologising for overreacting to a crime she didn't commit in the first place.

Despite knowing it was hopeless, Grace found herself wishing all over again that she really could talk to Rob, albeit without the Sylvain setting. To explain that she hadn't meant to hurt him. But how could she after having left it for so long? If she'd called Rob straight away … but she hadn't, and now she couldn't because any contact from her so late in the day wouldn't seem genuine; it would sound like a bunch of feeble excuses.

Daisy had always told Grace she was too stubborn for her own good. Grace knew her friend was right, but she also knew it was self protection. Loving a hero who was unable to escape from a poster on a wall was so much safer than a caring for a living, breathing human being. Robin Hood could never hurt her, and would never let her down. 'But then,' Grace whispered into her pillow, 'he can't hug me, laugh with me, or give me a nerve tingling kiss, can he?'

Grace sat up. She needed to finish her story. Now. This minute. Before the wedding. It had to end. For years she'd put off writing her novel. There had always been work to get on with, and the textbook to research for, plus the fear of being frowned upon for writing it in the first place. Maybe that was what had been holding her back.

Perhaps it was her desire to write Mathilda's tale that had been subconsciously consuming her attention since she'd been offered the chance to write her sorely neglected medieval textbook, and not her Robin Hood obsession at all. After all, she had proved to herself that she was capable of loving a real human being now, one that actually existed, not only in real life, but in her own timestream too. It may not have brought her happiness, but at least she'd done it.

'It's time.' Grace spoke into the mirror, ignoring her erratic bed-hair, 'Time to tie up loose ends and then start afresh.'

Feeling oddly comforted, if not totally convinced by this idea, Grace swung her legs out of bed, and grabbed her notebook, the scribbled on paper bags, and other random scraps of notepaper from her bag, that joined together to form the last part of her novel. It was time to sort this story out once and for all.

'Mathilda! How dare you? I told you to ...'

'My Lord, *please!*' Mathilda beseeched Robert, as she talked at top speed, 'Forgive my interruption. I was listening, and I know I wasn't supposed to be, but you must have known I would. And I *must* speak. It is very important. I think I know what this is all about.'

Eustace pulled out a chair and thumped down onto it. 'For St George's sake, Robert! If she is to be your woman you're going to have to learn to control her. Because I've damn well worked it out myself.' The second Folville brother crashed his palm down upon the table in frustration. 'Damn the man's hide! He'll be the death of all of us!'

Swinging around to Walter, who was already standing, his hand on the hilt of his sword, Eustace barked the instruction that Mathilda had already anticipated he'd make. 'Ride to Leicester. John, Thomas, and Laurence are there today. Tell them we need a family meeting. *Now.*'

Mathilda's raised her voice in warning, 'You can't just ... it isn't what you think ...' But her words were lost to the rapid flurry of activity.

Eustace had already left the hall. Mathilda could hear him shouting at Allward to find Sarah and bring her to the kitchen. Walter had vanished, presumably to grab whichever horse was the quickest to saddle, leaving Oswin standing looking from his sister to Robert de Folville and back again, his expression a picture of confusion.

The rushing past of Sarah as she hurried to the heart of her domestic domain, proved that Eustace's shouting had yielded results.

In the middle of this breakout of chaos Robert took Mathilda's hands. 'Are you sure it was him?'

'No, my Lord. I haven't named anyone anyway! I was trying to say that ...'

'No?' Robert roared the word, but gathered himself quickly, 'Mathilda, Eustace is gathering the family to sort this out. If you're wrong there will be hell to pay.'

Mathilda battled to keep her own fright-enhanced irritation in check as she responded. 'I was trying to speak, but no one was listening. Do *any* of you in this family ever

265

listen to a whole sentence before you jump to conclusions and bound off to act?'

To stop Robert charging off himself, Mathilda wrapped her smaller fingers around his, making him look at her, puzzled endearment putting an abrupt cap on his anger.

'I have been unjust towards you, and you have heard the rumours about me, and yet you take my hands anyway?'

'As I said, my Lord, you and your brothers are used to acting hastily and without thought. Perhaps you won't in the future?' She smiled at him, knowing that there was little chance of that as she added, 'As to the gossip, well the world is built on rumours. Most of them are wrong. Convenient lies to some; living hell for others. Why else would Our Lady denounce it as an abomination?' Mathilda stared into Robert's eyes, noticing how they were slightly mottled, more like the green of an oak leaf nearing autumn than just plain green, and spoke with more confidence than she felt. 'I think I know who the killer of Master Hugo is. It is the only theory that makes sense in the circumstances, but who is going to listen to the likes of me? We need proof.'

'We won't if Eustace get hold of him first. He'll wring his neck before any questions are asked!'

'But I think my Lord Eustace is wrong ... well partly wrong, my Lord!' A knot of panic tied in the pit of Mathilda's stomach, 'And anyway; the man isn't worth hanging for. Will you help me? Will you help me show them the truth about Hugo?'

Robert traced a hand over the girdle at her waist, the gleam to his eyes showing some of the potential affection he'd hinted at on their first meeting. A kindness and caring that had been missing since Hugo had lied about her work at the market. 'It really isn't true, what they say about me and Master Hugo.'

'I know. I think perhaps it may have been for Master Hugo though.'

Robert bristled, but Mathilda reached up and put a palm on his cheek. 'He was always going to be jealous of any

266

friendship you had, and I doubt he ever understood why, and that made him bitter and angry.'

'You speak about things you are forbidden to even think.'

'Says the man whose family operates its own brand of law, and has been personally connected to many felonies. Does that make you a forbidden thought as well, or simply a member of a family with the guts to fight back against a country so corrupt that even the Queen has risen up against her King?'

Looking at Mathilda as if he'd just seen her properly for the first time, Robert struggled to pull his mind back to the urgent matter at hand. He rubbed his forehead. 'So do you think my brother killed Hugo or not?'

'He didn't.'

'But Eustace said he'd reached the same conclusion as you, and that was ...'

Mathilda reached up on her tiptoes and placed a finger over Robert's lips, 'Your brother, the rector of Teigh, is in this up to his neck, but I don't think he was the one who struck out with a dagger, or indeed organised the death. We need Oswin and Allward to help us, and we *have* to move quickly. There isn't much time and they'll have to travel some miles.'

They moved fast. With a hasty explanation to Sarah, Robert buckled his sword to his side, and made sure his dagger was still where the housekeeper had hidden it. Meanwhile Mathilda gathered up some bread and some flasks of ale for Oswin and Allward, and stuffed them into their saddle bags as the boys clambered up onto the nearest horses as fast as the stable boy could saddle them.

'You know what to do?'

Oswin nodded at Mathilda as he and Allward whirled their mounts towards the gates, 'I'll see you soon, sister. Be brave.'

A lump formed in Mathilda's throat as she watched them leave, but she had no time to indulge in tears.

Robert was talking to Sarah. As Mathilda hurried over to

267

them she could hear Robert chastising the housekeeper for telling Mathilda about the rumours concerning him and Hugo, 'Of all people, I didn't want *her* to think I was like that!'

'And she of all people needed to know so she could be prepared for the back-handed comments.'

'And what if she believes it? What then?'

Mathilda rolled her eyes, 'We don't have time for this!' She pushed Robert towards the door as if he was a child refusing to go and fetch the firewood before a storm, 'I've already told you I don't believe it. Now go! If Eustace kills the rector, then we'll never know the whole truth for certain!'

As Robert vaulted onto his horse, Mathilda caught hold of his bridle, 'Stay safe, my Lord.'

Feeling unexpectedly warmed by the gratitude in his eyes as he held her gaze for a second, Mathilda watched Robert canter from the yard, trying to catch up with Eustace and Walter before they reached Leicester, and John Folville took the law even further into his own hands than usual.

Mathilda paced the hall, the kitchen, and the bedrooms, fussing and tidying as she went. Having given up any hope of resting after her sleepless night, she was supposed to be helping Sarah clean and prepare the food that was bound to be desperately needed by the time the family returned, some shattered after their own lack of sleep, others fuelled by anger. But after proving herself too distracted to be of any use in the kitchen, Sarah had sent Mathilda to attend to the fireplaces.

Her hands and knees were black from where she'd become careless in her agitation for news. As the hours passed, Mathilda went over and over her theory in her head, and with each rehash of her idea she became less and less certain. If only Allward would return and confirm her suspicions, but as she'd sent him on a long round trip she judged he'd be some time yet.

Mathilda began to consider what might happen if she

was wrong. And even if she wasn't wrong, what would she do if Father Richard managed to convince his brothers that she was a troublemaker bent on destroying his good name? As she returned to the hall to polish the well-worn wooden surface of the hall table for the second time that hour, Mathilda began to plan an emergency escape.

Grace was beginning to wish she hadn't left her laptop at home in her hurry to get away from the spectre of her evening with Rob. Pausing in her work, massaging some feeling into her tired wrist, and flicking back through her scattered notes, Grace decided she'd better number them, or she'd never get everything typed up in the correct order when she got home.

Flexing her neck, Grace realised that was the first time she'd thought about going home since her arrival in Hathersage without feeling vaguely nauseous. Seeing that as a good sign, Grace raised her gaze so she could see out of the window and across the hotel's well-kept gardens, speaking her thoughts aloud, 'I wonder how he's getting on in Houston.'

Without contemplating an answer to her question, Grace picked up her pen back up and turned to the next page in her notebook. 'Allward must be back by now.'

Having run though the house, peering around every door searching for Mathilda, Sarah eventually found her smoothing the covers on Robert's bed, 'Allward's back.'

The colour drained from Mathilda's face as she hurried back through the manor to find the servant boy sitting at the kitchen table drinking from a flagon.

'And?'

Wiping a sleeve across his mouth to dry his lips Allward, breathless from his gallop, said, 'You were right.' He pointed at the evidence he'd bought with him, now lying on the kitchen table.

'And Oswin, did he get to Twyford?'

The boy nodded. 'I met him as I left Bakewell. Your

269

father was tricked into a corner he couldn't get out of.'

'Are he and Matthew all right?'

'Oswin had them with him. They'll be safest at the Coterel manor until the guilty have been dealt with.'

Mathilda felt sick with shame. She hadn't considered the danger her accusations might have put her family in if Father Richard decided to ensure the silence of the only person who could point the finger at him with unshakeable confidence.

Placing a hand on Mathilda's arm, Sarah said, 'They'll be safe with the Coterels.'

'But they are felons.' Even as she spoke, Mathilda remembered how kind Nicholas Coterel had been to her by not taking her belt; and by sending Oswin to trail her, he may have already saved her life once before.

Smiling, Sarah said, 'They are felonious as the Folvilles; but only when they have to be. Only when there is no other action left to take.' The housekeeper paused before saying, 'I fear for one of them though – things have gone too far. The taste for the suffering of others has become a habit rather than an unpleasant, but necessary, tool to survival.'

A thunder of hooves from outside sent an exhausted Allward scurrying into the yard to help with the horses, followed by Sarah, her best haughty expression on her face, and an increasingly pallid and apprehensive Mathilda.

All the Folvilles were gathered in the yard.

Eustace, John, Thomas, Walter, Laurence, and Robert were moving as one. Right in the middle of them, like prey caught by a hunting pack, his face on fire with rage, stood Richard Folville, the rector of Teigh.

Chapter Thirty-four

Bundled from the yard into the hall, the rector of Teigh unleashed a feast of unholy verbal protestations as his eyes fell on Mathilda.

John, reverting to his role as head of the household, stood intimidatingly close to Mathilda. Towering over her, she couldn't help feeling as if she was the one on trial, rather than Richard. 'You had better be able to explain yourself extremely well, Mistress Twyford. I wish to know why you are besmirching the good name of my most reverend brother. He is, you may be interested to know, the very brother who was responsible for bringing you here to pay off your errant father's debt and his unworthy defamation of Robert. For that we owe the rector for upholding the family reputation, and therefore should be showing him gratitude not showering him with this suspicion.'

A smug expression passed over the churchman's face as he listened to his older brother cast suspicion on Mathilda's allegations.

Seeing the anxious look on Mathilda's face, Sarah laid a hand on her arm before addressing the head of the household herself, 'If you please, my Lord, it is the fact that my Lord Richard is responsible for bringing her here that first caused this suspicion to be cast. I truly believe you should hear what the girl has to say.'

John studied his housekeeper's face for a long time. The entire room seemed to have frozen, poised for the eldest Folville's reaction at this plea from his most trusted servant.

At last, although evidently not convinced he should bother, John gave a begrudging signal of agreement, and Sarah squeezed Mathilda's shoulder, 'Go on, Mathilda; tell my Lord John everything, just as you told me.'

With a glance at Robert's grave countenance, which was punctuated by a flash of an encouragement to his eyes that Mathilda hoped had really been there, that wasn't a trick of her imagination, she began to speak.

'My Lords, as I tried to say earlier, there is guilt with your holy brother, but I do not believe that he wielded the dagger that slew Master Hugo, he merely wished to ...'

'*What?*' John was ready to burst with anger, as Richard swaggered away from the dropped hold of his brothers. 'You, a *hostage*, had my kin hunting the entire Goscote Hundred, and across into Rutland to Teigh, for a *cleric*, and have them drag him here to be accused of – what, then?'

Mathilda was gratified to see that as Robert let go of the churchman, he appeared extremely uneasy about doing so, as he deferred to his eldest brother for instruction.

Burying her nerves as deep as she could, Mathilda bunched her fingers into her palms until her nails dug into her skin; the mild pain giving her an odd sort of reassurance. It seemed to be telling her that while she was still alive, she should feel every sensation possible. 'Please, my Lord, I can explain.'

'You'd better. For evil, unfounded accusations against a man of God are enough to send you to hell, Mathilda.'

Flinching, Mathilda stood her ground, and began to speak as fast as she could. 'My Lord, Father Richard did not strike the blow that murdered Master Hugo, but he knows who did, he knows why, and I believe he has used those facts to his advantage.'

Adrenalin pumped through Grace as she re-read the last few lines she'd written. In her haste to get the words down, her handwriting was appalling. Grace smiled as she remembered the course she'd taken in deciphering medieval handwriting. It would probably be the only thing that would help her read through this lot when it came to typing it up.

She had just over an hour before she had to pull on her faithful jeans and a T-shirt, and find Daisy for breakfast.

Grace pictured her friend in the neighbouring room. It had been her last night as a single woman. Was she still asleep? Or was she lying there awake, a bundle of nervous excitement? It must be a strange feeling, knowing that nights alone would be a rare thing from now on, and that there would be someone to share things with whenever she wanted to.

Shaking her head sharply to dislodge the feeling of loneliness that was trying to nudge its way into her heart, Grace was more determined than ever to bring Mathilda's tale to an end before breakfast. She wanted to be able to wave Daisy and Marcus off into their combined future with her story complete.

There could be no denying that Father Richard hadn't expected the girl to say that. He'd been braced to be accused of murder, something he could easily prove he didn't do. His face darkened, and he began to protest, but not fast enough for his sharp-eared brothers to have missed his split second of surprised hesitation.

Ignoring his younger sibling's blustered mutterings, John's eyes narrowed, 'Go on then, girl; tell us, which gullible fool do you believe to have been taken in by my reverend brother enough to kill for him?'

'And more important than that,' Eustace added, keeping his eyes trained on Richard, 'tell us why you think that happened.'

Mathilda had been all ready to blurt out a name and then run out of the hall as quickly as she could, sure that the room would erupt into a thunder of denial and threats of recrimination the second her accusation was made. It seemed though, that in her fear she'd forgotten the basis of the assembled brothers' motives for crime. Yes, they were violent, but they were only violent to those deemed deserving of such treatment.

Lines from one of her favourite ballads came to her. *'Robyn loved Oure dere Lady: For dout of dydly synne, Wolde he never do compani harme. That any woman was*

273

in.' [17]

Robyn and his men may have terrorised the rich and avaricious, but their devotion to Our Lady meant it would go against their principles to harm a woman. Mathilda hoped that was a principle Robert and his family upheld as well. When it came to the reverend, however, she rather doubted it. Something about the countenance of the man, let alone the way he spoke and acted, made her skin positively creep.

'It was the dagger in my cell that made me suspicious of the rector, my Lord.'

Mathilda was about to continue, but the reverend Folville had seen his chance, and pounced upon it.

'If anyone in this cursed hall would do me the justice of listening to me instead of that chit, I can tell you exactly why this child is hell bent on pointing the finger at me. She wishes to cover up her own guilt. For it was, without doubt, Mathilda Twyford herself who thrust the dagger into the chest of Master Hugo, and left him to bleed to death like a suckling pig.'

'What?' Mathilda opened her mouth for further words to come, but none did, for John had sprung forward and placed a gloved hand over her mouth.

'Your manners seem to be sadly lacking when it comes to listening to a man of the cloth, girl. You will allow us to hear him out.'

Mathilda had expected the rector to try and switch the blame to her, but she hadn't thought he'd jump in so fast. A new level of fear landed on her flesh, covering her in a cold clammy sweat. Why hadn't she started by naming the guilty party and working backwards from there? *Foolish!*

Striding towards John, Robert, with an expression on his face that could have withered the crops in the fields, said, 'I would consider it a great personal favour if you would remove your hand from Mathilda's mouth, brother.'

Again the tension in the air thickened as all eyes moved away from Richard to John and from John to Robert, as the eldest brother spoke with insincere calm, 'Can you assure me that your waif will remain quiet and give our reverend brother time to tell his side of the story before she utters another word in accusation?'

Robert placed his hand over John's and pointedly lowered it from Mathilda's lips. 'I can if you can assure me that, after Richard has spoken, Mathilda will be allowed to tell her side of the tale?'

John paused for longer this time. 'Agreed, but she must tell the truth, and be able to prove her words.' The elder brother paused again, before adding, 'On the surety of your place in this family?'

Sarah gasped, and looked at Mathilda, her eyes pleading with her to keep her lips closed whatever lies were about to be said.

Robert took over the questioning, his face etched with a menace his reverend sibling was either blissfully unaware of, or was simply ignoring, 'And what was Mistress Twyford's motive for murdering a man she doesn't know?'

'Surely it is obvious, dear Robert? Jealousy.'

Mathilda was struggling to remain silent, but the warning glance of Sarah kept her mute despite the injustice of the words she knew she was about to hear.

Taking a draft from his ale, Eustace sat himself on the nearest chair and put his feet up on the table, as if to prepare himself for the forthcoming charade, asking lazily, 'Jealous of what?'

'Master Hugo, of course.' Sneering out his words with relish, Father Richard then played his trump card, 'The leatherworker's ungodly affection for our *dear* Robert is well known. His very existence is a threat to young Mathilda, who has obviously set her sights far above her station at our family. Pointlessly of course, as dear Robert will never take more than a token wife.'

The dagger was drawn from Robert's side in a flash of mesmerising silver before the final word of the churchman's sentence had been uttered, and although John swiftly placed a warning palm on his shoulder, Robert didn't move the blade from the rector's throat. 'Go on then, cleric; carry on speaking your poison while you can.'

'You place a blade at my throat? You, who bring disgrace upon this family!'

Eustace's eyes turned to John, who said, 'Lower the knife, Robert, but keep it to hand. Now, Richard, tell your tale quickly before all our patience snaps.'

Holding himself as though shamefully affronted, the rector ignored all those present except for John. 'As I was saying, the girl wishes to up her family status. The removal of her only rival for Robert's affections is motive enough, and yet the girl is cleverer than that. She had a secondary plan. By implicating me in Hugo's death, she also took the opportunity to remove one of us, and therefore increasing her would-be husband's share of the family coffers. Greed. Jealousy and greed, John. I've seen it many times in the parish, I'm sad to say. Those believing themselves better than they are will go to any means to improve their standing.' The clergyman shook his head as he spoke, as if he was constantly surprised by the folly of his fellow humans.

Mathilda's lungs felt heavy. She'd barely taken a breath as he'd spoken. Surely the brothers wouldn't believe that? It was ludicrous, especially the last bit. Although people did kill to improve their position, there was no physical way she could have got to Twyford. She had been here all the time – locked in a cell no less!

'I myself saw the dagger by the Twyford girl's feet in the cell. Where, I should remind you, she'd been thrown for repeated insolence. A dangerous game to play indeed, especially as her help and good behaviour relates to how soon the debt her family owes is paid off. A fine example of how little she thinks of her father and brothers.'

Robert's hand gripped his dagger handle tighter as Mathilda bit her lips so hard together to prevent her protests that she was close to drawing blood. There was no way she was going to rise to the bait. She could imagine all too well how thrilled the rector would be to see Robert thrown from the family manor.

'Where did she get a dagger from?' Eustace spoke as if he was relishing the show he was watching. 'You yourself ensured the girl was weapon free when she was ushered here, and you are the one who escorted her to the cell on her arrival. Are you saying you were lacking in your duties?'

Mathilda relaxed her jaw a fraction. Was she imagining it, or was Eustace actually enjoying this? She'd certainly got the impression earlier that he had no trouble in imaging Richard having organised Master Hugo's death. On the other hand, the rector was his brother ...

'It is hardly difficult to pick up a dagger in this house, brother! She could easily have secreted such a small weapon within the folds or sleeves of her clothing.'

'And what know you of women's clothing, Father?'

Eustace's dig caused Walter to grunt derisively, as the gloating rector barbed his reply with heavy implication, 'I imagine I know as little as dear Robert does.'

It was a snide comment too far. Robert moved so fast he was a blur. The clatter of the nearest chair hitting the floor ricocheted around the stone hall as Father Richard found himself lifted off his feet and banged against the table with such force that Eustace had his flagon knocked from his hand. 'Enough! I've lived with your evil whispering long enough. No more.'

Keeping the flat of his dagger free hand pressed against the rector's chest, pinning him against the table, Robert addressed John. 'I believe you should let Mathilda speak now, my Lord. You have heard our reverend brother. His version of events has more holes than a broken fishing net.'

Instead John, rather than ask Mathilda to speak, turned to Sarah. 'You have been in charge of the girl while she has been here?'

'Yes my Lord. She has been a great help to me. I admit I wasn't sure of her at first, but she has earned my respect.'

'John, you can't take the word of a servant over ...'

The lord of the manor put up a hand to stem Richard's protests.

'And in your opinion, Sarah, is it even remotely possible

277

that Mathilda could have laid her hands on a dagger and escaped from this household for long enough to kill Hugo, or even arrange for another to do the deed. Has she appeared in any blood-soaked clothes? Had a weapon in her possession? Did this dagger in the cell even exist?'

Sarah glanced at Mathilda, before confirming that there had been no time in which Mathilda could have committed such a crime. The only time she had been separated from the girl was when she was being escorted to and from Derby market and the woods by Robert, when she delivered the messages to Nicholas Coterel.

Licking her lips, Sarah nodded towards Robert as she went on, 'My Lord Robert gave Mathilda a dagger to keep on her during her first trip to see Coterel.'

'You see! She did have a weapon.'

The reverend's cry resulted in Robert pushing him even further up the table so his feet where dangling off the floor, hissing through clenched teeth, 'Sarah has not yet finished speaking. She held her tongue as you uttered your lies, now you listen to some truth for once in your miserable life.'

Carefully Sarah continued, 'The knife was safely hidden under her cot on her return, awaiting the chance to be given back to my Lord Robert. It wasn't long after that that Mathilda was falsely accused of poor behaviour at the market when selling wares for Master Hugo, and was placed back in the cell. There was no dagger on her when she went in. I put her in the cell myself. There was, however, a dagger there when I took her food and drink. The girl had fallen asleep while she was in there. During that time, the dagger was placed by her feet. I can only assume that whoever had placed it there had searched her quarters and found it.'

John stared shrewdly at Richard. 'I believe you were at the manor that day. Did you check on our captive, by any chance, and add a little something to her cell?'

'As God is my witness, I did not! The housekeeper is bound to stick up for the girl. We all know she'd do anything to protect her favourite, and find a wife for her precious Robert.'

Ignoring the fresh outburst from the man pinned to the table, John refrained from mentioning that he thought God had more sense that to bear witness to his malevolent brother, asking, 'what did you do with the dagger once you'd found it, Sarah?'

'I hid it in the kitchen, and then later returned it to my Lord Robert.'

'I see.' John sounded solemnly. 'I think it is time we heard more from Mathilda. However, I feel it prudent to remind you, girl, that you are not a guest here, you are a hostage.' John closed his eyes for a moment as if to collect his thoughts before saying, 'You were telling us that there was a dagger in your cell when you woke up, but not beforehand. That was what alerted you to thinking that Father Richard was involved in this matter. Yes?'

Swallowing to lubricate some moisture back into her fear-dried throat, Mathilda nodded, 'That's right, my Lord. As Sarah said, I was in the cell when Master Hugo's body was discovered and ...'

'So what! You could have stuck him hours before then; we don't know the hour of the crime, just the hour of the body's discovery!' The withering glare that Robert gave the rector silenced the clergyman's new interruption.

Mathilda couldn't help noticing that which each fresh protest of his innocence, Richard was losing his red-faced flush of angry bravado. He was beginning to look pale. That meant he was getting rattled. Perhaps he was afraid she could prove he'd committed a crime after all.

Robert smiled kindly in Mathilda's direction, 'Go on, it's all right.'

'Thank you, my Lord.' Mathilda wiped her perspiring palms down the front of her dress. 'As Sarah said, the dagger was the one that my Lord Robert had lent me, but I hadn't seen it since I stowed it under my cot until I awoke in the cell.'

'And you believe that was the dagger that killed Master Hugo?'

'No my Lord, I think that is what everyone was meant to

think, and I wouldn't be surprised if it is a very similar weapon to the one used. You all wear daggers, and although I haven't been here long, I have noticed that they all look very similar. Not only that, but if they were made locally, then many other people could also own similar weapons.'

Eustace pulled his dagger from his side and held it up to Mathilda, 'They were a gift. We received one each when we came of age. Most of us have other daggers we favour, and keep these just for show. I rather like to keep mine handy; it has a useful short blade for hooking stones from my horse's hooves, opening stubborn doors, and such. They are more a tool than a weapon really.'

'But they *could* be used to kill, my Lord.'

The single stone in the hilt of Eustace's dagger shone red in the firelight. 'Indeed they could.' He turned to Robert, 'Where is your dagger now?'

'Wrapped in an old tunic at the bottom of the chest at the foot of my bed.'

John nodded, 'Sarah, fetch Robert's dagger from its hiding place, please.'

As Sarah left the hall, the expectant eyes of all the men fell upon Mathilda. 'When I learnt that Master Hugo had been stabbed while I was under lock and key it seemed too much of a coincidence for there to be no connection. I'd only recently been introduced to Master Hugo, he'd lied about me, I'd learnt that the Coterel family were suspicious of him, and a dagger had been put in my prison all within a very short period of time.

'It wasn't until I found out that it was Father Richard's idea to use me as a hostage to meet my father's debt that I began to wonder if he could be involved, although I didn't understand why.'

'But now you do?' The hall had become very tense. John spoke barely above a whisper. The fire had died down, and apart from the intermittent crackle as the logs snagged against the low flames, all that could be heard was the hush of suspense.

Chapter Thirty-five

Awake since seven, Daisy sat at the desk in the corner of her hotel room; her stomach fizzing with happy, excited energy.

The second she'd opened her eyes, Daisy had leapt from her bed and dressed in her usual jeans and jumper. In only a few hours she'd have to change again into the beautiful dress that Ashley had helped her find, and had somehow magically nipped and tucked in all the right places to make it appear as if the folds of ivory satin had been designed exclusively for her from the day the dress pattern was dreamt up.

Daisy hadn't expected to sleep much, but in fact she'd slept like a log. She wondered if Marcus had. He had plainly been exhausted from a day wrestling bovines and going through the short, but necessary, wedding rehearsal the night before. By the time Daisy had waved him off to her future in-laws' home, reluctantly keeping up the tradition of the groom not seeing the bride on the day of the wedding until it was time for her to walk down the aisle (or gap in the chairs as Daisy called it), Marcus had been all in.

Scanning her emails to make sure there were no last-minute cancellations from any of the wedding guests, Daisy reread the last message she'd received. Putting down her mobile, Daisy smiled. She was *almost* sure she'd done the right thing. However, in case she'd read the situation wrong in her keenness for Grace to experience some of her own hazy glow of happiness, Daisy was ready with a plan B – to deny all knowledge and tell Grace she couldn't possibly be cross with her on her wedding day!

Slipping on her trainers, Daisy fastened her laces, glancing over at the clock on the corner of the television screen as she did so. She'd agreed to go down to breakfast with Grace at half past eight, and as Grace was always early, she'd be knocking on the door any minute.

Grace was beginning to think that by the time she finally put on her posh frock, one of the sleeves would need shortening. Her right shoulder and wrist ached so much from her frantic scribbling that Grace feared she was in danger of wearing her arm down to the elbow. The ink in her pen was getting fainter as well, and Grace wondered what would run out first; the pen, or the time she had left to write in before breakfast with Daisy.

'It was after I'd spoken to my brother Oswin that it all began to become clear. You see, my Lord, unbeknown to me, Oswin had overheard my father talking to the rector in the workshop a few weeks before I was bought here. Being only a woman, I was not privy to the financial arrangements my father was about to make.

'The reverend had come for some cheap candleholders for his church. We were desperate, my lord. We only had enough money needed to buy the raw materials for his pottery order, so my father took up the rector's offer of a loan, and borrowed a small amount from your good selves.

'Father Richard told my father that if he would fan the flames of a rumour he had heard around the villages and towns about my Lord Robert, then he would ensure my family wouldn't have to pay back the full amount owed.'

'A rumour I have long suspected came from his foul tongue anyway!' Robert increased his pressure against the trapped cleric, his voice sounding incredulous as he turned back to Mathilda, 'and your father believed him?'

'Your brother is a churchman, my Lord. And, my father was desperate.'

'I assume that, rather than keep his word, my holy brother then reported to my Lord John that not only did your family owe us money, but that the Twyfords were the people who'd begun spreading the evil rumours about my friendship with Master Hugo?'

John nodded gravely to confirm the truth of Robert's allegation. There was no need for Mathilda to confirm Robert's statement.

The lord of the manor's steely eyes fixed themselves upon the reverend. 'Let me guess what happened next. You came up with another plan; a plan to make it appear that you remained loyal to this family by attempting to stop the rumours that could ruin my brother and Hugo's names.

By kidnapping Mathilda as a guarantee for the debt, it looked as though you were teaching the originator of the lies a lesson; with the added bonus of a sly suggestion in Eustace's ear that perhaps, despite being of lower status, the girl could be a suitable match for Robert. A move that would certainly quash the talk behind hands about his ungodly behaviour – which, I repeat, you started in the first place. I assume you thought Robert would be insulted by the suggestion of Mathilda's suitability for him – another fact you'd have enjoyed. How disappointing it must have been for you to see that despite the manner of her arrival here, the girl has been of considerable help to this family, and has obviously caught your brother's eye in truth.'

Raising a warning hand towards Robert, who looked ready to commit murder there and then, Eustace rose from his chair and sauntered closer to Father Richard, with Walter, Thomas, and Laurence following suit; boxing their reverend brother in.

'Is there more, Mathilda?' John seemed troubled rather than angry now. 'So far you have highlighted the dubious character of my brother; which is something that isn't going to surprise anyone. But what you've told us seems to have little to do with the actual murder.'

'Exactly!' Feeling the solid, menacing presence of his family closing in on him, Father Richard demanded, 'How am I supposed to have skewered the man while I was here supposedly planting a weapon on the girl?'

John was clearly losing patience as he repeated, 'Mathilda did not say you killed Master Hugo, but that you'd used the event to your advantage.'

'I did no such thing. The chit has far too much imagination.' Far from being relieved, the cleric looked more wary than before, 'I've had enough of this indignity. I have souls to save.'

'Any soul in particular, brother?' Robert let go of the rector with an expression of distaste. 'Your soul, perhaps? Or another soul? One that you might save all the way to the coast, so he can escape across the sea?'

'I have no idea what you mean!'

'Really? You don't seem to know much today, do you? You don't wish to take this opportunity to reveal the truth, then? You wish the girl to tell us more about how she saw through you?'

'John! How could you even think this of me?'

'Easily, after the number of crimes you've committed in the past.'

'As have you!' The clergyman puffed his chest in defiance.

'True. But usually for the good of the area as a whole, to do the job the officials should be doing, and *never* against a member of my own family!'

Mathilda thought back to the death of the corrupt Belers, and how much safer the region had felt after his removal, although the ripples of the terror of the occasion had been felt for a long time afterwards, and how she suspected that the recent meetings between the Folville and Coterel families were the build-up to the removal of another corrupt official in the near future.

John called for Allward. 'Go and fetch the sheriff, boy.'

'Are you mad?' Father Richard shook his head, 'He hasn't even bothered sending his men to investigate Hugo's death. Not a single soldier has been dispatched, nor a question asked, and the hue and cry was stood down before it had even begun. He couldn't care less.'

'And why do you think that was, dear brother?'

Richard's mouth dropped open. 'You?'

'Master Hugo was an unpleasant and objectionable man, but Sheriff Ingram knew of his war-forged friendship with Robert, so he consulted me on the matter of his death. He agreed to leave things alone. Having a member of this family implicated in this crime would not be in the sheriff's interests at the moment.' [18]

The rector's mouth dropped open, 'The sheriff is in your pay?'

'We have a plan afoot, do we not? We will need Ingram on our side. Anyway, he is a friend who helps me out sometimes,' John answered smoothly, 'and now I think we need him to come here.'

'No!'

Fear was now visibly emanating from Richard. John, eyeing his brother carefully, raised his hand, telling the travel-weary Allward not to head straight out on his new mission.

'Why not? Tell me, little brother.'

Richard searched the remaining family faces for a glimmer of help, but every expression was closed and sombre. Eventually he spoke with bitter resignation. 'You know full well why not. Ingram made it clear last time we met professionally that all my chances had run out. I don't wish to meet the hangman's noose.'

John gestured to Sarah for some ale as he sat back at the long table, 'I imagine I can persuade him not to stretch that neck of yours, but only if you tell us the truth now. I suggest you talk.'

The reverend remained silent. To Mathilda it was as if his malevolent eyes were searing into her soul.

'No? Then perhaps we should ask Mathilda?' Pausing long enough to be sure that no response would be coming from the rector, John once again addressed Mathilda. 'So who did kill Master Hugo?'

Summoning up all her courage, Mathilda said, 'I believe it was Geoffrey of Reresby, my Lord.'

'Because?' The original incredulity returned to John's

286

face, 'I can see no reason on this earth why Reresby would risk his neck to kill Hugo?'

Robert lowered his dagger a fraction, reassuring himself that his brothers weren't about to let Richard flee. He moved closer to Mathilda, and gestured toward her girdle belt. 'Would you be so kind as to remove your belt for me? And Allward, go and fetch the pitcher you collected from Bakewell.'

'Explain yourself, Robert.' John leant forward in his chair, his hand rubbing the stubble of his short, neatly trimmed beard.

'This brings us to the matter that Coterel and Oswin suspected, and led Mathilda to stitch the two sides of this puzzle together. Whatever you thought of Master Hugo, he was an excellent craftsman. If you look closely at the belt, and then at the borrowed pitcher, you will see that they bear exactly the same design. As you know, I was presented with the leather belt as a gift from Hugo some months ago. He was indeed, gruff, uncompromising, and given to being surly, but he was my dear friend, he saved my life when we were comrades in arms on the fields of Scotland. I owed him a debt of friendship, and I stuck by him, paying that debt.'

'A *friend!* You'll burn in hell! It just so happens that someone did the area a favour and sent Hugo there early!'

'Enough!' Eustace was bored with the drama he'd previously been enjoying. The glare in his eyes told Mathilda that there were now two brothers who would like to wring the cleric's neck there and then.

Passing the belt to John, Robert took the pitcher from Allward 'As you can see, the patterns are the same, even down to the leaves and vines that wind around the diagonal lines.'

Giving everyone but the rector the chance to examine the identical designs, Robert continued. 'When Mathilda worked at the market for Hugo she spotted Geoffrey of Reresby watching the stall. She believed that he was there keeping an eye on her. After all, he was responsible for the collapse of her family's pottery business with his cheaper imports and his own decorative wares, and, always jealous of her father's greater skill with clay, had remained a thorn in their side for some time.'

Mathilda was grateful for the constant presence of Sarah, who kept a comforting hand on her shoulder, as John asked her, 'Did Reresby speak to you, girl?'

'No, my Lord. I did my best to keep out of his way. But I'm sure Master Hugo saw him watching the stall; and of course he knew I was wearing his belt. I can only assume that Geoffrey *did* see me, and noticed that my belt bore the same pattern as had so recently begun to appear on his pottery.'

'Are you telling us that Hugo was murdered because of a pattern on a pot?'

'Prior to my time working with Master Hugo I had not seen more of his work than this belt. I had assumed that *he* had stolen the pattern from Reresby, but I was wrong. It was the other way about. Reresby had stolen the pattern. The design is Master Hugo's signature, my Lord. It seems he is known for the pattern. I have no doubt he saw Reresby's taking of the motif as theft.'

'Which is precisely what it was. Theft.' Robert handed the girdle back to Mathilda. 'To steal another man's craft, and to take custom from him that way, is dishonourable indeed.'

Refastening the leather around her tiny waist, Mathilda said, 'I didn't notice the connection at the time, my Lord. I was too worried about my meeting with the Coterels. It was only when I heard about the pitcher's pattern from Oswin that I finally made the link between the patterns on the leather and the pottery.'

'And how does this concern my brother, Father Richard?'

'Allward told me that a man had visited my father yesterday afternoon. He wasn't sure who this man was, as he'd not been there at the time. I sent Oswin to ask our father about the meeting. After some persuading, he told Oswin that the man was Geoffrey.

'He was livid, apparently, and not knowing that I'd been staying here, he believed my father had sent me to work

288

with Hugo to spy on him to gather proof that he'd stolen the pattern from Hugo, and to therefore get revenge for him taking most of our trade. He had assumed my father intended to blackmail him over the theft.

'Of course my father had no idea what Reresby was talking about, and apparently their argument soon fizzled to a discussion, with my father having no choice but to confide that I'd been taken into service here.'

'I'm sorry, Mathilda; but I still can't see what any of this meeting between Reresby and your father has to do with my felonious brother?'

'My Lord, in the meantime Hugo had learnt that Reresby had been using his trademark pattern. This was the reason for his poor behaviour towards me. Not jealousy, but a suspicion that it had been my family who had sold or given the pattern to Reresby out of spite.

'Fatefully, it was only moments after Reresby left my father that Master Hugo was on the road to the workshop to accuse my father of profiting from the theft. I believe they met on the road, argued, and a dagger was drawn with fatal consequences.'

'That I can confirm, brother,' Robert had the good grace to be a little shame-faced, 'Hugo did indeed believe that Mathilda had been avoiding being seen by Reresby because she had a guilty conscience, and not because she disliked the man so much and didn't want him to know of her family's disgrace.'

Mathilda, her whole being a mass of tension, took a swig from the mug that Robert passed to her while waiting John's reaction to what had been said. John, however, wasn't the first to speak.

'You see!' Triumph oozed from the cleric, 'The brat herself says I didn't do it. I wasn't even there. And I don't know Reresby beyond his name and trade.'

Tilting his head to one side John scrutinized his brother for a long time, each heart thudding second feeling like an eternity to Mathilda as she took another sip of drink to ease the dryness of her throat.

Robert, his expression calmer than it had been all day, said, 'But you did stumble across a situation that you could use to your advantage, didn't you. To use to blacken my name, and then to make yourself look good by appearing to clear it again! How was it, *Father* Richard? Did you come across a shocked and frightened Reresby with the body of Hugo at his feet, dagger in hand, wondering what in all hell he'd done? Did you offer to dispose of his blood-stained dagger, a dagger very similar in style from those we all own, and make him indebted to you for the rest of his life, before working out how to use this situation for your own gain?

'You'd already got Mathilda's frightened father to spread a rumour about me that, if true, could see me cut off and sent to hell. What better way to capitalise on that situation and to destroy my reputation further, than by implicating the woman who you had suggested might be a companion for me, in a murder, by placing an almost identical dagger in her cell? What a shame for you that Mathilda here has more intelligence than you have cruel cunning.'

In the quiet that followed Robert's allegations, John signalled to Allward, who disappeared out of the hall, presumably to fetch the sheriff.

'My Lord John,' Mathilda spoke, unsure if she should break the cloak of wordlessness that had fallen upon the hall, 'One point has not been addressed. Why was your holy brother was near my father's workshop at that time in the first place?'

'You know why?'

'If my father had carried out the rector's wishes and spread rumours about Master Hugo and my Lord Robert, I doubt we would have sold much leather at the market that day. No one wants to buy goods from a man who goes against God in the manner implicated, and yet we sold well that day.

'I asked Oswin to enquire further of my father. It appears he didn't tell anyone what the rector asked him to say. He had no stomach for such gossip, choosing instead to pay the full amount due. It is my suspicion that the rector was on

290

the way to my father to discover why his evil rumour was not flourishing as well as he'd hoped.

'I know he never reached my father to make his enquiries. I believe that on his way to the workshop he came across the scene of death described, and saw a chance to do more damage than mere rumour can do.'

John steepled his hands before him in contemplation before he spoke. 'Sheriff Ingram was only telling me the other day how the Crown needs a new force of arms to send into battle with the French. He has been charged to provide a force, and is at liberty to send felons alongside honest men, instead of them sending them to gaol. I believe he'll appreciate your holy ruthlessness swelling his numbers.'

'No, John!' Richard's face went far whiter than Mathilda's as he protested, 'I can't go back to that life, I've not long returned, and ...'

'You will go.' John pointed to Walter and Thomas. 'Take our reverend kin to the cell. He can wait for Ingram there.'

'But it's true! Richard spluttered as his brothers escorted him toward the door, 'Hugo loved Robert wrongly!'

This time it was Mathilda that put out a restraining hand to Robert before he could plunge his knife into Richard's heart. 'He did love Robert; but he loved him as a friend. Fiercely and loyally after their time fighting together, seeing horrors no man should see. Perhaps you didn't know that Hugo gave the girdle to Robert as a gift to pass on to the woman of his choice? I fear you understand the nature of affection and kindness between comrades, as little as you understand it between brothers.'

'And whose fault is that? Hers!' The rector of Teigh pointed at Sarah, the accusation in his voice full of a twisted bitterness. '*She* made me this way!'

Chapter Thirty-six

Only John, Eustace, Robert, Mathilda, and Sarah remained at the manor. The arrival of the sheriff and two of his men an hour ago hadn't been the noisy attention attracting affair Mathilda had thought it would be.

Ingram had come in, his dour face solemn. Curtly acknowledging all those present, the sheriff had had a private word with John, who had presumably filled him in on events, before his men were despatched to find Geoffrey of Reresby. Then the sheriff had enlisted the services of Thomas, Walter, Laurence, and Allward to help escort their now mutely sour brother from the premises, accused of covering up a murder.

Mixing together a stickily inviting honey tonic into a small pottery bowl, Sarah passed it to Mathilda. The housekeeper was still fuming as she passed it to Mathilda. 'I can't believe he had the nerve to blame all this on me! And to use a murder to do it as well! Whatever happened to the church's teachings on forgiveness and understanding? I tried to treat you all equally. I tried but ...'

Eustace, who'd been berating John from across the table for not having let them despatch Father Richard there and then for all the trouble he caused, shook his head. 'He'll blame anyone but himself, woman. The blame is not yours. Take no heed.'

Rising to his feet, Eustace pulled on his riding gloves, 'I think I'll go and make sure our holy kin has reached the holding cells at Leicester. I don't trust him not to have Bible talked his way out of trouble, and made a run for it. Anyway, I need a gallop to take the nasty taste left by our clerical brother from my mouth.'

'Please, my Lords,' Mathilda peered through the fringe of hair that had fallen over her face from where she'd been staring at her drink without really seeing it, 'Why wasn't Richard bought up here by Sarah, like the rest of you? I'm sorry, Sarah, but this really does seem to be the source of the rector's rancour.'

John shrugged, 'It's what happens. The eldest takes the title and runs the home and the younger brothers join the King's forces, help run the manor, find a trade, or are sent into the church.'

Sarah was still muttering to herself as she moved around her kitchen, 'How can I help it if he has developed a taste for causing harm! I blame that church of his. It's one thing to go in an unbeliever and learn to believe, but to take every word as zealous righteousness so any evil deed you do is all right ...' She crashed the jug she'd been carrying onto the table with such a thud that Mathilda feared it would crack.

'Be careful, Sarah,' Robert hadn't spoken since they'd watched the Sheriff, his unwilling guest, and his entourage disappear out of the stable yard. His expression remained grave despite the removal of the man who'd caused him so much trouble. 'That sort of talk could land you in trouble.'

'I know.' The housekeeper visibly sagged, and for the first time Mathilda could see that Sarah was probably a lot older than she appeared to be.

Exchanging a glance with Robert; and as if they were in unspoken agreement, Mathilda said, 'Sit down for a moment, Sarah. Have some of this, it's already made me feel much better. Thank you.' Mathilda passed her the remains of the honey drink.

Seeing that Robert and Mathilda so obviously understood each other without the need to speak restored the confidence of the housekeeper, and with a dip of acknowledgment to John at the head of the table, Sarah sank down. 'I've done my best. And I know I should care for Richard as much as the rest of you, but somehow he's just not ...'

John came to her rescue, 'Sarah, he's a blight on the face of this family, and I for one will be very glad when Ingram has got him safely out of the country. Let the cursed French

deal with him for a while! Now,' John scrapped his chair
back across the stone flags, 'I should get back to Leicester.
Robert, perhaps you'd accompany me to the stables. I think
it's time we made some improvements to his place, brought
it up to the standards of the Leicester house. I'd appreciate
your thoughts.'

Mathilda watched the men leave the kitchen. There was
no mistaking the fact they were brothers, despite the decade
that had divided them from birth; sandy-haired and
emerald-eyed, they stood shoulder to shoulder. John was
perhaps a fraction broader in the back, and stouter around
the belly, and his face had the lines of care etched into it
that came with being the eldest of such a high-maintenance
family, but otherwise he and Robert could have been twins
as well as brothers.

Feeling the gaze of Sarah on her, Mathilda turned her
attention back to the housekeeper, 'Why are you smiling at
me like that?'

'I hoped he'd come to like you. I believe my hope has
been realised.'

Mathilda blushed, 'It makes no difference though, does
it?' Getting up from the table, she collected the spent ale
mugs, 'What has happened today changes nothing. Geoffrey
killed Hugo in a fit of anger. All the rector did was use the
situation to his advantage; it was an opportunity he saw and
he seized it. The death was a happy coincidence for him, an
extra way to add polish to the slander he'd already set in
motion anyway to blacken Robert's reputation and get you
to love him as much as the others. My family, whether they
were duped or not, still have a debt to pay off.'

Observing Mathilda as she moved to the water bucket
and began to fill a bowl to clean the men's drinking cups,
Sarah said, 'There is one good thing that has happened
because of Father Richard's vicious meddling, though.'

'What's that?'

'He brought you to us.'

A treacherous thought at the back of Mathilda's head
took the smile from her face. *But what if they never let me*

go again?

The Folvilles may have been unusual gaolers, but whether she'd grown fond of Robert or not, which, Mathilda realised with a start, she had, the fact remained, gaolers was exactly what they were.

She had no idea why she liked Robert. He was a felon who had believed her capable of taking part in a blackmail plot. He was a robber, a kidnapper, had planned the death of Belers, and had maybe even taken part in that murder ... He was nothing but a criminal. But then so was Robyn Hode, and he was a good man ... mostly ...

Breaking the quiet that had fallen across the kitchen, Mathilda smiled at the housekeeper. 'Did you know you scared me when I came here? I'd never been made to bathe like that before. Was that really only a few days ago?'

Sarah laughed, 'Feels like an age has passed since then doesn't it? Sorry I was less than friendly, but I'd just been saddled with a girl who Father Richard had described to me as "the useless daughter of a malicious debtor." When Robert asked me to treat you like the lady of the house for a while on top of all my other jobs, when I firmly believed you to be from a family who'd spread wild gossip about him in the first place, I was resentful. Of course, I didn't know then, that the rector's snide suggestion that you be used to show the world Robert had a woman had been a plan to fan the flames of gossip.

'I suppose Robert actually taking his suggestion seriously, rather than just as the insult it was supposed to be, made Richard bitter enough to grab the opportunity to try and frame you for Hugo's death when Reresby so neatly handed it to him, although he must have known it was impossible.'

'Why was the suggestion an insult?' Mathilda felt herself affronted, but she wasn't sure why.

'Because you are a tradesman's daughter. To Richard, that would be a most unsuitable match.'

Mathilda knew Sarah was right, wishing she hadn't started to secretly contemplate becoming Robert's wife. She wasn't quite sure at what point that prospect had grown into an attractive one; but it had to stop. It was obviously simply a folly that the brothers had been happy to use to their advantage. She'd been foolish to think that Robert had become fond of her in return. She was merely someone who'd been useful to him.

'Why was I sent to Coterel? I'm sure any one of the brothers could have gone to hear that message at Bakewell.'

Sarah sighed, 'I suspect Eustace thought it would be a little insulting to Nicholas to send a servant. A kidnapped servant at that. It would show the Coterel family exactly how low in the Folvilles' esteem they stood.'

'But they are to work together? They're planning something big, I know they are.'

Two high points of red appeared on Sarah's cheeks. She spoke as if she was afraid of being overheard. 'They are. But I have asked to know nothing of the plan. I suggest you curb that natural curiosity of yours in this case, Mathilda. Knowledge like that could get you killed.'[19]

With her hands on her hips, stalling any further questions Mathilda might have, Sarah turned her mind to the domestic tasks of the day, 'Now, I think we should keep busy or the lack of sleep from last night will floor us before the day really gets going. Will you attend to the fireplaces properly this time, please?'

Kneeling at the grate of Robert's bedroom's fireplace, Mathilda began to pull apart the fire that she'd made up the day before. As they'd never gone to bed the night before, it didn't need more than a quick sweep, but she wanted time to think, and doing something with her hands while she did so always worked best for Mathilda.

Robert had been gone a long time for someone who was just going to have a word with his brother before he rode back to Leicester. Mathilda could imagine John telling Robert that she was to be kept here as a kitchen hand until every penny of the debt was repaid; or that now she knew that something big was brewing between them and the Coterels, that they'd have to think of a way to dispose of her body ...

Mathilda's stomach churned as each new idea that came into her head concerning her immediate future became more unpleasant. And what of her family? Had Oswin got Matthew and her father to the Coterels in Bakewell? Were they even safe there while Reresby was still at large, or would they end up working for that family, just as she seemed to be working for this one?

She was still on her knees, sweeping up a few dots of stray ash that had fluttered from the chimney flue, when Mathilda had the feeling of being watched. Spinning around on her knees, she found herself looking directly at the lower leg of Robert de Folville, and gasped in surprise, 'My Lord, you made me jump!'

'Something that is becoming a habit with us, Mistress Twyford.' Robert's eyes danced with a flash of mischief as he held out a hand to help Mathilda to her feet; an amusement that disappeared behind his usual more serious expression once they were face to face.

'Allward has returned with news from Ingram. Reresby is in custody, he was hiding in the church of Teigh. You were right. It seems the whole thing was an argument that got out of hand. He was expecting my brother to come with clean clothes to replace his blood-stained garments.

Relief flooded Mathilda from the heart outwards, 'What will happen to the potter? I thoroughly dislike the man, and his theft of Master Hugo's handiwork shows what a scoundrel he can be, but I doubt he ever had murder in his mind.'

Robert reached out and stroked a finger over the top edge of the leather girdle around her waist, 'You have a kind heart, Mathilda. Your family suffered because of Reresby's greed, and yet I think you'd still spare him the noose, wouldn't you?'

Not moving, Mathilda found she couldn't answer; she was too busy being torn between not moving away from the light masculine touch that ran across her waist through the wool of her dress, and the knowledge that it was improper to stay so close to the man she very much feared she'd unwisely fallen in love with. Instead she said, 'I'm sorry you lost your friend, my Lord.'

A cloud crossed Robert's face, turning his eyes from their bright emerald to a dull bottle green. 'I will miss him greatly, but I am very sorry he misled you. I am ashamed I believed him so readily when he accused you of betrayal. In Hugo's defence, he truly believed the accusation.'

'I know, my Lord. I understand that.'

An awkward silence descended before Mathilda came to her senses and took a step away from his caressing finger. 'I'm relieved my family can safely return to their home now, so they can get back to the paying off the debt, thank you, my Lord.'

Robert was shocked, 'But surely you don't think they still have a debt to pay?'

Mathilda's forehead creased, 'They owe your family money, my Lord?'

'The amount of money involved wasn't huge. Eustace and John are not fools. They know that money isn't as important as the family's reputation. You paid off the debt by exposing the true source of the rumours. Your father will supply us with ceramics at no cost for the next year. We will do well from this arrangement.'

'But?'

'You were only taken because we believed my holy brother's claims about the rumours. If we kidnapped a family member from every household that owes us a small fee then this house would be full to the rafters.'

Mathilda didn't know what to do. Could she leave now?

Robert grinned down at the top of her untidy tresses of red hair, 'You are still here until because I wanted to ensure that your family was safe. After all, your father didn't actually commit the crime of hearsay we were led to believe he did. No one has much choice in anything if the rector of Teigh decrees they act, and yet your father was brave enough to resist.'

'So my family truly is safe?'

'It is. And I suspect that it will now prosper with the removal of Reresby; whom I imagine will get the chance to know the rector of Teigh a great deal better while fighting at his side in France.'

'Yes, I suppose he will, my Lord.' She looked down at his hand, which had returned to the belt, feeling its warmth through the filigree patterns of butterflies. With far more effort than she would have thought possible, Mathilda said, 'I should go. My family will need me.'

Reluctantly lowering his arm, Robert moved away. 'John instructed me to let you leave. You have done this family; especially me, a great service. Thank you, Mathilda.'

Leaning down across the foot of height that divided them, Robert kissed her lightly on the lips, and then the top of her head.

Mathilda's heart beat faster as she dared meet his eyes for a second, before she gathered up her cleaning brushes in a flurry of activity, 'I, well, I should ummm ... yes, I must go home; so I should really ...'

'Should really what, Mathilda?' The light amusement had returned to his eyes.

'I should return this belt. Now Richard is gone, you don't have to pretend any more. Master Hugo meant it as a present for your future wife. She should have it.'

'So he did.'

Mathilda went to unhook the girdle's catch, but Robert's hands laid themselves on top of hers. 'And as such, I am rather hoping you'll agree to keep it.'

'But ... but ...' Mathilda wasn't sure she'd understood him for a moment, 'you're of noble birth, and I'm only a potter's daughter.'

'Mathilda,' Robert pulled her against his chest and held her close, his warmth enveloping her like a blanket of safety and protection, 'I'm the youngest brother in a family of seven, in a time of countrywide chaos. As long as I have my Lord John's approval, I can choose whom I marry. And anyway, you are *never* going to be, and I suspect never have been, "*only*" anything.'

299

Grace stopped writing.

The act of putting down the pen this time felt oddly freeing. She stared at the black biro lying against her satisfyingly full pad of words, and its adjacent heap of scrap bits of paper. She'd done it. She'd written a novel.

Although Grace knew Mathilda's story was only a draft, and that when she read it through there'd be hundreds of things to change and improve, she felt lighter somehow. Suddenly all her insecurities and doubts about whether she should have spent her time on this rather than the textbook which patiently awaited her on her office computer, disappeared.

Finishing this novel was a step towards her own freedom, not to mention Mathilda's. It had needed to happen.

Flexing her fingers, Grace stared out of the window. Seeing the sunshine hitting the rolling hills in the far distance, she couldn't stop herself from wondering if Rob would approve of her giving her novel such a romantic ending. He'd probably think that criminals like the Folvilles didn't deserve such a nice girl as Mathilda ... Which in truth they probably didn't, but Grace had wanted a happy ending for Mathilda as much as she wanted one for herself.

Pulling on her trainers, ready to dash next door to meet Daisy for the breakfast they were due to share in exactly one and a half minutes' time, Grace mumbled under her breath, 'I bet Rob will think that letting Mathilda marry her kidnapper is less a romance, and more Stockholm Syndrome!

'Ah well,' Grace stifled a sigh as she left her room, 'Not that it matters, I don't suppose he'll ever read it.'

Chapter Thirty-seven

Daisy was about to tell Grace she'd begun to think she'd bottled out of being bridesmaid and made a run for it when one glimpse of her friend's face changed her mind.

'You've finished your story, haven't you?'

'I think so. In rough anyway.' Worried she'd accidentally let her friend down, Grace asked, 'I'm not late, am I?'

'No need to look so worried, of course you're not! Come on.' Leading the way to the restaurant, a beaming Daisy said, 'So, did Robin Hood save the day then?'

'It isn't really about Robin Hood, Daze.'

'You're kidding?' Daisy was genuinely surprised.

'It was supposed to be; but somehow it isn't. Not really.'

'I'm sorry?'

'It was going to be about the influence of Robin Hood on the Folvilles, wasn't it? But it sort of drifted off course. Maybe I should add more outlaw stuff in the redraft?'

Propelling her friend along by the elbow, Daisy giggled, 'You'll be telling me you've written a love story next! Come on, my parents will be waiting for us. My mum will be looking forward to stopping me panicking about all the things she thinks I should be panicking about.'

Deciding to keep the shocking news that she *had* accidently written a romance, even if someone had died in the process, to herself, Grace hugged Daisy to her side, 'You aren't panicking though, are you?'

'Not even a little bit. But I'd hate to disappoint Mum. She is convinced that having decided to get married "so late in the day", I'll be a bundle of nerves, and who am I to disappoint her? What shall I pretend to be worried about?'

As they entered the restaurant, there was no mistaking their table. Someone, presumably Wendy the wedding planner, had decorated the middle of it with two surprisingly tasteful *It's Your Wedding Day* balloons.

Grace whispered to Daisy as they were ushered to the table, 'you could make out you're worried about the flowers drooping?'

'Why the flowers?'

'Because it'll give your Mum something to go and fuss over with Wendy, leaving you and me to get ready in peace.'

'Grace, you're a star! Perfect!' With a quick wink that only Grace saw, Daisy said in a louder voice, 'Are you *sure* the flowers will be OK, Grace?'

'I'm sure, but if it worries you that much, perhaps one of us had better go and check them after breakfast …'

Once their delicious breakfast was consumed, they left Daisy's mum to head off to Hardwick Hall to fiddle with the flowers at the end of each row of chairs.

With her dad promising to keep his kind but worrisome wife out of the way for as long as possible, Daisy and Grace headed to their rooms to get ready for the ceremony at twelve noon.

Grace circled her friend in admiration, 'It is such a gorgeous dress, Daze. Ashley did you proud.' She carefully smoothed out the back of the skirt.

Looking both voluptuous and feminine, Daisy's chest was flatteringly hinted at without giving anyone an unsubtle eyeful, while her curvy hips were smoothed into the perfect shape by the cut of the skirt, its ivory shade complementing the happy glow of Daisy's face.

Having declared a professional hairdresser a total waste

of time, as Daisy's short curly hair had proved a law unto itself ever since it had first grown through, Grace was tasked with making the ginger locks as presentable as she could.

Standing behind Daisy, reminding her friend for the umpteenth time that she was the worst choice for this job as she barely even brushed her own hair, Grace tousled it into place beneath a shoulder-length cream veil. Plain, all but for a tiny row of exquisite butterflies around the edge, a pattern which instantly reminded Grace of Mathilda's girdle.

Hiding the lump that had formed in her throat as the thought of Mathilda led predictably onto one of Robert, and then onto Rob, Grace jabbed one final pin into Daisy's hair.

'Right, Daze, I have no idea if you'll ever find them again in that mop of yours, but there are six pins to retrieve when it's time to take the veil off.'

Laughing, Daisy said, 'Check that! Six pins.' She turned to face her friend. 'Is it time for me to brave a peep in the mirror?'

'It is!' Pulling the desk chair out of the way, Grace wheeled forward the full-length mirror the hotel staff had put into Daisy's room especially for the day.

'Here we go then!' For the first time since they'd arrived at the hotel, Daisy was uncertain. Rather than step eagerly towards the mirror, she hesitated. 'Are you sure I don't look like one of those corny little brides they sometimes put on the top of a wedding cake?'

'You look amazing, I promise. Marcus is going to have one hell of a time keeping his hands off you until after the reception.'

Daisy blushed becomingly. 'Good!' Then with a slow exhalation of her lungs she moved forward to critically examine her reflection.

With only a touch of makeup to bring out the colour of

her eyes, and a discreet matte layer of foundation so her skin didn't go shiny under the flash of the photographer's camera, Daisy couldn't wipe the grin off her face. 'This really is it, isn't it? I'm actually getting married today! Me!'

Daisy's happiness, now her moment's unease about seeing herself in an outfit so foreign to her usual dungarees and jumpers had passed, was contagious. Grace beamed back at her. 'You are! Marcus is a lucky man.'

'And I am a lucky girl.' A couple of tears unexpectedly formed at the corners of Daisy's eyes. 'Oh God!' She went to wipe them away, but Grace stopped her, dabbing them away with a tissue instead so she didn't smudge her scraping of makeup. 'I'm a hormonal mess today! I'm so happy, and I so wish that you …'

Grace raised a hand to stop the words her friend was about to say. 'I'm fine as I am, thanks Daze. Now the novel is mocked up I can finally get on with the textbook. It seems less daunting and pointless than it did. If I don't want Professor Davis to sack me, I really have to get on with it, and believe me, it isn't going to leave me time for anything other than my job.'

Not giving Daisy the chance to argue with her, Grace moved to the wardrobe, where her own dress was patiently hanging on the door in its plastic cover. 'Time for me to go all Maid Marian then!'

From the moment Daisy had yanked together the lace-up back of Grace's dress, to the time until the wedding cars would arrive to take her and Daisy's mum, and Daisy with her father, the two miles to Hardwick Hall, ticked by with frightening speed.

Soon they were all standing outside the hall being greeted by a clipboard-wielding Wendy. As they waited for the signal to go inside, Mrs Marks fussed over Grace; such was her fear that the bridesmaid's breasts would make an escape bid of their own volition that she pulled her corset laces so tight that Grace feared she might pass out.

'There, you go, my dear..'

'Umm, thanks.' Grace knew her dress made the most of her boobs, and found herself having to bite her lips so she didn't apologise for them to Daisy's mum. She fished around in her mind for small talk, but her mouth dried as nerves assailed her. Grace desperately didn't want to let Daisy down, but had been so busy concentrating on not embarrassing herself by falling off her heeled shoes, she hadn't stopped to consider the possibility that she might escape from her bodice!

All the wedding guests were in position within the hall. Marcus and his best man were waiting at the front for Daisy to arrive, and Daisy's father was hugging his daughter proudly as they prepared for her big moment.

Staring down at the Lincoln Green she wore, Grace admired the flared skirt as it tucked her in at the waist, slimmed down her stomach, and caressed her hips. Would Mathilda's wedding dress have looked like this? *Of course not! Don't be so darn ridiculous, woman!* Now that Grace had allowed her romantic side a little freedom, it appeared there was no way she could switch it back off.

Grace was convinced she was right to have ended Mathilda's tale before the relationship between her and Robert developed towards a wedding, so that any readers she might one day have was free to imagine it for themselves, as the implication that there would be a wedding very was clear. Yet, as she stood there, staring out across the unspoilt landscape, Grace found herself picturing Mathilda and Robert de Folville walking together, hand in hand.

'Grace, are you OK?'

'Oh my goodness, I'm sorry, Daze! I was miles away.' Grace smiled. 'Are you ready for the off?'

'All systems go!'

Forcing a smile onto her face, Grace tried not to think about the fact she didn't know any of the guests beyond the bride, groom, and their parents. Daisy and Marcus had kept the wedding small, and only invited family – apart from her; and as she hadn't invited a plus-one of her own, the nearest Grace would get to a slow dance in her dream dress was with Daisy's elderly uncle and his walking stick.

Following her radiant friend into the stunning surrounds of Hardwick Hall, Grace was unable to stop her heart aching when she saw the look of love and devotion Marcus gave his almost wife as he caught his first glimpse of his bride walking towards him.

Grace felt as though her facial muscles had undergone some sort of living rigor mortis. Surely she was seeing things? It had to be her imagination playing tricks. She'd been so caught up in the romance of Mathilda's and Robert's story that she was hallucinating. Rob couldn't possibly be standing in front of the chair next to the one she was due to sit on once the procession reached the front of the aisle. Mrs Marks must have cut off the blood supply to her head with all that lace-tugging.

Struggling not to wobble and fall off her heels, Grace came to an abrupt halt behind Daisy, took her bouquet, and closed her eyes for a split second. When she opened them again she fully expected the chair in question to be empty.

It wasn't.

But Rob's in Houston. The thought stubbornly played itself on continuous loop through her mind despite the evidence of her own eyes, which told her categorically that Rob really was there, looking extremely handsome in a navy blue suit.

'I'm sorry if I startled you. Daisy said it should be a surprise.'

Much to Grace's relief, the quartet that had

accompanied the bridal party up the aisle from the balcony stopped, and the registrar began to welcome the guests, giving her an excellent excuse for not even looking at Rob, let alone replying.

Grace didn't hear a word of the ceremony. Fiddling with Daisy's' bouquet of cream roses, she stared unwaveringly at the back of the bride's dress, her mind so overloaded with questions it actually felt blank. Her lips moved in time to the words of the hymns, but no sound came out of her mouth, and as the registrar declared Marcus and Daisy man and wife, it was only the clapping of the guests behind her that pulled Grace back to her senses.

Speaking out of the side of her mouth, Grace finally muttered, 'But you're in Houston.'

'Apparently I'm not.'

'Why are you here, you hate me.'

'Hate you?' Rob shook his head, his expression heavy with regret, as he produced a piece of paper from his suit pocket. It was well creased and worn, as if it held words that he'd read, and reread, many times. With a half-smile he passed it to Grace.

Uncertain, Grace took it, and found herself confronted by a page of her own scribbled writing. It was obviously not the original, but a scanned or photocopied version of the list of things she liked about Rob that she'd made when she'd been staying in Daisy's spare room.

Speaking under his breath so as not to disturb the proceedings, Rob said, 'Did you know that even when you go pale, your freckles stay dark? It's as if they're tiny dots that someone has added on with a brown felt tip. Very cute.'

Letting the fact Rob had mentioned she was cute warm her heart for a moment, Grace kept her eyes on the list. 'Daisy sent this to you? She stole your email address off my phone?'

'She did.'

Grace looked across to where Marcus and Daisy were chatting to the registrar while they signed the wedding certificate, just as her best friend turned and winked at her.

'Why are you here, Rob?' Unwilling to allow herself to feel hopeful, Grace stared him squarely in the face. 'Why talk to me now, when you walked out on me then?'

'Daisy managed to convince me that you'd forgive me for being an idiot, that you felt guilty about Malcolm, but were too stubborn to ever say so.'

'I see.' Grace felt a smile nudging her, but she wasn't prepared to let him off the hook that easily.

'She also told me about Malcolm's stepmother, and how you'd been cornered into the coffee date.'

Grace fiddled with the petals of the flowers lying in her lap. 'You let Daisy explain, but not me?'

Rob sighed. 'My only excuse, apart from being an idiot, is that I've been hurt before. Sounds feeble, but it's true.'

'It's not feeble.' Grace glanced up at him, but turned away quickly. The way he was holding his hands out to her was redirecting her mind away from the matter in hand, and to their time together in her kitchen. Returning her gaze to the married couple, Grace said, 'but what *is* feeble is not giving me a chance to explain myself.'

'I …'

Grace stopped Rob in his tracks. 'We'll have to do this later. Daisy and Marcus are coming back to the front.' She stood up, ready to return the bouquet to Daisy, 'unless you intend to disappear again, that is.'

'Not a chance.' Rob grinned, his eyes twinkling in much the way Grace had described Robert's as he looked at Mathilda. 'For a start, Daisy would kill me!'

Grace wasn't sure how she got through either the photographs or the line-up before the reception. Daisy kept nudging her, 'Try and smile naturally, woman, you look like a waxwork model!'

'Don't blame me. It's your fault.'

Daisy wriggled her eyebrows, 'Don't tell me you aren't pleased to see him, Dr Harper, 'cos I won't believe you.'

'And I don't suppose I'm allowed to hit you on your wedding day, Mrs Stevens; so I suppose I'd better forgive you!'

Daisy smirked, 'I'll take that as a "thank you, Daisy, I'm thrilled you persuaded Rob to cut short his conference and fly thousands of miles to see me in my pretty frock", shall I?'

Unable to prevent her own smile now, Grace took two glasses of Bucks Fizz from a passing waiter, 'I think we need a drink! How long till the meal starts?'

'Just long enough for you to go and apologise to Rob, for him to apologise to you, and for me to make nice with my new mother-in-law.'

Not wanting to interrupt Rob, who was talking to Marcus and his brother, Grace took the opportunity to rest her feet. Sitting at the same table she'd sat at only twenty-four hours ago, dreaming of what might have been, she realised that thanks to Daisy, she'd been given a second chance.

'Hello again.'

Grace jumped, slopping her drink alarming as Rob appeared next to her. But rather than be cross as droplets of orange flavoured alcohol hit her dress, she burst out laughing.

Rob's face creased in confusion as he produced a handkerchief to dry her off, 'I'm so sorry. Why aren't you shouting at me?'

'You making me jump reminded me of Robert and Mathilda, that's all.'

'It did?'

'Yes; and that's the second time today my own life has

echoed that of my literary protagonists.'

'Does that mean you've finished your novel then?' Rob looked so proud and genuinely pleased that Grace mentally kicked herself. She had been just as much of a fool as he had.

'Yes,' Grace smiled, 'just a few hours ago in fact.'

'So what did you decided to call it in the end?'

Grace frowned. 'That's the bit I'm not one hundred per cent sure about. *Folville's Girl* is still in the running, but I thought I might go with *The Butterfly Girdle*.'

Rob's eyes twinkled mischievously as he sat down next to Grace, 'I can't deny that *The Butterfly Girdle* sounds very sophisticated, but as it happens, I have come up with the perfect title for you.'

'You have?'

'Yep! You should call your book *Romancing Robin Hood*.'

'*Romancing Robin Hood*?' Grace narrowed her eyes, not quite sure if her fellow historian was serious or teasing her.

Winking, Rob slid an arm around Grace's waist and squeezed her playfully, 'After all, that's what you and Mathilda have been doing all your lives, isn't it!'

Laughing, Grace shook her head, 'For one awful moment I thought you were serious.' Without waiting for Rob to expand on his thoughts for her title, Grace grabbed her chance to apologise before her bridesmaid duties called her away.

'I'm sorry, Rob. I should have told you properly about Aggie and her matchmaking. Thing is, I never took it seriously, so it didn't occur to me that you would. As Daisy told you, I didn't really have the heart to let her down, or get the opportunity to get out of seeing him.'

'You mean let Malcolm down surely?' Rob sat on the bench next to her and stared out across the landscape.

'Malcolm probably wouldn't have noticed if I was

310

there or not. He seemed happy as long as someone was making "I'm impressed" noises about his sporting and business achievements.'

'Oh, one of *those* men.'

'Sadly for Aggie, yes. But bless her; she loves Malcolm in spite of the whole self-centred arrogance thing. It was her feelings I didn't want to hurt.'

They sat for a while, admiring the gently rolling hills.

'You can see them can't you?' Rob placed a hand over Grace's palm, holding it as he examined the roll of the landscape with a historian's eye, 'the medieval population working the land; doing what they can to survive in a world that was, even by today's standards, cruel and relentless in its demand for hard work.'

As Rob but her own imaginings into words, Grace nodded but said nothing, not wanting to ruin the moment. After a while he said, 'I've finished something as well.'

'You have?'

'Our paper. I went ahead and wrote it using your evidence. I emailed it to you this morning, but if you hate it I won't submit it.'

Grace was gobsmacked. 'But I assumed ...'

'You thought because we had a teenage-style falling out that I wouldn't want to write a paper with you any more?'

'Well, yes. I mean, you did say so!'

'Well, I wasn't going to at first. But then I realised I was being unprofessional mixing up my personal feelings with my professional ones. You're an excellent medievalist. A moment of idiocy isn't the sort of thing that would want to stop me wanting to work with you. And doing much more than work, for that matter!'

The sound of the gong ushering all the guests to dinner interrupted just as the conversation was beginning to get interesting, making Rob sigh with resignation, 'You're back on duty now, and this isn't the place to talk properly.

Even afterwards you'll have the round of relatives to dance with and stuff, but I wondered …'

Grace looked up at him. Rob seemed anxious. 'Yes?'

Reaching into his inside pocket he pulled out another piece of folded paper and passed it to Grace. 'What do you think? I've never actually had the time to explore Nottinghamshire properly since I got back from the States, and somehow it seemed the ideal place to get to know you better.'

As Grace read the printout of a booking form, for a room in a hotel hidden away in what was left of Sherwood Forest – for that evening and the following two days – her mouth fell open.

'Daisy said you deserved a break. Will you come with me, Grace?'

Posting the piece of paper back into his pocket, Grace stood on her tiptoes and kissed Rob gently on the lips, before taking his hand and walking with him toward the dining room. 'I will, on two conditions.'

'And your conditions are?'

'That we share a room.'

Rob beamed; his expression telling Grace exactly how he approved of this clause in the agreement.

'And the other condition?'

'Oh that's obvious isn't it?' Grace squeezed his hand playfully. 'That we can visit the Robin Hood gift shop, of course!'

References

1. Roger Belers was murdered in 1326 in the field of Brokesby, Leicestershire. The incident was recorded in the Assize Rolls – *Just1/470*

2. Each county in England was split into hundreds, which served as individual administrative areas. By 1326 each hundred had its own court. Ashby Folville, Twyford, and Reresby were all in the Leicester Hundred of East Goscote.

3. *The Outlaw's Song of Trailbaston*, Dobson & Taylor, Rymes of Robyn Hood: An Introduction to the English Outlaw (Gloucester, 1989,) p.253

4. *Piers the Plowman*, Langland, W., The Vision of Piers the Plowman; A Complete Edition of the B-Text (London,1987), Passus XIX, line 245, pp242-3

5. Scattergood, J., 'The Tale of Gamelyn: The Noble Robber as Provincial Hero,' ed. C Meale, Readings in Medieval English Romance (Cambridge, 1994)

6. The steward of the Folville Manor at Ashby-Folville was John de Sproxton. I have only made Robert de Folville the steward for the purposes of this story.

7. Leyser, H., Medieval Women: A Social History of Women in England 450-1500, (London 1995)

8. *Robin Hood and the Monk*, Dobson & Taylor, Rymes of Robyn Hood: An Introduction to the English Outlaw (Gloucester, 1989), p.113

9. Bellamy, J., '*The Coterel Gang: An Anatomy of a Band of Fourteenth Century Crime*', English Historical Review Vol. 79, (1964)

10. Edmund de Ashby, sheriff of Leicestershire, was ordered to pursue and arrest Thomas and Eustace de Folville (with others) after they were indicted in the murder of Belers. Calendar of Patent Rolls, 1324-1327, p.250

11. Nichols, ed., History and Antiquity of Leicester, Vol. 3, Part 1, p.389 p.96

12. Hanawalt, B.A., Crime and Conflict in the English Communities 1330-1348 (London, 1979)

13. *A Song on the Times* is recorded in the '*Harley Manuscript*' No.913, folio 44. Wright, T., The Political Songs of England, From the Reign of King John to that of Edward II (Camden Society, First Series, Vol. 6, London, 1839)

14. *A Geste of Robyn Hode*, Dobson & Taylor, Rymes of Robyn Hood: An Introduction to the English Outlaw (Gloucester, 1989), p.112, stanza 456

15. *Robin Hood and the Potter*, Dobson & Taylor, Rymes of Robyn Hood: An Introduction to the English Outlaw (Gloucester, 1989), p.127, stanza 17

16. *Robin Hood and the Monk*, Dobson & Taylor, Rymes of Robyn Hood: An Introduction to the English Outlaw (Gloucester, 1989), p.117, stanza 22

17. *A Geste of Robyn Hode*, Dobson & Taylor, Rymes of Robyn Hood: An Introduction to the English Outlaw (Gloucester, 1989), p.79, stanza 10

18. Sir Robert Ingram was sheriff of Nottinghamshire and Derbyshire on four occasions between 1322 and 1334. <u>Lists of Sheriffs for England and Wales from the earliest times to AD 1831 Preserved in the Public Record Office</u> (List and Index Society 9, New York, 1963) p.102

19. The most scandalous co-committed crime by both the Folville and Coterel families was the kidnap and ransom of the justice Sir Richard de Willoughby. This is this felony that I allude to as the 'future crime' Mathilda becomes aware of the brothers' plotting. Eustace, Robert, Thomas and others were all indicted for this kidnap and ransom in the Assize Rolls, *Just 1/141b.*

Further Reading

If you are interested in learning more about Robin Hood and the historical felons of the English Middle Ages, there are many excellent reference books available. Here a few of my personal favourites.

Dobson & Taylor, Rymes of Robyn Hood: An Introduction to the English Outlaw (Gloucester, 1989)

Holt, J., Robin Hood (London, 1982)

Keen, M., The Outlaws of Medieval Legend (London, 1987)

Knight, S., Robin Hood: A Complete Study of the English Outlaw (Oxford, 1994)

Pollard, A.J., Imaging Robin Hood (London, 2004)

Prestwich, M., The Three Edwards: War and State in England 1272-1377 (London, 1980)

Other titles by Jenny Kane

For more information about **Jenny Kane**

and other **Accent Press** titles

please visit

www.accentpress.co.uk

Lightning Source UK Ltd.
Milton Keynes UK
UKOW02f2306180515

251808UK00001B/2/P